THE VALIANT GUNMAN

BOOKS BY GILBERT MORRIS

Through a Glass Darkly

THE HOUSE OF WINSLOW

1. *The Honorable Imposter*
2. *The Captive Bride*
3. *The Indentured Heart*
4. *The Gentle Rebel*
5. *The Saintly Buccaneer*
6. *The Holy Warrior*
7. *The Reluctant Bridegroom*
8. *The Last Confederate*
9. *The Dixie Widow*
10. *The Wounded Yankee*
11. *The Union Belle*
12. *The Final Adversary*
13. *The Crossed Sabres*
14. *The Valiant Gunman*
15. *The Gallant Outlaw*
16. *The Jeweled Spur*
17. *The Yukon Queen*
18. *The Rough Rider*
19. *The Iron Lady*
20. *The Silver Star*
21. *The Shadow Portrait*
22. *The White Hunter*
23. *The Flying Cavalier*
24. *The Glorious Prodigal*
25. *The Amazon Quest*
26. *The Golden Angel*
27. *The Heavenly Fugitive*

THE LIBERTY BELL

1. *Sound the Trumpet*
2. *Song in a Strange Land*
3. *Tread Upon the Lion*
4. *Arrow of the Almighty*
5. *Wind From the Wilderness*
6. *The Right Hand of God*
7. *Command the Sun*

CHENEY DUVALL, M.D.[1]

1. *The Stars for a Light*
2. *Shadow of the Mountains*
3. *A City Not Forsaken*
4. *Toward the Sunrising*
5. *Secret Place of Thunder*
6. *In the Twilight, in the Evening*
7. *Island of the Innocent*
8. *Driven With the Wind*

CHENEY AND SHILOH: THE INHERITANCE[1]

1. *Where Two Seas Met*

THE SPIRIT OF APPALACHIA[2]

1. *Over the Misty Mountains*
2. *Beyond the Quiet Hills*
3. *Among the King's Soldiers*
4. *Beneath the Mockingbird's Wings*
5. *Around the River's Bend*

TIME NAVIGATORS
(for Young Teens)

1. *Dangerous Voyage*
2. *Vanishing Clues*

[1]with Lynn Morris   [2]with Aaron McCarver

02A

THE VALIANT GUNMAN

★

GILBERT MORRIS

BETHANY HOUSE
MINNEAPOLIS, MINN

The Valiant Gunman
Copyright © 1993
Gilbert Morris

Cover by Brett Longley

Published by Bethany House Publishers
A Ministry of Bethany Fellowship International
11400 Hampshire Avenue South
Minneapolis, Minnesota 55438
www.bethanyhouse.com

Printed in the United States of America by
Bethany Press International, Minneapolis, Minnesota 55438

Library of Congress Cataloging-in-Publication Data

Morris, Gilbert.
    The valiant gunman / Gilbert Morris.
       p.   cm.—(The House of Winslow ; bk. 14)
    1. Ranch life—Wyoming—Fiction. I. Title. II. Series: Morris, Gilbert. House of Winslow ; bk. 14.
PS3563.O8742V28   1993
813'.54—dc20   93-2416
ISBN 1-55661-310-5   CIP

To Danny and Jan Meeks

The Lord give mercy to the house of Danny Meeks, for he oft refreshed me.

Someone once defined friendship as "two bodies—one soul." The years have slipped by, and with them many of my old acquaintances have faded from view. But in one of those mysterious alchemies of the spirit, we have grown closer—despite the miles that separate us.

I'm so grateful that God gives us fellow pilgrims to walk with as we travel toward home!

GILBERT MORRIS spent ten years as a pastor before becoming Professor of English at Ouachita Baptist University in Arkansas and earning a Ph.D. at the University of Arkansas. During the summers of 1984 and 1985 he did postgraduate work at the University of London and is presently the Chairman of General Education at a Christian college in Louisiana. A prolific writer, he has had over 25 scholarly articles and 200 poems published in various periodicals, and over the past years has had more than 20 novels published. His family includes three grown children, and he and his wife live in Baton Rouge, Louisiana.

CONTENTS

PART FOUR
WAR IN THE VALLEY

THE HOUSE OF WINSLOW

★ ★ ★ ★

THE
<u>HOUSE OF WINSLOW</u>

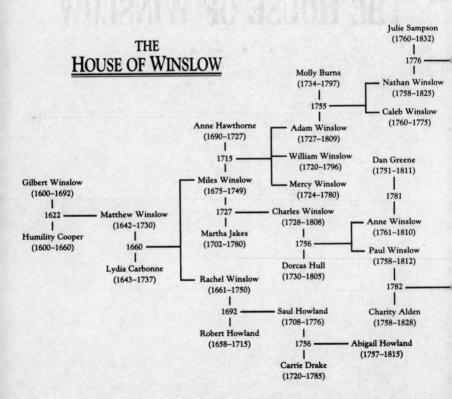

Julie Sampson
(1760–1832)

1776

Nathan Winslow
(1758–1825)

Caleb Winslow
(1760–1775)

Molly Burns
(1734–1797)

1755

Adam Winslow
(1727–1809)

Anne Hawthorne
(1690–1727)

1715

William Winslow
(1720–1796)

Dan Greene
(1751–1811)

1781

Mercy Winslow
(1724–1780)

Miles Winslow
(1675–1749)

1727

Charles Winslow
(1728–1808)

Anne Winslow
(1761–1810)

Gilbert Winslow
(1600–1692)

1622

Matthew Winslow
(1642–1730)

Martha Jakes
(1702–1780)

1756

Paul Winslow
(1758–1812)

Humility Cooper
(1600–1660)

1660

Dorcas Hull
(1730–1805)

1782

Lydia Carbonne
(1643–1737)

Rachel Winslow
(1661–1750)

Charity Alden
(1758–1828)

1692

Saul Howland
(1708–1776)

Robert Howland
(1658–1715)

1756

Abigail Howland
(1757–1815)

Carrie Drake
(1720–1785)

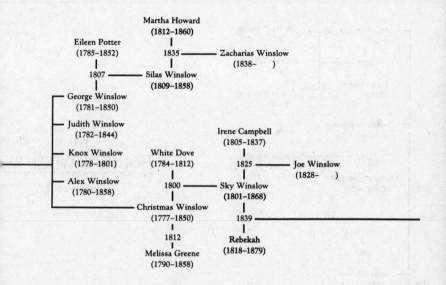

Martha Howard
(1812–1860)

1835 ———— Zacharias Winslow
(1838–   )

Eileen Potter
(1785–1852)

1807 ———— Silas Winslow
(1809–1858)

George Winslow
(1781–1850)

Judith Winslow
(1782–1844)

Knox Winslow
(1778–1801)

Alex Winslow
(1780–1858)

Irene Campbell
(1805–1837)

White Dove
(1784–1812)

1825 ———— Joe Winslow
(1828–   )

1800 ———— Sky Winslow
(1801–1868)

Christmas Winslow
(1777–1850)

1839 ————————————

1812

Rebekah
(1818–1879)

Melissa Greene
(1790–1858)

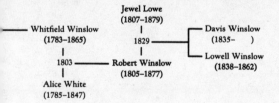

Jewel Lowe
(1807–1879)

Davis Winslow
(1835–   )

1829 ————

Whitfield Winslow
(1783–1865)

Lowell Winslow
(1838–1862)

1803 ———— Robert Winslow
(1805–1877)

Alice White
(1785–1847)

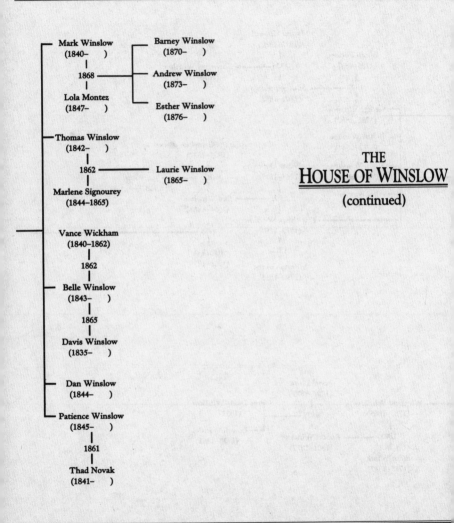

Mark Winslow
(1840–   )

Barney Winslow
(1870–   )

1868

Andrew Winslow
(1873–   )

Lola Montez
(1847–   )

Esther Winslow
(1876–   )

Thomas Winslow
(1842–   )

1862

Laurie Winslow
(1865–   )

Marlene Signourey
(1844–1865)

Vance Wickham
(1840–1862)

1862

Belle Winslow
(1843–   )

1865

Davis Winslow
(1835–   )

Dan Winslow
(1844–   )

Patience Winslow
(1845–   )

1861

Thad Novak
(1841–   )

THE
HOUSE OF WINSLOW

(continued)

PART ONE

TRAIL TO WYOMING

★ ★ ★ ★

CHAPTER ONE

A MAN FOR HOPE

★ ★ ★ ★

Hope Jenson Rogers had known from the instant Willis Malloy entered the house that he'd come for her—and it brought a tightness to her throat that made it hard for her to speak clearly. For months she had known he would come, and now that the moment was upon her, she had to force herself to ignore the spasm of fear that gripped her. Stepping back from the door, she said, "Come in out of the cold, Mr. Malloy."

"Thanks," Malloy said at once. He entered the simple room that served as kitchen, dining room, and living area for the Jenson family, shucked out of his heavy wool coat, hung it on a peg beside the door, then swept off his high-crowned Stetson and placed it carefully on another peg. Only then did he turn to face Hope, his black eyes sweeping over her. "I thought we got that all straight—about you callin' me by my first name."

Hope tried to smile. "I guess I forgot—Willis."

"Now, thet's more like it! I ain't no stranger, am I now?"

"No, not a stranger." Restless under the scrutiny of his dark eyes, she said hurriedly, "I was making up some sassafras tea. Come and sit."

"Where's your pa—and the boys?" Malloy was such a huge man that he made the room seem smaller by his bulk. He had a blunt-featured face, with large red lips, black eyes sunk deep under beetled brows, and a prow of a nose. His thick body strained the plaid wool shirt he wore, and as always, Hope was repulsed by the sight of his hands—huge and powerful with tufts of black hair swirling out behind the knuckles.

"Zane took Cody out to hunt rabbits," she said. "Pa's milking the cow."

The information seemed to mean something to Malloy, for his dark eyes registered the fact with a gleam of interest. He was a shrewd man for all his bulk, and now he said quickly, "Well, that's all right, Hope. I come to talk to you anyhow." Taking a step toward her, he said with a grin, "I guess you know what about, don't you?"

"Why—!" Hope faltered, and the impulse came to her to run out the door, but there was no place to hide. She said quickly, "I expect Pa will be back soon."

"Then I'll jest speak my peace before he does." Malloy put out a massive hand and gripped her arm before she could move. Despite his size there was a quickness in him, and as he looked down at the woman, he seemed to find an obscure pleasure in her obvious fear of him.

Willis Malloy was a man who liked to inspire fear in others. He was a notorious bruiser, his massive frame and thick skull able to endure considerable punishment, and few men were able to stand before the awesome strength of his fists. He provoked fights often, enjoying watching the fear leap into his opponents' eyes, and rumor said that he was hard on the women of the town as well—those who would tolerate him. Even now he increased the power of his grip, so that Hope blinked her eyes with the pain.

He eased up at once, saying, "Sorry, Hope. Didn't mean to hurt you none. Just don't know my own grip, I guess." But he held her arm fast as he said, "I ain't made no secret of how I admire you, have I? Been comin' around here for nigh onto two months now tryin' to get you to go with me to a dance or someplace." He shrugged, the motion bringing the huge muscles of his shoulders into prominence. "I thought for a while I had some competition—thet you was interested in some other man. But I don't reckon that's so, is it?"

"No. I—don't see any men."

Malloy paused thoughtfully, his gaze running over Hope as he thought about her statement. He was a man who had known many women, but there was something about this one that had intrigued him. All of the women he had known had been coarse and common. But Hope was different. She possessed a fineness that had drawn him.

Her face was heart-shaped, and her skin smooth and clear, save for one small mole on her right cheek close to her wide mouth. This blemish only served as a foil for the beauty of her complexion. Her eyes were blue with flecks of green, and when she smiled a small dimple appeared on her left cheek. His eyes traveled down her body, which was slim yet provocatively full-figured.

He had his look, then said, "I'm a man who likes things straight out, Hope. Not much fancy about me. I been thinkin' about you for a spell, now I come to ask you to marry me." He watched as alarm came into her eyes and said quickly, "Now, don't say nothin' till I git finished! I ain't no kid, Hope. I'm thirty-seven and I've kicked around a lot. I've known some women," he shrugged, "but a man's got to have his fun. Now I'm ready to settle down, and you're the woman I want."

"Oh, I can't answer you now, Willis!"

He brushed aside her protest with a sweeping move of his free hand. "Hope, I done thought all this out, and the way I see it, you gotta think of your family." His quick eyes caught the sudden expression that statement had brought to her eyes, and he nodded encouragement. "Things ain't been good for you, and thet ain't no secret. It's been a hard thing, this here reconstruction. Them carpetbaggers have stripped the South, blast 'em! This farm never was much, and with Amos gettin' sick, it's gone to pot."

"We're hoping for a good crop next year—"

"Cotton won't bring no money," he interrupted. "And even if it did, you owe so much on this place you ain't never gonna get it paid for. And how you gonna raise cotton with a sick man and one fourteen-year-old kid?"

Hope knew he was speaking the truth, for she had said the same thing over and over to herself. Her father seldom spoke of his illness, but he was past the sort of grinding work that raising cotton required. Her younger brother, Zane, was a hard worker, but he was not able enough.

Malloy saw the harried expression on her face. "And you need a man—a husband, Hope—just like your son needs a pa. You're jest bein' wasted, a good-lookin' woman like you without no man." He tightened his grip again as he thought of her past, then said with a teasing grin, "That husband of yours, he musta either been a good one or a bad one. Either he was so good you can't find nobody to measure up to him—or he was such a dud you got a bad taste in your mouth about marriage. Which one was it, I wonder?"

Hope shook her head, speechless. She had long ago managed to blot out memories of her first marriage. She had been barely out of girlhood, only sixteen years old, when she married James Rogers. He was older, nearly twenty-five. When Fort Sumter fell, he was one of the first to enlist in the Confederate Army—and then was one of the first to fall—at Manassas, the first battle of the war. Hope had been filled with girlish, romantic notions, and when he had asked her to marry him before he left for the war, she had trembled, then said yes. They had only a week together, and for a tender, untaught girl with no knowledge of marriage, it had been a terrifying week. Her mother had died two years earlier, and there had been no other woman to give her any help or instructions. James Rogers was a rough young fellow, selfish and taking, so Hope's first week of marriage had left her bruised and frightened.

When the news came that her husband had fallen at Manassas, her first reaction was one of tremendous relief that he would not be coming back to subject her to his rough hungers—and her second was guilt that she felt such a thing.

Her baby was born nine months after the wedding night, and she had shown no interest in men for the past ten years, though several had come seeking her, drawn by her beauty. Ignoring their advances, she had mothered her son, and cared for her brother and father in their small cabin on the hill farm in the Ozarks. After a while, the men of the hills had finally given up on her.

But now this! Hope trembled as Willis Malloy held her arm, despite her efforts to pull free. His very touch brought back vivid memories of her brief experience with James Rogers, and she whispered, "Please! Let me go!"

"Why, that's no way to talk to a man, Hope!" Malloy said. Instead of letting her go, he took her chin and forced her to look up at him. He lowered his voice, saying, "I think I know what's wrong with you. That boy you married, he didn't know how to treat a woman. You need a man who knows how to please you—and that's me!"

"I—can't leave my father and brother, Willis."

"Who said you had to leave 'em?" He grinned when his words caused her to open her eyes wide. "Thet's somethin' you didn't expect to hear, did ya? But I'm a careful man, Hope, and I've done a lot of thinkin' on this thing. Now look at this, your pa's gonna lose this place. Everybody knows he owes more on it than it's worth. And Gerald Tibbs, the banker, told me as much—private like."

"He didn't say that!"

"Shore did," Malloy insisted. "He's carried the note with nothin' on the principal ever since Amos got sick, but now he's gonna call the note." He saw the stricken look on her face and pulled her a little closer. "Now, don't let that bother you none. What I got in mind will be good for all of us. When we marry up, I'm pullin' out of Arkansas. Never did like it nohow!"

Hope stared up at him. "Where will you go?"

"Going to Wyoming, Hope. I bought a place there, a ranch, and got me enough money to go to Texas and buy up a passel of wild cattle. We'll drive 'em to Wyoming, take up some free graze. Now that the railroads are all the way into the East, we can feed out the stock, take it to the railroad, and make a lot of money." His eyes were gleaming with excitement, and he suddenly pulled her close and kissed her.

Hope, taken off guard, could do nothing, for his strong arms held her as though she were a child. He reeked of tobacco and whiskey and unwashed clothes, and as he pulled her closer, she could think of nothing but the touch of his rough lips.

Finally releasing his strong hold, he stared at her, then smiled. "You're a bashful little thing—but I'll teach you a few tricks after we're married."

"I can't marry you, Willis. I don't . . . love you!"

A smile parted his thick lips, and a hearty chuckle rumbled in his chest. "You been readin' some of them romance books, girl!

You need a man, and I need a woman, and thet's all there is to it! Now look," he spoke firmly. "When the bank takes this place, where will you go? You ain't got no place, have you? And no money? But I'm offerin' to marry you, and since I'm a generous man, I'll take care of your pa. He can go with us and stay as long as he lives. And Zane, he'll make a good hand. He's the best horse rider around here already, and I'll need him to git started."

Hope stood there, confused and frightened. She had thought many times of her family's future, and it was always a grim picture. They had no relatives to take them in, and she hated the idea of living in town, of being a maid or a waitress—which were the only jobs she could do.

But marry Willis Malloy? The very thought of it brought a wrenching sickness to her. Fortunately, at just that moment, they both heard steps on the porch, and Malloy said quickly, "You talk it over with your pa, Hope. I'll be back tomorrow." He gave her a careful glance with his black eyes, then nodded. "I expect you'll say yes. You ain't really got no choice, have you now?"

The door opened, and Amos Jenson entered with a bucket of frothy milk. He was very tall and thin as a rail. He had blue eyes and fair hair, and his fingers clutching the rope-handle of the bucket were long and sensitive—musician's hands, which was what he had been all his life. He could play any instrument, and during the first half of his life, he had played for dances all over Stone County, drinking and chasing the girls. When the war came he had joined the Stonewall Brigade and had gone through every major battle. It was at that time he was converted, and when he came home, he was as active at proclaiming the gospel as he had been at playing hoedowns. He had no education, and two children and a grandchild to support, so his preaching consisted of holding "protracted meetings," revival meetings in the rural areas.

After several years of preaching and farming, he had fallen ill and never recovered his strength. He tried valiantly, but the vitality of his youth was gone, and he watched his farm slowly deteriorate. Through it all he never complained but always said, "The Lord will care for us."

Now he came into the room and set the bucket of milk on the table before saying, "Hello, Willis. Cold for a man to be out visiting. Sit and have something."

"No thanks, Amos." Malloy shook his head. "Jest stopped in on the way to town. Thought you might need somethin' from the store."

"I guess not," Jenson said. "Come by on your way back. I expect the boys will come in with some rabbits—or maybe even a buck."

"Yeah, I'll do thet." He turned to put on his coat, then pulled his hat down over his rough thatch of hair. Placing his hand on the door latch, he paused to give Hope a sudden glance. "You think on it, Hope," he said, and then stepped out of the cabin.

Hope hurried at once to the stove and set the teakettle on to heat. She turned to look in the bucket of milk her father had set on the table, noted how full it was, and said, "Lots of milk, Pa. That's a good thing."

Amos Jenson was a quick man—always had been. If he had received an education, he could have been anything. He knew people, and he knew this daughter of his better than she knew herself. Moving carefully, he sat down in one of the cane-bottomed chairs. "I guess Willis came to ask you to marry him." He saw the sudden jerk of her head and the paleness of her face, and it hurt him. "You don't have to marry him, Hope."

The wind whistled under the door and through the thousand cracks of the old house. It rattled the shingles, which hung on by rusty nails that screeched at the pressure; and the stove belched a puff of woodsmoke as the wind forced its way down the chimney. It was a poor house, but it was all she had ever known. Hope glanced around with desperate eyes, then came to sit down across from her father.

"I guess maybe I do, Pa," she said. Her voice was unsteady, and she stared at her work-hardened hands as she told him what Malloy had said about the banker.

As she spoke, Amos sat before her, a familiar feeling of breathless pain growing in his chest. Whenever it came, he felt an enormous fragility, as if he were made out of thin glass and one stiff breeze would shatter him into tiny fragments.

But the pain was not bad this day. He knew it was his heart—and he also knew that no doctor could help him. Each day he measured out a little of himself, as a woman measures meal out of a container when the supply is low and there is no replacement. He had only so many days to live, so many words to say, so many sunrises to see. He had told himself that every man has limitations—but the difference was he *knew* that his were near the end.

He had been shocked when Appomattox came and he was one of the few ragged scarecrows who'd stacked muskets there. For years he'd lived with death at his elbow, seeing his friends go down one by one, and had assumed that his turn would come. But it had not come—and then when he had been laid low by sickness, rendered helpless by the sudden attack two years earlier, he had been caught off guard. He had made no provision for his children, and the pain that that knowledge gave him was worse than anything his illness had brought.

Now he was helpless, but still he said, "Daughter, don't marry him. We'll make out somehow." He knew his words were weak, and that she would have to be the strong one. He had discovered long ago that her first brief marriage had been a disaster for her, though he could only guess at the reason.

Hope kept her eyes lowered, and her voice was so soft that Amos could hardly hear it. "I—guess I got to do it, Pa. There's simply no other way."

The teakettle whistled a cheerful tune, and she got up at once. As she made the sassafras tea, she came to her decision. *It is not really a decision*, she thought, *for a decision means choice, and as Malloy said, I have no choice.* Had she been alone, she could have refused the man without a thought. Even if all she had was Cody, she would not have been afraid to find her own way. But the burden of her ailing father and of her brother Zane, who was teetering on the edge of wildness, was too heavy for her. She came to the table with the tea, and by the time she sat down, she'd gained control.

"We'll be leaving here, Pa, all of us," she said, forcing excitement into her voice. "Willis has bought a ranch and is going to get some cattle. We're all going to Wyoming. You always wanted to see the West, didn't you? Well, now you're going to see it!"

Jenson was not fooled for one moment by her forced gaiety, but he could say nothing. His heart was breaking, for he knew the sacrifice his daughter was making. She was like him, and together they would try to put as good a face on the thing as possible.

"Is that so? Well now, that'll be good, Hope! And won't Zane be excited? I've thought for the last two years he was gonna run off and be a cowboy! Now here he's got his chance."

"Yes, Pa—it's all going to be fine, real fine!" Hope got up again, turned away from her father, and stood looking out the window.

He got up from his chair and went to where she was standing, thinking how small her shoulders were for the heavy weight that had been placed on them. When he put his arms out, her face went stiff, then she fell against him, weeping as she had not done for years. He held her, each choking sob that wracked her body bringing him pain. But he said nothing—for there was nothing to say. Finally the sobbing stopped and she drew back. Her cheeks were stained with tears, but she wiped them away with a handkerchief, straightened up, and looked at him, her lips tight.

"It'll be all right, Pa. Cody will have a pa. And we'll have a place—all of us. That means a lot, doesn't it?"

"Yes, Daughter," he said heavily, but then he kissed her and moved away toward the bedroom where he could be alone with his thoughts.

★ ★ ★ ★

Zane's fingers were numb with cold, so that when the big jack-rabbit leaped up right under his feet, he had to fumble for the trigger of the old twelve gauge. The rabbit didn't run straight but made a zigzagging path across the snow toward a patch of under-growth. Flinging up the ancient gun, Zane shot instinctively; and as he was driven backward by the recoil of the heavy weapon, Cody yelled, "You got 'im, Zane! You got that big ol' scudder!"

Zane lowered the gun. He stood there as the boy ran across to pick up the limp carcass of the rabbit, then came back holding it up. "You sure did get 'im, Zane!" he announced proudly. "Ain't many who could've did it!"

Zane shrugged, saying casually, "Ain't too hard once you get the hang of it. Next year you'll be big enough to hold this gun, or maybe we'll get you a sixteen gauge." He pulled a gunny sack out of his rear pocket, stuffed the rabbit into it, then said, "We better git home. My feet are plumb froze, and it'll be dark soon."

"Aw, let's go just a little farther," Cody begged. "We might see a big ol' buck, Zane!"

"No, this scatter-gun makes enough noise to skeer every critter for ten miles. Here—you carry the rabbit."

A new four-inch layer of snow lay on the ground, transforming the dead brown woods into a crystal wonder. The two turned and headed back across the field, breaking through with each step. The two of them stopped several times, once poking in a hole that had been used by a vixen, then taking a shot at another rabbit that darted in front of them.

"Hate to waste a shell," Zane muttered. "They cost money!"

Most of his thoughts were centered around money, and he grew silent as he thought of the three shells that were left. They cost four cents apiece, cash money, and he well knew that there were no spare pennies in his father's pocket.

He glanced at Cody, noting the thin jacket, worn almost through at the elbows, and at the shoes that were held on by strips of rawhide he'd cured himself. *He's gotta have some warm shoes somehow* was his thought, and glancing down, he saw that his own footwear was little better. Zane Jenson longed for things with a raw hunger that gnawed at him. The hill people all around him were poor, for it was a poor part of Arkansas, and the state was prostrate after the war, as were all the rest of the southern states that had fought against the North. Nobody had much money, and everyone learned how to make things or do without.

But since his father's illness, things had gotten practically unbearable. Putting in a cotton crop this year had been impossible, for they had lost their mule, who was so old that he'd simply died in his sleep. They'd spent all summer raising a garden, putting up pickles and vegetables and berries. They'd killed a hog and salted the meat down, their last full-grown animal, and now that was almost gone.

I'm tired of thinkin' about where the next meal's comin' from! Zane thought rebelliously. He had often considered running away, for at the age of fourteen he was capable of many things. He was a fine rider, having a natural gift for it, but his father forbade him to race horses to make money for other men. That had made him bitter, but he could not stay angry at his father for long.

Busy with his thoughts as they approached the house, he was taken off guard when Cody said, "Zane, somebody's at the house."

"Hold on," Zane said, reaching out to draw the boy back. He had the natural suspicion of the hill people, inbred almost, and he stood there peering at the horse hitched to the tree just beyond the porch. They both stood watching, ignoring the cold, and finally the door opened. The boys stared at the man as he mounted the big horse and rode off at a gallop.

"That was Mr. Malloy," Cody said. He turned to look up at Zane and asked, "Why we standin' out here, Zane? I'm cold."

"Yeah, so am I." Zane moved across the yard, a frown on his face, but he said nothing to Cody. This too was typical of him, to speak little. "Let's go to the barn to clean this rabbit. Be warmer in there."

Twenty minutes later they stepped into the house, and Cody ran to his mother, who was standing at the stove. "Ma, we got a big fat ol' rabbit! You should've seen Zane hit 'im!"

"Did you now? Why, that's fine!" Zane watched as she stopped and gave Cody a hug, then came to him. "It's a good thing you didn't miss, Zane," she said with a smile. "I'm pretty tired of potato soup."

Zane saw the marks of tears on her cheeks and stiffened, but said only, "I missed one on the way back."

Hope hugged him and kissed him on the cheek. "Can't hit them all," she said, then turned to lift the carcass of the rabbit from Cody. "My, he's a big one, isn't he? Let me get started on him right now!"

"Where's Grandpa?" Cody demanded.

"He's resting," Hope said. "Why don't you go tell him about the rabbit?"

"Sure!"

Cody shot off, shedding his coat and hat as he went, and Zane picked them up. As he hung them on the pegs on the wall, adding his own, he said, "I seen Willis Malloy riding off as we come in, Sis."

Hope had her back turned and said, "Why, yes, he did stop by. He wanted to see if we needed anything from town."

They were close, these two, and Zane at once went and gently pulled his sister around to face him. She ducked her head, but finally had to look at him. He studied her, then asked, "I guess he wants to marry you, don't he?"

"Why—!" Hope intended to avoid the issue, but looking at Zane's drawn face, knew that he had to know. "Yes," she said. "He came to ask me."

Zane bit his lower lip, thinking hard, then asked, "You gonna do it, Sis?"

"Yes, I am, Zane—" and plunged at once into the advantages of the marriage. She spoke of how bad things had been and told him how Malloy was willing to take care of their father. "And I haven't told you the best part, Zane," she said. "Mr. Malloy's bought a ranch out west, in Wyoming. And he wants you to be one of his cowboys!"

Zane stared at her, and she saw the excitement in his eyes and was happy for it. "Gosh, really!"

"You'll learn all about ranching and cows, Zane. And Cody will have a pa."

Zane was thrilled about the idea of becoming a cowboy in Wyoming, yet something in his sister's face made him hesitate. He wanted to be sure that she was happy and asked, "Why've you been cryin', Sis?"

Hope forced herself to laugh. "Oh, Zane, don't you know women always cry at weddings? I'm just starting early!" She put her arms around him, saying, "Don't tell Cody. Let me do that."

"All right, Sis." He moved away, but a thought came to him, and he turned to her again. His young face was lean and sensitive, and his eyes reflected his concern. "Sis—"

"Yes, Zane?"

"Well, I wanna say—you don't have to marry him if you don't want to. I can get a job. We'll make out."

Tears started to rise in Hope's eyes, but she said, "Oh, you get along, Zane! I'm going to have a husband and we're going to be ranchers in Wyoming! I'm just excited. Maybe a little scared—but I want to marry Mr. Malloy. You go along now."

"Well, okay, Sis." Zane left to go outside and cut wood, happy with his thoughts. *Gosh, me, a cowboy!* And he chopped wood with the vigor and enthusiasm of a young boy who suddenly had been handed a great dream.

CHAPTER TWO

TRAIL TO CHEYENNE

★ ★ ★ ★

Despite the objections of Willis Malloy, Hope refused to marry him until spring. Malloy's hair-trigger temper was touched by her attitude, but he finally forced a grin, saying, "I see you've got a little iron in your backbone, Hope. Well, I like a woman with spunk. But it means no honeymoon, you know. I've gotta git down to Texas when this winter breaks, scour the country for the best buy in stock. Gotta be on the trail to Cheyenne early as we can. First herds get the good grass."

"I'll marry you in the spring," Hope had said firmly. He had visited infrequently during the rest of the winter, as most of his time was spent getting ready to leave Arkansas.

Amos sold the farm to a neighbor who had long wanted to add it to his holdings. "After the loan was paid off, we got a little over fifteen hundred dollars cash," he reported to Hope. "I'll keep it for Cody and Zane. Maybe they'll need it someday."

That was in December, and they celebrated their last Christmas in Arkansas as 1871 slipped away. It was a special time for them all, realizing as they did that things would never be the same. On Christmas Day, Hope cooked the big turkey gobbler that Zane had bagged, made a large pan of cornbread dressing, and used some of the peaches she had put up to make a rich peach cobbler. After they could eat no more, Amos announced,

"Been some lean Christmas times for you all the last few years. I made up my mind this year it was gonna be different."

"Pa, you didn't go spending your money on us!" Hope exclaimed.

"Keep your mouth off me, Daughter," Amos grinned. As he stood up and went to the bedroom, his face was touched with a happy expression such as none of them had seen in a long time.

"He sure looks happy, don't he, Sis?" Zane said. "Wish I had something to give him."

Amos returned with a pile of bundles, which he stacked on his chair. "Now, I ain't got no long beard, nor I ain't climbed down no chimney, but reckon I'm as close to Santa Claus as we're likely to get. Zane, I couldn't figure out no good way to wrap this so's you'd be surprised, but here it is—"

Zane's eyes grew large as his father handed him a long bundle wrapped in brown paper. Quickly tearing off the paper, he drew a sharp breath as a brand-new rifle emerged—a repeating Spencer. Taking it in his hands, he ran his fingers over the gleaming metal and the smoothly finished stock. It was quiet in the room, and finally Cody piped up, "Gosh, Zane, that's a fine rifle gun! You gonna let me shoot it?"

Zane appeared not to hear. He had admired the weapon for months, stopping at the case where it was displayed in Teller's Hardware Store in town, but he had no idea his father had known of his desire. He tried to speak, had to clear his throat, then finally looked up and said, "Pa—it's real fine!" He wanted to say more, to tell them all how he felt, but he was not one to talk much.

Amos had his reward, however, when he saw the shine in the boy's eyes and the tremble in his hands. "Well, I'm expectin' to git a return on that gun, boy." He smiled and put his thin hand on Zane's shoulder. "You know how partial I am to a fat young doe, so I'll be expectin' to sink my teeth into one of them pretty regular. Now then," he said, his own eyes shining with pleasure. "It's your turn, Cody, but you'll have to wait while I go outside and git your present."

He left the room, and Cody could hardly keep still. "What is it, Ma?" he demanded.

"I don't know," Hope smiled. "This is all your grandfather's doing." They waited, admiring Zane's Spencer, and then they heard steps on the front porch. The door opened, and Amos entered, dragging a large red puppy by a cord.

"Well, here he is, Cody," Amos grinned, shoving the dog toward the boy. "Aaron Biggers told me he was gonna be the best coon dog he'd ever bred. Come and get acquainted with your dog."

Cody stood stock still for a moment. He had begged for a dog for years, but times had been too hard. Now he couldn't seem to breathe. Then he uttered a small cry and ran to the dog, running his hands over the smooth red fur and laughing when the puppy yelped and began licking his face.

Hope felt the tears gather in her eyes and looked up to meet her father's eyes. They both smiled, and Amos said, "A boy's gotta have a dog, ain't he now? Cody, you'll have to think up a good name for that pup."

"His name's Buck!" Cody looked up at his grandfather, adding, "I done named him a long time ago."

"Well, that's a good name, I reckon," Amos nodded. "Short and handy like. Dog don't need no fancy name, no more'n a man." Turning to the remaining presents on the chair, he picked up a large, rectangular box wrapped in red paper and handed it to Hope. "This is for you, Daughter."

Hope shook her head, saying, "You shouldn't have spent all this money, Pa—" When she had unwrapped the paper carefully and opened the box, she gasped and lifted her eyes to him. "Pa! How beautiful!"

As Hope removed a light blue silk dress from the box, Amos said, "I had it special made. Swiped one of your old dresses for a pattern. Now, go put it on and give us a fashion show."

While Hope was changing, Amos had to give special attention to Buck, allowing Cody to point out his fine features, including his enormous feet, which Cody informed them meant that he would be a big dog sure enough when he grew into them!

Finally Amos had to call out, "Hope, git yourself out here!" And when she stepped through the door, he and the boys stared at her. None of them had seen her in a fine dress, not for years. They were so accustomed to seeing her in faded calico dresses that the sight of her was a shock to all of them.

The dress was full length, but a pair of new white leather shoes that had been in the bottom of the box peeped out from underneath the full skirt. The skirt billowed out, but the bodice was formfitting, trimmed with tiny dark blue flowers embroidered along the bodice line and the delicate cuffs of the sleeves. The glowing blue material was picked up by the blue of her eyes, and she looked like a princess.

"You're the picture of your mother," Amos whispered, shaking his head. "She wore a dress like that the first time I ever seen her."

"Gosh, Ma!" Cody said. "I didn't know you were pretty like that!"

Zane reached over and slapped the boy on top of the head, but he was grinning. "That's a fine thing to say to your ma," he said. "Now, *I* always knew she was pretty."

Hope was flushed with pleasure and ran to her father, throwing her arms around his neck. "Oh, Pa—!" was all she could manage. As Amos Jenson looked around at his family, he was happy—happier than he'd been for years. "Well, shoot! Don't make such a fuss over it!"

"Aw, Pa, it ain't fair!" Zane complained. He still held the Spencer tightly, as though afraid someone would take it from him. "Here you got us all these fine presents, and we didn't get you a thing!"

"Didn't get me a present?" Amos said with a show of surprise. "Why, Zane, that just ain't so!" He gave the three of them a solemn look, then said, "It appears there's one more package here. You must've forgot about this one, I reckon." He bent over the chair and picked up the last present and held it out for them to see the card on it. "Looky there—it says right on this card, 'Merry Christmas to Amos, from Hope, Zane, and Cody.' "

Cody stared at the package, a puzzled look on his face. "I don't remember that, Grandpa."

"Neither do I," Hope smiled. "I can't wait to see what it is we gave you, Pa."

"Neither can I!" Amos said, and then he ripped the paper off and stood there looking down at the rich wood of the fiddle he held. "Well, I'll be dipped!" he exclaimed. "Just what I wanted! How in the world you kids knowed I wanted this is sure hard to figure! But now we can have us some fiddle music any old time we take a notion."

Hope was smiling now, for she recognized the fiddle. It was one that her father had longed for for years, ever since his old one had collapsed of age. She knew it was one of the fine fiddles made by an instrument maker in Fort Smith, and that it cost almost a hundred dollars. She had seen her father look at it longingly at the General Store more than once.

"Let's have some fiddle music, Pa!" she said, and soon the cabin was filled with the rich tones of the instrument. Later, they all went out, and Zane gave them an exhibition of his prowess with the rifle, happy to discover that two boxes of shells came with it. Then nothing would do but that they must take a hike through the woods so that Buck could show them how he was going to find coons.

They found no coons, of course, but that didn't matter. They stayed up late that night, Buck curled against Cody in front of the fire, Amos touching the fiddle fondly, and Zane oiling the rifle, cleaning it until Amos said, "Boy, you're gonna rub the bluin' off that rifle gun! Now don't sleep with it and blow your foot off, hear me?"

Finally Zane and Cody were in their bed, and Hope sat on the floor in front of the fireplace with her father. She had been happy all day, but now as they sat there, she grew sad. "You'll hate to leave this place, won't you, Pa? It's been home for so long."

"Good memories," he answered quietly. "But life has to go on. I'm praying that this will be a good thing for Zane and Cody—and for you, Daughter." His eyes, hidden by the shadows, glinted as the flames leaped in the fireplace. There was a sadness in him, but he kept it to himself. "This farm is wore out. The West is the place for young folks like you and the boys. I'm glad to live long enough to see it come."

Hope was curled up beside him, staring into the fire, and he let his hand drop to her head, caressing it as he had done when she was a little girl. She reached up and held it, pressing it tightly, then said, "I'm afraid, Pa."

She had never spoken of the time ahead, not so honestly, yet Amos knew her fears. He wanted to tell her not to be afraid, that everything would be good—but he was too honest a man for that. Finally he said, "Hope, you're a fine woman. You're like your mother was. She was strong—stronger than most men, I think."

"I miss her, Pa!"

"Sure. Me too." Amos suddenly rose and left the room. When he came back from his bedroom, he had his worn, black Bible in his hand. Sitting down, he thumbed through the pages, found a place, then looked at Hope.

"When your mama died, Hope," he said, "her last words were about you."

"About me, Pa?"

"Yes. I was sittin' beside her, holding her hand. She'd been in some sort of a coma. But she just opened her eyes all of a sudden, and her mind was clear." Amos paused, his eyes grown gentle as the memories came to him. Hope said nothing, her face turned up to him. "She told me goodbye, and then she told me to take care of you and Zane. And then she said, 'Amos, one day Hope is going to have a great need. God has given me something to help her.' She was going out, Hope, the life just leaving her body, but with the last strength she had, she said, 'Give her this—from the Lord—For the Lord hath called thee as a woman forsaken and grieved in spirit, and a wife of youth when thou wast refused, saith thy God. For a small moment have I forsaken thee; but with great mercies will I gather thee. In a little wrath I hid my face from thee for a moment: but with everlasting kindness will I have mercy on thee, saith the Lord thy Redeemer.' "

Amos leaned toward Hope, his finger on a page of the Bible. "It's in Isaiah fifty-four, Daughter, verses six through eight."

Hope took the Bible, read the verses, then looked up. "What does it mean, Pa?"

"Well, I don't reckon I know. But Ellie got it from God, and I think sometime or other, it's going to mean a lot to you. I've pondered it ever since she gave it to me, wondering if it was time to give it to you, but it never seemed just right." He put his arms around her and held her close. "Daughter, it's time now, and I pray that you'll take this as your ma's last gift—something she got from God. She loved you more'n you'll ever know, and I think she saw something coming, and I think she asked the

Good Lord to undertake to keep you from it."

Hope rested her head on her father's chest, a little frightened, but the thought of her mother thinking of her and praying for her at the very moment she slipped away from earth brought her joy.

"I'll remember, Pa!" she whispered. "I'll always remember!"

★ ★ ★ ★

The South Platte River flowed north of Denver, a wide, shallow river nestled between mountains that shouldered their way from the earth, rising high to the north. Cody had begged to be allowed to trail the herd, and Zane had promised to look after him. Hope, driving the supply wagon with her father lying down inside, had gone ahead with the cook, a small, taciturn man with the unlikely name of Ozzie Og. They left the herd at dawn, drove the team at a fast clip, and set up on the bank of the river in time to build a fire and cook for the crew.

Ozzie gathered firewood and some large, flat rocks with which to make a fireplace, leaving Hope to unpack the supplies for the meal. Amos got out and stretched his legs, then began picking up firewood. By the time Og had made a suitable fireplace and started a fire, Hope had gotten out the supplies. The two of them made dough for baking powder biscuits, started a big roast in the black pot, mixed the ingredients for cream gravy, and made four pies to bake in a large metal oven buried in hot coals.

"I'm gonna start on my sourdough," Og announced, and Hope watched him carefully. The tight-mouthed cook's sourdough biscuits were the best she'd ever had, but he'd lost his starter back in New Mexico, crossing the Canadian River. Og took two potatoes and boiled them until they were falling apart, strained them through a cloth, and poured the juice into a wooden keg that had originally held kraut. He added a cup of sugar and then flour until he had a thin batter. Setting the keg close to the glowing coals, he clamped the wooden lid down firmly, saying, "Gotta keep this here keg warm all night. When this sourdough starts working, it'll be ready for making biscuits in two, three days."

It was the longest speech Hope had heard Og make since

they had left Texas, and she glanced at him with surprise.

"Where'd you learn to cook, Ozzie?"

"Around cow outfits in Texas—when I was a kid." That apparently was his conversation for the afternoon, and he clamped his lips shut like a purse.

Hope saw her father take his Bible and sit down in the shade of the wagon. "I'll take a walk down the river, Pa. Guess the herd won't be here until nearly dark." He nodded, saying, "Don't stray too far."

She left the campsite and made her way down the southern bank of the Platte, noting right away that it would be an easy crossing for the cattle. It came to her that this was the sort of thing she would never have noticed two months ago when the drive had started from Texas. It was one of the imperceptible changes that the last two months had made. She was not the same woman, she mused, stopping to poke into the shallows with a sharp stick picked up from the bank.

A fish broke the surface ten feet out, rolling out of the water, the sun striking its scales and turning them for one moment into flashing silver. She stared at the roiling water, wondering if the fish were good to eat and wishing that she could put out a line. But there was no time for fishing on this drive, and she continued downstream, enjoying the solitude. The sun was hot in Colorado, as hot as it had been in Texas and New Mexico. It burned her neck, and she glanced down at her arms, a warm brown, toasted by the days under the sun.

Finally she walked into a grove of cottonwoods and stopped to enjoy the shade. She took off her boots and waded in the river, enjoying the coolness of the water. The touch of it made her think of how long she had been dirty, and she realized that she hadn't had a bath for weeks. *Won't find a better chance than this*, she thought, and stripped off her clothing. The water was colder than she expected, the chill of it taking her breath, but after she grew accustomed to it, she reveled in the sensation. Finally she climbed back onto the bank, allowed the sun to dry her off, then dressed, wrinkling her nose at the dirty clothing.

She sat down on a flat rock, letting the sun dry her hair, and the thought came to her again that she wasn't the same woman she'd been when she'd left Texas. This was almost the first time she'd been alone since that day, and now the silence and the expansive landscape around her seemed to bring back memories.

She remembered how Willis had gone to Texas alone to buy his herd. When he returned he came for her, driving her into Fort Smith, where they were married by a Baptist preacher. The wedding was quick, for he was anxious to start the drive. Any hopes she had cherished that Willis Malloy would be a more gentle man in private than he was in public were shattered during their two-day honeymoon in a local hotel. She was greatly relieved when they headed back, picked up her family, and made a fast trip to Texas, where the cattle drive started at once.

The herd was small, no more than four hundred head, mostly young stock. Malloy didn't tell her that he'd lost a great deal of money in a poker game, and not only had to cut back on the number of steers he'd planned to buy, but could afford only two hands and a cook to make the drive.

They had left the end of March, following the Pecos north from Texas into New Mexico. It was slow going, difficult for Hope and more so for her ailing father. Amos rode in a wagon loaded with supplies, with Hope driving so that he could lie down and rest from the heat of the sun. The boys both did fine. Zane was furnished a horse and did his share of the driving, as good a worker as any man. Malloy said to Hope, "That Zane, he's gonna be a real puncher. Cody, too, when he gets his growth."

Hope made herself useful, helping with the cooking, and even riding beside the herd at times to keep the cattle from straying. The two hands Willis had taken on were both young. One of them, Randy Duggins, was a tall, rangy young man of twenty-five. He was not an accomplished rider, being new to the trade, but was cheerful and a hard worker. The other rider was a slight man of thirty, a native of Tennessee and a veteran of the Confederate Army. His name was Smoky Jacks, and he was the guide for the outfit.

The first week of the drive, Jacks had given them the history of the trail they were on. "This here is called the Goodnight-Loving Trail," he said as he squatted by the fire, drinking the bitter black coffee. "Charlie Goodnight and a hairpin named Oliver Loving decided to go around the Comanche country over in north Texas. Everybody said they'd never make it, but in '66 they drove two thousand head the way we're goin'. 'Course, there's one stretch 'bout eighty miles with jist about no water—but I'd rather go thirsty than entertain a bunch of them Comanches."

Smoky Jacks' stories of Indians made Hope nervous, but they saw none in New Mexico, and now that they were fairly close to Cheyenne territory, it seemed unlikely they would have any problems.

Hope lay back, growing sleepy in the sun, but soon rose and made her way back to the camp. Og was looking off into the distance and shouted, "Here they come."

A tiny spiral of dust rose from the south, and two hours later Hope could make out the herd clearly. Her husband was riding point, as was his custom, trailed by the herd, which were lowing and bawling as they followed. Zane was on the right flank and Smoky Jacks on the left, leaving Randy Duggins on drag—a job they all hated, for it meant eating the dust of the herd all day. Malloy led the cattle to the river, where they began to drink thirstily. He came riding into camp with Jacks, and the two men set about eating at once. "We made good time today," Willis said. "How much farther we got to go, Smoky?"

Jacks deposited a huge hunk of apple pie in his mouth, chewing it thoughtfully. "Mebby two, three weeks. Say, this here is good pie. I bet you made this Miz Malloy." He glanced at the cook slyly, adding, "Ozzie there, we can use his pies to shoe the horses with if we run short." Og glared at him but said nothing.

"I want to make better time than that, Jacks." The words were brusk, and Malloy made them sound insulting, as if the cowboy were somehow failing at his job. The big man had been excited and genial at the beginning of the drive, but as the days had passed, he'd grown surly, speaking only in clipped, angry phrases. He had treated his horses savagely and had been so brutally short with Zane and Cody that both boys dreaded him.

Jacks drew the makings of a cigarette from his vest, rolled one with an easy motion, then said softly, "These critters can't fly, Boss. They gotta take it one step at a time—and there's just so many steps to Cheyenne."

Malloy threw his head back and glared at the small puncher. "I thought you was a trail boss, Jacks! You ain't showed me much!" He got up and threw his coffee into the fire, making a sizzling sound. "Soon as you eat, go back and send them boys over to eat. Don't let them cows stray, you hear?"

Smoky Jacks' eyes were half-shut in a sleepy expression. He said in the softest of voices, "I hear ya." He rose, nodded to Hope, then mounted his horse and rode toward where the herd was drinking.

"Willis, I think we've done pretty good," Amos said. "Not lost any cattle and we're right on the schedule you set."

"No thanks to you, old man," Malloy grunted. He had been primed for trouble with Jacks, and when it hadn't come, he was edgy. "You don't do nothin' but eat and sleep in thet wagon."

Hope interrupted quickly. "Pa's not well. You know that, Willis."

He moved toward her, grabbed her arm with a grip that made her wince, then pulled her away from the fire. "Git in the wagon, woman. I'm takin' the midnight shift, so it's time for bed."

Amos looked away as the burly man half dragged Hope toward the supply wagon. Ozzie Og was silent as usual. Amos slowly rose and walked off down the river. When he came back nearly an hour later, he unrolled his bedroll but didn't get into it. Zane and Cody were crouched around the fire, and Amos listened to them talking. As usual, Cody was sitting with Buck's head nudging him.

Finally they rolled into their blankets and were asleep at once. Amos and Og went to bed, too. At midnight, Malloy roused Zane, and the two of them went out to relieve Jacks and Duggins. It was not a good system, for none of them ever had a full night's sleep, but it was the best they could do with such a small crew.

Amos awoke to the sound of Malloy's angry voice. Climbing out of his bedroll, he saw young Duggins getting up from the ground, with Willis Malloy standing over him, cursing. Hope stood to one side, pleading with Willis, her face pale. "He didn't do a thing! We were just talking!" Meanwhile, Smoky Jacks was silently emerging from his bedroll like a cat stalking its prey. He slipped his gunbelt on and came to his feet as Malloy struck Duggins again, a fearful blow that drove the rider's head back and knocked him flat. The young man rolled helplessly, blood streaming down his face.

"I'll teach you to fool around with my wife!" Malloy bellowed, a gray pleasure in his brutal face. He reached down and yanked Duggins to his feet as though he were a child, then struck him in the stomach with a massive fist. Duggins doubled over, and Malloy knocked him to the ground again with a blow to the jaw.

Hope screamed, "Willis! He wasn't—!"

"Shut your mouth!" Malloy shouted, "or you'll get some of what I'm gonna give him."

He lifted his boot to kick the helpless man, but at that moment, Smoky Jacks said, "Hold it right there, Malloy!"

Malloy glanced up to see the small puncher come to stand beside Duggins. His eyes were half closed, and his arms were lax at his side. "That'll be about enough of that."

Malloy swelled with rage. "As soon as I kick him to pieces, I'll have some fun with you, Jacks!" He drew his boot back but never finished the motion.

Smoky Jacks had drawn the .44 so quickly that Malloy froze, his eyes full of unbelief. "You kick that boy one more time," Jacks warned, "and it'll be the last mistake you ever make."

Malloy was wearing a gun too, and he blurted out, "Put that gun up! Give a man an even chance."

"Anything to oblige." Jacks dropped the revolver into his holster and stood there, relaxed as if he were loafing. His eyes looked sleepy, but there was a readiness in his slight frame and a small smile on his lips that made Malloy hold himself very still.

Finally Malloy licked his lips, then muttered, "A man's got a right to fight for his wife, ain't he?" Malloy was not a cowardly man, but there was something dangerous in the small puncher that made him back down. "All right," he grumbled, "we got cattle to drive."

"Let's get one thing straight, Malloy," Jacks said. "I'm of a mind to walk off and leave you, and I don't reckon Randy here will stay. You pay him off for the full drive, and I'll finish the trip. You can either hire another hand—or do Duggins' work yourself. Don't matter to me. I was lookin' for a job when I found this one."

Malloy wanted to curse the man and run him out of camp, but he had enough shrewdness to say, "I'll hire a man, Jacks."

Smoky studied him, then bent and looked at the fallen cowboy. "Amos, let's clean this boy up."

A few minutes later, as Duggins rested against a wagon wheel, his head still reeling from the blows, Malloy strode over and thrust a fistful of money in his face. "That's full pay for the drive." Without another word, he turned and walked away.

Amos asked, "Think you can make it back to Denver by yourself, Randy?"

"Sure. I'll be okay." Randy slowly gathered his things, mounted his horse, and paused long enough to say, "Miz Malloy—I'm real sorry!"

"It wasn't your fault, Randy. God bless you!"

The next day nothing was said about the incident. Malloy sent them all ahead, while he rode back to Denver and hired a thickset puncher named Fred Gibson to finish the drive.

Ozzie came sidling up to Jacks that night, asking, "Smoky, would you've shot 'im?"

Smoky studied the cook's face, then said, "Sure would, Ozzie. And it would have been a pleasure!"

Og glanced over at Hope, then said, "He's likely to take it out on her."

"Nothin' I can do about that. I can fumigate a fellow for kickin' my partner when he's down—but what goes on between a husband and a wife, that's where I count myself out!"

CHAPTER THREE

MEETING WITH THE SIOUX

★ ★ ★ ★

"Gosh dang it, Zane!" Cody exclaimed. "I don't care if we never get to Wyoming!"

The two youngsters were crouched behind a small rise watching for antelope. Both of them were darkly tanned, which made Zane's light blue eyes seem even lighter. He ran his hand along the gleaming barrel of the Spencer, looked out at the white rag tied to a bush fifty yards off, then back to Cody.

"It beats pickin' cotton at that," he remarked. He glanced down at Buck, who was crouched beside Cody, and shook his head. "Cody, if that dog don't stop growin', he's gonna be big as a Texas longhorn time we get to Wyoming!"

"Ain't he a caution, though?" The big dog had grown amazingly during the drive and never strayed very far from Cody. The boy ran his hand over the dog's silky chest, then pulled a piece of bacon out of his pocket and poked it into the animal's large mouth. Buck swallowed it whole, looked hopefully at Cody, and wagged his tail.

"Keep that biscuit-eater quiet, ya hear me, Cody?" Zane warned. He glanced out at the white rag and shook his head. "You reckon Smoky's pulling one of his tricks on us? This kind of huntin' don't make no sense!"

Smoky Jacks had seen the boys leaving camp to go out to

hunt and had told them, "You fellers ain't likely to sneak up on no antelope. What you'd best do is let them come to you." When Zane had asked how that could happen, Jacks had explained, "Well, them critters is plain curious, Zane. Anything out of the ordinary, they'll come pokin' around to see about it. So you just tie a white rag to a bush, then plump yourselves down a good rifle shot away. Keep quiet enough, and them antelope will come to investigate—then you can put meat on the table."

Zane and Cody had been suspicious of the rider, for he had pulled their legs several times, but he'd assured them that this was the truth. They'd gone two miles from camp and waited for a shot, and now even as Zane spoke his doubts, he broke off to whisper, "Looky, Cody! There he is!"

Cody peered cautiously over the edge of the rise, taking a look. "I can see two of 'em, Zane! Maybe you can get 'em both!"

That was the way it happened, for as soon as the two antelope had come close enough to touch the rag with their inquisitive noses, Zane put a shot through one, which fell dead instantly, then threw another shell into the chamber and knocked the other animal down before it had gone ten feet.

"Apostles and prophets!" Cody yelled, leaping up, his eyes big as silver dollars. "You plugged 'em both, Zane!"

Zane felt inordinately pleased with himself. "With a rifle gun like this, a feller can do some real hunting!" he grinned. "Let's get these two back to camp."

As they rode back with the carcasses of the antelope tied behind their saddles, Cody talked incessantly. But as they drew nearer to the camp, he grew quiet. Zane noted his silence and knew what was the matter with the boy. "Don't let Mr. Malloy get you down, Cody," he said finally.

Cody gave him a quick glance, then shook his head. "He's a mean ol' scudder, ain't he, Zane?"

The older boy made no answer at first. His eyes were on the hills that rose sharply over to their left, and he studied them carefully. "Cody, keep your eyes goin' all the time. Smoky said we could run into some Injuns around here, and we don't want 'em to come up on us sudden like."

Cody looked around at once, his eyes shaded by the brim of the floppy hat he wore. "Would you shoot 'em if they came at us, Zane?" he demanded.

"Depends on how many there was. This here Spencer only holds seven shots. If they was eight of 'em, I don't see how we could win—besides, I might miss one of 'em."

"Naw, you wouldn't miss none of 'em," Cody said, with boundless optimism in his tone. He watched the hills carefully until they passed them, then murmured, "I *hate* that ol' Malloy."

Zane glanced at the boy quickly, noting the stubborn set of Cody's lips and the half-shut eyes. "He's a mighty hard man, all right, but we gotta get along with him, I reckon."

"But, Zane, he's mean to Ma!"

The remark brought a quick streak of anger to Zane, and he thought about the bruises he kept seeing on his sister from time to time. She would put him off whenever he asked about them, claiming that she had run into something, but he knew better. Now he could only say, "Nothing we can do about it, Cody." He tried to think of something better to say and finally added, "It's a pretty tough business, bringin' up a trail herd like this, and he ain't never done it before. He's scared of Injuns and that the cattle might get sick or lost in a river. When we get to the ranch and things settle down, he'll be a mite easier."

Cody was staring down at his hands and muttered, "I don't think he will. If a man's mean, he'll be mean anyplace."

They were close enough to see the smoke of Ozzie's fire now, and Zane warned, "Don't give him no trouble, Cody. We'll make out all right."

When they rode into camp, Hope and Ozzie both stopped their work and came over to admire the antelope. Hope gave the boys a hug, saying, "I guess we don't have to worry about a square meal around here, do we? Not with hunters like you two!"

Ozzie was pleased, but too contrary to show it. "You don't expect me to clean them things, I hope?" he asked pugnaciously.

"No, I'll do it," Zane grinned. "Can we have 'em tonight?"

"Naw, you cain't. We're having something better'n a stringy old antelope tonight," the crusty cook grumbled. The closest thing to a smile that ever appeared on his lips showed itself briefly, and he added, "Tonight you're gonna git something better'n you ever had before—my own special stew."

"What's it called, Ozzie?" Hope asked curiously.

Og gave her a crafty look. "It ain't fittin' to say its name, not with women and young'uns around," he announced. He stalked off, leaving them mystified, and Zane whispered to Cody, "Must be a pretty bad name, huh?"

Og was, in a way, an artist—when it came to preparing decent food for the crew. A young steer had broken its leg, so Ozzie butchered it at once before Malloy had a chance to notice. Malloy was so stingy with his cattle that the crew had lived on game and hardtack for weeks. Og himself was heartily sick of it and had determined to have a meal fit for a king. He cut up the beef liver and heart into one-inch cubes, then sliced the marrow gut into small parts. He placed this into a Dutch oven and after covering it with water let it simmer for three hours. He then added salt, pepper, and hot sauce as carefully as a scientist doing an experiment. The main stew he cooked in a larger pot; then an hour before supper, he took the sweetbreads and brains, cut them into small pieces, and added them to the stew.

He timed his meal well, for Malloy and the two hands had come in when the finished stew had been simmering for an hour.

"Is it all right to leave the cattle all alone?" Zane asked Malloy.

"Not for long," Malloy grunted. "You and Gibson go watch 'em after supper."

Smoky pulled off his hat and wiped his forehead. "They ain't going no place," he remarked. "Not with that good grass and water."

"Maybe they ain't going anyplace," Malloy snapped. "But they could get stolen mighty easy." He was in a surly mood and trudged over to take one of the tin plates Hope had set out. He helped himself to a large portion of the stew, then walked off and sat down by himself, eating in silence.

Smoky waited until Hope, the boys, then Gibson had gotten their stew before taking a plate. But as soon as he had filled his own plate and taken a bite, he looked across at Og, chuckling with undisguised admiration. "Ozzie, you old bandit! This is—!"

Og glared at him. "Shut your mouth, Jacks! It ain't polite to say the name of this here stew in front of a lady!"

Jacks looked surprised. "Well, that's its name, ain't it? I never heard it called nothing else."

"Don't make no nevermind," Og snapped. "Jist eat it and don't call it nothing!"

The cook's attitude amused Jacks. He looked over at Hope and said, "I'm just an ignorant cowboy without no fine manners. But from now on I'll call this fine stew something real genteel. How 'bout—jelly bean soup?" He rolled his eyes toward Og. "That fancy enough for you, Ozzie?"

Both Cody and Zane were grinning widely, and Hope herself smiled. "Well, it doesn't have any jelly beans in it, Smoky," Og fumed.

"Don't matter, as long as it *sounds* nice," Jacks said. "Ozzie here, he's used to fine company, you see. Guess I'll have to quit chewing tobacco in his presence. Don't do to offend the cook on a drive."

For the next three days things went well, and Hope commented to Smoky as the cowboy rode in, weary and dusty from a long day's trailing the herd, "It looks like we're going to make it without any trouble."

Smoky lowered his coffee cup and considered the sight of the cattle a few hundred yards to his left. "Well, it might be so. But a drive ain't over till it's over."

"Aw, don't be so blasted gloomy, Smoky!" Amos said. "God's watched over us all this way. We'll be on the ranch in a week, Willis says. And we've enjoyed Ozzie's jelly bean soup."

"Yeah, I reckon," Jacks said reluctantly. "Got to admit it's been an easy drive." He drank the rest of his coffee, stood up, then said blandly, "Well, if the cattle don't stampede, or get drowned in a river—and if they don't get tick fever, and if the Sioux don't raid us, or if we don't have a hail storm—"

"Aw, git out of here, Jacks!" Og snapped. "We don't need none of your palaverin'!"

Jacks left, grinning at the cook and winking at Hope. "Jest funnin' ya, Miz Malloy. I reckon we'll make it fine."

That night Hope tried to be especially nice to Willis, but he shook his head in a surly fashion, ignoring her efforts. When he left to go back to the herd, she sat in front of the fire, poking it with a stick from time to time, watching the sparks fly up in myriad showers of miniature stars. She was very tired and also depressed, though she concealed this as well as she could from the others. The two months on the trail had been physically wearing, but it was her marriage that threw a dark cloud over her spirit.

She had known that Willis Malloy was not a gentle man before she married him, but somehow she had conceived the hope that beneath the rough exterior lurked something finer. Her brief and unpleasant honeymoon, and now the two months with him on the trail, had completely extinguished all such hope. He had shown nothing except a callous selfishness. She felt degraded, for he used her as he used his horses, cruelly and with a vicious temper. At first she had hoped that their marriage would be some sort of union that went beyond sex, but he had never once inquired as to her needs as a woman. She had food and a place to sleep—what more could she want? This insensitivity, along with his physical brutality, had crushed the lightness of Hope's spirit. She lived now with the certain knowledge that there was nothing better to expect in the days and years to come.

"You sorry we came?"

Hope started, turning to find her father standing beside her. She brushed her hair back, saying, "No. It's been hard, but when we get to the ranch things will be easier." She reached up, took his hand, and pulled him down to sit beside her. "How do you feel tonight?"

"Tolerable," Amos said quietly. He was, in fact, feeling very weak, but he never complained. Now he sat there, looking up at the stars gathered overhead, and uttered reverently, "The heavens declare the glory of God." He put his hand over hers, saying gently, "The stars have glory, but we have to live in a pretty grubby world, don't we, Hope?"

She glanced at him quickly. It wasn't like him to be despondent. Since her marriage, he had been different, and she knew he blamed himself for forcing her into it. "Why, Pa, it's a beautiful world! Think of the people having to live in tiny, dirty places in the city! And we have space and the big blue sky and rivers!"

Amos Jenson sat there, listening to Hope, and was proud of her. He knew the terrible sacrifice she had made, and it grieved him to the heart that this delicate, fine daughter of his was yoked to a brute who abused her.

"The boys are doing well," he said. "Both of them love it out here. It'll be a better life for them than back on that wore-out farm in Arkansas."

"But you miss it, don't you, Pa?"

"Well, a man gets used to a place, sure enough. But this is a good country, Daughter." He longed to say more but couldn't find the right words. He slowly stood to his feet and sighed. "Guess I'll turn in. Willis said we'd be at the ranch in a week, huh?"

"That's what he said. I'll be glad to get there. Maybe there'll be a church close enough for us to get to. You could preach a revival meeting." Hope tried to smile, but the effort was a failure. "Don't worry about me, Pa," she said quietly. "I'm all right."

The next day was cloudy, and Smoky observed to Fred Gibson, "Looks like we got a little weather comin', Fred. Don't like the looks of them clouds."

He proved to be correct, for a drenching rain swept across the plain two hours later, accompanied by a lightning storm. It was brief, but the jagged bolts and the resounding peals of thunder terrified the cattle, which broke into a blind run. Zane pulled his horse up as the animals tried to bolt, and Smoky yelled as he went sailing by, "Zane, I'm gonna try to turn 'em! Stay on the flank!"

It was a nightmarish experience, and Zane fought down his fear. The churning hooves of the stampeding cattle would cut a man to pieces in a minute, he knew, but he did as Jacks had instructed him. Glancing over his shoulder, he saw that the wagons were not in the path of the herd and was grateful for that. The cattle, though angular and ungainly to look at, ran with surprising speed, their hooves pounding as they thundered along. A steaming heat rose from the herd as they ran wildly, the thin light reflecting on their horns and tails.

Zane saw that Jacks had reached the front of the stampede. The puncher began firing his revolver in the air, and when that was empty he yanked his slicker off and began flailing it in the faces of the leaders. It was a daring business, for one slip and Jacks would be down under the thundering hooves. Even though Zane was terrified as he watched, he thought, *I wish I had the nerve to do that!*

He saw a couple of the leaders dodge and some of them went down, but gradually the herd turned to the right, in Zane's direction. He gave way to let them come. As the huge animals tired, they could no longer maintain their speed, and the mad run finally gave way to a loping gallop, then slowed to a walk.

Malloy came charging from the rear, crying out, "Hold 'em! Hold 'em!" But there was no need, for the lightning had faded and the cattle moved with their heads down, bawling but no longer in a running mood.

The men rode around the herd for an hour, ready to contain another outburst, but finally Malloy said, "Guess they're all right. I'm goin' back and see how many we lost."

Zane gave him a hard look. "Be nice if you'd say a word to Smoky," he said in a spare tone. "If it wasn't for him, they wouldn't have stopped."

Malloy wiped the rain from his face, gave Zane a hard look, then snarled, "That's what he gets paid for," and galloped off.

Shaking his head in disgust, Zane moved to where Jacks was trying to roll a cigarette and said, "Wish *I* could do a thing like that, Smoky—stoppin' the herd, I mean."

Jacks grinned at him. Strain drew his mouth tight and there was a slight tick in his right eye, but he said, "Why, boy, that weren't nothin'. Once when I was over in New Mexico—" He began to spin a tall tale about a drive he'd once made, and Zane listened, wishing he'd done some of the things Jacks had done.

They continued to watch the herd carefully, but the run had taken all the starch out of the cattle. When Smoky and Zane were relieved by Gibson, they rode to the chuck wagon and downed a hot meal—antelope steaks and spicy baked beans. Zane was telling Cody and Hope about how Jacks had stopped the herd when suddenly Malloy leaped to his feet, yelling, "Look out—!"

All of them looked up, and Cody's heart seemed to stop as he turned to see a small band of Indians standing no more than fifty feet away. He and his mother moved closer to Zane, who had gotten to his feet and was gripping the Spencer in his right hand.

"Careful, Boss!" Smoky warned as Malloy put his hand on his revolver. "These are Sioux, Malloy. I ain't sure we got the best hand in this game."

Malloy asked tersely, "You speak their lingo, Jacks?"

"Not a whole lot of it—but I'll give it a shot." Jacks walked away from the chuck wagon, stopping in front of the line of warriors and lifting his hand, palm upward. He spoke a few words in a guttural tone, then waited.

One of the Indians immediately got down off his horse. He came forward carrying a rifle, his eyes opaque. "Me White Wolf." He studied the whites, then declared boldly, "Hungry—want cows."

At once Malloy stepped forward saying, "No—!" but as he did, several of the Sioux lifted rifles. Two of them fitted arrows to bowstrings.

Jacks said sharply to Malloy, "Ain't no choice here, Malloy. It's your wife and family we got to think about. I'll make the best deal I can." He turned to White Wolf and began talking trade. Even though Hope could not understand much of the dickering, which was carried on mostly in Sioux and sign language, she understood that the Indian wanted too much. He kept raising his rifle as a bargaining power, but Jacks kept shaking his head.

Jacks had argued the chief down to four cows, telling Malloy they could take the two killed in the stampede. Finally it seemed to be settled, but then White Wolf nodded toward Buck, who was standing beside Cody, and added, "Dog—go with White Wolf!"

Cody cried out, "No! You ain't takin' Buck!"

For some reason the Indian had made up his mind to have the dog, perhaps as a matter of pride. White Wolf raised his rifle over his head and the others followed suit. "Give dog—or we fight!"

"He means it!" Malloy hollered, and went at once and grasped Buck by the scruff of his neck. When Cody tried to stop him, he knocked the boy to the ground with a backhand that brought a cry from Hope, who ran to help him up.

"Don't let them have the dog, Willis!" she cried.

"Shut your mouth, woman!" Malloy spat out roughly. He moved to where White Wolf stood and shoved the dog at him. "Take the dog," he said grimly.

White Wolf laughed at Buck who was struggling in vain to get at the chief. The Indian said a word, and one of the younger warriors slipped from his horse and came to get Buck. He strode back and mounted his horse with ease, holding Buck securely in the crook of one arm.

"Let them have another steer," Hope begged. "It's Cody's dog."

"They'd take that deal," Jacks said at once. "They'll probably eat the dog anyway." He hesitated, then added, "If it was my boy, I'd give 'em the steer."

Malloy glared at him, then shook his head. "Plenty of dogs around. Tell 'em to get out."

White Wolf had watched this with interest. When Jacks told him, "I'll get your cows," the Indian nodded and turned to go, but at that moment Cody broke loose from Hope and went hurtling across the space. He hit White Wolf with his fists flailing, and the Indian staggered back, anger in his eyes. Hope cried out, "Cody—!" and Jacks' hand dropped to his revolver.

It was an explosive situation, but suddenly the big Indian laughed. He pulled Cody away, with one hand grasping the boy's hair, and studied him. Cody kept trying to fight but could not get close enough. "I'll kill you!" he was shouting, and even White Wolf knew what this meant from the boy's tone and the fire in his eyes.

A laugh ran along the line of Indians, and one of them said something that amused White Wolf. He shoved the boy toward Jacks, who caught Cody and held him fast. "Good fighter," White Wolf observed, obviously pleased by the scene. Then he said, "Give cow."

Cody stopped fighting, his face red from the struggle. Hope was weeping, and at that moment Zane spoke up. "Mr. Malloy, give 'em the cow. I'll work it out."

Malloy glared at him. "You'll work anyway!"

Zane drew himself up, his eyes filled with anger. "No, I won't. I'll run off and get a job. Let 'em have the cow."

Malloy was seething with rage. He was a man who couldn't stand to be crossed. "You keep your trap shut or I'll wale ya!"

Zane looked at Cody, then without hesitation walked straight toward White Wolf. The Indian's face instantly grew tense, for the boy had the Spencer in his hand. A sudden mutter ran along the line of Indians, but Zane was holding the rifle out. "The gun for the dog," he said harshly.

White Wolf stared at the boy's face, then nodded slowly. He took the rifle and said a word. The Indian holding Buck bent down and released the dog, who ran straight to Cody. White Wolf studied the boy carefully, then said, "We go now."

Fred Gibson went along with the Indians to watch them butcher their cows. As they all disappeared over the ridge, Hope went quickly to Zane and put her arms around him, but he was stiff and unyielding as a tree. Cody came to say, "Zane—I won't never forget it—!"

Malloy glanced toward Jacks and couldn't mistake the look of scorn he saw on the lean rider's face. He couldn't do anything about that, so he turned on Zane. "You fool kid! That Spencer was worth twenty curs like that!"

Zane stepped away from his sister and stood there, his eyes cold. "And one cur is worth twenty of you, Malloy!"

Willis Malloy took a step forward, an insane rage on his face, but a voice stopped him in his tracks. "Hold it there!" He looked around to see that Jacks had drawn his revolver and pulled the hammer back. Malloy froze in his tracks, caught by the threat in Jacks' words. Taking a deep breath, he said, "If I'd have knowed it meant that much to you boys, I'd have let them have another cow."

"No, you wouldn't," Zane said. "You're cheap and a liar, Malloy."

"Get out of this camp!" Malloy yelled, his face crimson. "If I ever catch you—"

"Here, that's enough!" Jacks nodded to the cook, saying, "Ozzie, fix up a big sack of grub." As Og moved quickly to throw groceries into a sack, Jacks spoke to Zane. "It ain't but a day's ride to a ranch I know. Owner's name is Wells. Tell him I sent you, Zane, and that it'd be a favor to me if he'd give you a job."

He began telling the boy how to get to the ranch, and when Og came with the supplies, Smoky offered, "Take that big roan I been riding."

"Hey, that's *my* horse!" Malloy yelled.

Smoky looked at him, then said, "All right, I'll go with the boy. We can ride double."

Malloy gasped and shot a look around the circle. He knew he had no choice and muttered, "All right, he can borrow the horse."

"Make him out a bill of sale and sign it, Malloy," Smoky demanded. "And hurry it up, or I'm gone."

Malloy wanted to tell Jacks to get out too, but knew he had

no chance of getting the herd through without the experienced rider. He turned to the wagon and disappeared inside.

Hope cried, "Oh, Zane, you can't leave!"

"Gotta do it, Sis." Then Zane turned to his father. "Pa, I'll find us a place and come and git you, I promise."

Amos came over to stand by his son. He put his arm around the boy's shoulders. "Zane—I was never prouder of you. The Lord will take care of you." Then he moved to the chuck wagon and lifted his rifle out. "Take this. It ain't no Spencer, but it's true as steel." He waved off Zane's protests, saying, "Man's got to have a gun in this world, son." He reached into his pocket, pulled out a wallet, then removed several bills. "Got to have a little cash, too, until you draw a paycheck," he said. "You can pay me back sometime."

"Pa—" Zane said tightly, but then Malloy was back. He held out a piece of paper and yelled at the boy, "Don't show up on my place—*ever!*"

Zane threw a saddle on the roan, tied the groceries on the back of it, then mounted. "Thanks, Smoky," he said briefly. He tried for a grin but without much success. "Cody, you look out for your ma, ya hear me?"

"Sure!"

Cody watched with the others as Zane rode out, and then Malloy said loudly, "Well, that's that!"

But it was not, and they all knew it. Malloy could feel the antagonism in the camp and muttered, "I'll take the first watch."

"I hate him, Ma!" Cody said, staring at the horseman. "Let's run off, you and me and Grandpa. We can get Zane and we'll get us a place."

Hope shook her head. "We can't do that, Cody." She left his side, and Cody looked at his grandfather. "Why does he have to be so mean, Grandpa?"

Amos shook his head. "Don't rightly know, boy." He turned aside as well, and Cody sat down by the wagon wheel and fondled Buck's sleek head, thinking of Zane. It made him feel sad that Zane had lost his Spencer. "When I grow up, I'll get rich and I'll buy him ten rifle guns like that!" he whispered. Then he got up, and the dog followed at his heels as he walked away from the wagon.

CHAPTER FOUR

ARROW MAKES AN OFFER

★ ★ ★ ★

After White Wolf's visit there had been no more trouble on the drive. The weather had mitigated and no other Indians had appeared. Two days after Zane left, they reached the South Platte and turned the herd west, and on the third day following, Malloy led them to a broad flat plain that seemed to stretch on endlessly.

"This is the place," he said to Hope, looking around eagerly. She was sitting in the wagon, her father resting in the bed under the canvas. Malloy was riding alongside, keeping pace with the wagon. "That red chimney rock over there—that's the marker for the southeast corner." He pulled a map out of his pocket, studied it, then called out to Jacks, "Turn 'em north!" Replacing the map inside his pocket, he pointed on ahead. "House ought to be right beneath that slight rise over there." When Hope said nothing, he grew irritated. "Well, cain't you talk? A man gits tired of nothin' but the sound of his own voice, blast it!"

Hope turned to look at him, somewhat surprised at his outburst. Since Zane had left she'd not said a word to him—nor had anyone else for that matter. Their silence had grated on him, she realized, but she wondered why it bothered him so much. "It looks fine," she said evenly. "I'll be glad to be in a house again."

He rode silently for a moment, considering her response. "It probably ain't much of a house."

"It doesn't matter. We'll make out."

He hesitated, obviously wanting to say something, but changed his mind. Finally he said, "I'll go on ahead and locate the house."

"All right, Willis."

As he spurred his horse on and rode over the rise, she pulled the team to a stop, then climbed back under the canvas. Kneeling by her father, she asked, "Pa, how do you feel?"

Jenson's face was pale, and he appeared to be asleep. But his eyes opened when she spoke to him, and he smiled faintly. "Makin' it fine, Daughter."

She took the stone jug that rested on the bed of the wagon, poured some of the tepid water into a tin cup, then lifted him into a sitting position. "It's warm, but wet," she smiled. He drank a little, then she let him lie back. "We'll have you on the home place tonight." Taking her handkerchief, she moistened it with the water, then carefully wiped his face.

There was little of the bright spirit in her that Amos had loved to see, and he asked, "Are you worried about Zane?"

"Yes. He's too young to be away from home."

"That's a fact," Amos agreed. "But God knows where he is. And you and I have agreed in prayer that he'll be kept from harm. So it'll be fine with him."

"Yes, Pa."

Hope had always envied the simple faith that her father possessed. He had the gift of faith, it seemed, more than anyone she'd ever known. When things were at their worst, he would pray, then say, "Well, it's up to God now—and He ain't never failed us, has He?"

One of the few times Hope could remember her father getting angry with her had been the occasion when she'd asked, ". . . but what if it doesn't work? What if prayer doesn't work?" He had snapped at once, "That's *doubt and unbelief* you're atalkin', Daughter! It's what got all the Israelites killed, doubtin' that God was able to take them out of Egypt! There ain't no good reason to doubt someone as lovin' and merciful as God. So don't let me *ever* hear you talk like that again, you hear?"

Hope looked down at her father's pale face, wished that she

had his faith, then smiled as she rose. "You feel like riding on the seat with me, Pa?"

"Well, I think I do." She helped him to the seat, then the two of them looked around at the open country that would be their home.

"Big, ain't it, Daughter?" Amos shook his head in amazement, eyeing the broad sweep of the land. Very few trees interrupted the vast gray-yellow expanse that extended to the horizon. "Didn't know a man could see so far," he remarked. "Always had trees and mountains in the way back home."

Father and daughter sat silently together—the wagon bumping and swaying across the rough land—both lost in their own thoughts as they contemplated their new surroundings. Two hours later, Malloy came galloping back in a cloud of dust. "House is right over there—" He signaled for them to follow him toward a stand of cottonwoods that lined the banks of a small creek. He pulled up where the creek made an elbow-shape at the foot of the slowly rising hills. "There it is," he nodded. "Get down and let's see what we got."

Hope climbed down off the wagon, stretching stiff and sore muscles, then turned to help her father down. But she realized that he would rather do it himself, so she turned to look at her new home. It was a poor excuse for a house, not nearly as good as the cabin they had left in Arkansas. It was a simple single-story structure, built of roughhewn lumber that had weathered to a drab gray over the years. The unpainted boards were warped by rain and sun, some of them lying on the ground, some hanging on only by a rusted nail or two. All the windows were broken.

The inside of the house was in even worse condition. Pieces of broken furniture lay scattered about; the floor was littered with old papers, broken glass, and nests made by pack rats. The broken windows had not stopped the endlessly blowing sand and dust from piling up in every corner and on every surface.

"Well, it's a mess," Malloy stated matter-of-factly. "But it's bigger than I thought it would be." They examined the rest of the house—four rooms besides the kitchen. All were in equally poor shape, and Hope found herself overwhelmed and depressed by the thought of trying to make this into a home.

"Guess Og and the boy can help you clean it up" was all

Malloy had to say to her. "At least we got a good cookstove and plenty of water nearby."

"It'll be fine," Hope assured him, not wanting Willis to see her inner turmoil. "I'll get started right away."

Malloy left then, returning to the spot along the creek where Jacks and Gibson had taken the cattle to drink. He pulled up to the chuck wagon, ordering, "Ozzie, go help my wife get the house cleaned up."

Smoky Jacks was sitting in the saddle with one leg crooked around the horn. He had just rolled a cigarette and lit it. "So long, Ozzie. I'll sure miss that jelly bean soup of yours." Og nodded at the rider, and as he drove the wagon away to carry out his boss's orders, Jacks turned to face Malloy. "Guess if you'll pay me off now, I'll be movin' along."

Malloy hesitated, then reached into his pocket. Pulling out a wad of bills, he counted out Jacks' wages, then shoved the money back into his pocket. He said reluctantly to the wiry puncher, "You did a good job. I'm much obliged."

"Sure." Jacks jammed the bills carelessly into his shirt pocket, then dislodged his foot from the saddle and stuck it in the stirrup. He took a deep draw on the cigarette, studied the cattle for a moment, then asked suddenly, "You see them cows with the arrow brand?"

"Shore do," Malloy answered. "Quite a few of 'em—and some of 'em grazin' on my grass." His eyes narrowed, and he asked, "What about 'em?"

"They belong to Silas Head. He owns the biggest ranch around here—and claims most of what he don't own. He's a rough old cob."

"Well, he'll have to get his cows off my graze."

"Yeah, well, good luck, Malloy." Jacks picked up his reins, but something was on his mind, and he stopped and turned to Malloy again. "None of my business, but if I was you, I'd be careful about Arrow. Head's hired a rough crew. Big outfit like that likes to crowd the small fellows."

Malloy's temper, never far from the surface, was aroused. He flushed, saying, "I don't care how big Arrow is, they cain't use my grass."

Jacks saw that his warning had been useless, so he merely

59

nodded. "Yeah, well, I'll be movin' on." He turned his horse and rode away, stopping only long enough to speak to Cody, who was on his pony, watching the cattle with Fred Gibson. "Hey, Cody, I'm pullin' out," he said, stopping beside the boy. "You tell your ma and your grandpa goodbye for me, will you?"

"You're leaving?" Disappointment clouded the boy's eyes, and he looked up at the cowboy, asking hopefully, "Will you see Zane?"

"Might just do that," Smoky grinned. "You keep your eye out for him and me. Mind your ma and your grandpa. You're gonna be some punkins, Cody. Any fellow who'd tackle White Wolf—why, he's a fellow to tie to." Jacks winked at him, then nodded at Gibson, "So long, Fred," and galloped away. As he left, he was sad, for he saw no happy ending for this family.

★　★　★　★

"New bunch moved into the Carlin place."

As Ash Caudill had known, his casual remark struck a raw nerve in the owner of the Arrow spread. Caudill had been the foreman of the huge ranch for four years, ruling over the crew with an iron hand. He had recruited them as an officer collects a company of fighting men, and only a man of Caudill's skill with a six-gun could have controlled them. There was little in his appearance to reveal the deadly killer instinct and the absolute coolness under fire. He was not tall, no more than average in height, but he was compactly built, well-muscled, and perfectly coordinated. He looked at the world out of slate-gray eyes, speaking softly as a rule, but he had a set of hair-trigger reactions and a temper like a land mine, unpredictable and violent. He was a handsome man of twenty-nine, with brown hair always neatly slicked down and neat features, a ladies' man—it was said, though he kept that part of his life separate from his job as foreman.

He was standing in front of Silas Head's desk in the big, rangy room used by the cattleman for a study. Once a week, Caudill came to give Head a summary of the conditions of the range and to apprize him of any other details he thought he should be aware of. Caudill had saved this one bit of information until last, knowing that it would set the big man off. When the explosion came, Caudill had expected it.

"Clear Creek's the only water in that part of the range," Head bellowed, speaking as if he were addressing a town meeting, though only the two of them were in the room. "We'll have to use that graze if we're to meet the government contract—and we can't use it without that water."

Silas Head was a huge, burly man—in his sixties but still hale and healthy. He had come to Wyoming years earlier, fought the Sioux for the land and the rustlers who came like hyenas to glut themselves with his cattle. The battles, no less violent than those fought at Gettysburg or Shiloh, had not left him unmarked. Physically, he carried part of an arrowhead in his back, too close to the spine for the doctors to risk removing it, and several bullet tracks scattered in various parts of his huge body. Spiritually, the damage was worse, for in the deadly fight to build Arrow into a great ranch, he had become a despot. Not an enlightened despot, but one who had managed to avoid annihilation by striking his enemies as hard and quickly as possible. The stubbornness of his spirit was reflected in the truculence of his chin, the set of his jaw, and the steadiness of the blue eyes that drilled men who crossed him like twin bullets. He had been a fighting man in his youth, accounting personally for those who tried to stop him, and now as the titular head of the largest ranch in eastern Wyoming, he used hard men to do that sort of thing for him.

Now he glared at his foreman. "You'll have to get them off that claim, Ash!"

Caudill shrugged in a casual manner. "I told you we should have bought that claim from Carlin. After we softened him up, he would have sold out cheap."

"So now it's my fault?" Head demanded. He was not a man who could bear censure, but he gave Caudill more leeway than he did most men. There were two reasons for this: first, because Caudill was one of the few men he knew who was hard enough to keep the crew in line, and second, because there was some possibility that the foreman would be his son-in-law one day. These two facts gave Head pause, and he rubbed his chin. "Fact is I did plan to buy that place, just for the water. But Carlin got sore and left before I could get to him." He stood to his feet and moved around the desk to look out the window. A group of cowboys were sitting on the top rail of the corral, yelling like Comanches as a rider tried to stay on top of a paint horse. "That all they got to do?" he muttered.

Caudill ignored the question. "What d'ya want me to do about this new fellow? Run him out?"

"No. We'll go make him an offer. Come along." Head grabbed his Stetson from the horns of a monstrous elk head and stomped out of his study. As the two of them left the house and stepped into the saddle, a young woman riding a fine mare tore around the corner of the barn and headed toward them. She pulled the mare up so abruptly that the horse threw back her head and reared her front legs in protest.

"Diane, I told you to quit riding like a wild Indian!" Silas Head's words were hard, but his eyes were not angry. This was his only surviving child, his wife having died five years after his daughter's birth. There had been a son, too, but he had died in the war at Cold Harbor. Now it was too late for him to have other sons, so he had placed all his hopes of holding his empire together in Diane and the man she would marry.

"Where you headed, Dad?" Diane smiled, patting the silken neck of her mare. She was an attractive woman of twenty-six, with black eyes and black hair, and the kind of coloring that made that combination spectacular. Her mouth was mobile and somewhat willful, which seemed to please most of the men she met. She wore a tan cotton riding outfit that clung to her body, the divided skirt permitting her to ride astride.

"Just a ride," Head said. "You wouldn't be interested."

"She might be, Mr. Head," Ash put in, smiling at Diane. "It's her business. Besides, it'd give me a chance to convince her what a fine husband I'd be."

Diane laughed. "All right, Ash, you do that." She swung her horse around and the three of them left the ranch, headed for the bench country. It was a long ride, but they never tired of looking over Arrow property. Ash and Diane did most of the talking, all of it in a light vein and mostly about the ranch. Ash related a story of an attempted holdup in War Paint, the small town ten miles from Arrow, and when he finished, Head asked, "Did they get the bandits?"

"Sure did," Caudill nodded. "Sheriff Rider was standing across the street all the time. He heard the shots inside the bank and pulled his rifle from his horse at the rack—then when the three bandits came out, he picked them off with three shots."

"Pretty good for an old fellow like Sheriff Rider," Diane laughed.

"Old?" Head snapped. "Rider's two years younger than I am!"

Ash winked at Diane, who smirked, "I just meant that he's no spring chicken, Dad."

Head glared at her suspiciously, then said, "Me and Bill Rider stood off a bunch of Sioux two days after you was born!"

They rode on past the Arrow herds, stopping to talk to the hands from time to time. Finally they came to the edge of the hills, and as they approached the house set at the base, Diane asked, "Isn't that the Carlin place?"

"Carlin left a while back," Ash said. "Guess he sold out to this new man. Don't know anything about him."

"Well, I know he's sitting on the only water in this part of the valley," Head snapped. "We've got to buy this place, or we can't meet our contract with the army."

Diane looked at her father, then at Ash. "Dad, don't lose your temper."

"Why would I lose my temper? I'm going to make the man an offer he can't refuse." He stood up in his stirrups and squinted through the blaze of the afternoon sun. "Not much of a place. We ought to get it for three or four thousand. All Carlin filed on was the section along the creek."

When they rode into the yard, they saw a big man standing on the porch watching them. A woman stood close by him. Pulling up to the porch, Head stepped out of the saddle, tied his horse, and spoke to the couple. "I'm Silas Head, owner of Arrow. This is my daughter, Diane, and my foreman, Ash Caudill."

"Willis Malloy—my wife, Hope."

Head had expected to be asked in, but when the offer didn't come, he said stiffly, "Got some business to talk, Malloy. Maybe we could go inside?"

Malloy shrugged. "Guess so—but the place ain't much yet."

He turned and led the way inside, saying, "Hope, give these folks a drink of that water."

As Hope brought the water, all three of the visitors were studying the pair. Caudill and Head were sizing up the man, noting that he was a tough-looking fellow who wore his gun inside the house. There was nothing soft about him, Caudill observed, and as was second nature for him, he was wondering how fast the man could draw the weapon and get off a shot.

Diane watched the woman, puzzled by the contrast between her appearance and that of the man. There was no way to judge a marriage, yet something didn't fit between Malloy and his wife. Taking the water and murmuring, "Thank you," she saw that the woman was much younger and that there was a sensitivity about her that clashed with the brash arrogance of Malloy. *She'd be very pretty*, Diane thought, *if she'd take care with her hair and get some decent clothes*. Then she realized that the woman would never do that. She'd be too busy working long hours to be able to take time for herself, and Malloy didn't seem the type to spend money on pretty dresses.

After Head took his drink, he plunged ahead in typical fashion. "Malloy, I'm no man to waste time. I'm going to come right out and make you an offer for this place."

"Not lookin' to sell," Malloy said at once. He had taken an instant dislike to Head, for no other reason than the fact that he always disliked men who were powerful. If Head had been a smaller, more humble man, Malloy might have been more agreeable. He was not adverse to the idea of selling in order to make a profit but was determined to call the shots himself. He might even sell to a man like Head, but only if he could gouge him for the place.

Head looked up, a flash of anger in his eyes. He opened his mouth to speak, but then caught a slight movement and saw Diane shaking her head in a warning. He immediately softened his response. "Now, don't say that, Malloy, until you hear my offer."

Ash stood back listening as Head talked, but he knew the answer would be no. He could read faces better than most, and the obstinate expression on Malloy's told him Head had no chance. That was fine with Caudill. Just one more opportunity to show Silas Head that *he* was the man to run Arrow—and to show Diane as well.

"... so I wanted to buy Carlin out, but he left before I could buy the place," Head concluded. "Now, I suppose you've come a long way and spent a bundle on the cows you brought. I can't expect you to take a loss, but I need this place. It's the only water in this valley, which you well know. Tell you what, I'll give you four thousand dollars—no, make that five thousand. Give you all the time you need to find another place. Now, that's fair, isn't it?"

Malloy knew that it was fair. He had paid Carlin only two thousand, but he was a stubborn man. "I'll take twelve thousand," he grinned. "And you won't run me off this place like you did Carlin."

A faint flush touched Head's cheeks, and he glanced at Caudill. "We may have had a little trouble with the man, Malloy. But we didn't—"

"You ran him out," Malloy said flatly. "Carlin and me were old friends. He warned me when he sold me the place I couldn't hold on to it. I may not be as easy to push around as he was. So, twelve thousand and the place is yours."

The rancher threw his head back, glared at Malloy, then bit his words off. "I won't pay it!"

"Then it looks like we're gonna be neighbors," Malloy said. "And some of your stock is watering on my creek. You can take them back with you when you leave."

Head gave him a killing look. "Malloy, I've fought for this land. I'm still fighting for it. I came out here to make you a good offer. Now, I'm going to do something I don't do as a rule. I'm keeping my temper, and I'm raising my offer. I'll give you eight thousand—and that's five times what the place is worth."

"It's worth twelve thousand to me," Malloy grinned, a mocking light in his eyes.

Ash said quietly, "It won't be worth fifteen cents to you if you're dead, Malloy."

Malloy dropped his hand to his gun and turned to face Caudill. "I heard about you from Carlin," he sneered. "The hatchet man for Arrow—that's what he called you. But you won't run *me* off, Caudill!"

Caudill smiled and would have taken the challenge, but Diane interrupted. "Dad! Ash!" Then she turned and apologized to Hope. "I'm sorry for this, Mrs. Malloy." She walked out the door, taking Caudill's arm and almost forcing him to follow her.

Head stood there, anger written on his face. He stared at Malloy, then muttered, "Think it over. It's a lot of money, and there are other places as good as this."

He left the house, mounted his horse, and the three of them spurred away from the house. Caudill was irritated. "Don't ever come between me and a man I'm dealing with, Diane!"

She gave him an angry look. "I should have let you kill the man? Then you could have shot his wife, too, so she couldn't testify against you in court!"

"Diane's right, Ash," Head interrupted. "It was no place for gunplay."

"So we let him alone?" Caudill demanded.

Head answered, "Give him a day or two. He's not that flush. I'll offer him nine, and he'll take ten."

Caudill shook his head but said no more. Though it was Silas Head who seemed to be the more stubborn of the two, it was Caudill who was actually the more determined. He had brought Arrow through some hard battles, and all of them had been won by his aggressiveness. He was a secretive man, sly in his ways. In this thing he saw a way to prove once again to Head—and perhaps finally—that he, and no other man, was able to lead Arrow. A plan began to form in his mind, and he thought, *If I can save Silas a big chunk of money for Clear Creek, that ought to swing it.* A smile turned the corners of his mouth upward, and he suddenly became cheerful, persuading Diane that the two of them had to go to the dance in War Paint the following week.

Hope had tried to reason with Willis after the three left. She had heard Smoky Jacks tell how strong Head was, and she pleaded, "Willis, it's a lot of money. We can go someplace else. This isn't a home to us."

"He tried to force my hand," Malloy grumbled, his temper still raw. Then he gave Hope a hard look. "I'll probably sell the place—but I'll get some of Silas Head's hide with it!"

"That man Caudill—he's a gunman, isn't he? If it hadn't been for the woman, he might have killed you."

"Or I might've killed *him*!" Malloy snapped. It had grated on him that Hope had seen Jacks make him back down. He was a tough, hard man, and sooner or later he intended to show Hope just how tough he was. He smiled to himself, thinking about how he was going to work this out. "We'll play this thing easy. Just settle down like we intend to stay here forever. Head'll scream because he's *got* to have this water."

"I'd rather not stay," Hope said, worried. "It'll mean trouble."

Malloy grinned and went to her, putting his arms around her. "You don't know what a tough feller you married, Hope! Nothin's gonna happen to *me*!"

Despite her obvious resistance to his touch, he kissed her roughly, then left the house. Hope watched him leave, her fears not for him, or even for herself, so much as for Cody and Amos. She nervously paced around the room, wishing that Willis would change his mind, but she knew his stubbornness. Finally she took off her apron and went down to the creek where Cody and Amos were fishing. Buck was lying quietly by Cody's side, intently watching the proceedings.

"Catch anything?" Hope asked, tossing a stick for Buck to run after so she could sit beside Cody.

"Sure!" He pulled up a string of sunfish that glittered in the reddish glow of the sun.

"Who was them folks?" Amos inquired.

Hope said, "It was Silas Head, the big owner Smoky told us about." She hesitated, then added, "He offered Willis a lot of money for this place, but he wouldn't take it."

Amos shook his head. "No, he wouldn't." He pulled in a fine fish, took him off the hook, then got to his feet. "Let's go cook these fish up, Hope. I'm hungry."

"I wanna catch a few more," Cody pleaded. When his mother said he could, he watched them go, then whistled for Buck, who had forgotten the stick and was now sniffing out a small animal burrowed in the bank of the creek. Cody pulled his hook from the water. He considered the worm that was wiggling wildly, then spit on it.

"Now then—!" he said firmly, plopping it back into the clear water. "You git down there and do like you're supposed to!"

CHAPTER FIVE

FIRST CASUALTY

★ ★ ★ ★

As Hope stepped out of the house at dawn, Buck came to nuzzle her, nearly upsetting her. In the two months since they had arrived at the Circle M, he had grown into a startlingly enormous dog with heavy muscles and a deep chest. "Get away, Buck," she commanded, but when she got to the door, he edged himself inside before she could stop him, going at once to his spot behind the stove. He fell to the floor with a loud thump and watched her as she moved around the kitchen.

As she got out the flour and began putting her biscuit mix together, she thought, *It'll be Christmas in a few months*—and her mind went back to the last Christmas they'd had in Arkansas. She thought of the sight of her father's face as he'd given Zane the Spencer, but then she thought of what she'd heard of Zane recently and her face grew sad. Smoky Jacks had found a job with a rancher named Dave Orr not too far away, and he'd stopped to tell her that he'd run across Zane. "Working with Oscar Wells. He's doing fine."

As she rolled out the dough and cut out circles with an empty can, Hope thought of the one letter they'd gotten from Zane. It came a month after they'd settled in and had been only a few lines. *I got a job. Not much, but I'll make out. I'll see you when I can get away.* He had added a few details, but the only personal note was at the end: *I sure do miss you all!*

She arranged the biscuits in a pan and put them into the oven. When they were almost done, she went to wake up Cody and Fred. The two of them shared a bedroom, and they came stumbling out as she finished fixing breakfast. "Wash your hands, Cody," Hope said automatically.

"What for?" he grumbled, asking as he always did when told to wash. "I ain't touched nothin' dead." He dabbled gingerly with the tips of his fingers in the wash basin beside the door, then dried off and came to sit down at the table. "Seems like I spend half my life washing!"

Fred Gibson washed his hands, too, doing little better than Cody but teasing the boy nonetheless. "For a kid that can't stay away from that creek, you sure do hate water, Cody." He smiled behind the heavy beard he'd started a month earlier. "When I was your age, I took a bath every day and twice on Sunday."

"You didn't neither!" Cody challenged. He liked Gibson, but the big man teased him constantly. "You ain't had a bath now since you fell in the creek last month!"

"That's enough, Cody," Hope broke in, lifting the heavy frying pan off the stove. She came to the table and deposited several fried eggs on their plates—two for Cody and four for Fred. "Are you ever going to stop arguing about washing yourself?" She came with the hot biscuits and sat down, then said a brief blessing.

Cody could hardly wait until she was finished before stuffing his mouth with half a biscuit. Chewing it noisily, he argued, "I'll bet Elijah didn't take a bath, Ma. You said he was a great man, so if he didn't take baths, why do I have to spend half my life washing?"

"Cody, I don't want to argue about taking baths!" Hope gave the boy a strict look that he recognized as being the end of the discussion, then asked Gibson, "Can you take care of the cattle by yourself today, Fred?" Malloy and Og had gone to War Paint the previous day and were not due back until late.

"They're right peaceful, Miz Malloy," Gibson said. "Me and Cody can handle it." He reached over and tousled Cody's hair, grinning. "This cowboy's getting to be quite a hand. You show your ma how you learned to use that rope, Cody?" The cowboy speared himself another biscuit, then got up and harvested the two remaining biscuits, turning as Amos came into the room. He looked down regretfully at the eggs, and Hope said, "Go on and eat them, Fred. I'll fix Pa some more."

"Why, thank you, ma'am," Gibson said, brightening up. "I don't like to mess my plate up fer less than half a dozen eggs." He sat down and began to devour the rest of his breakfast, tossing the food far back in his throat.

Amos watched the puncher as he swallowed the food, then shook his head in disgust. "Fred, you ain't never actually *tasted* no food. A man tastes with his tongue, and you throw your grub back and swallow it whole—just like a snake swallows a chicken egg." He looked tired but brightened as he turned to Cody. "I seen you rope that heifer yesterday, Cody. That was a good job."

Cody grinned and smeared apple jelly on another biscuit. "I'm goin' to try a big ol' steer pretty soon," he boasted loudly.

"No, you ain't, not till I say so," Fred spoke up, then got to his feet. "Come on. We got to milk that cow." Cody rose, still chewing the biscuit, and the two of them put on their hats. As they walked out, Buck following close behind, Hope and Amos could hear them arguing about what was the best bait for catfish.

"Glad Fred's here," Amos observed. "He's good with Cody."

"Yes. Sometimes they act like they're just about the same age." Hope fetched the coffeepot from the stove and poured coffee for them both, then sat down again. "Don't forget to take your medicine," she warned. "It's doing you some good."

He shrugged but nodded. At Hope's insistence soon after their arrival, he had gone to see War Paint's only doctor, Walter Matthews. The doctor had looked him over, then said critically, "Not much I can do for you, Mr. Jenson," to which Amos had replied, "I know that. Just give me some sort of sugar pills. It'll make my daughter feel better."

Now as he sipped his coffee and picked at the food Hope put before him, Amos said, "If this is a hard winter, we'll lose some cows. I been talking to Dutch Shultz at church. He says we ought to try to warn Willis about winters."

"He won't listen, I reckon," Hope shrugged. "Emma Shultz told me the same thing. I tried to talk to Willis, but he just laughed at me."

There was nothing more that Amos could say about the matter. They had settled into a pattern at the ranch, and it had been hard on them. Arrow had begun putting pressure on them almost at once. It had not been a violent thing, but the threat was always there. At one time or another, the men of Circle M had been challenged—which usually came in the form of a conflict over the range or the water. Since the range itself was open, Arrow had as much right to use it as Circle M. But time after time Caudill's men would deliberately mix their cows with those of Malloy's, which forced either Willis or Fred to go through the herds held by Arrow to get their own cattle back. When this happened, the Arrow hands usually had some crude, salty remarks to make. Malloy himself was tough enough to face the riders down, but they had quickly discovered that Fred Gibson was no fighter and had made his life miserable. Once when Og had been challenged, he had simply pulled out the huge shotgun he carried in his boot, and that had ended the argument.

There had also been a number of instances concerning water, when Arrow had allowed their cattle to crowd into the narrow strip where the creek ran along the edge of the hills. This never failed to enrage Malloy, and he'd gone twice to Arrow to complain but had gotten no satisfaction. Silas Head had merely said, "You ought to know that you can't stop thirsty cattle from going to water," and then had pressured Malloy to accept his offer to buy the place. He had not, however, raised his bid, for Caudill had convinced him that sooner or later the Malloys would get fed up and sell as cheap as others had done.

If the problems with Arrow were bad, matters at the Circle M itself were worse. Cody had never forgiven Malloy for offering Buck to the Indians, and though Hope forced him to be civil to his stepfather, he was never more than that. Malloy was hard on the boy, and it was only by a determined effort that Hope was able to keep the big man from whipping him. He had done so once, when Cody had glared at him and spoken impudently, and it had been a frightening thing. Willis had yanked off his belt and grabbed the boy by the arm, then beaten him in a blind rage. It was only when Amos had tried to come between them bodily that Willis finally stopped. "You're gonna learn to show some respect, boy," he had bellowed, "or I'll bust you so hard you'll be in bed for a month!"

Hope had been badly shaken by the whipping and constantly worked at keeping such a thing from happening again. Amos had been a help, spending a lot of time with Cody. Together, the two of them had been able to keep Malloy from physically venting his anger at his stepson again. It was, however, like walking a tightrope, and the tension in the house was thick.

As for Hope, she had come to the point where all she could do was endure Malloy's attentions. She never complained, but she dreaded the nights and his heavy hands on her. Her only response to him was fear and revulsion, and she gave up ever expecting to feel anything else.

Once, after his usual rough treatment of her, he'd demanded, "What kind of a woman are you? Don't you ever *feel* anything? I might as well be married to a stump!" Finally he had taken to going to town, coming back smelling of liquor and cheap perfume. He hinted of his success with other women—never coming right out with it—but when he found that Hope never responded, he'd become sullen, grumbling, "I wish I'd never seen you, Hope! I need a *real* woman, and you sure ain't nothin' like that!"

He had, more or less, left her alone since that time, and far from being angry, Hope was tremendously relieved. She liked best the times when he left to go to town—and dreaded to see him return. From time to time she wondered what it was like to know real love for a man, but her two experiences with marriage had been so traumatic, she could no longer nourish any tender or hopeful thoughts of such a thing.

Amos watched her as she drank her coffee, noting that she was still a good-looking young woman. The strain of being married to a brute like Willis Malloy had erased her quick smile, he noted. She had lost weight over the summer, but so had they all. What concerned him most was that she didn't have the gaiety of spirit that had always been such a part of her character. He blamed himself for this, but that was past praying for, so now he did his best to ease her pain as best he could. He asked, "Think we'll have a crowd at church Sunday?"

Hope reached over and put her hand over his. "I don't know, Pa. That was a pretty rough sermon you preached last Sunday. May have thinned out the lukewarm folks a little." A playful light appeared in her fine eyes, and she asked, "What was the title of that sermon? 'Turn or Burn,' wasn't it?"

Amos grinned ruefully, rubbed his chin, and admitted, "Well, maybe I did get carried away, Daughter. Dutch told me he could almost smell the brimstone during the sermon."

"Maybe you can preach on love next Sunday," Hope suggested.

"Sort of average out?" Amos slapped the table and laughed. "Well, I'll do that. They're good people, and they deserve a better preacher than me."

"No, they don't," Hope said instantly, shaking her head stubbornly. "You're a fine preacher—a little outspoken sometimes, but it's always from the Book!"

They had found a small congregation meeting in an old store building on Sundays, but there had been no pastor for two years. The congregation, having subsisted on itinerant preachers, had welcomed Amos Jenson and his family to their fellowship. And when they had discovered he'd been a preacher for years, they asked him to pastor the church, which he'd refused. "I'm not strong enough for that," he told the deacons, "but I'll do as much as I can." His refusal to take a salary had surprised the congregation, and they responded by bringing gifts. This was called "pounding the preacher," and it was a time of joy for the church when they got together and filled Amos' lap with all sorts of gifts—vegetables from their gardens, fresh milk and eggs, various and sundry household items, and even chickens and hogs.

"You know, Daughter," Amos remarked, sipping his coffee and musing about the services, "I think the congregation just puts up with my preaching to git my fiddle playing and your singing." The two of them had brought a great deal of pleasure to the church with their music, and he added, "Let's work up something for next Sunday."

"All right, Pa," Hope agreed at once. Soon the house was filled with the hymns of Zion, Amos playing his fiddle and Hope strumming a mountain dulcimer. They had not played for long before the door burst open, and Cody came tumbling in, hollering, "Ma—it's Fred! He's hurt real bad!"

Hope and Amos jumped to their feet, startled by the frightened look on the boy's face. "What happened, Cody? Did he get thrown?"

"No, it was some of them Arrow cowboys. They come up and started hurrawing Fred, and when he sassed them back, they pulled him off his horse and beat him up! He can't even git on his horse, Ma!"

"I'll hitch the wagon," Amos said. "He'll probably need to see Doc Matthews."

He was right about that, for when they got to the Fred, Hope took one look at his face and said, "We'll go right into town." She had brought blankets and a pillow, but it took all three of them to get Gibson into the wagon bed. He was limp, and his head lolled helplessly as they struggled with him. Amos said, "We'll have to go slow. He don't need no rough ride."

They made the ten miles into War Paint by noon, and Fred never recovered consciousness. Amos drove straight to the doctor's office, and by good fortune, Matthews was there. He came out to the wagon, looked at the still form of Gibson, then grunted to some of the men who had stopped out of curiosity, "Well, don't stand there like ninnies! Alf—Benton—take him into my office—and be careful with him!"

Doc Matthews was a stubby man of fifty with round cheeks and wild white hair. He was a good man for fixing broken bones and gunshot wounds, but was less successful with the baffling ailments of the ladies of the town. His office was two rooms—an outer office that was rarely used, and a larger room with three single beds, a desk, and two equipment cabinets.

After the men had placed Gibson on one of the beds, he waved them out but said to Hope and Amos, "You two stay. You're going to have to take care of him, so you might as well know what's wrong with him. Son, you wait in the other room," he said to Cody.

He worked on the unconscious man swiftly and efficiently. When they stripped his shirt off, and he saw the ugly bruises, he said, "Looks like they used their boots on him." While he was examining Gibson, the puncher groaned and began to thrash around.

"Hold still now—!" Doc Matthews ordered. "You're going to be all right. Just see if you can move your arms—this one first."

When he was finished, the injured man began to whisper, and Hope bent over to catch his words. "Tried to stop them— but there were—too many!"

"You did fine, Fred," Hope said, taking his hands. "Just rest now."

"Well, he's alive," the doctor stated bluntly. Rolling his sleeves back down, he lit his stubby pipe and shrugged back into his coat. He opened one of his cabinets and began rummaging through the assortment of bottles. "Got a busted nose, some busted ribs, some loose teeth, and he's going to be stiffer than he's ever been in his life. I can give you some laudanum for the pain, but the main thing is making him lie down and take it easy for a spell. I want him to stay here tonight, then I can look him over in the morning. If he's not any worse tomorrow, you can take him home then."

"Thanks, Doc," Hope said. She watched while the doctor poured out a large spoonful of dark liquid, lifted Gibson's head, and gave him the laudanum. He laid Fred's head back, then motioned toward the door. "Let's go to the outer office." When they got there, he took a bottle of whiskey from his desk, took two swallows, then shoved it back into the drawer. He gave Cody a long look, then asked abruptly, "Who beat Gibson up?"

"Some Arrow punchers," Amos answered.

"Figures," Matthews nodded, staring at them. "What do you plan to do about it?"

"Why, tell the sheriff," Hope said.

"Well, you better do that, though it will do no good. Sheriff Rider's authority stops with the city limits."

"Well, then, I'll go find my husband," Hope said. "He'll want to handle it."

Doc Matthews lifted his eyes quickly, then said, "No, let me find your husband. You and the boy stay here with the patient."

He left the room, accompanied by Amos, who asked as they stepped out onto the street, "Why didn't you want her to find Willis?"

"Because the last time I saw him—which was this morning— he was all wrapped up with one of the girls from the Frontier Saloon." He gave Amos a sharp inspection, then demanded, "She know he's seeing other women, Jenson?"

Amos nodded. "I reckon so—but thanks for sparing her having to see it."

They found Malloy in the Frontier playing poker, a buxom

woman hanging on to his arm. When he looked up and saw Amos, he scowled. "What're you doing here, Amos?"

Doc Matthews' answer was brief, and there was scorn in his tone. "One of your men was hurt. Thought you might find time from your busy social life to look into it."

Malloy shoved the woman away and got to his feet. "Who's hurt?"

"Fred," Amos said. "Come on outside, Willis—"

But Malloy demanded, "What happened to him? He get piled by a horse?"

"No, he took a bad beatin' from somebody," Amos said. Everyone in the saloon was watching now, and several of the men were Arrow punchers. "We'll tell you all about it outside," he said quickly.

Malloy just stared at him. "Beat up? There's only one bunch who'd do a thing like that, I reckon." He turned to face two men at the bar. "You two have anything to do with it?" he demanded.

One of them, a tall man with a long face and a droopy cavalry mustache, shook his head. "Not us, Malloy. We been in town since day before yesterday."

"Well, tell that yellow-bellied foreman of yours, I'll be around to collect for this." He glared at the two. "Take exception to that remark?"

The shorter of the two shook his head. "We're just a pair of innocent bystanders."

Malloy spit on the floor, then spun on his heel and stormed out the door. "Come on. We'll see about this!"

Sheriff Rider could offer no help. They found him in his office, a tall man in his sixties with hazel eyes and a firm mouth. "Say this took place out on Circle M? Nothing I can do, as I guess you know." He shook his head adding, "I been expecting this, Malloy."

"Have you? Well, you just keep on expecting, Sheriff," Malloy nodded with a hard glint in his eyes. "Only next time it'll be one of the Arrow crowd who gets hit!"

Sheriff Rider had seen every sort of trouble that could take place in the West. He'd watched the struggle build up between the big ranchers, who'd come to thrive on the free range, and the smaller ranchers and farmers. Now he shook his head, offering the only advice he could. "Don't jump into anything too sudden, Mr. Malloy. I seen a couple of range wars, and there wasn't no winners."

As he had expected, however, Malloy snorted and walked out of his office. "Too bad, Ray," he murmured to his deputy. "Looks like the ax is about to fall in this county, and there ain't a blessed thing we can do about it."

"Malloy, he ain't got no show at all," Ray Shotwell observed. He was a short fireplug of a man with a face that had undergone just about every disaster possible. "If he goes after Arrow, they'll cut him off at the knees, Sheriff."

"Likely, Ray. Very likely."

When they were outside, Malloy turned to Amos and ordered, "Go find Og. He's somewhere in town. I've got some ridin' to do."

"Don't you aim to go by and see Fred?"

"I'll see him when I get this chore done."

"What about the cattle? There ain't enough of us to watch 'em with Fred laid up."

"I'll bring some help with me. The herd can't stray far." He turned and walked away, leaving Amos to stare after him. Instead of looking for Ozzie, Amos went straight back to the doctor's office and told Hope what had happened.

"What's he going to do?" Hope asked.

"He's been talking to some of the small ranchers ever since we got here. They're mostly in the hills, or on the fringes of the open range. Most of them are like Dutch and his family, good people, hard workers just trying to get by. Some of them come to church—the Millers, the Cox family, and the Proctors." Amos paused, then added, "But some of the folks Arrow's pushed around are borderline cases—like the Littleton boys. It wouldn't take much to get them riled."

A crease appeared in Hope's forehead, and she shook her head. "I wish this whole thing would just quietly blow over."

"So do I. Anyway, this whole valley is like a powder keg. Only take one spark to set the thing off."

"What's Willis going to do?"

"Try to get them all together and fight Arrow. But that's just what Head and Caudill want. They've built up a small army over at Arrow, and all they need is an excuse to sweep this country clean of small ranchers and farmers. The law's too far away to do anything, and it'd be too late anyhow."

A cold fear came over Hope, which she struggled to ignore. "Why don't you find Ozzie, and the two of you go back to the ranch. I'll bring Fred out tomorrow."

"Might be best. You be all right, Daughter?"

"Yes, I'll be fine."

The rest of the afternoon Hope stayed close to the patient. One of the merchants, L.C. Chance, was also one of the deacons in the church. He stopped by soon after Amos left to offer his help. "Mrs. Malloy, let Cody come home with me. Him and my boy Sam get along fine. He can bunk with Sam, and you can pick him up when you're ready to go back home."

Cody agreed, but whispered to his mother before leaving with Chance, "Ma, please come and get me. Don't go home without me."

Hope nodded and smiled. "I wouldn't do that, Cody. You be a good boy."

The hours ran on, and there was little for her to do. Doctor Matthews had no patients calling. He came by and sent her to get supper at the cafe at six. When she returned, he said, "Use one of the beds and get some sleep, Mrs. Malloy. No sense wearing yourself out."

"Yes, I'll do that."

The day had been long, and Hope slumped wearily into a chair by the window overlooking the street below. It was a bleak enough view, for War Paint was like a hundred other small western towns. The main street was a dusty stretch between low buildings whose square fronts and overhanging board awnings had long ago lost the shine of fresh paint. As dusk fell, lanterns were lit, making a foggy shining out of dusty windows and casting eerie shadows through the locust trees that formed an irregular line along the walks. Saddle horses stood here and there before hitch racks, and the wide mouth of a stable yawned down the street.

The pace picked up as the night wore on. Riders came and went, and the tinny jangling of a piano arose from the saloons across from where she sat. The raucous clamor of laughter—

both men's and women's voices—punctuated the night and grated on her as she tried to rest. Once there were two quick shots fired, and a man ran out of a door, threw himself on a horse, and headed out of town at a dead run.

She heard Fred making some noise, so she got up to check on him. He was mumbling in his sleep but seemed to be in little pain. She shuffled to the bed across the room, slipped off her shoes, and lay down. The sounds of the busy night life of War Paint surrounded her, but she was thinking of her family now. She knew her husband was such a violent man that he would never think of the safety of anyone—not even his wife.

Finally her weariness began to overtake her. As she dropped off, she thought of a day long gone, a faint memory from her childhood. She had been wading in a small creek near the cabin where she lived with her family. It had been hot, and she could vaguely remember how cool and fresh the water had felt on her feet and legs. Her mother had come for her, and she remembered clearly saying, "Oh, Mother, I wish I could wade in this creek forever! It's so nice and peaceful here!"

And she remembered her mother's answer. *All of us would like to wade in a nice creek and have fun, Hope—but we've all got to eat our peck of dirt before we die.*

As the memory faded she fell asleep, unaware of the tears that gathered in her eyes and rolled down her cheeks.

CHAPTER SIX

"A MAN'S GOT TO FIGHT FOR WHAT'S HIS!"

★ ★ ★ ★

Willis Malloy stared around the crowded room with disgust. Over twenty small ranchers and farmers had come to Dutch Shultz's house, and now after two hours of argument they were no closer to action than when the meeting had begun.

They were crammed into the biggest room of the Shultz house, the combination kitchen and living area. Emma Shultz had fixed coffee, using all three of her coffee pots, but then had left the men and gone outside. A few of the men were seated, but most of them were standing, leaning against the walls.

The tension in the room was almost palpable, for some of these men were natural enemies—cattlemen and farmers. Malloy had known that the two groups were distrustful, and now as he looked around the room trying to think of some way to bring them all to one purpose, he saw that they had arranged themselves as much as possible into representative groups. One group centered around Shultz, a big German of forty with mild blue eyes and yellow hair. These were the small farmers, all possessing calloused hands and wearing worn overalls. Lowell Cox, Malloy sensed, was the leader of the group—he and Shultz. Cox was a balding fat man in his early fifties. He was one of the mildest men in the room as a rule, but he had been a tough sergeant in Grant's army. He let his wife and four children boss him around, yet there was steel in the man, buried beneath the placid exterior.

He spoke up now, saying in a mild tone, "Malloy, I can't go along with what you're saying." He was sitting beside Dutch Shultz, and as he spoke he rubbed his enormous stomach as if it were an old friend. "I'm a farmer, not a rancher. I can't see myself going to war with an outfit like Arrow because Silas Head is making it hard on you ranchers."

Most of the farmers agreed, and Malloy kept a tight rein on his temper. "You think that now, Cox, but how many of your fences has Arrow pulled down? How many times has that bunch ran their cattle over your crops and ruined 'em?" He saw that his words had touched a raw nerve and went on to say urgently, "There's room in this valley for all of us. But Head don't believe that—and he won't be satisfied till he's sittin' right on the whole thing!"

"In that, you're probably right, Malloy." The speaker was Gus Miller. He was leaning against the wall and had said almost nothing during the meeting. He had been listening, his black eyes alert and clear, but now he showed a trace of temper, running his hand through his thick black hair. "I had a run-in with some of Ash Caudill's hard-nosed hands last week. They're pushing me pretty hard."

"Sure, Gus, but not as hard as they will if we don't do somethin'," Malloy said instantly. Gus Miller had been a pretty tough hand, he knew. He'd smelled plenty of gunpowder in his day, and Malloy knew that the other ranchers looked up to him.

Dave Orr, a tall, thin man of thirty-two, spoke up. "You're probably right about that, Malloy, but I don't see that we can do much about it." Orr had fair hair and blue eyes, and there was something of a scholar about him. He didn't fit well among these men, yet the fact that he was educated meant that they held a lurking respect for him. He was the owner of a fairly large ranch, his crew of five men effective as far as running cattle were concerned. He spoke of that now, doubt shading his voice. "I've got a good crew, but they're not gunmen. Most of us in this room aren't." Looking around, he said, "Except for you and Gus, Malloy—and a few hands like Smoky Jacks—I doubt that any of us are."

A mutter of agreement rippled around the room, but then one of two men who had been standing in a far corner spoke up. They had said nothing at all; in fact, they had not even joined in the small talk that the other men had engaged in when the meeting began. The speaker was Charlie Littleton, a smallish man of less than thirty, with tow hair and startling green eyes. He looked a little like a cat with those eyes, and the compact shape of his body and the smooth way he moved added to the impression.

"Them Arrow hands, they still put their pants on one leg at a time, don't they?" His voice was soft and had a Texas accent. His words dropped into the conversation, bringing the eyes of every man in the room around to him. He drew tobacco and a paper from his shirt pocket, fashioned a cigarette with small, tapering fingers, then lit it and added casually, "I guess a bullet will make a hole in them boys, no matter how tough they are."

Shultz studied the small rancher, his eyes filled with doubt. "That's right Charlie, but they make holes in us, too. And I ain't had the practice those fellows have."

Charlie Littleton and his brother Dion, a huge hulking man who rarely put two sentences together, ran a small ranch that bordered on the Blue Hills. It was rough country, and dangerous, for the Indians had used it for years as a hunting ground. But when the Littleton brothers had moved their ranch there, the Indians had learned to give the place a wide berth.

They were a strange pair, having the same father but different mothers. Charlie, small and quick and intelligent; Dion, strong as an ox, but not bright. They had one thing in common, and that was the smell of danger about them—which had been proven in several gunfights—and by a reputation they'd brought with them from Texas.

Charlie shrugged, answering Shultz's doubt. "Sure, Dutch, but you can learn. Like Malloy says, things won't get any better in this valley as long as Silas Head is alive."

"Even if he dies," Gus Miller nodded, "it'll be Ash Caudill we'll have to face—and he's worse than the old man!"

"That's exactly right!" Malloy said eagerly. "We gotta stand up for ourselves. The law won't do nothin'."

"Maybe we could take some of these things to court," Dave Orr suggested.

"Court!" Charlie Littleton laughed softly. He turned his eyes on Orr. "When's the last time you heard of any court in this county bringing a judgment against Silas Head?"

"That's right enough," Lowell Cox nodded, a thoughtful look on his round face. "At the same time, if we step out of line and Head brings *us* into court, you can be blamed sure how that will go!"

The argument went on for another hour, and Malloy finally said, "We'll have to stay together. One man can't do much, but if we get organized, we can put up a fight." He was thoroughly disgusted with the crowd, but knew it would be foolish to show it. "You fellows think on it. We'll meet and talk again."

"Guess that's a good idea," Dutch nodded, relieved at the outcome. He was a ponderous man and hated the idea of change.

The meeting broke up abruptly, the ranchers leaving at once but the farmers staying to drink more coffee and visit. As Malloy mounted and turned his horse, he was joined by the Littleton brothers. Charlie Littleton said, "Might ride a piece with you, Willis."

"Sure." Since the Littletons' ranch lay in the opposite direction from his own, Malloy understood at once that it was not a casual whim. When they had passed out of sight of the Shultz farm, Malloy ridiculed the others. "Seemed like a big waste of time, Charlie. Those fellows will never make a move."

Charlie Littleton shook his head, then gave a sly glance at Malloy. "Oh, they might, if they got hurt bad enough."

"Bunch of dumb dogs!" Dion grumbled in his chest.

"I don't mind doing business with dumb people," Charlie smiled lazily. "A man needs some of the dumb ones to get the work done."

"And then the smart ones take the cream?" Malloy asked.

"I think you're smart, Willis," Charlie nodded. "I like smart people."

Malloy asked cautiously, "What's on your mind, Charlie?"

"Making money—the same thing that's on yours."

Malloy turned in the saddle to give his companions a keen

study. Finally he smiled broadly. "You two are crooks."

Charlie Littleton looked more catlike than ever as he smiled back. "Why, sure we are, Willis. We make a good living at it."

"I've heard some rumors 'bout Arrow losin' cows over your way. Better be careful. That old pirate would string you up in a minute if he ever caught you."

"Ain't ever caught me," Charlie said lightly. His hat brim shaded his eyes, and for a time he rode along, saying nothing. He seemed to have forgotten that he was talking to anyone, but finally he remarked, "I ain't interested in anything small."

"No? What would it take to satisfy you, Charlie?"

"All of the graze west of Buffalo Springs."

Caught by surprise, Malloy blinked his eyes and hauled in on his reins. He stared at Littleton, speechless, then said slowly, "That's about a fourth of Head's best rangeland. Why don't you just take it all?"

Ignoring Malloy's sarcasm, Littleton said in a cool tone, "Because I'm not strong enough to take it all."

"How you plannin' on doin' this? Nobody ever took an inch of land from Head."

"Why, I'm a smart fellow, Willis!" Littleton dropped his smile, then said, "I've got a pretty tough crew. Paying them top wages, but they understand they might have to bust a cap sooner or later. I'm out to bust or get busted, Malloy. Like Dion said, those fellows back there—they're dumb. Way I see it, that's good. We can use 'em, then when we get what we want, they can look out for themselves."

"Too much talk, Charlie!" Dion broke in.

Charlie glanced at his brother's brutal face, then nodded. "Maybe you're right, Dion. What do you say, Malloy? You want in?"

Malloy was still cautious. "I ain't heard you tell how you plan to do all this, Charlie. I'd like to take Arrow down—but I value my skin."

"All right, here it is." Littleton spoke rapidly. "We start a war, and when the smoke clears, we'll take over what we want. First thing, we get Arrow stirred up so they begin putting the pressure on those fellows. Make Head so mad he starts shooting. Then, we get the small ranchers and farmers to shoot back. They're like a bunch of sheep now, but when they get hurt, they'll shoot back. We whittle away at Arrow, me and you and a few more. That outfit's scattered all over the country! Got men in line shacks, don't they? We hit them and Head will hit back."

Malloy nodded, his eyes thoughtful. "That might work, Charlie."

"Are you in?"

Malloy had made up his mind. "Sure. But how do you know you can trust me?"

"I don't trust you, Willis," Littleton shot back. "You don't trust me either. Fellows like us can't afford to trust anybody. You'll watch me and I'll watch you. That's all right. Just remember, when this thing is over, we'll be the big moguls in this valley." His sharp white teeth gleamed. "Sound all right to you?"

"Let's do it!" Malloy nodded. "Arrow beat up one of my hands. I'd like to pay 'em back. Got any ideas?"

"I might just have one. Maybe we can build a fire under this thing—and pick up a nice bunch of change at the same time."

★ ★ ★ ★

Diane Head was conscious that she made an attractive picture, but it pleased her when Ash Caudill said, "You look mighty pretty in that outfit, Diane."

"Compared to what? You haven't seen anything but smelly old cows in so long that *any* girl would look good to you."

Caudill grinned at her, shaking his head and rolling a smoke. "Well, I'd have to admit that you're prettier than any cow I ever saw."

The two of them were watering their horses at a small creek lined by cottonwoods. They'd made a circuit of some of the younger steers at the far eastern border of Arrow's grass. It was only ten in the morning, but the sun was getting hot. They had dismounted, enjoying the cool shade and the trickling sound of the creek.

Diane leaned back against a tree, took off her hat, and threw it on the ground. "Dad wouldn't think so," she said in response to Caudill's compliment. "He thinks a cow is the most beautiful thing in the world."

"They're useful," Caudill smiled. He was a handsome man,

and looked his best in the distinctive regalia of a range rider. He was wearing a pair of dark trousers, a tan shirt, and a black hat with a rawhide cord, now pushed back so that his crisp brown hair fell down on his forehead.

Diane glanced at him and gave him an arch look as she remarked, "You're a good-looking scoundrel, Ash."

"I'm a scoundrel?"

"Of course you are. Did you think I didn't know?"

His gray eyes showed a flash of humor, and he said, "It'll take a rough fellow to ride herd on you. Anyway, you wouldn't be interested in a mealy mouth type."

"No, that's right."

She seemed tall; the riding trousers helped to create that illusion, shaping her in a slim, boy-figured fashion. She wore a man's shirt, open at the neck. It fell carelessly away from her throat revealing the smooth, ivory shading of her skin. Her features seemed sharp, but this was only another illusion caused by the flickering shafts of sunlight that touched her as they filtered through the leaves. Her lips were slightly parted as she looked up at him, her eyes like ebony pools that had no bottom. The strongest impression she made on people was of a temper that could swing suddenly from laughter and softness to anger. There was, Caudill knew, a deep capacity for emotion in her, and he asked hopefully, "What about it, Diane?"

"What about what?" she smiled, feigning surprise.

Caudill moved so quickly she had no chance to react. One moment he was standing still, the next he was pulling her into his arms, and even before she could protest, his lips closed on hers. He had kissed her before, but always she had provoked it, and she had been the one to break it off. Now, as his arms drew her closer, she found herself helpless—and enjoying it.

Without knowing it, Diane Head had tired of men who were half-afraid of her. She had long known that many of the men who admired her were drawn more by her father's wealth than by her own qualities. She had become cynical, putting men to the test—which most of them failed. None of them had been strong enough, but now as Caudill made his demands on her, she sensed his strength, and was both drawn and repelled by her own response.

Drawing back, she glared at him. "Don't do that again, Ash. I don't like it!"

"I *will* do it again," he said easily, "and you'll like it, Diane— just like you did just now."

"You *are* a conceited man, aren't you?"

He shook his head. "Don't you think I've been here all this time, watching how you handle the men who've come for you?"

Diane stared at him, her shoulders unconsciously straightened, opposing him, and her hands tightly closed. Ash still held her at arms' length, appreciating the supple lines of her body and knowing that she was calculating him in a way she'd never done before. She had a quickness of mind matched by a stubborn streak, and now he saw something rise in her eyes. "Yes, I liked it," she admitted suddenly, but then she laughed at him and pulled herself free from his grasp. "So, how *do* I treat men?" she inquired curiously.

"You like to make them jump when you speak. And most of them will, but not me, Diane."

"No, you won't," Diane said, her voice quiet and a thoughtful look in her eyes. Then she shrugged and bent to pick up her hat. "Come on, let's get back."

"All right." Caudill swung to the saddle, too smart to press his advantage. He knew his embrace had stirred her—and he knew as well that it had challenged her. Now she would try hard to control him. He was a man who liked challenges himself, and now more than ever, he felt that sooner or later this girl would choose him.

They made the ride back to the ranch without incident, but as soon as they rode into the yard, both of them saw that something was happening. "Trouble of some kind," Ash murmured.

Then the booming voice of the owner came across the yard, "Caudill! Come here!"

The pair dismounted, going at once to where Silas Head was standing. Deuce Longly was with him but let Head do the talking.

"What's wrong?" Caudill asked.

"We've lost some stock, that's what's wrong—and we've got a man shot as well!"

Even in the tension of that moment, both Caudill and Diane

noted that Head mentioned the lost stock before the wounded man. "Who got hurt?" Ash demanded. "Where was this?"

At a nod from Head, Deuce Longly explained. "Me and Legs was at the line shack over near Simmons Bluff. Got those two-year-olds feedin' there. Well, we was in the shack last night, and Legs heard somethin' outside. I thought it was some kind of a critter, but then we heard the cattle start bawlin'—like they was bein' driven." Longly was so fair-skinned and had such pale blue eyes that he came close to being an albino. He was a cool hand and a hard one, so Ash listened to him carefully.

"Well, we got our guns and popped outside—and it was light enough to see some riders. They were movin' the cattle out."

"Rustlers?" Caudill demanded instantly, his eyes growing angry.

"Well, they weren't takin' those cows out for no midnight stroll, Ash," Deuce said sarcastically.

"What'd you do?"

"Why, we opened up on 'em, of course! But they was waitin' for us. Soon as we fired, they cut down on us from two or three spots. They knocked Legs down with the first volley. I dropped and they kept on firin'. It was all I could do to get him back in the line shack."

"Why'd you take so long to get back to the ranch, Deuce?" Caudill snapped.

Deuce was one of the few hands who had no fear of Ash. His pale eyes never wavered as he shot back, "Because some of 'em kept us pinned down all night while the rest of 'em took the cattle. I ain't gettin' paid to commit suicide, Mister Caudill!"

Caudill stared at him, then waved his hand. "Sure, Deuce. How's Legs?"

"Shot in the leg. I hauled him back in the wagon."

Caudill looked at Silas Head. "I'll go after them, Mr. Head."

"Bring the rustlers back dead," the rancher snapped. "We've been nibbled at for a long time by those little fellows. This is different."

"Won't be easy to find 'em, Mr. Head," Deuce shrugged. "You know how them hills are around that country. Lots of draws and blind canyons. I took a little look-see before I brought Legs in. Seems like they took some of the stock into hiding, then stampeded the rest all over creation. I don't reckon even an Indian could pick up that trail."

A wild look came into the eyes of Silas Head. "I want them hanged, you hear me?"

"Dad, we've got to catch them first," Diane protested.

"We know who's behind it." Silas shook his ponderous head. "This isn't just a few cows. This is organized rustling, and I won't have it."

"I'll take the Indian and see if he can pick up their trail," Caudill said quickly.

"Be careful you don't come up on 'em too sudden," Deuce warned. "Those hairpins can shoot."

Thirty minutes later, Ash mounted his horse with the Indian hand and six other men, but Head called to him, and Ash dismounted and moved to stand before the owner. "Yes, Mr. Head?"

"Ash, this thing has got to be taken care of."

"Sure."

Head studied his foreman carefully. He was calmer now and lowered his voice to say, "I doubt you can pick up this bunch. They got too long a start on you. They'll be halfway to Cheyenne by the time you get lined out."

"I'd guess that's right," Caudill said. He gave the big man in front of him a quizzical look, then asked, "What do you want done, Mr. Head?"

Silas Head stood there thinking of many things, but mostly of the hard days when the very range he stood on had been riddled by rifle fire. He had seen his good friends shot to death, and for just one moment he hesitated. But he had put his life into Arrow, and now he knew he would have to fight for it one more time.

"We'll have to grind them down," he said grimly. "I could live with the few we've got now, the small timers, but there's no end to them. Once you let them take root, they breed like insects! And now they've got somebody to follow—which leaves us no choice."

"You want me to take them out, Mr. Head?"

"Yes, and I hate to see it. Some of those poor farmers are going to get hurt, just like some of us will go down. But a man's got to fight for what's his." That was the code of Silas Head—"A man's got to fight for what's his." Now as he spoke it, a bitterness clouded his eyes, and he looked sternly at Caudill. "Do what you've got to do, Ash."

Caudill, nodded. "All right, Mr. Head. I'll take care of it."

Head stood watching the crew ride out, and his heavy shoulders drooped. He well understood what he had set in motion by his order to Caudill, but there was no other way. Slowly he turned and disappeared into the house, not wanting to watch the spiral of dust made by Caudill and the men as they rode into the distance.

★　★　★　★

Zane Jenson, after being laid off by Oscar Wells and asking every rancher in the country for work, was down to his last quarter when he met a puncher who suggested, "Well, you might try the Slash R." He was a thin cowboy with a lantern jaw and a hard eye. "If I was hungry as you, thet's where I'd go, at least till I got a stake. But it's a tough outfit, kid, and you could get into trouble."

"What kind of trouble?" Zane asked.

But the puncher only said, "I ain't recommendin' it—but it beats starvin', I reckon."

Zane was lightheaded with hunger, and getting instructions from the rider, he made his way to the hills, losing his way more than once. He was riding with his head down and nearly fell off his horse when a voice broke out suddenly, "Hold it right there—!"

Two men bracketed him, then one of them demanded, "Where d'ya think you're going?"

"Lookin' for the Slash R," Zane muttered. "Feller told me I might get a job there."

The two men exchanged glances, then the older of the two grinned. He was a short, muscular puncher with a shock of blond hair and a drooping mustache. "Guess he ain't dangerous, Ray," he said.

"Ain't worth takin' back, Keno," his companion answered. He was a tall, thin man with bad teeth and a sour look. "Get back where you come from," he grunted.

"Wait a minute," the one called Keno said. He examined the boy with a sharp eye, then asked, "Don't reckon you can cook, can you, boy?"

Zane thought of the times he'd helped Hope, and he'd learned a lot from Ozzie Og on the drive from Texas. "Try me," he nodded. "If I don't suit, you can always run me off."

Keno laughed, his teeth very white against his tanned skin. "I like a man who'll speak up. What's your name?"

"Zane Jenson."

"Come along." He turned his horse, ignoring the protests of the one called Ray. "We lost our cook three days ago, and if I have to eat any more of my own cooking I'll go loco."

The two led Zane through a maze of hills, finally leading him up to a ranch house and several large corrals to stand before two men sitting on the front porch. "Found us a cook," Keno announced.

Charlie Littleton examined Zane, questioned him, then shrugged. "You can take a shot at it, kid. If you don't suit, you'll have to leave. Show him the kitchen, Keno."

The scrawny puncher led him to the kitchen, then left saying, "Hope you do good, Zane." As soon as he left, Zane found some canned meat and some cold, hard biscuits and promptly stuffed himself. It restored his strength, and he spent the afternoon doing his best to prepare a meal. He found the larder well-stocked, including a quarter of beef from which he carved a big roast. He got a fire going in the big stove, threw the makings of corn bread dressing together, then made pie dough.

He had no idea of how many to cook for, and he was not sure of the timing, but when five o'clock came, Littleton entered the kitchen. "Crew's on the way, kid. Supper ready?"

"Yes, sir. I'll put it on the table."

He put out the food, and when the crew came in and sat down, they pitched in with a vengeance. He'd made a big pot of beans with hot peppers to go with the roast and dressing, and Littleton exclaimed after sampling the food, "You're hired, kid!"

When he brought out the three pies, two apple and one peach, even the surly puncher named Ray had loosened up. "Well, now, this ain't bad at all."

"You better send us out to do the hirin', Boss," Keno mumbled, his mouth full of pie. "If Ray and me can find a good cook lost in the bushes, we ought to be able to find any sort of feller!"

Afterward, Charlie Littleton let the rest of the crew leave the dining room, then asked Zane, "How does forty a month sound to you?"

"Real good, Mr. Littleton," Zane agreed quickly. "But I gotta tell you—I did my best meal tonight. I'll have to practice on other stuff."

"Sure," Littleton nodded. He looked at the boy with an odd expression. "Keno said you was looking for my place when they found you. Who sent you here?"

"I run into this puncher in town. Told him I was lookin' for a job and he said you might be hirin'."

"He say anything else?"

It was an innocent question, and Zane didn't try to lie to the man. "Well, he said it was a tough outfit."

Littleton stared hard at Zane. "You do the cooking, Jenson. Keep the hands fed and your nose out of everything else. Safer that way."

Zane swallowed hard. "Sure, Mr. Littleton."

It was a strange time for Zane. He threw himself into the job of learning to cook, but he soon sensed that the Slash R was more than just a tough outfit. They were that, and he had to take abuse from one or two members of the crew. On one occasion, Keno finally stepped in, beating one of the punchers into insensibility. "Any of you want the same, just lay a hand on the kid," he threatened, and there was no more trouble.

Zane couldn't help but overhear the careless talk of the crew, and within two weeks, he knew for sure that the Littleton outfit did more than raise cattle—they stole from others. He said nothing, of course. Sooner or later he knew he'd have to leave, but first he had to have a stake.

The weeks rolled by, and Zane saved every penny he earned. During that time, the men came and went—sometimes being gone for a week or more—and when they came back, he heard their boasts about the job they'd pulled off. One of the hands, an older man named Bill Tippit, didn't come back. When Zane asked Keno if he had quit, the puncher gave him a hard look, warning, "Don't poke your nose into things, Zane."

Zane wrote to his sister, mailing the letter at a small town where he went to get supplies. He never went alone, and the puncher who accompanied him was suspicious. He grabbed the envelope, studied the name, then demanded, "Who's this Hope Malloy?"

"My sister."

The puncher handed it back with a shrug, saying no more.

More and more Zane felt like a prisoner. He had time on his hands and spent most of it at the corrals, riding the rough stock. There were always half-broken horses, and when Charlie Littleton saw that he was good at breaking them, he offered him ten dollars for every horse he broke. He earned enough to buy himself another horse, a rangy gray with an easy gait that ate up the miles.

He'd been at the Slash R for nearly three months when the whole crew rode out late one afternoon. Dion Littleton had come for them, saying to Zane, "You keep an eye on the place, boy." Zane had watched Dion lead them all out and was surprised that no one stayed back. Usually at least one or two of the men were kept on the place, mostly as guards, Zane knew.

They didn't return that night, but Zane didn't expect them back. The next day he kept watching the horizon, but still there was no sign of them. He worked with the horses, ate at noon, and later went hunting in the hills. He got nothing and came back to find the men still gone. He went to bed, vaguely alarmed.

He awoke with a start, brought out of a deep sleep by the sound of horses' hooves. Springing out of bed, he pulled on his pants and boots. He stumbled out of his small room off the kitchen, and when he stepped out on the porch, the crew was dismounting.

"Get them into the big room," Charlie Littleton commanded. There was a hard edge in his voice that Zane had not heard before. He peered across the yard and saw by the pale moonlight that some of the men were hurt, and then Keno called out, "Lend a hand, Zane—!" He hurried across to help the cowboy ease a man down from the saddle. "Easy—he got it in the side," Keno said, and when they had carried the wounded man into the big room, Zane saw that it was Ray. His shirt was soaked with blood, and his face was white as bone.

"Get some hot water and some clean rags," Keno ordered, his voice flat.

Zane ran out of the room, noting that two other men were being helped into the room, but he didn't wait to identify them. He stirred up the fire, heated water, and then returned. One of the men, a young puncher named Pinto Smith, was sitting in a chair with his wounded leg propped on another chair. Charlie Littleton was saying, "Didn't hit bone, Pinto. Ought to be all right." He saw Zane enter and waved him over. "Bring that stuff over here, Jenson—" He began at once to clean out the wound while asking Keno, "How's Ray doing?"

"Not so good. Lost a lot of blood."

One of the hands had been bending over the third man. He suddenly straightened up and said, "This one's finished."

Dion Littleton went to look down at the man, reached out and put his heavy hand on the man's chest, then nodded. "Malloy's dead meat." He shrugged, then went to get a swig from the whiskey bottle that was going around.

Zane seemed to freeze where he stood, for none of the crew was named Malloy. He stared at the dead man, but the face was turned away from him. He moved slowly across the room, his chest tight, and when he came to stand over the still form, he saw at once that it was Willis Malloy.

The room seemed to reel, and a faint humming sounded in his ears. Looking down on the gray face, he tried to feel something, but death had taken away his hatred for the man.

Charlie Littleton had finished the dressing on Pinto's leg. When he turned, he got a glimpse of Zane's face. A frown creased his brow and he went to stand beside the boy. "What's the matter, Zane? You never saw a dead man before?"

Zane licked his lips and had to clear his throat before he could speak. Finally he said in a thin voice, "That's—my sister's husband!"

His words drew the eyes of all the crew, and Charlie Littleton's eyes were alert. "You never told me you had folks around here."

"He kicked me out—back on the trail," Zane said. "I wanted to kill him—but I guess it's over now."

Littleton didn't answer, and Zane left the room, feeling sick and frightened. He went to sit on the back porch, trying to think, but he was not able to get his thoughts together.

Finally Charlie Littleton came out and stood over him. "Ray didn't make it." The news didn't seem to mean much to Zane, who looked up and said nothing. Littleton hesitated, then shrugged. "We gotta bury him. What about Malloy? You want us to bury him, too?"

Zane tried hard to concentrate, then shook his head. "I—guess I better take him home, Mr. Littleton. He wasn't no good—but he's my sister's husband. If he gets buried, I guess the ranch will be hers, but if he just disappears, I dunno—"

"I guess you know what happened, Jenson. You're not dumb."

"I reckon you were rustlin' cattle."

"That's it. And you know about it."

The threat hung in the air, and Zane knew that he was on a fine thread. "I've never seen any rustling. All I've done is cook. Nobody even knows I've been here at the Slash R."

Littleton nodded slowly. "I'm giving you a break. Take Malloy out of here. If you ever squeal on me, I'll kill you or have it done. You understand that?"

"Yeah, I won't say nothin'."

"All right. But Arrow was the outfit that shot us up. When they hear about Malloy getting shot, they'll put two and two together. Tell your sister to bury the man, but wait a week. Then let the word get out that he got killed by a bad horse or something like that."

"I'll tell her and my pa."

"I'll have the boys tie Malloy onto your spare horse."

Twenty minutes later Zane rode out of the yard, the body of Malloy secured to his gray. There were no farewells, except from Charlie Littleton, who warned, "You're a dead man if you let this get out, Jenson!"

"I'll keep quiet—but I don't even know how to get to my sister's place." He listened as Littleton gave him directions, then rode out.

Dion came to stand beside his brother. "Should've shut him up, Charlie."

"He won't talk, Dion," Charlie shrugged. "He knows he's dead if he so much as peeps."

Zane followed Littleton's instructions, but he was scared as he made the trip. If anyone saw him, he would be in trouble. He rode for the rest of the night, and kept to the hills and timber all morning. At three o'clock he came over a rise that Littleton had described and saw a ranch house in the elbow of a small stream, exactly as the rustler had said.

Still he was nervous, so he tied his spare horse, with Malloy's body still slung across its back, securely to a sapling, then rode off down the slope. As he crossed the creek, he saw Cody come out of the house and called out, "Cody—it's me—Zane!"

He rode into the yard, and by the time he got there, his sister and his father were there to greet him. They were babbling and pulling at him, but he could not say a word. He hadn't realized how much he had missed them.

Finally his father said, "Come in the house, son."

Zane asked, "Where's Ozzie?"

"Why, in town, Zane."

"I—gotta tell you something, Pa—all of you."

"Are you in trouble, Zane?" Hope asked anxiously.

"I think we all are," he said. Quickly he told them about working for the Littletons. "I didn't know they was crooks when I went there, and they never asked me to do nothin' wrong. All I done was cook." He bit his lip, then continued, "But they went out two days ago, and it was to rustle some cattle. When they came back last night, some of them was hurt."

They were staring at him, and he said nervously, "Two of them died—and one of them was Willis."

Hope gasped, grabbing at Zane's arm. "Zane! It can't be!"

"I—got him with me, sister. Tied on a horse back there. He's dead."

Amos said at once, "We'll have to take him to town."

"We can't do that, Pa," Zane said. "They'll know he was shot stealing cattle." He hesitated, then suggested, "How about if we bury him, wait a few days, and then tell people he got killed in an accident?"

Amos shook his head firmly. "No. We can't do that. The scripture says, 'He that covereth his sins shall not prosper.' We'll take him in. Where'd you leave him, Zane?" When the boy told him, he said, "You got to stay out of this, Zane. I want you to get away from the ranch. All I'll tell the sheriff is that he rode off, and he come back shot. I can say I found him almost back to the ranch. That won't be a lie."

"But I want to stay here, Pa!"

"You can come back in a few weeks." Amos shook his head. "Arrow is going to know Willis was shot, but they can't prove it."

Hope agreed with their father. "Yes, Zane. You have to stay clear of this."

"You go back and take him off the horse, son. Og and me will put him in the wagon. Take the horse with you."

★　★　★　★

Sheriff Rider lifted the tarpaulin covering the dead man. He studied the face, then let the tarp drop back in place. Walking to the front of the wagon, where Hope and Amos sat, he asked, "Where'd you find him, Amos?"

Hope spoke up. "He was about a quarter of a mile from the house, up on the rise above the creek, Sheriff. He was sprawled on the ground and his horse wasn't there."

Rider's face was sad. "I hate to see this, Miz Malloy." He chewed the edge of his mustache. "I got to tell you, he was probably shot by one of the Arrow hands. Ash Caudill and his crew caught a bunch of rustlers making off with their stock."

Hope looked at him steadily. "He's dead, Sheriff. There's no proof that he was a rustler—but if he was, he's paid for it."

"I guess that's right, ma'am." Rider reached out his hand toward Hope. "Let me help you down, Miz Malloy. I got to file a report. It's out of my territory, but the U.S. Marshal will want to know about it."

Amos sat in the office beside Hope, and the two of them told the sheriff the truth—that Malloy had been gone from the ranch for several days. "He was talking to some of the small ranchers and farmers, I expect," Amos said.

"He did that, all right," Sheriff Rider nodded. "I talked to Gus Miller, and he said Malloy was at a meeting at Dutch Shultz's place. But nobody saw him after that." He gave them a sharp look. "Mr. Head is gonna tie this to the rustling, you know."

"I thought he might, but none of us know anything about that," Hope said. She was hoping that the sheriff would not ask them how they happened to find her husband's body and was relieved when he did not.

As they left the office, the sheriff said kindly to Hope, "I'm right sorry about your husband, Miz Malloy. Let me know if I can do anything."

"Thank you, Sheriff Rider," Hope said. They left Malloy's body at the funeral home, and the next day there was a brief ceremony at the graveside with more people than Hope expected. The crowd was composed of church friends and towns- folk who'd come for her sake and out of respect for Amos. She felt nothing as the coffin was lowered into the raw mouth of the grave, and afterward she forced herself to respond to those who came to express sympathy.

As they drove out of town, Hope sighed, greatly relieved to have the ceremony over with. "I'm glad we left Cody at home, Pa. He didn't need to be there."

"No. It's been rough on the boy."

When they came in sight of the ranch, Amos put his arm around Hope. "Well, Daughter, looks like we've got to start over again."

She was silent for a moment, then staring straight ahead she burst out, "I'll never let a man touch me again, Pa!"

Amos looked sharply at his daughter. Her face was tense, her lips drawn into a tight line. "Well, Daughter," he said gently, "I guess you got good reason for that." A great sadness came over him, for he knew that Hope had a deep capacity for love.

She'll never know what it means to love a good man, he thought as they pulled up in front of the house. *No man will ever lay a hand on her—not the way she is now!*

A DREAM DEFERRED

★ ★ ★ ★

PART TWO

A DREAM DEFERRED

CHAPTER SEVEN

A MAN'S DREAM

★   ★   ★   ★

Dan Winslow never had any trouble remembering how he celebrated his thirtieth birthday, for on the first day of the year 1874, he was run out of New Mexico by a posse.

Not that the posse had a great deal of legal standing, being composed of twenty or so hardcase gunmen that a big rancher named Angus McClellan had recruited to throw against the small army of punchers hired by Olan Deal. The two ranchers had fought over a huge slice of land—too small for both of them but just right for one—and it had been by pure chance that Winslow had hired out to Deal instead of to McClellan. For years he wondered what his life might have been like if he had chosen the winning side in the range war, but he well understood that no man could go back and change things.

Dan Winslow had enlisted in the Confederate Army at the age of seventeen and had fought all the way through to Appomattox. After the war, his father, Sky Winslow, had tried to persuade him to stay in Virginia and help rebuild the plantation, Belle Maison. But four hard years of war had done something to Dan, and he'd left Virginia for Texas.

Somewhere along the way during the war, a dream had been birthed in him—one which he never shared with any of his family or his companions in arms. All his life he had been intrigued by stories he heard from those who went west, and at some point between Manassas and Gettysburg, he'd made up his mind that if he lived through the war he would become a cowboy.

It had been a pleasant enough dream, one that could make him forget the carnage of war and the loss of friends. As he trudged along the roads to battles, with barely enough clothing to cover him and shoes tied on with strings, he would turn his mind to the open spaces of the western ranges. He could see himself riding a fine horse, sitting tall in a Mexican saddle shimmering with silver, and wearing a pair of matched Colts tied down low. Many nights as he sat around a campfire waiting for the battle at dawn, he blotted out the grim knowledge that the odds were against his being alive for the next campfire, and he dreamed of owning a herd of cattle, watching them grow and prosper.

It was a fine dream for a Confederate soldier, for after the first excitement of enlisting, when the young women came with pies and cakes and lemonade to see them off to battle, there was little but a bloody struggle that most of them knew could not be successful.

Manassas, Seven Days, Fredericksburg, Second Manassas, Chancellorsville, Antietam, Gettysburg—

The gray ranks grew thinner, while the armies in blue swelled, always coming with fresh men and gleaming new equipment. Later, men would say that the miracle of that time was the spirit and determination of the scarecrow men of the South who never gave up.

During those turbulent years, Dan said nothing of his dream, not even to his brothers, Mark and Tom, who were in the same regiment. In his letters home, he spoke not at all of his dream. Once, he mentioned his desire to go west to his sister Pet, but she paid it little heed, being so much in love with a young man named Thad Novak that she was not hearing too well.

Only to one individual did Dan ever truly reveal what was inside him, and that was to a young corporal from Texas. His name was Logan Mann, and he joined Dan's company late in the war, after most of them realized it was lost. Mann had been attached to General Hood's Texas Brigade but had been wounded at Gettysburg. He'd recovered slowly and was assigned to Dan's

Virginia Company, since Hood had gone on to fight in Tennessee.

When they first met, Logan was a slight young man of twenty-four with brown eyes and dark brown hair. On his first day in camp, he was put on guard duty with Dan Winslow, and Dan discovered that Mann had the same ideas he did about heading west.

"I'm aiming to get me a few head of cattle, Dan," Mann had said as they peered out across the river, keeping a sharp lookout on the bluecoats camped on the other side. "Get me a place somewhere in the Panhandle, not too big. Then I'll just set around and let them fat up. Drive them to Abilene, sell them, then go back and do it again. That's what I'm going to do soon as we whip the Yankees."

Dan had said at once, "Why, that's what *I'm* going to do, Logan!"

From that moment the two had marched together, forming one of those friendships that sometimes occur in wartime, forged by hardship and danger. Since Logan had been a puncher before the war, Winslow liked nothing better than to listen as the small man spoke of ranching and cattle. Nor was Mann reluctant to dwell on that time, though he didn't realize that the present hardships were causing him to romanticize the life of a cowboy.

He would speak of the work as a sort of pleasure—riding a fine horse, drifting along lazily as the cattle plodded on, gathering around a campfire with good fellows who knew how to laugh, and going into the small Texas towns and shooting them up with a boundless energy.

What he had forgotten—or chose not to remember—was that he had been a dirty, overworked laborer who fried his brains under a prairie sun, or rode endless miles in rain and wind to mend fences or look for lost calves. It was much more pleasant to think of himself and his fellow punchers in a slightly heroic image—hard-riding, fast-shooting young men, as they appeared in some of the fiction of the day.

Dan found a book about the West by Mark Twain on the body of a dead Yankee major, and read it by the light of the fire to Mann. "This Mark Twain fellow thinks the West is a sorry place, Logan," he commented once as they ate parched corn and washed it down with an imitation coffee made from roasted acorns. "Listen to what he says—" Dan tilted the book and read: " 'Sometimes we have the seasons in Nevada in their regular order, and then again we have winter all the summer and summer all winter. It's mighty regular about not raining though, but as a general thing, the climate is good—what there is of it.' "

"Aw, that's in Nevada, Dan!" Logan protested.

"He says it's worse in Texas," Dan grinned. "But I'll be glad to get there, no matter how hot or dry or wet it is."

The next week, Lee's Army of Northern Virginia—what was left of it—tried to break out of Richmond. Harried by the legions of Grant, they were brought to bay, and two days later, Grant and Lee sat down in the parlor of Wilmer McLean. When Robert E. Lee left that room, the Civil War was over.

When General Lee broke the news to his troops, Dan Winslow was one of those who crowded around him to shake his hand. He was standing no more than five feet away when Lee said with a voice shaking with emotion, "Men, we have fought through the war together. I have done my best for you. My heart is too full to say more." Lifting his hat, he rode through the weeping army to his home in Richmond.

That scene stayed with Dan Winslow, but he wanted to forget the war, and after a brief visit with his family, he'd left for Texas. His intention was to find Logan Mann, because the two of them had spoken many times of being partners. But Mann had gone down toward the Mexican border, and Dan found a job on a ranch in the northern section, close to the border of New Mexico Territory.

He learned his new trade with enthusiasm, and though he made no money and the work was hard, it was a welcome relief from the war. The months turned into years, the scars that the war had put on him began to heal, and he became a good puncher. He had been around guns all his life, and the violence of the war had hardened him. It was a rough life, and he slipped into the ways easily, becoming a hard-drinking, fighting man.

In 1872 he left Texas, drifting to New Mexico where he got a job with the huge Slash W spread, owned by Olan Deal, one of the pioneers of the cattle business. Deal's troubles with Angus McClellan had already begun, and the two outfits went to war over grazing and water rights.

It was a bitter time, worse than the Civil War for Dan, for then he had gone to war with noble ideals. The range war, however, was a matter of money, none of which would go into the pockets of the men who fought and died in it.

In the end, McClellan had won, for he had better political connections. It was due to these that he managed to get his own man put in as U.S. Marshal, and that official chose a posse from McClellan's men and hit the Slash W on January 1, 1874, wiping out half the crew. Dan managed to fight his way out, along with a few more punchers, and slipped back over the border into Texas by the light of a pale moon.

As he rode along that night, nursing a bullet crease along his ribs, he thought bitterly about his life over the past nine years. He had one dollar and sixty-five cents in his pocket, the clothes on his back, and the horse he rode. No more than that—for nine years of his life!

Making a dry camp, he crouched over a small fire to keep from freezing, and as the Texas wind whistled across the plain, numbing his face, he found that he had given up on most things. Finally he threw a stick onto the fire, watched it ignite, then stared at it until it was consumed. Bitterness welled up in him, and he said hoarsely, "I guess that's what dreams are good for, to bring a man down!"

★　★　★　★

No ranches hired in winter; in fact, most of them had to lay men off. Dan Winslow found a job of sorts that allowed him to survive the winter. He rode into a little town called San Isadore and asked the owner of the livery stable to let him sleep in the barn.

The owner, a rotund fat man with the vein-netted nose of a heavy drinker, gave him a quick glance. "Busted and broke?" he asked.

"Just so," Dan shrugged.

"My name's Boley Minton." He stood there a minute, rubbing his stubby whiskers, then said, "Shore, you can sleep here tonight. Clean the place up and I'll take you out for a good meal." When Dan nodded, Boley said, "I've got an errand. Anybody comes in, take care of their horse, will you?"

Dan cleaned the stable out, his stomach aching from hunger. Three customers came in, and he stabled their horses. When Minton came back at five o'clock, his face was rosy from his visit to the saloon, and he moved carefully. Looking around, he said with surprise, "That's a good job you did, Winslow. Let's go eat."

He took Dan to a cafe, ordered them both a steak with beans and potatoes. Dan made no attempt to conceal his hunger. While he ate, he took the money he'd gotten from the customers and handed it to Minton. Dan didn't notice the surprised expression on the man's face, being too occupied with his food.

After they had finished their pie and were drinking coffee, Minton asked him about his plans. When Dan told him he didn't have any, Minton said, "You can get work around here in the spring." His black eyes narrowed and he added, "But I guess you'll get hungry before then. Tell you what, I know most cowboys get their feelings hurt if they're asked to do any work without a horse. But you can work for me until spring—just for bed and board," he added quickly. "You can fix up a room I been using for harness, and I'll give you five bucks a week for tobacco."

Dan said at once, "You've got a man, Minton."

"You won't get rich at it."

"I didn't get rich in the Confederate Army, and I didn't get steaks like we just had. I'm grateful for the offer."

It worked out very well for both of them. It gave Minton a chance to spend all his time at the saloon drinking, and Dan Winslow gained weight on the regular food. The work was negligible, and he spent long hours reading or just dozing in his bunk. It was the easiest time he'd had for the past thirteen years. The war years had demanded every ounce of his strength, and the years he'd spent punching cattle in Texas and New Mexico had been harder than he'd realized.

The days were dull and slow, and he took long rides when the weather permitted. Sometimes at nights he would go to the saloon, not to drink, but just to be with men of his own kind. It was a peaceful time for Winslow, and one night as he was standing outside the livery stable, he had one of those unusual moments that come to a man. He had put aside all ideas of ever having a place of his own, but now it came back to him, came with such force that he could not understand it. He had no money, no real job to speak of—and yet somehow he knew that he was going to try for it.

He said nothing to Minton and knew no other men that he could share it with. He thought of writing to his family, but pride kept him from asking for help. For weeks as winter began to wind down, he thought of it; then when spring came, he said, "Got to thank you, Boley."

"You moving on?" the stable owner asked with surprise. "Well, I wish I could have paid you more, but winter's a pretty dull time for business. Might do a little better now," he said hopefully.

"That's charitable of you, Boley," Dan smiled. He liked the little man, but his mind was made up.

"Going to get a job, I guess. Go out to the Running Y. Tell Tal Bonner I said you'd be a good hand. He's a fair man, though he works his men hard."

The next day Dan rode out to the Running Y and got a job. For the next year, he worked harder than he'd ever worked in his life and spent nothing. He stopped smoking, and bought clothes only when the rags he wore no longer covered him or kept him warm—and then he bought used ones for a few cents or took the cast-offs from the other hands. Boots that he normally would have thrown away he mended himself. He avoided barber shops, cutting his own hair, hacking it off with a pair of shears. On the few occasions he did go into town for ranch supplies or for his own bare necessities, he didn't even look at a saloon. Once his business was finished, he simply turned his back and rode out.

It wasn't easy, but as he scrimped and saved every penny, his dream came back to him, stronger than ever. He had a restlessness that drove him to work when other men were taking it easy, and the other hands all thought he was crazy.

The owner, Tal Bonner, didn't think so, and he made it a point to get acquainted with Dan. He was a towering man in his early sixties, wise in the ways of men and cattle. When he saw that Dan Winslow was a man who could be trusted, he raised his pay and offered him extra work. Somehow he came to understand that it was Winslow's ambition to own his own place, and he approved.

"When you get ready, Dan, I'll sell you some stock dirt cheap. But don't try to make it in Texas. Take them up north, to Montana or Dakota. Land's cheap there, and the railroad ties in to the East."

When Winslow came to tell Bonner that he was ready to try it, the big man said, "Stay with me, Dan. I'll make you foreman in a few years. You'll be set for life."

"Thanks, Mr. Bonner," Dan answered. "Nobody ever treated me as fair as you have. I'm probably crazy, but—"

"You've got to have your own place," Bonner smiled. "Sure, Dan, some of us are like that. Well, go after it. How much money you got saved?"

"Just under twelve hundred dollars."

"Well, I'll do my best for you. I like to see a young man with your spirit. Come along, and we'll see what stock would take the trip and those cold winters up north—"

Bonner did his best, better than any other stockman would have done. He and Dan rode his range for a week, hand-picking a small herd. Finally, the two of them stood looking at two hundred and forty-three head of stock milling around, and Bonner shook his head, "That's the strangest-looking herd I've ever seen, Dan."

"I'm not buying them to put in a show, Mr. Bonner," Winslow grinned. "They're tough, and that's what counts." Many of them were longhorn-hereford crossbred two-year-old heifers, but added to those was every cow that didn't fit into the pattern for a big rancher like Bonner. There were wild steers with an eight-foot sweep of horns, undersized cows that would never be first-class stock, and mavericks and half-grown calves who'd lost their mothers. They were red, brown, spotted, and streaked, but they were cows, and Dan Winslow felt that his dream at least had hooves and horns. He had agreed to send back five hundred dollars when he sold part of the herd, and he knew that Bonner was losing money on the deal.

He chose the name Circle W for his brand, and the crew, ordered by the owner, branded them and slit the ears. Most of them were doubtful about his venture; one of them offered his advice: "Be good to your ma, never vote Republican—and never start your own spread, Winslow. Reckon you'll find out about that right soon!"

It was a small herd, but too big for one man to drive. Winslow had kept enough money out to pay for one hand and hired a short, morose cowboy named Leon Wilkins to make the drive. Wilkins was not a good hand—and was of a surly disposition—but there was no line of applicants for the job at the small wages Dan could offer.

Bonner rode up as Dan and Wilkins started the herd moving just after dawn. He pulled alongside and stuck his hand out, saying, "Good luck, Dan. I'll be praying that you make it."

"Can't ever thank you enough, Mr. Bonner," Dan said. "If I had any sense, I'd stay right here with you. But I got to try this thing."

"Sure. Well, hang on to your scalp." Bonner looked at the lowing cattle, remarking, "Quite a few of those calves are too young for a long drive. You'll lose them." Then he turned and rode away, calling back, "Let me hear from you, Dan—!"

"Sure thing!" Dan called back, and then turned to say, "Let's head north, Leon." He expected no answer and got none.

The sun was hot and the trail in front of him was long and dusty, but Dan Winslow didn't care, for there was a new hope in him. He began to sing a song about a poor young cowboy who lost his sweetheart, and laughed out loud at himself. He hadn't sung for years, but there was a good feeling in him that he had to express, and he ignored the sour glances he got from Leon Wilkins. He sang as he rode along, some ribald saloon songs, and some hymns that he'd sung when he was a boy in Virginia. The dust billowed up under the hooves of his cattle, caking his face, but he spit it out and kept on singing. It was a fine time for Dan Winslow—the best he'd ever had!

CHAPTER EIGHT

AN OLD FRIEND

★ ★ ★ ★

"Ain't never gonna get these cows to Dakota Territory."

Dan Winslow looked across the small fire at Leon Wilkins, wishing for the one hundredth time he had never laid eyes on the man. He was tired to the bone and hadn't had over two or three hours sleep on any night since leaving the Running Y.

"We'll make it, Leon," he said. Taking a swig of the bitter black coffee in his cup to wash down the hardtack they'd stopped to eat, he nodded toward the herd, adding, "We'll cross the Red River tomorrow or the next day."

Wilkins spat out a mouthful of the hardtack and got to his feet. "That puncher said the Red was out of its banks. Ain't no way jist the two of us can get 'em across—not without losin' half of 'em."

Winslow rose, forcing back the angry retort that gathered in his throat. Wilkins had not said one encouraging word on the drive, and Winslow knew at that moment that taking the puncher on the long drive north would be more than any man could bear. However, he could not afford to lose him until he could find more help, so he said quietly, "We'll get across. Let's get moving."

They reached the Red the next day, and as Winslow had feared, the river was high. He sat there studying the swirls in the water, knowing that they needed at least two more hands to safely make the crossing. Yet there was nothing they could do but to try. It might be days before the river went down, and he couldn't wait. "I'll find a good crossing," he called out to Wilkins, who shook his head, responding gloomily, "Not on this river you won't."

Winslow rode the banks, going downstream, where he found a bend that slowed the river down. Urging his horse into the stream, he felt the power of the water, but he got over halfway across before the river deepened so much that the horse had to swim. "Come on, Duke!" he urged, and the big black horse swam powerfully, his hooves touching bottom not far from the opposing bank. Winslow looked around quickly and was pleased to find that the bank made a gradual slope. It was sheer good luck that had brought him here, for much of the riverbank was composed of high banks eaten away by the river, too steep for cattle to climb.

When he got back to the herd, he said to Wilkins, "We're in luck, Leon. Good spot to cross no more than a quarter mile downstream."

"We can't handle this many."

"That big red steer with the bent horn," Winslow motioned. "He's a herd leader. We'll start him across, and the rest will follow. We'll get downstream and drive any strays back into line."

"Won't work."

Winslow gritted his teeth, but said only, "It'll be all right. Get 'em moving."

As the herd turned and started downstream, Winslow took the lead, keeping his eye on the big red steer. He was a cantankerous animal, and Bonner had thrown him in for nothing. "He's a pest around here," the cattleman had said. "But he's beef, and I think he might be useful to you on the trail."

Winslow had named the animal "Old Bent" for the peculiar shape of his horns. One of them pointed out then turned upward, while the other was turned downward about a foot from his head. Now Winslow looked at him fondly, saying, "Well, Bent, looks like you're the boss." He grinned suddenly despite the pressure, adding, "We ain't much, but we're all we've got.

You get us across that river, and I'll retire you. Lots of green grass and water—how's that sound?"

Old Bent turned his head, fixed a malevolent eye on Winslow, and snorted. This delighted Winslow, who nodded, "You and me, we'll make us a ranch."

When they reached the crossing, Winslow yelled, "Get downstream! I'll get 'em started." As Wilkins moved to the right, Dan spurred Duke, moving ahead until he was beside Old Bent, who took a swipe at the horse with a quick sweep of his horns. Batting him across the nose with his hat, Dan yelled, "Turn, you mossyback!" Old Bent bellowed but turned and plunged into the river, and the cattle behind followed him. Winslow moved Duke downstream and made for the bank, he and Wilkins yelling like maniacs as they chased strays back into line.

Out of the corner of his eye, Dan saw Old Bent reach the deepest part of the river and begin swimming strongly. The bawling of the herd grew louder, but the mass of horns above the water seemed to press forward, and soon Old Bent was pulling himself out of the water. Dan turned his attention to the strays and young calves who were having trouble. Two calves, he saw, were being overcome by the current, and he made for them at once. He put his rope over one of them, hauled him across, then got the other who was about to be carried away. For the next fifteen minutes he was busy, but there was no real problem.

But as he turned to cross, he saw Wilkins' horse go down, spilling the puncher into the deepest part of the river. Wilkins came up choking and spluttering, fighting to keep his head above water. It was obvious that he couldn't swim. "Duke—!" Dan yelled, and the big horse turned and plunged into the roiling waters.

Dan kept his eye on the struggling puncher, saw him go under, and timed his approach to a spot twenty feet down the river. He did a good job, for just as he arrived Wilkins bobbed to the surface, his eyes glazed and his mouth open. Winslow leaned down, threw his arm around the drowning man, and hauled him out of the water and across the front of his saddle. He urged Duke to shore, where he dismounted and eased Wilkins to the ground. The puncher had taken in quite a bit of water, but after some gagging and retching, he sat up and stared around with wild eyes.

"You're okay, Leon," Dan said. "You rest here. I'll get your horse."

Mounting quickly, he caught up with Wilkins' horse, brought him back to where his owner sat with his head down. He put hobbles on the horse then turned his attention to the herd. They were still moving forward, and he rode at once to where Old Bent was forging ahead steadily. "Here—Bent!" he yelled and turned the steer to the left. The herd followed obediently, and soon he'd brought them to a stop. He kept circling them as they milled around restlessly then began feeding.

When he got back to the river's edge, he found Wilkins in the saddle—hatless, pale, and angry.

"I quit!" he said morosely.

Dan sat there, staring at him, but said only, "All right. When we get to the next town, I'll find somebody else."

"I'm leaving now!"

"No, you're not."

Wilkins looked up, startled, and something he saw in Winslow's eyes made him say, "Well—I'll stay till you get another man."

Winslow nodded. "I'd appreciate it." He studied the herd, then said, "We'll push on in the morning. You fix supper while I watch the critters."

The cattle were tired and unlikely to give any problems, but Dan took no chances. He moved slowly around them until he was convinced they weren't going anywhere. Then he helped himself to a supper of bacon and canned beans and coffee. "You watch 'em till midnight," he told Wilkins. "I'll take 'em till morning."

He sat there after Wilkins left, trying to make plans, but he was so tired his brain refused to function. Finally he put the tin plate and cup aside, stretched out, and fell asleep at once. He had pushed his body to the limit. There is some point at which no matter what is in a man's mind, the body simply refuses to obey, and Dan had passed that point.

When Wilkins called to him at midnight, he seemed to swim upward out of a deep pool, every muscle and nerve crying out to ignore the call and drop back into the warmth of unconsciousness. Fighting to get his eyes open, he struggled to his feet and drank the last of the coffee from the pot. It was cold and bitter, but it helped him to get moving. He rode out on his one spare horse, a small mare, in order to rest Duke, and found the cattle resting.

The stars were cold and brilliant in the sky—faint pulses that diluted the coal blackness of the earth. Glancing back toward the camp, Winslow saw a tiny amber-orange cone of light that broke the velvet density of the night. Wilkins had made a small fire, and the tiny flickering dot of flame broke the unity of nature in a startling fashion. He watched it glow for a while, then as his eyes grew heavy, he dismounted and led the mare slowly around the herd.

Time passed slowly, and it was all he could do to stay awake. He knew the day would be hard, and in his half-awakened state, doubts began to come. It was a thousand miles or more to the heart of Dakota Territory. The trail was lined with danger all the way. Hostile Indians, resentful of the infringement on their hunting grounds by whites, would be quick to see an opportunity in a small herd led by two men. One war party of Comanche or Sioux could swoop down upon them, killing them almost instantly; or if less fortunate, they could be staked out with their eyelids cut off staring up at the merciless white sun. The rivers could drown men and cattle, or the long stretches without water could mean disaster and death to the herd. But there was a resilient streak in Winslow that refused to be crushed, and he said aloud, "Men can get killed crossing the street or picking blackberries." His voice sounded hollow and small, shrunk by the vast, open spaces that surrounded him.

A thought came to Dan—of his father, Sky Winslow. He'd crossed the desert with a wagon train in the days when there was no army to protect travelers, and his grandfather Christmas Winslow had pitted his youth and his strength against the Sioux as well. He thought of them for a long time, and of his mother who'd made the crossing with his father, braving the danger of the trail. Then came thoughts of the long line of Winslows that had produced him. He knew their history, all the way from Gilbert Winslow, who had crossed the ocean in the *Mayflower*. That one had left a journal, and Dan's father had read it to his children many times.

A memory came to Dan, clear and sharp, of one of those times. He saw his father, trim and handsome with the trace of Indian blood from his mother reflected in his high cheekbones and coppery cheeks, sitting in a horsehide chair in his study, and around him were his boys, Mark and Tom and Dan, his two daughters, Belle and Pet, and his wife, Rebekah, in the rocker, sewing as always. It was winter, and outside the wind whistled, clawing at the windows with icy hands, and the fire answered by popping and groaning as the big logs settled, sending myriads of white and red sparks swirling up the chimney.

His father had read of the terrible first winter in Plymouth when more than half of the First Comers had died, and when it seemed likely that all of them would die. He got to the place in Gilbert Winslow's journal when only a half dozen were able to walk, when those few struggled to tend the others, and when they buried the dead at night so that the Indians outside wouldn't know how few they had become. Dan could still remember the words of Gilbert Winslow as he recorded them at night, so tired he could hardly move:

> We buried four more tonight, in the frozen earth. Mister Bradford is so ill he can barely stand, but he goes about washing the dirt and soil from those too sick to turn over. He knows I am not a man of God—yet he never tries to force his religion on me. Yet tonight, when I came back with John Alden after burying our dead, he did say something. He was so weak he had fallen beside his bed, and I picked him up and put him there. He opened his eyes, and said, "Gilbert— our God is able to do all things. Do you believe that, my son?" What was I to say? I have given up on God—and yet when I see a man who is dying, yet who still sees God in all things—! I could not answer him, but I know he sees something that I cannot see, that the God I have given up on is there for John Bradford and for these others who have come to this terrible land for God, and even when He allows them to die—they die with praise for Him on their lips!

Dan remembered how shocked he'd been that night to see tears on his father's cheeks. He'd never seen his father cry, never! Yet that night Sky Winslow, who had faced the guns of his enemies without blinking, let the tears roll down his cheeks. They had all grown very still—not a sound in the room except the ticking of the clock, the clawing of the wind outside, and the hissing of the fire.

Finally his father had closed the book, looked at his family, and said, "Gilbert Winslow found his God. And Rebekah and I have found ours. Tonight my heart is full. I want to pray for each one of you, that you will not leave this earth without finding the pearl of great price—the Lord Jesus Christ." He had risen then and gone to each of his children, putting his hands on their heads and praying for them.

It had been a moment none of them ever forgot, and as Dan Winslow sat under the glittering stars, he lived it again; in his fancy he could almost feel his father's hands pressing lightly on his head and hear the prayer his father had whispered in his ear. It had been a prayer of love, and the last of it came to Dan now: "And you, my son Daniel, may run from God. But I ask God tonight to pursue you, to dog your steps wherever you go, to never give up on you, so that when you have fled from Him as far as you can, you will turn to discover that the One you've been running from is the best friend you'll ever know on this earth— the One who loves you the most, and who loves you forever!"

Somewhere off in the far distant reaches of the flat Texas plain, a coyote's lonesome cry broke the silence. Dan brushed the back of his hand across his eyes, shook his head with a quick motion, and said, "I guess if God could get Gilbert Winslow across the whole ocean, he can get me and these smelly old steers as far as Dakota!"

* * * *

Leon Wilkins didn't run away, but that was only because there was no place for him to run to. That and the fact that he was fairly certain that if he did try to make a break, he'd look over his shoulder sooner or later and see Dan Winslow standing there.

Two days after crossing the Red River, they came to a settlement where they learned of a town called Jason, twenty miles to the east. It was, the old Mexican with bright black eyes told Dan: "—a big place, señor. Muchas cantinas, plenty whiskey." When pressed, he also added that Jason was the center of some large ranches—was used, in fact, as a departure point for herds on the way from western Texas to the railheads at Dodge City and Hays, Kansas.

Winslow and Wilkins turned the herd and late that evening camped five miles outside of town. The next morning, Dan mounted Duke, saying, "I'll be back as soon as I get a man to take your place, Wilkins."

The town was small—one main street composed of saloons, shops, and a hotel. Winslow had passed at least one herd being held outside of town, and went at once to the general store for a few supplies and then to the saloon. It was, he knew, as good a place as any to find cowmen, and when he entered the swinging door, he was greeted at once.

"Dan! Dan Winslow!"

Winslow stopped abruptly, not expecting such a thing, and turned to see a man leave the bar and come toward him. He thought at first it must be one of his old riding partners from New Mexico, but he didn't recognize the man who came smiling toward him.

"By gum! I sure didn't expect to see an old reb like you in this here place!"

Suddenly Dan grinned. "Logan Mann! You no-good sidewinder! I see you under that hat! Now come down out of there!"

The two men ignored the looks of the customers who lined the bar and sat at the tables playing cards. Mann threw his arms around Dan Winslow, and throwing back his head, let out a wild cry that almost rattled the glasses in front of the mirror behind the bar.

One of the card players, a tall man with a pair of light blue eyes, called out, "Last time I heard a rebel screech like that was at Antietam! Ain't you heard the war was over, reb?"

But Mann paid no heed to the remark. He was wearing a full beard, so that only his lips could be seen, but his brown eyes above the brush were as bright as ever. "My Aunt Sadie's garters, Dan!" He shook his head. "What in the name of common sense you doin' in this place? Here, have a drink, and let's get caught up on our visitin'!"

They sat down, and Dan drank a beer as Mann plied him with questions. Finally Winslow said, "Well, Logan, I reckon you're looking at the latest edition of the prodigal son. I left Virginia right after Appomattox and lit out for Texas." He smiled wryly as he recounted his history, then chuckled, "I guess I won't be writing any books entitled *King of the Texas Cattle Barons* for my biography." He took a swallow of the warm beer, then asked, "What's your story, Logan? Made your first million yet?"

"Not yet," Mann shook his head. "I guess you and me should have stayed together and watched out for each other, Dan. I spent a lot of time runnin' Mexican cattle over the Rio Grande. Poor things was hardly worth stealin', to tell the truth. Did some freightin', and went broke at that, or almost."

"No family?"

"Well—" Mann clawed at his whiskers, then gave a sigh. "I got married once, to a Mexican girl in San Saba. We got one girl—but my wife, she never cared all that much for me. She left me. Hard to believe, ain't it, Dan? Handsome fellow like me, with all my charm and money?"

Winslow read beneath the light words. Mann made a joke out of it, but he was hurting over the thing. "Can't you put it back together, Logan?"

Hope sprang to Mann's eyes. "Just what I got on my mind. You always could read me like a book, Dan Winslow!" He pulled a small tablet out of his vest pocket and the stub of a pencil. Drawing on one of the pages, he said, "This here is Wyoming Territory—here's the North Platte, up from Cheyenne. Now right here—" he made a heavy X with his pencil "—I've got me a place bought."

"A ranch?"

"Sure! Got good water and some land, about a hundred acres, at least."

"Won't handle too many cows," Winslow observed.

"It's right in the middle of a million acres of free government graze, Dan," Mann said. His eyes gleamed and he added, "Some day all that land will be for sale—cheap. If a man was there, he could buy him enough for a few dollars an acre. It's better than anything down here in Texas."

"Gets cold, don't it?"

"Oh, they got weather." Mann shrugged carelessly. "Got a few Indians, too, but I hear General Custer's working on running them all out."

Dan nodded, then sipped his beer. "Glad to hear you're doing so well, Logan. How many cows you got to start with?"

Mann dropped his eyes, crestfallen. "Well—that's the hitch, Dan. I only got about twenty-five head. Took most of my money to buy the place, so I guess I'll get a late start."

Dan Winslow looked at his friend, something coming into his mind. He was not a man who spent much time thinking on how men's lives took direction, but now was one of those times when he thought he saw a pattern.

"Logan, you got a ranch and no cattle. I got two hundred fifty head of good stock—and no ranch. That give you any ideas?"

Logan Mann stared across the table, dumbstruck. Finally he whispered, "You ol' rebel! I cain't hardly believe it!" Then he slammed his fist on the table with a force that nearly overturned their glasses, and once again let loose a wild yell. A heavy man came over, scowling at the two. "Listen, if you want to yell like a catamount, go outside to do it, you hear me?"

"Yeah," Mann nodded and watched as the bouncer went back to the bar. Then he turned back to say, "You ain't lying to me, are you, Dan? You really got that many cows?"

"They're five miles outside of town right now. I got one hand, but he's going to quit on me. That's why I rode in, to hire another man."

"Two hundred and fifty head!" Logan Mann almost gloated over the figure. Then he said, "You and me, we got to figure some, Dan! Now—"

An hour later the two of them left the saloon and rode back to the herd. While Mann rode around looking at the cattle, Winslow paid Wilkins off. The man took the money, and surly to the last, mounted and rode out of camp without a single word to Dan.

Dan cooked some fresh pork chops he'd bought from the butcher, and the two of them ate hungrily. When the meat was gone, he opened up a can of peaches and they speared the yellow fruit with their knives, letting the juice dribble down their chins. Then they shared the thick syrup left in the can and settled back to smoke and drink coffee.

"Dan, I got me an idea. Seein' as how we're partners now,

lemme hear what you think." He lit his pipe with the glowing end of a stick from the fire, got it going, then said, "About fifty miles south of here there's a big thicket. Nothing much but cactus and rocks and some grass. Thing is, it's as full of half-wild steers as a dog's full of ticks. Now if a man was tough enough, he could take a couple of hands and go down there. He could collect maybe a hundred or so of them cows and bring them to the Circle W."

Dan said, "I don't see how we can get another herd and take care of this one at the same time, Logan."

"Done thought of that. What we do is split up. One of us takes your herd to the ranch. The other one makes the gather and follows soon as he can."

"It would take some money, Logan. I'm broke."

"Well, I got just about enough to hire a few hands. You can hire some bean-eaters to collect them mavericks in that thicket. They do it better than white men anyway. Hire a couple more to make the drive with your cows. What's your thought on it, Dan?"

"It sounds like a pretty chancy business, Logan," Dan said after a long pause. "I been worrying about making *one* drive—and you're talking about *two*."

"Sure, but we'll start out with a good-sized herd, Dan," Logan urged. "It'd take three to four years to breed that many from what you got now, but if we got four to five hundred head, why, in two or three years, we'll be shipping a thousand head to the market!"

They talked until dark, then cooked supper and talked some more. Dan was reluctant, but finally Mann's exuberance convinced him. "All right, Logan," he finally grinned. "You always could talk me into anything, you old grayback!"

Logan put out his hand, saying, "Here's to us, Dan Winslow, two rich old codgers sittin' on the front porch and lettin' poor cowboys do all the work! Now, which you want to do?"

"You take what cows we got," Dan said at once. "I'll make the gather and come as quick as I can. Some of the stuff is too young to take the trail good. Leave them with me, and by the time I pull out, they'll be in good shape."

Logan nodded. He leaned back, puffed at his pipe, thinking

hard. "Seems like a million years ago . . . the war . . . don't it, Dan?"

"More than that. Seems like another life. But I can remember one night just like this. We were sitting around a fire, the night before we went up Little Round Top at Gettysburg. Remember that, Logan?"

"I reckon I do! Lots of good boys wasn't there the next night, Dan. I've thought about that a heap." He puffed at his pipe, letting the silence run on, then said, "I was sittin' beside Harlow Killegrew that night. He shared his last piece of bacon with me. And he got killed goin' up the hill. Why him, and not me, Dan? I've wondered that a million times! Old Harlow was a better man than I'll ever be."

Dan shook his head. "Can't say, Logan." He poked at the fire, watched the sparks fly up, then lifted his head, his eyes thoughtful. "Maybe you didn't get killed because God knew I'd need you and your ranch. And maybe I didn't get killed so you could have some cattle to start your ranch."

"Shore would like to believe that, Dan," Mann said quietly. Then he said, "I'm an ungrateful scamp—but I thank the good Lord you walked into that saloon, Dan."

Winslow nodded. "I feel the same way, Logan. My father would say it's God trying to run me down." He grinned crookedly, adding, "You're no angel in disguise, are you, Logan?"

"Fraid not." Mann shook his head. "I'm just a poor cowboy tryin' to put things together."

They sat there thinking of the future, and finally Mann said, "Well, Dan, we went through a whole war, and the Yankees couldn't kill us. So I'm just believin' that God will take us the rest of the way."

"Amen to that," Dan Winslow murmured. Then he lay back and the two of them slept under the silent stars that looked down on them from high in the sky.

CHAPTER NINE

ROSA

★　★　★　★

By the end of the first day's gathering, Dan realized that hiring his Mexican crew was the smartest thing he'd done in a long time. There were four of them, all small dark men, wearing tight-fitting clothing, including heavy leather trousers called *chaparreras*—which Americans called "chaps." Their saddles had a high cantle rising to their belts in the back and a sharply curved pommel in front, so that it was almost impossible for a rider to fall out. Not that they were likely to—for they were the best riders Dan Winslow had ever seen. They used braided rawhide lariats, strong enough to hold a roped 1,200-pound steer. Those lariats could be dangerous, for they were as taut as a blue-water fishing line when the steer hit the end, and any man who got his fingers trapped would see them sliced off as neatly as with a knife.

Their method of bringing down the steers for branding startled Dan. He was accustomed to the head-and-heel catch in which one cowboy put a loop around the steer's head and another snared the hind legs. Then the two riders backed their horses off while the branding iron was slapped on.

But the *vaqueros*, as they called themselves, employed a rougher method. A single rider would enter the broken-up country, rutted with gullies and rocks, and spiked with cactus that could tear a man's clothing from his body and blind his horse.

Riding at top speed, he would turn a steer that had learned to run like a deer through the brush, and drive him into the open. When he got him there he would drop a head catch over his horns, then flip his rope over the steer's flank. Then he would throw out all the slack of his rope and angle away forty-five degrees from the steer's path. The loose rope would tighten, twisting the animal's head back and lifting its hind legs, reversing its direction and throwing the animal in a violent corkscrew somersault.

More than one steer never got up but lay there with its neck broken. Those that survived the maneuver were meek enough after that to be handled easily.

"I thought I'd seen some good roping, Diego," Dan said to his chief vaquero, admiration shading his tone. "But I've never seen the likes of you fellows."

"Ah, Señor Dan," the small rider smiled. "Gracias! You would make a good vaquero yourself with some training."

"No, I'm headed north, Diego. Soon as we get as many of these critters as we can. Sure wish I could hire you to drive them for me."

"That is possible, señor," Diego nodded. Nothing more was said, but when the number of steers bearing the Circle W brand grew, Dan made the deal with the slight Mexican. They agreed on wages, and Diego indicated that three of them would make the drive with Dan.

It was a relief to Dan, for the Mexicans worked more cheaply than American riders. They agreed to brand twenty or thirty more steers, but late that afternoon a rider came into camp.

"You Dan Winslow?" he demanded. He was a skinny young fellow, no more than sixteen, with a fair skin burned red by the sun. "Got a telegram for you," he said. Fishing a piece of paper from his pocket, he handed it to Dan. Opening it, Winslow read:

> *Dan. My wife died. You got to bring my daughter, Rosa, when you come. She's in San Saba, on Pecos River. House of Delores Fluentes. Don't argue. Tie her across your horse if you have to. Give messenger ten dollars. Meet you in Wyoming at our ranch.*

Dan reached into his pocket, counted out ten silver dollars to the messenger. "Much obliged," he said, and the young man turned and rode away without a backward look.

He stuck the telegram into his pocket and went to where Diego was working. "Diego, I've got to go to San Saba. You know it?"

"Sí, señor," Diego nodded. "Small town village, about two hundred miles south of this place. On the Pecos."

Winslow came to a quick decision. "I've got to go there and pick up my partner's daughter, Diego. Will you finish the gather and hold the herd until I get back?"

"But of course, señor. I hope it is not trouble."

"It's trouble—but I got to do it," he said grimly. "I'll take four horses so I can spell them. Draw me a map, will you?"

He left twenty minutes later, rode hard all day, changing horses every three hours. That night he camped beside a creek that had shrunk to a trickle, rested for four hours, then was riding before the sun arose. He resented every mile but had no choice. He thought often of Logan's admonition: *Don't argue. Tie her across a horse if you have to.* It sounded ominous, and he wanted no part of getting into a family feud. The Mexicans were a touchy people, proud and quick to anger—especially where family was concerned.

"I'll do the best I can," he thought grimly, "but I'm not kidnapping any child—not even for Logan!"

He rode into San Saba an hour past noon and asked at the general store for the house of Delores Fluentes. The owner glanced at him quickly. "She died, you understand?"

"Yes. Can you tell me how to get there?"

"Back down the road you came in on. Turn off west first trail. You'll see the house set back—adobe with a big garden beside it."

"Thanks."

Dan swung into the saddle, rode out of town, and ten minutes later took the turn west. The house sat where the merchant had indicated, and he slowed down, studying the place. It was a touchy situation, and he wanted to make no sudden moves.

The house was a low structure with a flat roof, whitewashed at one time but now dulled by weather and time. There were two corrals, each of them containing several horses, which told him the family was not completely broke. Several women were working in the garden beside the house, all of them stopping to watch him with suspicious eyes.

As he rode up to the house, several men appeared. They formed a line along the front of the house, saying nothing, but all of them carried weapons, rifles or six-guns in holsters. One man stood slightly in front of the others, an older man with white hair and jet black eyes, which he kept fixed on Winslow.

"I am looking for the family of Señora Delores Fluentes. My name is Winslow," Dan said, speaking easily and keeping his hands carefully away from his gun.

"What is it you want, Señor Winslow?" The older man was taller than most Mexicans and straight as a soldier.

"I'm a rancher. My partner is a man named Logan Mann."

The dark eyes of the Mexican changed, and he said, "Get down, señor. I am Ramon Fluentes." He waited until Dan dismounted, then said, "My sons will see to your horses. Come into my house."

Dan handed the rope to one young man and another took Duke's reins. Winslow followed Fluentes into the house, welcoming the cool air of the large room. "Bring some wine and some cool water," Fluentes said to an older woman who waited for his order. She nodded, and soon Dan was seated in a comfortable chair, drinking alternately from the *olla* of water and the bottle of wine that his host set on the table.

"That tastes mighty good, Señor Fluentes," he said. "I've had a hard ride."

"The desert is dry," Fluentes said. He studied his guest but asked no questions.

Dan decided to lay it out at once. If this man decided that the girl was not going—then she was not going, that was evident. "As I said, señor, Logan Mann and I are partners in a ranch far in the north. He left a month ago with one herd, and I have been gathering another. It was my plan to leave at once, but I received a telegram two days ago." He drew it out of his pocket and offered it to Fluentes, who shook his head, saying, "Read it to me, señor."

Winslow read the telegram aloud, then stuffed it back in his pocket. "I knew that Mann had been married and had a daughter, but he never told me anything about her."

"You came for the girl then?"

"I came to speak with you and to see what would be best, señor," Winslow said pleasantly. "Family is family—and I am a stranger. I come at the request of my partner, but you know what is best, of course."

Fluentes stared at him, then his lips parted in a thin smile. "You are a wise man, Señor Winslow. I appreciate your manners. Not all gringos are so well-spoken."

Dan grinned. "Well, Señor Fluentes, when I see myself out-gunned as badly as I am here, I am likely to use my very best manners."

The Mexican laughed aloud at that. "An honest man, too! That is even more rare than manners in a gringo." He took a sip of the wine and said, "I will speak with you frankly, Señor Winslow. You know nothing about the marriage?"

"Not a thing."

"Mann married my daughter Delores against my will. She ran away with him, knowing I would never consent. It was a bad marriage for her, as she soon realized. She came home and I took her back, her and the child. I allowed Mann to come for visits, but Delores wanted no more of him. She married again, a fine man, one of our own people. They have five children." His eyes showed sorrow, and he said softly, "She died last month, giving birth to the sixth."

"I am sorry, señor," Winslow said honestly. He could see the grief in the old man's eyes. He was also trying to understand how to approach the problem. "How old is the child, señor?"

Fluentes' mouth suddenly grew tight. "She is not a child, Señor Winslow. She is fifteen years of age."

Winslow blinked in surprise. "I—I thought she'd be six or seven, though Mann never gave me any reason for thinking that." He'd just assumed that Mann had gotten married after the war. Now he knew that it was something that had taken place before the Civil War.

"That's not what I expected," he said frankly. "I could take a child—though it'd be a hard trip. But I can't take a young lady."

Fluentes sipped his wine, and Winslow could see that he was caught in some sort of conflict. Finally the old man said, "I think it would be best if you did take her—best for me and my family."

He shook his head sadly, adding, "I do not know *what* would be best for Rosa."

"Surely she'd be better off with her own people."

"That is the problem, señor—she is *not* with her own people!" When Fluentes saw the surprise in Winslow's eyes, he calmed himself and explained. "She *feels* that she is a stranger. She is half-gringo, and she is very touchy, very quick to blame anything bad that happens on that. If any of us say a word to her, she says we are mistreating her because she has white blood. And that may be so, I'm afraid."

"But it'll be the same, won't it, if she goes to live with her father? Some Americans will taunt her about being half-Mexican."

"That is probably true," Fluentes sighed. "But she will not stay here long in any case. She hates the country life, and I'm afraid—"

When Fluentes broke off suddenly, Winslow stared at him, asking, "What are you afraid of, señor?"

"It is my shame, but I will tell you. I cannot let you decide without knowing the worst." Fluentes drummed the table with his fingers for a moment. "She is a beautiful girl—or woman—señor. Men are drawn to her. She likes this, and very soon she will leave to go into town. She will become a common woman, you understand? I can do nothing! I cannot keep her here against her will, not for long. But if I let her go to the town, she is doomed!"

"What does your daughter's husband say about the girl?"

"Ah, he loved my daughter Delores very much—but he has never cared for the girl. She has been very difficult, a bad influence, Juan feels, on his other children."

The two men quietly talked, sipping the wine and cool water for over an hour. The old woman came once to bring fresh water, then passed through the doorway again, making no more noise than a ghost. The sunlight streamed through the open window, a strong white shaft of light, filled with millions of dancing motes.

Winslow finally shook his head. "I cannot decide what is best. If the girl doesn't want to go, I can't force her."

Señor Fluentes sat still in his chair. Age had passed over

him—in the shadows his face looked almost sphinxlike—his eyes sunken into deep sockets, yet still they glowed with intelligence. "Let us ask the girl," he said heavily. "If she agrees, I think it would be best if you took her with you. She might have some chance there. She has none here."

"Is she here?"

"No, she is at the house of Juan Cordoba. He is her stepfather, my Delores's husband. Come, I will take you there."

Winslow followed the old man outside, where at his command two horses were brought, his own and another. They mounted, and on the way to Cordoba's house, Fluentes said very little, except to ask about the ranch in the north. "I could not stand that cold," he commented finally. "Only you gringos can stand those winters."

They arrived shortly at a house much like the one they had left, and dismounted. A tall, thin Mexican came to greet them, and Señor Fluentes introduced the two men, then said, "Juan, we must speak with you—inside." Winslow entered the room, but discovered that Cordoba's English was very poor. Fluentes spoke rapidly, then paused for Juan's reply. The two men talked for some time, once seeming to grow angry. Then Fluentes turned to Winslow. "My son-in-law is very bitter just now."

"Tell him I am sorry to come at such a time," Winslow said.

Fluentes interpreted, then turned again to Winslow. "He says if the girl will go, he thinks it will be best. But he wants me to make it plain that if she goes, she is no longer his responsibility."

"I understand. And I know her father will make a good home for her, the best he can."

After Fluentes repeated this, Cordoba nodded and called, "Maria!" A woman appeared, and Cordoba spoke to her briefly. The three men sat there, all of them ill at ease. Winslow had made up his mind that the girl would have to agree, or he could not take her. And he was hoping that she would *not* agree, for as he thought about the situation, problems loomed ahead in his mind.

A girl came into the room, and Winslow got to his feet and took off his hat.

"This man wants to take you to your father, Rosa," Fluentes said.

The girl looked at Winslow directly. She *was* a beauty, so much so that Dan was startled. Her cheeks were oval and her black hair ran smoothly back on her head. She had large, lustrous eyes and a mouth rounded and soft. Her skin was very light, a smooth olive, and her thin dress revealed well-formed curves.

"Tell me," she said to Winslow. There was a directness in her gaze that bordered on boldness, and Winslow was somewhat shaken.

"Your father and I are partners. He was on his way to Wyoming—very far north. He asked me to come and see if you would be willing to live with him." He saw a flicker of humor in the old eyes of Fluentes and knew he was thinking of the telegram. But he saw no use in threatening the girl. He ended by saying, "If you wish to go, and if your people agree, I will take you to him."

"Is it a big ranch?" she asked suddenly.

"It is a new ranch, Rosa," he said carefully. "With much work and some luck, it will be a fine ranch. But you must know that it is a hard land. Very cold in winter. And your father and I are not rich. Times will be a little hard for a while."

Rosa looked at her grandfather, not to her stepfather. "What have you said to him?" she asked.

Fluentes shrugged, a Latin gesture that no North American could imitate. "I told him that you are an unhappy girl—and likely to be more unhappy if you stay here. I think you should go with him."

Rosa looked at Cordoba, but said nothing to him. She turned to Winslow and said, "I will go with you. I will get my things."

The suddenness of it startled all three of the men, Winslow the most. He said, "Well—you can think it over, Rosa. It's a big decision."

"I have nothing here," the girl shrugged. She left the room, and Winslow turned to the two men. He sat down, stunned by the girl's decision.

He ran his hand through his hair, thinking that he had acted too impulsively, but the thing was done. Shaking his head, he said, "I don't know if this thing is right or not."

"None of us knows, señor," Fluentes said softly. "All things are in the hands of God. I will choose to think the Lord God will use this to help the girl find her way."

There was little to say, and when Rosa came out in less than ten minutes, she carried two canvas bags—all of her possessions apparently. "I am ready," she said firmly.

"I'll take your things. You can say goodbye to your family." Winslow took the two bags and walked outside. He tied them with rawhide thongs and waited, but not for long. The two men and the girl came out—and one woman who was weeping. Rosa's face was set, but she turned suddenly and threw her arms around the elderly woman. Winslow looked off, not wanting to watch, and finally Fluentes said, "We are ready now."

A horse was tied to the rail, and Cordoba nodded toward it, speaking to Fluentes, who replied, "I will send the horse back."

Rosa mounted easily, and the trio rode out of the yard. Rosa, Winslow noted, never looked back. Nor did she speak on the return to her grandfather's house.

"The hour is late," Fluentes said as they dismounted. "You will stay the night." When Winslow tried to protest, the old man shook his head. "You need food and rest. You can leave at dawn."

Dan said, "Thank you, señor. I am tired and the way back is rough."

He went into the house and later ate a simple meal. The table was crowded, and afterwards, Fluentes said, "You need to sleep. Come with me." He led Winslow to a small room with a single window and a simple bed. "Good-night, my friend. Sleep well."

Fatigue caught up with Winslow, striking him almost like a blow. He undressed, fell into the bed, and knew nothing until a tapping at his door and a voice pulled him from sleep. He rose and dressed, then went to the table where he'd eaten supper. Rosa was there, but she didn't speak to him. He ate the food the old woman put before him, then rose, saying to Fluentes, "Thank you for your hospitality, señor."

"It was nothing." Fluentes led the way outside. It was still dark, but dawn was not far away. Two of the young men had saddled two horses and put the spares on lengths of rope.

Winslow mounted, then saw the old man take the girl's shoulders. He spoke to her gently in Spanish, kissed her, then stepped back. "*Vaya con Dios, Señor Winslow*," he said.

Winslow nodded, repeating the phrase, then looked steadily at the girl. "Are you sure this is what you want, Rosa?"

The girl stared back at him, her eyes enormous. "It is not what I want. It is the only thing I can do."

Winslow shrugged, touched his spurs to Duke, and they rode away. Again he noted that the girl never looked back . . . not once. But Winslow did look back and saw the old man lift his hand in a gesture that was somehow sad and final. Then the dust swirled, blotting him out, and the two continued on without a word.

CHAPTER TEN

DAN MAKES A RULE

★ ★ ★ ★

The journey back to the herd from San Saba was very uncomfortable for Rosa, who was not accustomed to riding long distances. Winslow kept up a steady pace all day, stopping at noon to swap saddles and change mounts beside a small stream. "Better give the horses a rest," he said to Rosa, who had not volunteered a word all morning. Twice he had tried to start a conversation, but she had answered in brief monosyllables. Dan decided that she was naturally silent.

He filled the canteens, then opened a sack of food that the older woman at Fluentes' ranch had given him as he had left the house. Finding some dried beef and canned fruit, he said, "Let's eat." Sitting down beneath the shade of some skinny alders, he took out his knife, divided the beef, then cut off some slices of the bread. When he held out the food to Rosa, she took it but began to eat standing up. The long ride had tired her, and the skirt was not made for riding. She had been riding astride—which was only possible because her skirt was very full—but now her legs were chafed and painful, and she knew there was a long way to go.

She ate the bread and beef slowly, then took the can of fruit he'd opened with his knife and ate some of the peaches. They were sweet and delicious to her, and she wished there were more.

"We'll cook up something tonight," he promised when they were finished. A thought came to him, and he said, "We better get you one of those riding skirts, the divided kind. Be more comfortable for you on the trail." She nodded but made no answer. He rolled a cigarette, not looking at her, then got up and removed a blanket from behind his saddle.

Rosa watched carefully as he walked over to her, her eyes alert. He handed her the blanket, saying, "Better rest for a little. I'll take a walk and see where this stream goes."

"You don't have to stop for me," she said.

"Horses need a rest. Reckon I do, too. You can wash up some in the creek."

Rosa watched as he walked downstream, not looking back. When he was far down the stream, she quickly went to the horse she was riding and removed one of the sacks filled with her possessions. She rummaged inside, then brought out a small tin box, painted bright red and yellow. Opening it, she found a small jar of ointment. Pulling up her skirt, she gently applied the ointment to her raw and irritated thighs. The salve was a remedy her grandmother, the wife of Fluentes, had taught her to make from the pulp of cactus and some herbs. A sigh of relief escaped her lips as the cooling sensation spread over the raw spots. Quickly she took an old undergarment and made two bandages, which she then tied in place. There! That would make the ride easier. She replaced the salve, closed the tin box, and put it in the sack.

The stream made a pleasant gurgling sound, and she went to kneel by it and take a long, cool drink. The land was flat, and she could see the man far away, still walking along the stream. Taking her handkerchief from her pocket, she began to bathe her face and neck, enjoying the coolness of the water. Finally, she mopped her face with her skirt, then picked up the blanket and spread it in the shade. As she lay down, she relaxed and was asleep almost at once, lulled by the coolness of the shade and the musical voice of the water that bubbled in the small stream. . . .

"Time to go, Rosa—"

The girl awoke at once, striking out blindly at the touch she felt on her arm. Her hand struck Winslow's arm, and he jumped back, watching as Rosa scrambled to her feet. Her eyes were wide with alarm, and she drew back from him as if he were some sort of dangerous animal.

"Don't you ever put your hands on me!" she said hotly.

Winslow shook his head, half-angry at the girl. He'd done his best to make the trip easy, and had spoken to her twice before touching her, but she'd been in such a deep sleep that she had not awakened.

"Look, Rosa," he said, trying not to show his irritation. "I know this is a hard time for you. I'm a stranger, and I don't doubt you've been taught to mistrust strangers. But we've got a long way to go, and it's going to be pretty miserable for you if you don't settle down."

"You are right, Señor Winslow. I don't trust strangers." Rosa held her head high, and her dark eyes were flashing as she spoke. "I have learned that lesson very well!"

Winslow had an impulse to spank the girl, but she was not a child—not this one. He stood there, perplexed, then shrugged his shoulders. "Well, Rosa, all I can say is that you don't have anything to worry about from me."

"I have heard that before!"

He shifted, the scorn in her voice a disturbing thing to him. But he tried again. "I guess maybe you have," he nodded, "but you haven't heard it from me. Your father asked me to bring you to him, and that's what I intend to do." It was difficult for him to speak, for the suspicion in the girl's eyes did not waver, but he added, "I know it's tough, losing your mother and then getting dragged all over the country to a place you've never been— and with a stranger. But I'll do the best I can for you, and if you'll just relax a little, it'll be better for both of us."

Rosa was tense—she had been afraid since she'd left San Saba—but she would have died rather than let the big man who stood in front of her know it. Her life had been unpleasant at home, but it had at least been familiar. Here alone with this man she didn't know, she felt she had to keep a wall between the two of them.

"I will give you no trouble," she said finally. "But never put your hands on me again."

"I can promise you that, Rosa," Winslow said. He picked up the blanket, put all the gear back on the horse, and mounted. He led out, heading north, and she followed him. The ointment and the bandages helped, and she thought of his suggestion about the divided skirt. None of her people wore such things. If women rode at all, it was sidesaddle, but most of them were poor riders. She could see that such a garment would be much more sensible, and she looked forward to wearing one.

They traveled at an even pace, sparing the horses. Late that afternoon, Winslow yanked his rifle from his boot and got off a shot. He knocked down a big rabbit and went to retrieve it. Later, when they camped at another small creek, he skinned the rabbit and made a small fire. When he started to cook it, Rosa said suddenly, "I can do that."

He gave her the rabbit and the frying pan, and soon the smell of cooking meat filled the air. They ate the rabbit and what was left of the bread, washing it down with coffee that Rosa found too bitter but drank anyway. Winslow hacked open another tin of peaches and divided them with her.

After he ate, he put more wood on the fire, pulled the blankets off the horses, then said, "I'll look around before I hit the sack." He strolled away, and she quickly washed her face, then spread her blanket out far back from the fire. She lay there wide awake until, after what seemed a long time, he returned. She watched as he sat down by the fire and poured more coffee from the pot. As he sat there, idly staring at the fire, she noted that he was a big man. He had a very deep chest and wide shoulders, and his hands around the cup were thick and strong. His hair was black and he had a deep tan. It was his eyes she watched, for they were the most startling shade of blue, light as one of the delicate desert flowers she had often collected and put in small vessels. Against his tanned skin they seemed to leap out when he turned them on her.

There was strength in the man, she knew, and because of this she was both drawn to him and repelled by him. This dual response was, perhaps, a natural result of her entire life—especially the last few years as she had grown out of girlhood. She had always been conscious of being different from her brothers and sisters, and her mother had made this more evident by her attitude. Delores had loved Logan Mann at first, but it had been a romantic impulse that had caused her to marry him, and the romance had soon died away. Logan Mann had taken her from her home to a small town on the northern Texas border where there were few Mexicans. Delores had never felt accepted by the white community, and six months after they were married, she had begged her husband to take her back to San Saba. But Mann had refused and had gone off to fight in the war soon after Rosa's birth. Delores had returned to San Saba on her own, and never considered taking Mann back as her husband. She always spoke of Mann with disgust, giving Rosa the impression that he had been a cruel husband.

Rosa had always been the odd child in the family, the half-gringo. It had caused her to feel unloved—which, in fact, she was. Only her grandmother—Abuelita, as she was called—loved her.

If her early childhood was difficult, her life after she blossomed into a youthful beauty was even more so. Girls married in her world at an early age, and by the time she was thirteen, the young men were beginning to notice her. This attention had pleased Rosa, and she had encouraged it. As she grew older, however, she was aware that the men who paid attention to her only wanted her to satisfy their own desires. If a young man had come seeking marriage, she might have been different, but none did, and she became cynical about men, aware of her power over them—and using it. The stern warnings of her mother and the whippings administered by her stepfather had only hardened her, so that she had determined to leave as soon as possible.

Now, lying wrapped in the blanket and regarding Winslow, she thought of what sort of man he was. In her world, the only choice a young woman had was to marry—or become a common woman. There were no jobs for such as her, so it was natural that she would see every man as a possible suitor.

Winslow was rich, in her estimation, and a fine-looking man. He was strong, which frightened her, for she knew that she was totally at his mercy in the desert. But that strength drew her as well, for all her life she had been alone, with no one to watch over her except those who treated her harshly.

Winslow fascinated her, and now in repose she saw no sign

of cruelty on his face. The firelight threw its flickering shadows on his form, and she admired the smooth planes of his jaw and the steadiness that now appeared in his eyes. He was much older than she, but she knew of young girls who married men much older; it was common enough, and she was aware that this man, though older, was in the prime of his life.

Finally Winslow straightened up, glancing toward her. Rosa stiffened instantly, a stab of fear running through her, but he got up and went to the opposite side of the fire, wrapped his blanket around himself, and settled down. Rosa relaxed and soon dropped off to sleep, thinking of how different this night was from all others in her life.

★ ★ ★ ★

"You've done a fine job, Diego!"

Dan looked over the herd, noting the fresh brands and the notches in the ears of the cattle. He was tired from the five-day trip to get Rosa, but the sight of the cattle gave him pleasure. "How many do we have?" he asked.

"Two hundred and four, Señor Winslow," Diego beamed. "All strong animals."

It was far better than Dan had hoped, and he smiled at the small vaquero. "Maybe I can find a little bonus for you. You sure deserve it."

"Gracias, señor!" Diego bobbed his head, making the huge sombrero fan the still air. "We will leave soon?"

"Tomorrow—daybreak if we can. We'll have to pick up a wagon in town and fill it with supplies." He hesitated, then added, "I figure the young lady can use it for a bed, too."

"It is a hard trip for a young lady, but we will do our best to make her comfortable." Diego had said nothing when Dan had ridden in with Rosa, but now he seemed to have something on his mind. "I would not offend, señor, but it might be best if we make some rules. My men are young and will be drawn to such a beautiful girl. We must have no fighting over Señorita Rosa!"

"My thoughts exactly, Diego," Winslow nodded. "I guess one rule should be plenty—no romancing the girl!"

"Ah, that is simple—and very easy to say, but it may be that a little reminding will have to be done, not only for my men, but—"

Diego paused, and Dan stared at him. The man's meaning came to him, and he said hastily, "No problem with me, Diego. She's just a child, and I'm just looking out for her."

"You are her protector, that is true—but she is no child," Diego shrugged. "I do not think she should be treated as one. But I will explain the problem to Pedro and Mateo." A humorous light touched his brown eyes, but he didn't smile as he suggested, "Perhaps you will explain your *rule* to Señorita Rosa?"

"Why—!" Winslow stammered uneasily, then finally nodded, "I guess I'll have to do that, Diego."

They made their last camp beside a small pond large enough to water the stock. Mateo, the younger of the two new hands, slaughtered a calf too weak to make the drive, and that night they had fresh beef. Since neither Mateo nor Pedro knew much English, most of the conversation was in Spanish. Winslow, who had only a smattering of that language, felt somewhat left out. He spoke with Diego about the supplies they'd have to pick up at the small town of Sandstone twenty miles north, but soon Diego spoke to the two younger men, and they moved to a discreet distance to unroll their blankets.

Dan looked across to where Rosa was sitting and said to her, "I'm hoping we can pick up a wagon at Sandstone. We need one for supplies on the drive." When she made no answer, he said, "It'd be a good bed for you, Rosa, a chuck wagon. We'll have some weather, I'd guess. Besides," —he took a deep breath and plunged into his "little talk" with her—"a young woman on a cattle drive can cause problems."

This last comment caught her attention. "Problems? What sort of problems?"

"Why, you know," he said quickly, "it's a rough sort of thing, not too bad for men, but for a young woman, it can be uncomfortable. I mean—well, a girl needs some privacy." Winslow was groping for words, feeling about as awkward as a man could feel, but it had to be said. "I guess if we can get a wagon, you can fix up a bedroom and have that—but I need to talk to you about other—problems."

Rosa sat up and leaned forward. The firelight threw her into relief, her face smoothly carved and almost golden by its gleam. "What problems are you talking about?"

"Well, I don't expect any sort of . . ." he faltered, almost using the word *problem* again, but it seemed to have been overused. ". . . any sort of difficulty, but where there are men and a young woman on a long trip, it might be best if we kind of made some sort of rule."

"I see." Rosa slowly reached up and took a pin out of her hair, a graceful motion that caused Winslow even more discomfort. "A rule," she repeated, and as her hair was freed from the pins, it spilled over her shoulders. It was very long and glossy black, but Winslow could see some reddish gleams in the long luxurious tresses—the heritage from Logan Mann. Pulling a brush out of the small pouch near her, she began stroking her hair, and there was something sensuous about the motion, as when a cat stretches and extends her claws.

"Tell me more, Señor Winslow—about this 'rule' you speak of."

Dan shifted uneasily, trying to find words to put the thing, and finally could do no better than to say, "Well, you know that young men sometimes get into fights over young women, Rosa." He saw a tiny smile on her lips, the first he'd seen from her, but it didn't make him feel any more comfortable. "The two young men, Mateo and Pedro, they can't be blamed for noticing that you're a very attractive young lady."

"No?"

"Why—!" Winslow felt her eyes on him and dropped his own. To conceal his nervousness, he moved around to find his cup, filled it from the pot, and tasted it cautiously. "That's good coffee Diego made," he remarked.

Rosa continued to stroke her hair, and the slight curl in it made glossy waves. It fell over her shoulders almost like a silken cloak, and from time to time, she would change hands. Her eyes were lustrous and picked up the glow of the fire, and now she asked again, "What is the *rule* you speak of, señor?"

"Well—it might be best if you sort of—keep away from the young men while we're on the drive."

"I see. And why do you not tell them to keep away from me?"

"Diego's already done that, Rosa." He sipped the coffee and tried to make the thing seem ordinary. "It's unusual for a girl to be on a drive. I've never seen it happen. What I have seen is that men, all by themselves, get pretty tough. Not much in the way of manners. We talk rough—which doesn't matter when it's just men. But with you along, we'll all have to be careful of our speech and—and other things," he ended lamely.

Her hair was brushed out now, and she lifted her arms and began to braid it. The action threw her young figure into prominence, and she asked curiously, "What *other things* do you mean?" Her voice was soft, yet the emphasis on the words revealed to Winslow that he was not going to put anything over on this young woman.

"Rosa, men anywhere will try to make up to pretty girls. Not just on a cattle drive. I'm sure you've had it happen to you. At a party or a dance at home, I'd guess, young men have tried to— to get your attention. I mean, put their arms around you—things like that."

Rosa didn't take her eyes from Winslow's face. "And you are making a rule against that for me?"

"Well—yes. But it's for your own good, Rosa. I'm not expecting any trouble from Mateo or Pedro—but we'll be meeting up with other outfits. When we do, there'll be young fellows there, and I'd be surprised if some of them didn't try to romance you."

"And your rule is that I must not let them?"

Winslow nodded, relieved to have the conversation over. "I knew you'd see it my way."

Rosa stared at him, her hands busy with the braids. The silence ran on as she wound the thick plaits around her head and pinned them into place. Only then did she remark, "You evidently think that women are like dogs." Her dark eyes narrowed. "That the females must be locked up to keep them away from the males."

Dan understood then that he had insulted her, and he retorted, "That's not fair, Rosa! I only want to be sure you're safe."

"No, you only want to be sure that the men are safe from *me*! Or is it perhaps that you wish to keep the others away from me so that you can—how did you say it? You can *romance* me yourself?"

Her lips curled with scorn, and she rose and moved back into the darkness. Her accusation had caught Dan off guard, so that he sat there speechless. Then a wave of anger rose in him: *Blasted fool girl!* he thought savagely. *I wish she'd stayed home where she belongs!* He rose and stalked out of camp, and Rosa listened carefully to his retreating footsteps. She thought of his face as he'd tried to explain his *rule*—so serious! And she'd known all the time exactly where he was going. Suddenly she giggled, pleased that she had embarrassed him, and at the same time relieved that she would not have to worry about the young men. But even as she lay back, she thought, *He's so—so awkward! Just like a gringo! All that talk, as if I were a child who needed a lecture!* She smiled again, then thought, *It could be much worse. He could be fat and ugly—and always out to get his hands on me.* And then she considered the fact that he had shown no interest in her at all, not the sort of attention a man would show to a woman.

The campfire cast its gleam over the prairie, and as she lay there thinking, listening to the occasional soft lowing of a cow, another thought came to her. *Perhaps he does not think I am attractive at all.* The thought disturbed her, and it was followed almost at once by another: *I can make him notice me—he's a man, isn't he?*

She was still awake when Winslow returned, and she listened as he went to his blankets. Even though the campfire was between them, he was close enough that she could hear him sigh as he lay down, using his saddle for a pillow.

A smile touched her lips, and she snuggled down into her blanket, thinking: *We will see how well Señor Winslow observes his little 'rule'!*

CHAPTER ELEVEN

HARD-LUCK TRAIL

★ ★ ★ ★

When they were ten miles from Sandstone, Winslow rode up to Diego, who was riding point, to say, "I'll go on ahead and try to buy a wagon, Diego. Anything else you need that's not on the list?"

"No, Señor Dan. We will rest the herd for the night at the river, yes?"

Winslow nodded. "We've made good time. I'll take Señorita Rosa with me to get the things she needs." He wheeled his horse and rode back to where Rosa was walking her horse slowly off to one side of the herd to avoid the dust. "Rosa, we'll ride on ahead."

She smiled brightly. "That will be nice." She spoke to her horse and pulled up beside Dan as he moved ahead. They left the herd behind and headed for Sandstone. It was an old trading post, consisting of no more than half a dozen stores, two saloons, a blacksmith shop, a livery stable, and several weathered houses scattered almost at random on the flat plain. "We'll see about a wagon first," he said, pulling up at the livery stable. "Then get our supplies."

The owner came out, a stocky man of fifty with a huge mop of black hair and a pair of sharp gray eyes. "Howdy," he greeted them. "I'm Hooper. Help you with something?" He listened as

Dan told him he needed a wagon, then nodded. "Well, I got jist the thing fer you. C'mon around to the back." Leading them around the stable, he waved his hand toward a wagon, saying, "There she is—ready to go."

He was a talkative man, and as Dan walked around the vehicle, Hooper kept on talking. "Big herd came through here 'bout two months ago, from Del Rio, they was. Boss was a big Texan, anyways, and fancied hisself a gambler. We locked horns in a big game one night, and I jist about lost my shirt! But finally I figgered him out, and when the smoke cleared I won this wagon and that Texican's fancy gun with silver handles, on three eights. Well, what you think?"

"Pretty good wagon," Dan shrugged. "I guess it might make it through to Wyoming."

"*Might* make it through!" Hooper scoffed. "Lemme show you this wagon, mister—" He began pointing out the fine points with enthusiasm, and Dan tried to look unimpressed. It was, in fact, a much better wagon than he'd hoped for. It had iron axles, and to the basic wagon bed, where bulk goods such as foodstuffs and bedrolls could be stored, had been added three handy trail-drive appendages—on one side a water barrel big enough to hold two days' supply of water; on the other a heavy tool box, and on top of that, bentwood bows to accommodate a canvas covering for protection against sun and rain.

But even better was the chuck box! It was a structure built on the back of the wagon facing the rear. It had a hinged lid that let down onto a swinging leg to form a worktable. Like a Victorian desk, the box was honeycombed with drawers and cubbyholes. Here—and in the boot, which was between the rear wheels— the cook stored his utensils and whatever food he might need during the day.

When Hooper finally ran down, Dan shook his head. "It's a good enough wagon, but just not what I'm looking for. Thanks for your time."

Hooper had few customers and was anxious to make a sale. He immediately named a price, at which Dan laughed. Dan kept moving away, giving the appearance of a man who was on his way, but after about half an hour, he agreed to pay thirty dollars and two prime steers for the chuck wagon. After another half hour he had traded four more steers for two fine mules.

Hooper shook his head sorrowfully as he took the cash from Dan. "I'm no trader," he stated. "You got a good buy, mister!"

Dan tied their horses to the rear of the wagon and drove to the general store, where he spent some time buying supplies. Fortunately, the wagon had come equipped with cooking gear, grease, a lantern and kerosene, so he confined his purchases mostly to groceries. Not being a cook, he had to estimate, and wound up with green coffee beans, flour, pinto beans, sugar, salt, baking powder, molasses, lard, vinegar, dried apples, onions, potatoes, and grain for the work team. One of the drawers in the chuck box was called "the possible drawer." For it he bought castor oil, calomel, bandages, needle and thread.

"Well, Rosa, that's all I can think of. How about you?"

"You better get some chewing tobacco and whiskey," she nodded. "I never saw men who didn't need those."

Smiling, he added that to his order, then said to the clerk, "Fit this young lady out with some clothes, will you? You have any of those riding outfits for ladies—the kind with divided skirts?"

"Yes, sir, we sure do!" the clerk nodded.

"You get what you need, Rosa," Dan said. "I'll go down to the blacksmith shop and get the shoes checked."

"What will I get?" Rosa asked.

"Why, something for the trail," he answered. "Better get some new boots. Those shoes you're wearing won't hold up. And you'll need some sort of bonnet, and—and whatever else a woman needs." He turned and left the store quickly, saying, "I'll be back pretty soon."

Rosa turned to the clerk. "Let me see the riding outfits, please."

The next hour was one of the most pleasant of her life, for aside from a small article or two, she had never been allowed to choose any of her clothing. True, she was not going to buy any of the party dresses she had always longed for—but they would have nothing like that in this small store isolated on the western plains anyway.

She tried on several divided skirts and finally chose one made of soft light brown leather. By some miracle it fit her perfectly.

While she was trying it on in the back room, her cheeks glowed as she examined herself in the cloudy mirror fastened to the wall. Since she had reached her teens, she had worn nothing but shapeless, full dresses, and when she saw how the soft leather fitted itself to her figure, she gasped. At once she knew she had to have it.

Going through the small stock of the store, she chose a brilliant red silk blouse that satisfied her need for color, and a green cotton shirt that was more practical. She found, also, a man's vest in a very small size, apparently made for a man who admired foppish attire, for it was black with silver threads along the seams and an embroidered silver dragon over the left breast. The high-heeled boots she picked out were also made for men but were small enough for her, and she admired the black sheen of the highly polished texture. As for a hat, she ignored the shapeless cotton bonnets the clerk offered, choosing instead a low-crowned black hat with a medium brim to keep the sun off. It had a leather thong with a silver concho that slid smoothly up and down to fasten under her throat, and a snakeskin band around the crown.

She donned the entire outfit, preening again before the mirror, her cheeks glowing, for her eyes told her that never had she looked so attractive! Stepping out of the dressing room, she enjoyed the slight gasp that the clerk could not restrain and the startled look in his eyes. "I will take these," she said, then proceeded to choose some undergarments. She could not resist one rather fancy nightgown, although she knew she could not wear it on the trail.

A little fearfully, she examined the stack of clothing, asking, "How much is all this?"

The clerk made a list, totaled it up, then said, "$38.20, miss."

Rosa kept her face straight, but her heart sank. Money had been scarce at her home, and she was tempted to have the clerk take some of the items off. Just as she stood there struggling with the thing, Winslow entered. She turned to face him, but the look on his face made her pause.

Dan had given little thought to what Rosa would wear, and when he entered and saw her decked out in the new outfit, he was stunned. When he had left her barely an hour before, she had been wearing a drab, shapeless brown dress. Now as he took in the fringed riding skirt and crimson blouse that clung to her rounded young figure, the embroidered vest and the black hat crowning her raven hair, he was speechless. The new garments made her look older and considerably more provocative.

"You look fine, Rosa," he nodded. "Real nice."

She smiled at him, a full smile on her lips, the first he'd seen. But she said in a worried tone, "Señor Dan—these clothes, they are very expensive, almost forty dollars."

"Your dad would want you to have them, I reckon." Dan paid the bill, and the two of them left the store. Placing her purchases in the wagon, he said, "Let's get something to eat. Last chance we'll have to eat at a restaurant for a while."

They moved along the wooden sidewalk, Winslow very much aware of the overt stares Rosa drew from the men they passed. They found a cafe with red-checkered tablecloths and ordered a meal. The waitress brought them steak and potatoes, with greens and fried squash. They both ate hungrily, and he spoke idly of the trip.

As they were eating, a man entered the door, leaning heavily on a cane. He had a boot on one foot, but the other was heavily wrapped in bandages. He was young, not more than twenty-five or six, but looked pale, and there was a hollowness in his cheeks that spoke of sickness or malnutrition. As he glanced around the cafe, the waitress came to tell him, "Got a table for you, mister."

"Is the owner here?" the young man asked.

"Yeah, he's in the kitchen. This way."

As the young man passed by, walking awkwardly with his cane, Dan saw that he was a puncher; there was no mistaking the rope-burned hands and the dress of a cowboy—worn jeans, checked flannel shirt, and brown Stetson stained by rain and sun. What attracted Dan's attention was the look on the man's face. He had chestnut-colored hair and hazel eyes, but his wide mouth was pulled into a tight line, as if he were in pain, and there was a bitterness in his expression. When he passed through the door into the kitchen, Dan and Rosa could hear the conversation easily.

"My name's Kincaid," they heard him say. "I'm looking for work."

"You ain't no cook," another voice said at once. "Anyway, I do all the cooking here."

"I thought I could wash dishes—maybe clean up the place."

"Sorry, cowboy. Me and my wife do all that. Can't afford no help. Place is too small for that."

A small silence ensued, then: "Well—thanks, anyway."

The door opened and the man came out, his face flushed with shame. He tried to hurry out, but Dan got up quickly, jerked a chair from the table and smiled at him, saying, "How about a cup of coffee?"

Kincaid halted abruptly; he turned sharply to face Dan. The young man was humiliated, and Dan saw that he was about to refuse his offer. But the friendliness on Winslow's face made him change his mind. "Well, that would be all right." He sat down, put the cane on the floor, then said, "I'm Sid Kincaid."

"Dan Winslow, and this is Miss Rosa Mann." Kincaid nodded, uttering a brief greeting, and Dan asked, "You get piled up by a horse?"

"That's it. I was on drive with Charlie Goodnight. Was roping a big steer and my horse stumbled. Stove in some ribs and broke my ankle." Kincaid shrugged his shoulders, adding, "Mr. Goodnight paid me off, but I been here for four months."

"Reckon you could wrestle one of these steaks down?"

A faint smile touched the rider's lips. "Think I might," he said. He sat there as Winslow motioned the waitress over and ordered another meal, then said, "I guess you heard me hit the owner up for a job." He shook his head in disgust, adding, "Never thought I'd try for a job as a dishwasher—and get turned down!"

Dan said, "I washed dishes once, in San Antone. Lost every dime I had in a poker game—worked two weeks for a stake—then lost that to the same gambler! Man's a frail creature and prone to error."

When the waitress brought the food, Kincaid had to force himself to eat politely. He cleaned his plate, ate the apple pie down to the last crumb, and then leaned back. "First square meal I've had in a month," he said. The food had brightened his eyes, and he took the makings from Dan and rolled a cigarette expertly.

Dan studied the young man with a fresh interest. He'd offered the meal on impulse, having been broke often enough himself to know what this man was feeling. Now he began to speak of the drive to Cheyenne, giving a brief history of his endeavor. "You've made the drive, I guess?"

"Sure, five times," Sid Kincaid nodded. "It can be tough, but if a man knows the water holes and how to dicker with the Indians, it's not too bad."

Dan made a quick decision. "You won't be riding for a few weeks, I reckon—not with that foot."

"Got nothing to ride, Winslow," Kincaid shrugged. "Sold my horse and saddle and everything else just to eat."

"But you could drive a wagon—and maybe cook some?"

Hope sprang into Kincaid's eyes. "If you'd take me along with you, Mister Winslow, I'd do just about anything!"

"Well, I can't pay anything, Sid," Dan was quick to say. "But I need someone to drive the chuck wagon."

"I can help with the cooking," Rosa said suddenly.

Kincaid was unable to speak. Dan stood up and smiled. "Well, I take it that's a yes. Let's get your stuff and we're on our way."

"Nothing much to get," Kincaid said. "I been sleepin' down at the stable. I had to give the owner my gun for that."

Winslow paid the check, and the three of them left the cafe. The stable was only half a block away, and when Kincaid went inside to get his bedroll, Dan asked the owner, a thin man of fifty, "How much for the gun you took for his board?"

"Oh, ten dollars, I guess."

Dan paid him the money, then handed the gun belt to Kincaid. "Might need this, Sid." Then to avoid the man's thanks, he quickly strode out of the stable and swung up on the wagon seat.

Kincaid hobbled out, tossed his bedroll into the bed of the wagon on top of the supplies, and climbed up to sit beside Rosa. He said nothing until they were out of town; then he turned and looked back on the scrubby buildings. "Sure ain't much of a place." Kincaid took a deep breath, and Rosa noted that if he were shaved and well-dressed, he'd be a handsome fellow.

★ ★ ★ ★

The first half of the drive went so well that Winslow remarked to Kincaid, "I can't believe we've come this far with no problems, Sid. Sure hope troubles aren't all stacked up in front of us in a clump."

"Don't say that, Dan!" Sid responded instantly. "It's bad luck."

Bad luck and trouble were a part of the long drive, which was the climactic event in the life of a cattleman, be he owner or puncher. It was a chance to prove a man's mettle, moving herds of longhorns from the home range where they were worth four dollars, to a point where they might bring forty a head.

Those times did not last long, only about twenty years—from the end of the Civil War to the mid–1880s. But in that brief era, ten million cows walked the trails from Texas to railheads in Kansas and Missouri, some farther into Wyoming and Canada.

A small herd might number no more than three hundred head, but the biggest included 15,000 animals that moved out of Texas in a massive exodus. Sometimes several herds would get crowded together, jammed into a single milling, moving mass at a river crossing. Whatever the size of the herd, each drive seemed to generate its special measure of trouble. Steers would bog down in sinkholes at the river, and Indians constantly tried to beg or steal cows. Settlers drove the herds from their fields with guns. A clap of thunder might set off a stampede during which half a dozen calves could be trampled. There was rarely enough water for the cattle and never enough sleep for the weary cowhands.

Little of this had come to them since leaving Texas. After crossing the Canadian River, water had grown scarce, but Sid Kincaid had earned his keep by guiding them through the arid stretches to water holes and streams that they would have missed otherwise.

Now they were at the Colorado line, with Pueblo, which was touched by the Atchison, Topeka & Santa Fe Railroad, and not much farther Denver, which fed beef to the East via the Kansas Pacific Railroad. There they would cross the South Platte, and after an easy drive, cross over into Wyoming, with Cheyenne only a day or two from the border.

It had been early morning at breakfast when Winslow had

made his remark about their lack of trouble and been rebuked
by Sid. All day he had walked his horse at the slow pace of the
steers. The idea on a long drive was to allow the cattle to pick
up weight on the drive so they'd bring a higher price, but even
though he planned to sell none, he wanted them to reach Cheyenne in good condition.

He thought of the routine of the drive, allowing the cattle
some time to graze during the early morning, then covering another five miles or so in the course of the morning. Sid would
move ahead with the chuck wagon to find a good noonday pas-
ture where no other outfit had stopped or bedded down. Winslow or the hands would see a curl of smoke and move ahead to
find dinner prepared. After an hour's rest, the herd would be
back on the trail. All afternoon they would move northward,
accompanied only by the sounds of the drive: the muffled crack-
crack of the cows' ankle joints, the steady thudding of hooves,
and the occasional clatter of long horns swung against each
other.

Those afternoons passed almost hypnotically, the prairie un-
folding before them in a slow, majestic panorama. For mile upon
mile Winslow and the others could see nothing but an undulat-
ing expanse of seared brown grass through the rising clouds of
dust.

Winslow called out, "Diego, there's the chuck wagon. Sid
says there's not much water, just some scattered pools."

He moved on ahead, sensing the gradual coming of twilight.
As he got close to the chuck wagon, which was located beside
some stunted alders lining an old creek bed, he heard Kincaid
singing. The puncher had a fine voice and knew more songs
than anyone Winslow knew. The one he was singing now was
one of his favorites:

> Little Joe, the wrangler, was called out with the rest;
> Though the kid had scarcely reached the herd,
> When the cattle they stampeded,
> Like a hailstorm 'long the field,
> Then we were all a-ridin' for the lead.
> The next morning just at daybreak, we found where his
>   horse fell,
> Down in a washout twenty feet below;

And beneath the horse, mashed to a pulp,
His spur had rung the knell,
Was our little Texas stray, poor Wrangler Joe.

Winslow slid off his horse, stamped the ground to relieve his tired legs, then grinned at Sid, who was busy stirring a big black pot of simmering beans. "Sid, don't you know any *happy* songs about cowboys? "

"Ain't any," Sid grinned. "We're all poor unfortunate souls." He tasted the beans, then called out over his shoulder, "Rosa, bring some more of those hot peppers, will you?"

Rosa was kneeling over a Dutch oven, examining the biscuits critically. She got up, remarking, "How much longer are you going to keep using that foot as an excuse for making a slave out of me?" She crossed to the chuck box, pulled some peppers out of a sack, then returned to toss them into the pot. Feigning annoyance, she said, "I think your foot is all right. You're just too lazy to go to work."

Winslow poured himself a cup of coffee, squatted on his heels, and nodded. "I think you're right, Rosa. All cowboys are lazy."

"Why should I wrestle with a bunch of smelly old steers when I can sit down on a nice wagon seat with a pretty girl all day? I ain't had *all* my brains kicked out!"

Rosa smiled at his compliment. She liked Sid, though at first she had been offish with him. When he offered no attentions toward her, she had spent the long days on the seat with him pleasantly enough. He rarely asked her to do anything, but was always quick to notice and thank her when she did gather wood or help with the cooking.

Kincaid had been an invaluable asset on the trail. He'd found the best grazing spots and water and had proved to be an adequate cook, even if somewhat limited in his choice of meals. Winslow acknowledged his contributions now, saying, "You've sure enough saved our bacon, Sid. Don't see how we'd have managed without you on this drive."

Sid kept stirring the beans, not answering for a few moments. Then he lifted his eyes to Winslow. "Not many bosses would have taken a cripple along" was his brief comment. "Why, this is just a vacation—lots of fresh air and sunshine! And if you'll cut me out a horse, reckon I can do some herding. This foot's still a little touchy, but not bad."

"You just cook the beans, Sid," Dan smiled. "I'll go wash up."

When he was gone, Sid said, "He's a square sort of fellow, Rosa. You were pretty lucky—having him come to get you." She had told him her history, and he added, "Lots of men wouldn't do for this job—to take a handsome young lady all the way to Cheyenne with a bunch of tough hombres like us." He tasted the beans critically, found them satisfactory, then added, "Did I ever tell you about the sermon he gave me about you?"

"No, Sid."

"Told me to treat you like a lady or he'd break my other leg and leave me for the buzzards. Reckon he might just do it, too. He's a hard nut, Rosa. But he's sure took good care of both of us."

"Yes, he has." Then she pursed her lips in an oddly restless manner. Suddenly she asked, "What if he hadn't told you to stay away from me? Would you have tried to kiss me?"

Sid looked startled, then laughed out loud. "You ever know a cowboy who would leave a pretty girl alone? I'd have made a pest out of myself, you bet."

She cocked her head, studied him, then laughed. "No, you are not a bad man with girls."

"Aw, I've got you fooled," Sid grinned. "Give me a chance when this drive is over, and I'll be in the line of poor cowboys comin' to get their hearts busted."

Rosa looked up as Winslow appeared. "*He* will never do that," she said so softly that Sid barely caught the words.

Winslow ate, then rode out so that Diego and the others could come in. He stayed out until midnight, and when they relieved him, he came in and got a plate from the wagon, piling it high with beans. He was eating slowly when Rosa's voice suddenly came from behind and made him jump.

"There is some peach pie. I will get it."

"Great guns!" Dan exclaimed. "Don't sneak up on a man like that, Rosa! I thought you were asleep in the wagon."

"I didn't mean to startle you." She got the pie, brought it to him, then sat down in front of the fire. She was wearing one of her old skirts and a white blouse; her hair was down, falling almost to her waist. Holding her knees with her arms, she watched him eat, saying nothing.

"You make this?" he asked.

"Yes."

"Fine cooking." He finished the pie and stretched. "You remember your dad, Rosa?"

"Yes. He came to San Saba twice. I was very young the first time. But he came again when I was twelve." Her voice was soft and her eyes thoughtful as she stared into the glowing coals. Despite her mature appearance, there was still an innocence about her that Dan admired. "He took me to a show and bought me a new dress and some shoes."

"He's a fine man. I've known him a long time." He sipped his coffee as he sat there telling her about his youthful days with Logan in the army. He was tired and sleepy, but this was the first time he'd spoken to her so freely. Finally he rose to his feet, put the dishes back, then turned to say, "I know you've had a hard time, Rosa, but your dad wants to make things better for you. I think that's why he wants a ranch—to have a place for you."

She had risen when he did, and now she stood looking up at him. She was barefooted and he was wearing boots, so he towered over her. For days she had been worrying about what would happen when they got to Cheyenne, and now she put her fears into words.

"Maybe he will not like me. He's young enough to marry again. If he does, his wife wouldn't want me around."

"Now, that's foolish talk," Winslow protested. "Logan needs you, and if he marries again, his wife will love you, too."

Tears came into her eyes, and when he saw them he was alarmed. "Why, Rosa, there's no need for you to cry."

"I'm afraid!"

It was the first time she'd ever admitted a weakness, and the confession seemed to cause something in her to break loose. She began to tremble, then to sob uncontrollably. Without thought Dan put his arms around her and she fell against him, pressing her face against his chest and holding to him fiercely.

Dan, caught off guard by the girl's vulnerability, held her, not knowing what to say. Finally she grew quiet and lifted her head. Tears ran down her cheeks, and her dark eyes were enormous. "Nobody has ever loved me—" she whispered.

He stopped and kissed her cheek, saying, "Why, Rosa, that's all over!"

She was holding his arm tightly, and more than anything she'd ever wanted, she longed for this strong man to hold her, to care for her.

But Dan was suddenly aware that this was no child he was holding, but a woman, desirable and beautiful. He took a sharp breath and stepped back. "You're just worn out from the trip, Rosa." He patted her shoulder awkwardly. "We'll be at the ranch in a few days, and you'll be fine."

She stared at him with a strange and unfathomable look in her eyes. She had never felt toward a man what she had just felt toward Dan Winslow. And he had not responded, except to pat her shoulder. She said good-night in a strained voice, then walked away and climbed into the wagon.

Dan stared after her, knowing that she had been offended, but he had been too conscious of her for his own comfort. He went to bed at once, but sleep came slowly to both him and Rosa that night.

Sid Kincaid, who had observed the entire scene from his blankets under the wagon, thought: *The big fellow may know how to handle cows—but he sure don't savvy women!*

CHAPTER TWELVE

END OF A DREAM

★ ★ ★ ★

The first sign of trouble came the second day after they had crossed the South Platte, and it came so mildly that Winslow paid almost no heed to it. He was eating pancakes and molasses at the time, and when Diego rode in with the report that three of the cows seemed to be ailing, he had not given it much thought. "Probably that alkaline water they had didn't agree with them," he told Diego.

"Me, I don't think so," Diego shrugged. "They don't look so good."

Winslow finished his breakfast and nodded toward Rosa. "Good pancakes, Rosa." But he got no answering smile from her, which bothered him. She had been quiet—even morose—for a week, not speaking with him except when forced to. Winslow decided that she was still worried about leaving her people and how it would be when she was with her father. Getting to his feet, he saddled his horse and rode out to relieve Mateo and Pedro, saying, "I can handle them. Both of you go get some grub."

He rode around the herd, which was grazing quietly, and soon found the ailing cattle. They did look sick, just as Diego had said. All three of them were standing motionless with their heads down, not eating. Dan dismounted, and when he walked toward them, they didn't shy—which was unusual. He went over them carefully, finding nothing obviously wrong. Their eyes looked yellowish and they seemed to be overheated, but not excessively so. Puzzled and a little worried, he wondered if they would be able to keep up. "Have to keep an eye on them," he murmured as he got back on his horse.

An hour later they were on the move, and as he had feared, the three sick cows lagged behind. "Keep them moving, Pedro," he called out sharply. When they stopped at noon, he went to eat but said almost nothing. He returned to the herd after lunch, and immediately Diego rode over to him, his face tense. "Señor Dan, four more of the cows are sick."

Dan stared at the thin vaquero, and a fear began building in him. He said nothing, but followed Diego to look at the cattle. They were listless, and now it was obvious that the first three that had taken sick were running a fever. "What do you think?" he asked Diego.

"Could be not too bad," Diego said slowly. "We will maybe have to slow down until we see if they get well."

But the next morning, one of the first three animals to get sick was down; there was no question that she was dying. The others had gotten worse, and Dan's lips grew thin. "It's bad," he said. "We'll cut the sick ones out and leave them, Diego. Maybe it won't spread to the rest."

But it did spread, and when they found more than twenty sick head the next day, they knew the worst. Sid Kincaid had a look at the afflicted cattle and said to Diego, "It's Texas tick fever, I'm afraid."

"Sí, señor," the Mexican agreed. "I have seen it before. I feel very bad for Señor Dan."

"He'll lose this herd, or most of it," Kincaid nodded. "I was with Shanghai Pierce on a drive to Abilene three years ago. We got hit by tick fever, and lost half the herd—over three thousand head had to be shot."

"It is in God's hand," Diego said softly, then added, "but my heart is sad that such a thing should happen to a good man like Señor Dan."

At first Rosa knew nothing about the extent of the sickness. She thought that it was only a matter of a few cows. But finally it became obvious that something was seriously wrong with the whole herd, and she asked Sid, "What's happening to the cattle?" When he explained, she sobered at once. "Will they all die?"

"Most of 'em, I guess. When it gets started, tick fever is just about like a plague. Spreads like wildfire, and there's no way to treat it. Just shoot the sick animals and hope it burns itself out."

"How awful!"

"Going to be hard on Dan," Sid said slowly. "He's worked like a slave to build up this herd. Hate to see it."

"Maybe it will stop," she said hopefully, but saw that Sid had given up. "We *can* hope, can't we?"

But as the days went by, she heard the cracks of revolver shots each morning as the sick cattle were destroyed. She found herself counting them, willing them to stop—but each day there were more. All the fun went out of the drive, and Winslow said nothing at all to anyone. He never smiled now and slept little. Rosa tried to get him to eat, but he merely sampled the food, not even hearing her, apparently.

It could not continue long, and two weeks after the first cow went down, there were fewer than fifty healthy cattle left. The Mexicans were embarrassed, not knowing what to do with themselves. Finally, one morning, Winslow said, "Diego, no sense you and the boys hanging around here." He stepped forward and handed some bills to the men, saying, "You did a good job."

Diego was stricken and tried to argue. "It is too much, Señor Dan," he said. "We agreed on this for the whole drive."

"Not your fault," Dan shrugged and forced a smile. "You get on back to Texas. Maybe I'll come down and pick up another herd next year."

"I would like that very much, señor," Diego said quietly. There was nothing more he could say to this big man whom he respected more than any gringo he'd known. He spoke to Pedro and Mateo, and when they had gathered their belongings and tied them to their horses, they mounted and with a wave rode out of camp.

Feeling the eyes of Rosa and Sid on him, Dan turned to face them. "Those are fine people," he said quietly. Casting his eyes toward the shrunken herd, he said, "I don't think we'll make it with any of these. It'll be a real disappointment to your dad, Rosa."

Wearily, he climbed on his horse and left, and soon Rosa heard the sound of gunshots. She and Sid counted them. "Seven more dead," she said.

Sid shook his head. "Too bad, Rosa." He was standing beside

the wagon, looking toward the herd but thinking of Winslow. "Hope this don't get him down," he murmured. "Seen it do that to a few."

"Do what, Sid?"

Sid put his weight on his right foot, testing it carefully. "Almost well," he said, then looked up and answered her question. "When a man's got a big dream, and it don't happen—it can eat him alive. Sure would hate to see that happen to Dan."

"He won't give up," she said quickly. "He's a hard man."

"You think so?" Sid asked. Shaking his head, he said, "Maybe so, in some ways. But when a thing like this happens, it's like getting shot. I got shot once, down in Val Verde. Knocked me down and I was wide awake. I wanted to keep on fighting, but my arms and legs wouldn't work. I was trying to get up, but it was like all my nerves were dead, and all I could do was just give up."

Rosa stared at him. "It's only cattle, Sid."

"No, it's Dan's dream. And if a man's got a dream, it don't matter much what it is. Can be climbing a mountain or having a son or breaking the bank at a gambling joint. It ain't so much *what* the dream is, Rosa. What means something is that he's actually *got* one. That's what keeps us going and makes the mornings good and the air smell sweet. But if it gets smashed—" He shook his head, a sadness in his hazel eyes. "I seen quite a few whose dream got ruined, and they lived for quite a while, but they wasn't really alive."

Rosa couldn't believe what Sid was saying. "But there are more cattle. My father is up ahead with the herd he brought. Dan can get more cattle. He said so to Diego."

Sid slowly rolled a cigarette and lit it. "Sure do hope so, Rosa. I'm right partial to that big fellow!"

★   ★   ★   ★

They crossed the line that divided Colorado and Wyoming with twenty-seven head, all that had survived the virulent fever. Two days later they crossed the Union Pacific Railroad, a long sweep of track stretching east and west. That night at supper Sid spoke to Winslow about leaving.

"Dan, if you'll stake me to a horse, I'll leave you here." He nodded toward the east, adding, "I can find some sort of a riding job, maybe in the stockyard in Cheyenne."

Dan glanced at him, but shook his head. "Your foot's not ready for hard work yet, Sid."

"It's all right."

Rosa was frying potatoes in the large black skillet. She shifted them with a fork, and said at once, "No, it's not. If you try to work cattle, you'll be back on crutches again."

Sid snapped angrily, "Well, I can't sponge off you the rest of my life, Dan!"

"Don't guess you eat enough to be a problem, Sid. And when we get to the ranch, you can start in slowly. Rosa's right. You don't need to twist that ankle around too much for a month or so."

Rosa brought the pan to where Sid was sitting. "That's enough talk about leaving. Hold your plate out."

Sid muttered, "And you don't have to treat me like a child, either."

Rosa ignored him, moved to Dan and filled his plate with fried potatoes. He had been eating better, she had noticed, and gave him a double portion. "How much farther is it to the ranch?" she asked.

Dan stabbed a big bunch of potatoes with his fork, shoved them in his mouth, and sputtered, "These are *hot*, Rosa!" He spat out half of them and chewed the rest carefully, thinking about the trail ahead. "Best I can figure, less than a hundred miles. We can make it in a few days." He stabbed another smaller forkful of the hot potatoes, blowing on them this time before putting them in his mouth. "Sure be glad to get there. Losing the herd was a hard thing for me. I'd like to get it behind and start with something fresh."

It was the first time he'd commented on the loss of the herd, and his remark caused Sid and Rosa to exchange a swift glance. They had been worried about Winslow, for he had taken it hard. But now he seemed more cheerful. Later Rosa said to Sid, "See, he's all right. I told you he would be."

That night Sid insisted on taking a turn on horseback to watch the cattle. "Got to keep in practice," he said, allowing Dan to saddle up for him. He got into the saddle carefully, but once mounted, he grinned. "Well, if I don't fall off, I'll see you after a while."

He walked his horse off, and Rosa said, "I'm glad you didn't let him go to Cheyenne." She was washing the dishes with water from the creek that ran close by, her nightly chore. "He's not ready to work yet."

"Don't guess there'll be enough work to hire him when we get to the ranch," Dan shrugged. "But he can rest up until he's able to get a riding job." He poked at the ground with his knife, cleaning the blade in the sandy soil. Looking up, he remarked, "Guess I've been pretty poor company lately."

She lifted her eyes to him and said gently, "I'm sorry about the cattle. I know what it's like to lose everything."

"Why—it was only cattle, Rosa," he protested.

"I know, but you'd worked so hard for them," she said. "I didn't like to see you hurting."

Her words brought his eyes up, and he said, "Well, it'll pass." He folded the knife and put it away. "You feeling better about being with your dad?"

"I—think so." She tried to smile, not quite successfully. "It's just that I'll be a stranger—and a foreigner, Señor Dan."

"Hey, that's not right!" he protested. "You'll have a dad and me and Sid. And will you please stop calling me *señor*? Makes me feel like some kind of a government official!"

She laughed at that, and there was an ease between them. "All right—Dan. But I'm half-Mexican. People will call me 'bean-eater' or 'greaser.' "

Winslow said grimly, "Not when I'm around!"

She crossed her arms and gave him a sly smile. "Didn't you ever call a Mexican those names?" Then she laughed at his expression. "Oh, Dan, it's all right. You should hear some of the names we call you gringos!"

As the fire burned down, they sat there talking quietly as the darkness closed in, drinking the black coffee. A little later they heard Sid singing in his smooth baritone:

> I'm up in the mornin' afore daylight
> And afore I sleep the moon shines bright.
> No chaps and no slicker, and it's pouring down rain,
> And I swear I'll never night-herd again.
> Oh, it's bacon and beans most every day—
> I'd as soon be a-eatin' prairie hay.
> I went to the boss to draw my roll,

He had it figured out I was nine dollars in the hole.
I'll sell my horse, and I'll sell my saddle;
You can go to blazes with your longhorn cattle.

Finally Winslow rose and stretched. "Well, guess I'll sleep a little." He looked out into the dusky night, shook his head, and remarked, "I've lost enough sleep over that herd. Man can't go around with a long face forever because he has a little bad luck. Good-night, Rosa."

"Good-night, Dan."

★　★　★　★

A light rain fell as they broke camp the following Friday, laying a silver glaze on the land. It settled the dust and brought a fine vigor to Winslow as he climbed into the saddle. They had made good time, and now he was anxious to find Logan and put an end to the drive. He had not let it sour him, but disappointment had been a keen pang, for he'd wanted to bring a fine herd to the new ranch.

Rosa had asked him to saddle her horse, and the two of them got the cattle started. All morning they traveled steadily, always on an inclined plane. At noon they took a break, and Sid built a fire and heated some beans and the meat they'd had the night before. As they ate, Rosa asked, "How much farther, Dan?"

"Not far." He pulled a folded piece of paper from his vest pocket, smoothed it out, and pointed at it as he spoke. "See that bluff right over there—the one with the red face? Here it is on Logan's map. 'Course this map was made by the fellow he bought the place from, so he couldn't guarantee how accurate it is, but it looks like we ought to hit the ranch by dark."

They moved ahead all afternoon, and both Dan and Sid were impressed with the quality of the country. "If your place looks like this," Sid said, "you'll be able to raise good cattle. Never saw a better piece of country."

Finally at four-thirty Dan drew to a halt beside a small creek. A few cows were drinking, and Dan squinted at the brands, then grinned at Rosa. "We're close. Those are Circle W cows." He studied the lay of the land. "This is Clear Creek, I think. See how it follows the line of rising ground that goes to the bench country? Just like on the map. Sid, it's getting too late to move the cattle. You and Rosa camp here and keep an eye on them while I find the place."

"Oh, Dan, let me go with you!" Rosa begged. "I want to see it."

"Guess you can," he grinned. "Give old Logan a surprise."

They left, and Rosa grew more excited and a little nervous. "He hasn't seen me since I was twelve," she said, searching the distance for a house. "I wonder if he'll be satisfied."

"He'll probably faint," Dan said. "I imagine he's got a little girl in pigtails in his mind. Now he'll have to oil up his shotgun to keep half the punchers in this valley run off from chasing his grown-up daughter."

There was an air of expectancy in them both, and in less than an hour they crested a rise. There in the valley before them lay a small ranch house. Winslow looked up, nodded toward a sheer bluff that rose in the west, and said, "That's the place, right where the map shows it. Let's go see your dad."

They rode down the slope, passing many cattle, mostly bearing the Arrow brand but with a few Circle W cows among them. "Don't know about this," he said. "What are all these Arrow cows doing mixed in with our stock?" His nerves began to tingle, and even Rosa was alarmed and puzzled. When they got to the house, two men came out to greet them. The one who spoke was young, no more than twenty-five, and wore a fancy vest and hat. "You looking for the way to War Paint?" he asked. He was very blond, his hair worn long like Custer's and Wild Bill's. But he was more than a dandy, Dan sensed. There was something dangerous about him. He wore two guns low on his thighs, something that Winslow noted with interest.

"No. We're looking for Logan Mann's ranch."

"Mann?" The puncher pushed his hat back, then shook his head. "Don't know any owner by that name."

Dan looked around at the landmarks. "You should. This is it we're standing on. He's my partner—and those cows with a Circle W are our stock."

At once the man's light-colored eyes fixed on Winslow in a different manner, and there was a slight tension as he shifted his weight. "You're wrong there, mister. This here is Arrow land. Has been for years. You look closer you'll see those Circle W cows have been vented. They're Arrow cows now."

Dan was aware of the custom of laying a line with a hot iron across a brand, called "venting." A new brand would be placed below, signifying that the cow had been sold to the owner of the new brand. Angry at this surprising turn of events, Dan dismounted, and Rosa followed suit. He wished she were not with him, but there was no help for it now. Advancing until he stood in front of the blond man, he said carefully, "I'd like to look around inside the house."

"That's too bad," Deuce Longly grinned. " 'Coz you got no more chance than a snowball in Hades of doin' it. Not unless Mr. Head says so. You go get a note from him, and you can look all you please."

Dan had an impulse to force the thing, for he knew that if there was anything in the house that would give a clue to the mystery of Logan's failure to be on the spot, it would be gone by the time he returned. But he was acutely conscious of Rosa's presence and said, "Looks like you got the best cards."

He turned to go, but as he did the other man moved from the porch. He was a tall, burly man with the pushed-in nose and scarred eyes of a fighter. He was running to fat, but he was not slow. Winslow had swung onto his horse, but in that moment, the big man had come to take Rosa's arm, holding her fast.

"You're a pretty little thing," he leered. "Me and you ought to get on fine!"

Rosa gave a short cry of fear and looked to Winslow. Deuce Longly, Dan saw, was laughing, his attention on the big man.

Without hesitation, Dan drew his .44 in one smooth, fluid motion and slammed the barrel down on the balding head of the bruiser, who collapsed without a sound; then he swung the gun to cover Longly, who had reacted with a fast draw. But Longly stopped abruptly, his gun only halfway out of the holster when he saw the black muzzle of Winslow's revolver looming in front of him. He pulled his hands clear and held them away from his guns. "I'm not drawing!" he said quickly.

Winslow ordered, "Take those guns out and lay them on the porch—by the barrels." When Longly had carefully placed them down, Dan said, "Now turn around, kneel, and put your hands as high as you can reach." He got a glance of pure hate from Longly, but when Winslow said quietly, "Better mind," the gunman did as he was told. Dan reached back and pulled a length of rawhide from his saddlebags, then stepped down out of the saddle. He pulled the gun from the holster of the unconscious man and stuck it in his own saddlebags. He quickly bound the man's wrists and cut the rawhide with his knife. Moving to the porch, he tied Longly's wrists, then collected the man's guns. "Put these in my saddlebags, Rosa."

"Get up," he snapped, and Longly struggled to his feet, his pale eyes glowing with rage. "You'll never get away with this," he whispered.

"Let's take a look inside." He noted that the man he'd hit was coming out of it, so he walked over to him and hoisted him to his feet. "Get inside," he said, forcing him to the porch. "You two first." Dan shoved the pair through the door. "Sit down on the floor, and don't even think about anything rash." He began to search the house, hoping to find something that would at least prove that Logan had been in the house, but found nothing. He looked at every scrap of paper, but none of them were to Logan or were written by him.

Finally he gave up, saying to Rosa, "We'll find him."

Longly demanded, "Untie me! I told you, there ain't nobody named Mann been here."

Dan considered the two, then asked, "How far to Arrow?"

"Ten miles."

"Get up. We're going to see your boss."

The two men began to curse, but in the end they had no choice. Dan untied their hands and said sternly, "You two will ride in front of us. There's plenty of daylight left, so don't get ambitious and try to get away. Get your stuff, because you won't be coming back here."

Fifteen minutes later the four of them left the ranch house, and an hour later they pulled up in front of a large log structure. At once a voice challenged them, and Dan moved his horse forward, laying the muzzle of his gun on Longly's ribs. "Be polite and you might make it out of this thing," he said quietly.

"It's me and Ollie," Longly called out. "Got some people who want to see Mr. Head."

The man who had challenged them called out, "Well, bring them in here."

"Nice and easy," Dan said, and he dismounted, keeping his gun in his hand. "Let's go see the man."

They moved across the yard, and when they reached the porch they were met by a man who peered at them, trying to make them out in the deepening twilight. "Who are you? What d'you want with Mr. Head?"

"I'll have to tell him that personally."

"He's got a gun on us," Longly burst out.

The information caused the shadowy figure of the man to straighten up. "You're not going in this house with a gun!" he said abruptly.

"Then ask Mr. Head to come out on the porch."

There was a brief silence, then the front door opened and Head stepped outside. "What's going on here?" he demanded.

"Mr. Head?" Dan asked.

"Yes. Who are you?"

"My name's Winslow. I found your crew on my place. Thought we'd better talk about it some."

"He means the old Gunderson place," Deuce broke in. "He knocked Ollie in the head and got the drop on me. Gimme a gun—!"

"Shut up, Deuce," Head said impatiently. He paused, then said, "Come in the house—all of you."

Dan waited until the men of Arrow were inside, then stepped through the doorway. At once he heard his named called—"Dan Winslow!"

Winslow wheeled to meet the astonished gaze of a man he recognized instantly. A brief smile touched his lips. "Hello, Ash. Didn't expect to find you here."

Head was watching this carefully. "You know this man, Ash?"

Caudill nodded. "Reckon I do. We worked together on a small ranch in Texas many years back."

Dan motioned quickly toward Rosa. "This is Miss Rosa Mann, my partner's daughter."

Deuce Longly was glaring at Winslow balefully. He broke out, "He busted Ollie on the head and threw me down! Then he busted into the house and searched it."

Ash glanced first at Head, then at Winslow. "What's all this about, Dan?"

Dan faced the two men squarely. "Maybe you better tell *us*. Logan Mann left Texas three months ago with a small herd, all branded Circle W. When I got to the ranch this afternoon, I saw a few Circle W cows mixed in with a lot of Arrow cows. These hairpins claim those cows are all Arrow cows now and they never heard of anyone named Mann. I asked to look around, and Longly said I'd have to get your okay. When we started to leave, that one started to force himself on Miss Mann, so I knocked him down and took Longly's guns away." Winslow's eyes grew fierce. "I guess you better start talking, Mr. Head. Your men were in *my* ranch house and jumped us when we tried to talk to them. Apparently, my cows are vented with your brand on them, and there's no sign of my partner."

"I don't know anything about it," Head said at once, his face growing red. He was a man who could not abide opposition and now said angrily, "If you attack my men again, I won't be responsible."

"Let me see the bill of sale for those cattle with your brand on them," Winslow said promptly.

"Get off this ranch," Head broke out. "That place has been empty since the last owner left!"

"Show me the bill of sale," Winslow demanded.

"Get out!"

"Wait a minute, Mr. Head," Caudill interrupted. He turned to Winslow, saying, "Dan, we found those cattle straying on our graze."

Winslow's eyes grew harder. "And you slap a brand on any cow that strays on your place? You know better than that, Ash!"

Head broke in. "I'll have no man invading my range! Get off the place—and if you're at that cabin tomorrow, I'll have you *put* off."

Winslow wheeled to face Silas Head. He fixed his eyes on him, and there was a readiness in his face that made Caudill stiffen.

"I have certified copies of the bill of sale and the deed for that ranch. Your brand's been illegally vented on my cattle. I'll be there tomorrow and the day after. I'll be looking over the rest of your herds for any vented Circle W stock."

"Get out! Get out!" Head shouted. "You'll not go through my stock!"

"Let's go, Rosa," Dan said. He wheeled and took her out of the house without a backward glance.

"You ain't lettin' him get by with this, are you, Mr. Head?" Deuce Longly's face was flushed, and he was almost trembling with rage.

Head stared at him. His lip curled as he said, "Looks like I'll need tougher men than you to stop him."

Longly flushed, but before he could answer, Caudill ordered, "You two get out of here."

"Ash—!"

Ash gave him a contemptuous look. "I said get out!"

Longly and Ollie stumbled out, and when the two were gone, Head demanded, "What do you know about all this, Caudill? Is Winslow telling the truth about that vented stock?"

Caudill explained quickly, "Sure, there's a few cows we picked up. Not many." He tried to remember, his brow wrinkled with thought, and finally said, "Ed and Shorty found them wandering around over close to the Red Hill country. I said to let them graze, and a month later Shorty asked me what to do with them. I told him to vent them and put our brand on them."

"What about this fellow Mann?"

"Nobody of that name I know of."

"What about that ranch of Gundersons? We need it?"

"We need it bad," Caudill agreed, then looked the owner right in the eye. "But we don't need it bad enough to fight Dan Winslow for it."

Head stared at his foreman. "He's tough, then?"

"Too tough to fool with. But he'll sell, I guess, if we pay enough. Let me handle him, Mr. Head. We went through some tough times together. I can bring him around." He hesitated, then added, "He's not a bad fellow. Rather have him on my side than against me. But if he gets stubborn, we put pressure on him. How much can I offer him for the place?"

*   *   *   *

As they headed away from the Arrow ranch, Rosa rode silently beside Winslow. The scene had shocked her. She had seen Winslow handle the two Arrow hands almost contemptuously, though she knew they were both dangerous. It was a side to him she had not suspected, and finally she asked in a small voice, "Dan, where is my father?"

"I don't know, Rosa. But if he's alive, I'll find him."

"You think he might—be dead?"

Dan hesitated, then said, "It's something we have to consider. If Logan were alive and able, he'd have gotten in touch with us. He wouldn't just run out without letting us know something."

Rosa said nothing for a few minutes. Finally she asked, "Dan, what will happen to me if we don't ever find him? I heard what my stepfather said—that if I left I could never come back."

Dan drew his horse close to hers and put his hand on her shoulder. "Rosa, I'll take care of you. I promised Logan I would."

"Will you, Dan?" She turned to look at him and put her hand out for his.

Winslow took it, noting how small it was. "Rosa, we'll find him if we can. But whatever happens, I'll be around for you to lean on."

There was a silence, and then she whispered, "Thank you, Dan—!"

They rode through the night, each thinking their own thoughts. Dan was aware that his dream of a ranch was only a fragment now. If he had had no obligations, he would have ridden away from it all, but he'd given his word. And the memory of Rosa's small hand in his, resting there trustfully as a child's, was fresh and strong. He put his own weariness out of his mind, knowing that he would never stop until he'd done whatever a man could do for his friend.

Rosa was aware that she should be afraid, and she was—for her father. But as they rode on, she seemed to hear Dan's voice, like a tiny echo—*Whatever happens, I'll be around for you to lean on.*

PART THREE

STORM CLOUDS

★　★　★　★

STORM CLOUDS

CHAPTER THIRTEEN

WINSLOW PAYS A CALL

★　★　★　★

Sheriff Bill Rider considered his visitor with hooded eyes, saying, "Have a seat, Winslow." He waited until the big man sat down in one of the three cane-bottomed chairs in the small office, then added, "Been expecting you to come by."

"News travels fast."

"Bad news quicker than any," Rider agreed. He got up, walked to the stove, and picked up the ancient coffee pot. "This coffee's about as bad as coffee can be," he said, picking up a heavy mug and passing it to Winslow. "But the worst cup of coffee I ever had was pretty good." As he filled the two cups, he studied Winslow carefully, knowing that he'd have to deal with him in one way or another.

What he saw was a man taller than the average rider, heavier of bone, and more solid in chest and arm. Winslow was trimmed down to muscle, and exposure to rain and sun and cold and dust had built within him a reserve of vitality. He was not a man, Rider recognized instantly, who would be easily stopped at anything he threw himself into. He had a head of black hair; the blue eyes were direct, and his skin, with all its weathering, was unwrinkled. His nose was long and his mouth heavy, and though he showed no sign of hurry or strain, his face had a melancholy shadow on it.

Dan saw that the elderly sheriff knew more than he was likely to say, so Dan smiled faintly, remarking, "I'm probably going to be a downright nuisance to you, Sheriff. But I guess you know about that."

"I hear you've already stirred up Silas Head."

"We had some words," Winslow nodded. "We'll have more, I expect."

"A powerful man around here, son," Rider said idly enough, but there was a warning in his hazel eyes. "Pretty well used to having his own way."

"I know, he's the big mogul in tin pants, and he's got fur on his knees," Winslow shrugged. "I'll be going over to collect any more vented Circle W cows from him. Be calling on all the ranchers for that same reason."

"Might run into some trouble."

"They're my cows." The words might have been carved in stone, and Winslow moved on to say, "My partner, Logan Mann, came up the trail with three hundred head of good stock two months ago. I'll be asking around for him."

"I run into most people who come into this valley," Rider said. "I never met him, never heard his name until you mentioned it."

Winslow knew the old man was speaking the truth. There was an air of honesty about Bill Rider that he recognized, and he nodded at once. "Sure—but the cattle are here, Sheriff. They didn't get here alone."

"No, I guess not." Rider was troubled and said so. "It don't look too good, does it? I take it he wasn't the kind of man who'd just take a notion to ride off and leave stock to wander?"

"Not Logan." Winslow sipped the bitter coffee and spent the next ten minutes giving Rider a brief history of their partnership. Winslow appeared relaxed and idle as he sat in the chair, but there was a latent power in his posture. Finally he got up, saying, "I know you don't have any authority outside War Paint, Sheriff Rider. Just wanted to stop by and tell you I'll be nosing around. You'll probably get some complaints."

Rider rose to his feet, a thin man worn by time but still vigorous. "Wish I could be of more help, son. I'll keep my ears open. If I hear anything, I'll let you know. Meanwhile, come and see me from time to time—and try to keep from stirring up more hornets than you can swat."

Dan grinned, and it made him look younger to the sheriff. "Good advice," he said. "Do the best I can."

As he left the office and walked to his horse, he considered questioning some of the businessmen about Logan, but he was totally convinced that the sheriff was an honest man. *Rider knows this town*, he thought. *If Logan had spent any time here, he'd have met him—or at least heard about him.*

A pair of punchers were leaning against the wall, watching him from under the brims of their hats. On impulse, Dan asked them, "You know the way to Arrow Ranch?"

His question caught them off guard, and there was a noticeable hesitation before one of them finally pointed west. "Out that road. Go six miles and take the west fork."

"Much obliged," he nodded, and rode out of town in a leisurely fashion. He glanced back as he turned off the main street, just in time to see the two mount and drive their horses at a dead run down one of the side streets. Later he saw dust to his right, then in front of him, and knew that they were on their way to give notice of his coming.

"Nothing ever changes," he murmured. It was an old game to him, and he knew he had no choice but to allow himself to be drawn into what was coming. But he put those thoughts away, having learned that a man can't let trouble control his actions. There was a dark streak of fatalism running through him, put there by the hard times he'd encountered. They had not soured him, but he was always conscious of the possibility of a tragedy around the next bend, so as he rode toward Arrow, he gave little thought to what might happen there, but rather studied the country.

All the way up from Texas he had thus studied the land, so that now he could draw a map upon the ground of each river and creek he had crossed, each hill and pass. He could describe the quality of grass along the way, the brands of the various trail herds seen. There was this map in his head, filling out day by day. For him the world was a natural environment of weather and grass and beef, and of this world he was an active scholar. He recognized that there was another world where men lived crowded together, worked according to the clock, and surrendered their freedom to authority—and all that made a terrible picture to him of stunted souls sweating in an endless treadmill.

The dust of the two riders in front of him drifted back, settling on his face, and when he came to the turn to the west, he noted the trail they left. Two miles down that road, he came to a small creek lined with alders. Dismounting, he loosed the cinch of his saddle and let the horse enjoy a leisurely drink. It was indicative of Winslow that he would be so considerate of a horse. Most men would only have let their horse drink briefly, then jerked his head up and gone on their way. He had learned to take time in small doses, and now he relaxed as Duke snorted and drank noisily, enjoying the shade and the sight of the hills that lifted off to his right. A rider was approaching from that direction, and his attention sharpened at once. He was surprised to see it was a woman, and when she drew near she stopped her horse on the far side of the creek and studied him. He removed his hat—a gesture she noted at once.

She was riding a fine gray mare with a pure white mane, and she was dressed in a light green divided skirt and a darker green blouse. She examined him frankly, her black eyes going over him in a practiced manner. Her dark hair was bound into a single coil that hung down her back, and she wore a low-crowned white hat with a narrow brim.

"Looking for Arrow?" she asked suddenly.

Dan nodded. "Yes. Down this road, isn't it?"

"About four miles." There was something almost masculine about her manner, at least in the steadiness of her gaze. She was, Winslow saw at once, accustomed to the company of men. "I'm Diane Head," she said. "Come along and I'll take you to the house."

Winslow cinched his horse's girth snugly, swung into the saddle, and crossed the creek to where she was waiting. She turned her mare, and the two of them galloped along the dusty road, sending up more fine dust.

"I'm Dan Winslow," he said. She turned her head at once, giving him a sharp look. He smiled, adding, "Yes, Miss Head. I'm the curly wolf with the long white teeth you've been hearing about." There was a flicker in her dark eyes that told him he'd been discussed, and he added, "A face to scare the children with, a voice like a rough file, and no good through and through."

Diane allowed a slight smile to touch her lips, then asked, "What's the other side of the picture?"

"Isn't any."

She nodded, amused at his openness. "Just as well you think so then." When he didn't answer she said, "I'm a little surprised to find you headed for Arrow. Some of our hands have been breathing fire and brimstone at the mention of your name. Good thing I'm along, Mr. Winslow. They're a pretty tough bunch, and you might not like the reception they've got planned."

He looked up, traced the flight of a high-flying hawk, then said softly, "Why, Miss Head, each day brings its troubles and a man seldom has a warning. Sometimes he has to make an answer when things fall through."

"What if his answer's not good enough?"

"In that case, he has to hold to his answer until the sky falls in—which is about the extent of my philosophy, I reckon."

Diane Head sat in her saddle easily, thinking of what she had heard about Dan Winslow—and was perplexed. Her father had described him as an arrogant boaster, and Deuce Longly had said worse. Ash had been more cautious, saying that Winslow was a tough one, not to be discounted.

What none of them had mentioned was how fine-looking he was, but she knew that only a woman would take notice of that. *He is a handsome thing,* she thought, stealing a glance at him. *But he doesn't seem to know it—not like most men would.* She waited for him to show an interest in her and was piqued when he did not.

"What happened at your ranch? You have a woman there, I understand."

Dan surmised that she put the matter in those words to anger him, and he was amused. "My partner's daughter is there. She's fifteen. I had to correct Ollie when he grew impertinent."

"I saw the gash in his head where you 'corrected' him, Mr. Winslow," Diane answered. "You understand he won't forget what you did?"

"I hope not," Dan said mildly. "Miss Head, you don't really have to ride with me. I can find the ranch, and your father wouldn't like you to be in my company."

His words angered her, and she shook her head in an imperious gesture, saying quickly, "My father knows I can take care of myself."

"In that, Miss Head, he's correct. But he probably wouldn't like your choice of society."

Diane thought she caught a sly note of cynicism in his voice. She rode beside him for a few moments, then asked, "What will you do if you can't find your partner? I understand you've found a few strays from the herd he brought from Texas—but you can't make a ranch on those, can you?"

"I'll find the cattle. But I'd rather find my partner. He's a good friend, and Rosa needs him."

"I hope you do," she said at once. "It must be very hard on you—and on the daughter."

Dan turned to face her and saw that the remark was genuine. She was, he decided, a strong-willed young woman, spoiled by good looks and wealth—yet he noted that her lips were gentle as she spoke, and it made him like her more. "That's kind of you, Miss Head," he said quietly.

She grew rosy, as if he had paid her a great compliment, and turned the conversation to a neutral ground. By the time they rode up to the headquarters of Arrow about twenty minutes later, she had grown easy in his company. As they crossed to the big house, four of Arrow's crew appeared and formed a line across their way. Two of them, Winslow saw, were the punchers he'd spoken to in town; the other two were Deuce Longly and Ollie Peace.

It was Ollie who called out, "Get off that horse, Winslow!"

But it was Diane Head who said angrily, "What do you think you're doing?"

"You don't know this joker, Miss Head," Longly protested. "He jumped Ollie and me—"

"Deuce, get to work," Diane snapped, her eyes flashing. "And take the rest of these gentlemen of leisure with you." When she saw them hesitate, she cried out, "Do you hear me? Get to work or get off the ranch!"

At that moment Ash Caudill walked out of the bunkhouse and called out, "Do as she says, all of you!" He came to stand in front of the pair as the hands moved sullenly away, then said,

"Sorry about that, Dan. Get down and come into the house."

Winslow dismounted, and as he tied his horse to the rail, said, "Sorry to get you caught up in my troubles, Miss Head."

"Call me Diane," she replied, and he saw that she was still angry. Turning to Ash, she said, "If you can't keep the men in hand, I'll do it myself!"

Her words caused Caudill's head to jerk, and he flushed angrily. When he spoke, Dan saw, it was only with effort that he was able to maintain any semblance of ease. "Why, I wouldn't have let them jump on a guest, Diane," he said finally. Then he turned to face Winslow. "Dan, I've been wanting to talk to you. Come and sit down."

"Can't do it right now, Ash," Dan said, smiling to take the edge off his refusal. "Got some chores to do. Just stopped by to tell you that I appreciate the way you moved your stock off my graze."

The previous day three Arrow hands had appeared, cut the vented cattle out, and moved the Arrow stock away from Circle W range. It had surprised Dan, and he'd come expressly to make it plain that he appreciated the gesture.

Ash nodded eagerly. "Why, Dan, it was only right. We were wrong to vent your brands in such a hurry, but we just figgered they'd wandered off from some herd. If we find any more, I've told the boys to drive them to your place."

"Appreciate it, Ash," Dan said. "You can tell Mr. Head I'm grateful."

"Sure, Dan, I'll do that. How about you come over later and you and him and me can sit down and talk some. He'll be back in three days."

"Be happy to." Dan turned to the young woman. "Thanks for keeping the wolves from chewing me up, Diane." He mounted and with a smile and a wave pushed Duke to a fast gallop as he left the yard.

Diane watched him go, then said, "He's not like I thought he'd be, Ash."

Caudill glanced at her, catching something in her tone that made him ask, "What did you expect?"

"Just another hand. But he's more than that, isn't he, Ash?" She caught his look and was taken by an impish desire to tease the man. "Why didn't you tell me he was so good-looking?"

"Didn't notice."

"Well, he is," Diane nodded emphatically, then added, "Tell Deuce and those others to leave him alone."

Her command didn't sit well with Caudill. "I'm the foreman here, Diane. I'll take care of the hands."

"See you do it, then," she snapped. She liked Ash Caudill, but there was a streak in him that had made her keep him at arm's length. She turned and walked into the house, leaving him to watch her, anger glinting in his eyes. Then he cursed and moved toward the bunkhouse, wishing he'd never set eyes on Dan Winslow.

★   ★   ★   ★

"Did you find out anything about my father, Dan?"

"No, Rosa, but I talked to Sheriff Rider," Dan said. "He knows everybody in the territory, and he promised to ask around."

"He must have left some kind of a trace," Sid put in. "We know he got as far as this valley."

Dan had been met by the pair as soon as he returned from the Arrow ranch, and now the three of them were eating the dinner Sid had put together—barbecued beef ribs and beans. They had moved into the house, giving Rosa one of the bedrooms while the two men shared the other. But all of them were uneasy, feeling the lack of permanence about the thing.

Dan finished eating and stood up. "I'm going to make a few calls."

"I'll go with you," Sid said instantly.

"No, you stay here and watch the place. I'm just going to do some riding, visit around and see what I can pick up. But while I'm—" He broke off, glanced out the window, and at once moved to put on his gun belt before going out onto the porch. Sid grabbed a rifle and limped after him.

Two men on horseback were approaching, and they had brought some cattle, which they now left milling around. "Hello the house!" one of them hailed, lifting his hand in a friendly gesture.

Dan let them approach, then said, "C'mon in. Beans in the pot."

The two men dismounted, and one of them answered for both. "We done et. You Winslow?"

"I'm Winslow. This is Sid Kincaid—Miss Rosa Mann, my partner's daughter."

"I'm Gus Miller—and this here is Dave Orr." Miller was a short man with black hair and hard black eyes, who spoke in a husky voice. "Heard about you moving in. Brought some of your cattle back that drifted on my range a while back—fourteen head with a Circle W brand."

Orr spoke up at once, adding, "I found twelve, Winslow. May be a few more, but this was all I could find."

Dan said, "Why, that's handsome of you both! Come in for coffee at least, and maybe some pie."

Soon the two visitors were seated at the table, eating apricot pie and drinking coffee. Orr was saying, "Ole Gunderson was a good friend of mine. I wanted to buy this place, but he took off before I had a chance." Then he grinned wryly. "Well, to tell the truth, I couldn't have bought it, anyway. But I guess Arrow would have."

"I don't expect they would," Gus Miller grunted. "It was easier for them to run Ole off. That way they got his graze without paying for it." He chewed stolidly on the pie, then said, "Your partner, he brought the herd from Texas?"

"Nearly three hundred head," Winslow nodded. "You ever meet up with him?"

Both men shook their heads, and Miller said, "I've seen a few of these vented Circle W cows scattered around, but nothing like three hundred head. I reckon your partner—"

Dan cut in quickly, knowing what Miller was about to say. "I'll be doing some hunting. I'm hoping to find him and the cattle."

Miller realized that Winslow had cut him off to save the feelings of the daughter. "Sure, I'll keep my eye out, and we'll pass the word around."

"Would you draw me out a rough map?" Dan asked. "Might save me some trouble."

"Might save you from getting shot," Miller grinned. He took

a piece of paper that Rosa found, sketched a map on it, pointing out the ranches and homesteaders' locations as he drew. "That's Dutton's place—and here's the Shultz homestead—Lowell Cox here. Here's the Jenson place, not far from your ranch. And this is the Draws—the Littleton boys got a ranch there. Matter of fact, I saw a few of your cows up there last month. Didn't know they were yours then."

Dan took the map, and they all stood up. "Nice to know we have neighbors," Dan said. "I'll hope to repay you someday."

When they left, Dan said, "Rosa, I'll start looking around. Sid will be here to look out for you."

"All right, Dan. Be careful."

"Sure." Dan went outside and saddled a fresh horse, a rangy bay with a rough gait but a lot of endurance. When he swung up into the saddle, Sid came to say, "Wish I could go with you, Dan." Then he glanced toward the house where Rosa was standing. "Think he's alive—Rosa's dad?"

"No, I think he's dead and buried somewhere in these hills. And somebody has a lot of Circle W stock—if they haven't sold it off." His lips grew tense, and he shook his head. "It's been two months, and nobody's seen Logan. He wouldn't run away, and I doubt anybody could keep him away by force for that long."

Sid looked down, not wanting to see the pain in Winslow's eyes.

"Tough," Sid said finally. Then lifting his head, he said quickly, "If you find something, don't try to handle it. Come back and we'll raise us an army."

Dan looked at the rider, a warmth coming to him at the loyalty he saw in Kincaid's face. "Sure, Sid," he nodded. "You hold the fort. I'll be back by morning or tomorrow afternoon at least."

He rode out, and soon the ranch was lost to his sight. He rode steadily all afternoon, stopping at two small ranches and meeting the owners—Pie Dutton and Birch Bingham. They were cautious, and Dan saw that they were accustomed to being so. Both of them said they'd seen a few vented Circle W cows, but denied having any. Nor did either of them have any information about Logan Mann.

Later in the afternoon the country grew rougher. Before him

lay the deep slash of a canyon, and he had to ride carefully to get to the bottom of it. A small creek flowed there, with another canyon leading away like the downstroke of the letter T. This he followed until he found a traveled path. Angling up he reached timber again and at six rode out into a meadow. He moved forward, but at that moment a bullet's slug struck at the bay's hooves with a brief *thwut*, and the sound of a hidden gun, delayed by distance, began to roll its metal echo all across the bowl of the canyon.

At once, Dan wheeled his horse around and made for the cover of the timber. Another shot came, then a third, but he reached the timber safely. At once he moved down the slope, and when he had covered three hundred yards, pulled up. He dismounted and tied the horse, then yanked his rifle from his boot. He could hear the sound of a horse approaching and ran to the edge of the tree line. A horseman was coming at a dead run, a rifle in his hand. Dan let him get a hundred feet away, then quickly took aim and sent a slug over the man's head, yelling out, "Hold it!"

The rider yanked his horse's head up so abruptly that the animal reared, throwing the man to the ground. He dropped the rifle, but when he made a wild grab at it, Dan yelled, "Don't do it!" and he halted at once.

Dan stepped forward, and as the man got up, he warned him, "Don't make any mistakes."

The man was small but well-built, with tow hair and green eyes. He looked around to see if Winslow was alone, then demanded, "What's the idea of throwing a slug at me?"

"I might ask you the same question."

"This is *my* place!"

"You shoot at every man who comes for a visit?" Dan demanded. He looked down at the house and saw three men getting on their horses. "Step over here," Dan said, motioning with his rifle.

"This is good enough," the man said defiantly. "You won't shoot me."

"I'll put a bullet through both your knees and leave you to squirm the rest of your life!" Dan said wickedly. "Now *move!*"

"All right—all right, take it easy!"

Dan slipped the revolver out of the man's holster, saying, "Don't get ambitious when those fellows get here."

"Who the blazes are you?"

"Dan Winslow."

"Winslow? The fellow who bought the Gunderson place?"

"Yes."

"Well, why didn't you say so instead of sneaking around! I'm Charlie Littleton."

"I was just trying to pay a friendly visit. But you took a shot at me."

"We been having some trouble," Littleton shrugged. "Sorry about that, Winslow. It was just a warning shot." He turned, saying, "Let me stop those fools—" He waved his hands in the air as the riders approached, yelling, "It's okay! Don't shoot."

Dan watched as the riders drew up in a half circle, and waited as Littleton told them to cool down. He handed back Charlie Littleton's gun, saying, "Sorry I didn't send an engraved letter of my intention to visit."

Littleton grinned. He was a handsome fellow, and no fool. He introduced his crew, including his brother Dion. "C'mon to the house. We'll feed you and put you up for the night."

"The grub would be welcome," Dan nodded, "but I've got to get home by morning."

"I'd be careful ramming around these draws after dark," Dion Littleton said gruffly. "Fellow could get hisself killed."

"Shut up, Dion," Charlie said easily. He led the way to the cabin, and as Winslow ate, he told them his errand.

"None of them Circle W cows up here, I'm afraid," Charlie Littleton said. "We'll keep our eyes open, though."

An alarm went off inside Winslow, but he let nothing show on his face. "I'd appreciate it."

"You're going to have trouble with old man Head," Dion nodded. "He thinks he owns every blade of grass that grows in Wyoming."

"Some of us have been meeting," Charlie said carefully. "Trying to find out some way to hang on to what we've got. Like to see you there next time. We little fish have gotta stand together."

"Sure. I'll be there."

Winslow stayed around for another thirty minutes, and when

he rose to go, he saw the relief in the eyes of the pair. "Got to head home. Sorry about the misunderstanding, Charlie. I'll sing out next time."

"Sure, no hard feelings. And you come to the meeting next week. It's at the Jenson place."

Dan didn't relax until he was clear of the place, and in the darkness he was having to move slowly. Finally when he exited from the draws, he pulled up his horse and took a deep breath. "Pretty close, Dan," he murmured softly. "Something about those two won't hold up."

He managed to get home at three in the morning, and as he dismounted stiffly, he heard Sid hit the door calling out, "Dan—!"

"What's wrong?" he demanded instantly.

"It's Rosa! She went off for a ride on her mare, and she didn't come back." Sid was angry and scared, Winslow saw. "She was just going for a short ride. Well, she didn't come back, so I went out to look for her—but it got too dark for me to track her, Dan."

"Which way was she headed, Sid?" Dan asked, feeling sick.

"Over toward the hills. But we can't track her until first light." Sid smashed his fist into his palm. "I ought to be shot—but she's been taking a little ride for days now."

"She must have gotten lost," Dan said. Looking up, he said, "Two or three hours before we can follow." He saw that Sid was in torment and said quickly, "Not your fault, Sid. We'll find her."

But as the two of them waited for the dawn, Dan Winslow was aware that a fear gripped his own spirit. He had to grit his teeth to keep from showing what he felt, and once he thought, *It's at times like these when a man knows how little and helpless he is!*

CHAPTER FOURTEEN

ARROW HITS BACK

* * * *

As soon as Zane came into the house, Hope knew that he was angry. She poured a glass of water from the olla she kept hanging on the wall, then handed it to him, saying, "You don't drink enough water, Zane."

He took the glass, drained it thirstily, then handed it back. "Sis, some of our cows are gone."

Hope looked at him with a startled expression. "Stolen?" she asked quickly.

"I guess not really," he said. His lean face showed fatigue in the lines around his mouth, and his shoulders drooped beneath the faded blue shirt. For months now, he had worked night and day trying to keep the ranch going. He was the only rider to see to the stock, though Cody was old enough now to help some, and Amos did a few of the easier chores. But the hard work could be done only by a strong, active man, and Zane had been worn thin by it.

Now he said bitterly, "Arrow let some of their stock drift onto our graze over by the buttes. They shoved 'em onto our grass, and we had twelve cows get mixed up with their stock. When I went to get 'em out, they wouldn't let me. Now they've taken their stock away—and our cows with 'em."

"I'll go see Mr. Head," Hope said. She put her hand on his

shoulder, adding, "You can't do everything, Zane." His shoulder was hard and muscular, but thin beneath her touch.

"He won't do nothin'. I'll have to go find that herd and bring our stuff back." Hope argued with him, but he shook her off. "I may not get back tonight, so I'll need some grub." He waited until she fixed a sack of food, then left the kitchen.

As he rode off, Amos came in through the back door carrying three sticks of wood for the cookstove. Dumping them into the box, he asked, "Where's Zane off to in such a rush?" He straightened up, listened as Hope explained, then shook his head sadly. "Too much on that boy, Hope. We've got to have some help."

"How would we pay them, Dad?"

"I've still got a little money left from the sale of the farm."

"We'll need that to get through another winter." Hope scanned her father's face, noting that he looked as tired as Zane, though he did little work. "I'm going to have to start doing some of the riding," she said. "You and Cody can help with the house." She had seen for some time that it would come to this, and now she added, "I can ride and keep track of the cattle. If I run into something I can't handle, I'll come and get Zane to help." She glanced out the window. "I wish Zane wouldn't go after those cows. Those Arrow riders like nothing better than to stir up trouble."

Zane was thinking along the same lines as he rode steadily toward a set of hills that peaked in the distance. He realized that Arrow had taken the cows deliberately, for they had done such things before. He dreaded coming up to them, for they would taunt him as they always did. He'd get the cows, but only after they had their sport. He knew that it was part of Silas Head's policy to make things as rough as possible on small ranchers, and his orders were carried out with glee by his workers.

He let his hand fall to the .44 that he wore on his right hip, but knew that the worst mistake he could make was to let the Arrow hands lure him into a fight of some kind. If he fought with his fists, he had little chance, for they were all tough men and would have no compunction about piling on him in numbers. As for using a gun, he had little skill there, though he practiced regularly.

No, he would have to let them have their fun, no matter how

humiliating it got. As he rode along, he tried to put out of his mind the scene that would take place. He was so tired he rode half-asleep, coming awake with a jerk when he felt himself slipping out of his saddle. Once he stopped to water his horse, and as he looked around, he saw that the sun was dropping fast. "Should have waited until morning," he muttered aloud. He thought of going back but decided that he could get the cattle back on his own range even in the dark.

An hour later, he came up to the herd, glad to see that it was not a large one—no more than two hundred head. One rider was in front, one was riding drag, and the third turned at once to face him. Zane felt his stomach knot up when he saw that it was Jack Hines, but he rode up to say, "I guess a few of our cows got mixed up with your stock."

Hines leaned on his saddle, grinned, and shook his head. "Now, you ain't calling me a rustler, are you, kid?" Hines was a tall, muscular man of thirty, with tightly curled coppery red hair and a bold face. He had a bad reputation with fists and guns, and was proud of it. Now he was enjoying the sight of the boy, who had no chance at all against him. The cruelty in him came out in the shine of his light blue eyes and the twist of his wide mouth.

"I didn't say that," Zane mumbled. He looked at the cows and then pointed, "Look—there's one of our cows."

Hines looked, then turned back to Zane. "I didn't see it."

Zane sat there helplessly, knowing that there was no way he could force the rider to do anything. His lips were drawn tight, and there was a trembling in his legs. It was not fear but humiliation that brought that reaction, but he could do no more than say, "If you'll let me go through the herd, I'll cut our stuff out."

"You'd scare our stock," Hines commented. "Might stampede them. Can't take no chances." One of the other riders came over, the one who was riding drag, and Hines said, "This fellow says we've got some of his stock, Luke. Think we ought to let him cut 'em out?"

"Let him go to the devil!" The speaker was a tall puncher named Luke Mott. He had a hatchet face and a pair of close-set brown eyes that gleamed with malice as he looked Zane over. "Light a shuck, boy. Run home to your momma."

Zane endured their taunts, and finally they tired of it. "Well, if you act nice," Jack Hines said, "I'll let you get your cows. Say 'pretty please, Mr. Hines.' "

Zane's face burned, but he mumbled the words. Both men laughed, and Hines said, "Hurry it up—and don't get them cattle stirred up."

It was a difficult chore, separating his own cows from the herd, but finally Zane cut them out, twelve as he had reckoned. When he left, Hines said, "Now, kid, you keep your stock from getting in with our stuff from now on, you hear me?"

"I hear you."

Hines taunted, "You ain't said, 'Thank you, Mr. Hines, sir.' "

Zane knew if he refused, the tough puncher would take the cows and mix them back with the herd, so he said evenly, "Thank you, Mr. Hines, sir."

"Git outta here, you punk kid!"

Zane turned his horse and didn't look back, not wanting Hines to see the expression on his face. He began moving the cows along at as fast a clip as he could manage, but they scattered, individuals running off in different directions, so he had to slow them down to a walk.

Dusk caught up with him, and he stopped to let the cattle rest. They were tired and his horse was moving slowly, so he finally decided to spend the night by a small stream. He had had nothing to eat, so he built up a small fire, cooked some bacon, and made coffee. Then he wrapped the single blanket around him, stretched out beside the fire, and dropped off at once into an exhausted sleep.

He awoke with a start, not knowing where he was. He had been awakened by some sound, but as he listened there was nothing. He had no idea what time it was, having no watch, but thought it could not be past midnight. He began to gather a few sticks to replenish the fire, and as he did so he heard something. It was not one of the usual night cries one would hear on the prairie, and it was so faint and thinned by distance he could not make it out.

He stood to his feet, straining to hear, and it came again— almost a ghostly sound on the stillness of the air. The moon shed a silvery light on some cattle that stood quietly close by, and

Zane waited until the sound came again. He saddled his horse, mounted, and moved away toward what seemed to be a stand of timber. When he had gone perhaps two hundred yards, he heard the sound again—and recognized it as someone calling. He moved ahead at a faster rate, moving carefully through the saplings that appeared. The timber grew thicker, larger trees beginning to loom in front of him, and finally he stopped his horse and listened. When he heard nothing, he shouted, "Where are you?"

At once a voice to his left came: "I'm over here!"

He moved toward the sound and soon heard someone cry, "This way—over here."

When he had gone a little farther into the timber, he stopped when someone spoke, almost at his feet. "Here—!"

Zane glanced down. In the darkness, he could barely make out a huddled form beside a large alder. He dismounted, moved closer, and discovered that it was a woman. He couldn't see her face clearly, but she said huskily, "Thank God you've come!"

"What happened?" Zane went to one knee, bringing his face down to her level. She was young, but aside from that impression, he could tell nothing about her.

"My horse ran away," she said. "A limb raked me off."

"Are you all right?"

"I twisted my leg when I fell—and the limb cut my head."

Zane said, "Get on my horse. I've got a fire going."

She tried to get up but cried out in pain. "My ankle—!"

"Here, let me help. Lean on me and put your good foot in the stirrup." He took her weight, noting that she was small but was firmly rounded. She moaned slightly, but when her foot was in the stirrup, he lifted her as carefully as he could into the saddle. "Let's get out of these woods," he said, and led his horse through the timber. When they got back to the fire, he stopped the horse and moved to her side. "I'll be as easy as I can," he promised. She slid off the horse, falling into his arms, and he let her down gently. When she was sitting down, she looked up, her eyes shining in the moonlight. "I thought no one would come." Her voice was raw and husky.

Zane said, "I'll bet you're thirsty." He grabbed a tin cup, ran to the creek, and hurried back to her. She took it eagerly and drained it without stopping for breath. He got another, which she drank more slowly. When she finished, he asked, "What's your name?"

"Rosa Mann."

"I'm Zane Jenson. What about your folks? They didn't come for you?"

She shook her head. "I went for a ride when it was nearly dark. I think they're looking for me, but I rode in a different direction from my usual way." Rosa was feeling a tremendous relief, for she had been badly frightened. She'd never been in the outdoors alone at night and knew that there were wolves and bears in the region. "If you hadn't come when you did," she said, "I don't think I could have stood it."

Zane was suddenly aware that she was a most beautiful young woman. Her eyes were large and dark, and her hair was black. With her lips half-parted she made an attractive picture as she gazed at him. He wondered how old she was but was too shy to ask.

"Well, it's no fun being lost in the woods," he said finally. Then he added, "Look, I'd better go to your house and get help. Where is it?"

"Oh no!" Rosa was flooded with fear at the thought of being left alone. She reached out and grasped his arm, begging, "Please—don't leave me here by myself!"

"Why, I won't then," Zane said, startled by her action. "We can ride double. Think you could do that?"

"I think so," she said. "But I'm so hungry. I didn't eat anything since breakfast."

Zane said at once, "Why, I'll fix you something, Rosa." He pulled a quick meal together from his small store—bacon, cold biscuits, and coffee. He sat back on his heels, watching as she ate hungrily. "What about your family?" he asked. "Your folks will be about crazy with worry."

She stopped eating and looked across the fire at him. "I—don't have any parents—" She hesitated, and he was puzzled by her manner. "I mean, my mother's dead, and I don't know where my father is."

"Well, gosh, that's tough!" Zane exclaimed. "Do you live with relatives?"

"No. I live with my father's partner. His name is Daniel Winslow."

"Winslow?" Zane thought for a moment, then nodded. "Sure, I heard about him—and it's your pa that's disappeared?"

"Yes."

Zane dropped his gaze uncertainly. "That's too bad, but maybe he'll be found."

"I don't think so. I think he's dead." Rosa had not admitted this to Dan or to Sid, but she was aware that neither of them had any hope of finding her father alive. She spoke out of the harrowing experience of being alone and helpless. Now that it was out, she suddenly realized it was this suspicion that had been dragging her spirits down. Tears welled up in her eyes.

Zane was appalled by her grief, which he felt that he had caused by prying into her family life. He stood up, looked off into the darkness, then moved around the fire to take her plate. As he bent over, he saw that she had hidden her face in her hands and that her shoulders were shaking. The sight of her brought the sharpest kind of pity to him, and he awkwardly sat down on his heels and put his hand on her shoulder. "Rosa—please don't cry!"

For an answer she leaned against him, giving way to a paroxysm of grief. She had been alone for a long time, even with her family in Texas, and had put all her hope of happiness in her father. Now that she had faced up to the fact that he was probably dead, she was left with nothing. The grief flooding through her was so black and bitter that she was totally unaware of the boy; leaning against him was only a reaction.

Zane put his arms around her, shocked by the deep sobs that racked her body. She was totally vulnerable, without defense, and he was held by an emotion that he had never known. Her sobs were deep at first, but finally they subsided, and then she pulled away and looked up at him. "I'm sorry, Zane Jenson," she whispered. The tears made silver tracks down her smooth cheeks, and she was more lovely for her helplessness. "I—didn't mean to do that." She pulled a handkerchief from her pocket and dried her eyes. "I guess you never expected to run into something like this way out here, did you?"

He was relieved that she seemed better. "Never did before.

All I ever found out here was cows."

She smiled at that, then asked, "Where do you live?"

"Over that way, about five miles." He motioned toward the ranch. "I came out yesterday to get some steers that got mixed in with another herd, and I got caught out after dark."

"I'm glad you did, Zane," she said. "I'd called until my throat was raw. When I saw you coming for me, I thought you were the best thing I'd ever seen!"

"Well, you won't think so after you get over being scared," he said.

"You look better than I do," Rosa smiled. She touched the bump on her head, winced, then said, "Let's see if I can ride."

Zane nodded, and after putting out the fire and packing the gear on the horse, he helped her mount. It was obvious she was in severe pain, and he asked, "Which way to your place, Rosa?"

"Why—" Rosa looked around for a moment, then said with confusion, "I don't know. The mare got scared and ran for a long time before I got knocked off by that limb."

Zane hesitated, then said, "I'll take you to our house. My sister can take care of you, and I can ask around to see if I can find Mr. Winslow." He put his foot in the stirrup and swung himself up behind her. "Does it hurt—your ankle?"

"Just go slow, please."

He spoke to the horse, and as they left, Rosa asked, "What about the cattle?"

"They're all right. We're on our land now."

As they made their way toward the ranch, she asked him about his family. He gave her a few details, and then she asked, "You take care of the ranch all alone?"

"Well—pretty much so."

"How old are you, Zane?"

"Eighteen."

"Why, I thought you were older," Rosa said. "Twenty at least."

Zane didn't feel compelled to inform her that he had been eighteen for only four days. Instead he asked, "How old are you, Rosa?"

"Fifteen." She turned around to face him, smiling. "It's nice to have people close to your own age around, isn't it?"

"Yeah," Zane muttered. He was aware of her firm body pressing against him, and said to cover his confusion, "Maybe our folks will be neighbors, and we can spend some time together."

It was, for him, a daring speech, and when she replied, "Oh, that would be wonderful," he felt at least eight feet tall.

When they pulled up in front of the ranch, Zane said, "I'll wake my sister up. She'll want to take a look at you." He slipped out of the saddle and helped her down, but when her foot touched the ground, she cried out with pain. "You can't walk on that!" he exclaimed. "I'll carry you inside." He ignored her protest, saying, "You don't weigh as much as a pesky yearling." Scooping her up, he crossed the yard and pushed the door open. Hope had left a lamp burning low, and he moved to the couch and carefully set Rosa down.

She kept her hold on him for one moment, whispering, "Zane—before anyone comes—let me say thank you." Her face was close to his and she suddenly gave him a hug, holding him close in a way that startled him. Then she leaned back on the couch, and he straightened up with confusion.

"I'll get my sister," he muttered, his face red with embarrassment. But even as he spoke, the room got crowded, for Hope came in, followed by Cody and Amos, and then Ozzie Og came in to stare.

"This is Rosa Mann—" With some apprehension Zane explained the situation, and Hope went to the girl at once, her face alive with sympathy.

"How terrible for you, Rosa!" she exclaimed. "Now, let me do something about that bump, and we'll take a look at your ankle."

Thirty minutes later Rosa was feeling more pampered than she'd ever felt in her life. Hope Malloy had bathed the bruise on her head with cool water, then had carefully removed her boot and put her foot to soak in a bucket. The old cook had fixed a fine breakfast of oatmeal, eggs, toast, and bacon, and Cody had moved his chair as close to her as possible as she recounted her adventures.

Amos Jenson had studied her ankle and pronounced it twisted but not broken. "I've got some liniment that my grandma concocted," he nodded firmly. "A little of that and you'll be fit to dance a reel, Miss Mann."

Rosa was, of course, somewhat overwhelmed by all the attention. She looked up from her meal, smiling at Zane. "You didn't tell me what a nice family you had, Zane," she said. "I'd have managed to get thrown from my horse a long time ago if I'd known you were going to come along and rescue me and bring me here."

Ozzie Og grinned at the boy's red face. "Never seen no knight in armor who rode around rescuing young gals in distress, Zane. You figger to make a career out of such?"

When the others laughed, Rosa said quickly, "Let them tease you, Zane, but when you found me last night, I thought you were something like that."

After breakfast, Rosa said, "I think I'd better go home. Dan and Sid will be worried about me."

"Let me go get them," Zane urged. "You can't ride with that foot."

But Rosa insisted, and finally Amos said, "I'll hitch up the wagon. You can drive her home, can't you, Zane? Or are you too tired?"

"No, sir!" Zane said instantly. "I feel fine."

"I remember when I could stay up all night and be ready to go the next day," Ozzie mused. "I'll hitch the team, Amos."

When Ozzie brought the team to the front door, Rosa stood up slowly but could put no weight on her injured limb. "Could you help me one more time, Zane?" she asked with a small smile.

Face flaming, Zane picked her up and carried her out to the wagon. As he placed her on the seat, he was aware that four men had ridden up and were watching. When he turned, he saw with a shock they were all Arrow hands. Jack Hines and Luke Mott were grinning at him, and beside them were Deuce Longly and Ollie Peace.

"Well, what do we have here?" Longly grinned, winking at Ollie Peace. "We meet again, don't we, Rosa?"

Hope moved forward at once, asking, "What do you want?"

Longly was enjoying his moment. He got off his horse, and Ollie did the same. "Why, Jack and Luke tell me that your boy there's been makin' trouble. Stampedin' our cattle, he says."

"That's a lie!" Zane said bitterly. "They took twelve of our cows. I just got 'em back."

Jack Hines dismounted and came to stand beside Deuce. "You callin' me a liar, boy? I don't stand for that even from a punk kid."

Amos said, "Get off the place. The boy's done nothin'."

"Shut up, Grandpa," Deuce said contemptuously. "You better get in the house."

When Amos turned and went into the house without a word, Longly was surprised but laughed at the sight of the old man leaving. "He's got sense, Grandpa has," he commented. Then he turned to Rosa, who was watching fearfully. "Well, now, Honey," Longly grinned. "Looks like you're in luck. You can take a ride with a gentleman."

He started to get into the wagon, but Zane stepped forward and pulled him around. "Stay away from her!"

Ollie Peace stepped up, grinning, his eyes cruel. "You always got somebody to fight for you, sweetheart? Well, this one don't look like much to me. You deserve more of a man than this kid."

"Get out of here—all of you!" Hope cried. "Leave us alone!"

"I'll get to you next time I come for a visit," Longly said. "I heard there was a good-lookin' widow woman out here. Been meanin' to call." He ran his eyes up and down Hope's trim figure, then shook his head. "Right now we'll take the little tamale for a ride. Don't worry, now, we'll take her right back to Winslow. But first we'll show her a good time."

"And we'll see what Winslow can do with his fists," Peace grunted. "I'll break his face this time!"

Longly turned to the wagon, and Zane made a grab for him, but Ollie Peace was expecting it. He grabbed Zane's arm, swung him around, and drove a powerful blow into the boy's face. Zane went down, sprawling in the dust. Both Rosa and Hope cried out, but when Hope moved toward him, Longly caught her. Holding her fast, he grinned at the other riders. "Bust him up, Ollie. He needs a lesson in manners."

Zane climbed to his feet and staggered toward Peace. Blood was running down his chin, and his eyes were glazed, but he didn't hesitate. It would have been better if he had, for Peace handled him with contemptuous ease. He struck Zane in the face repeatedly, and when the boy fell, he yanked him up and propped him against the wagon. "Teach you to mind your own business!" he growled and began mercilessly striking him in the body. Zane would have fallen, but Peace held him fast, and the sounds of his brutal fists pounding the boy's helpless body sickened Rosa.

A sudden explosion rent the air, and all the Arrow hands involuntarily ducked. Peace released Zane, who sprawled in the dust, and Hope wrenched free from Longly and ran to fall on her knees beside her brother.

"What the—!" Longly's hand reached for his gun, but he found himself looking into the muzzle of a very large shotgun. A chill went through him, and he cried out, "No—!"

"Just be still," Amos said quietly. "You might even live if you do."

"You fellers hold still!" The two riders who had not dismounted had started to draw but froze when Ozzie stepped outside and stood on the porch. He was holding another shotgun aimed at them, and he said, "I bet I can cut you both down with one shell."

The Arrow hands were tough men, but they had seen what a shotgun can do to a man at close range. "Now just a minute—" Longly began, but Amos cut him off short.

"Drop your gun belts—all of you." When Longly hesitated, Og added, "All right, I'll do it the hard way—"

Longly saw the old man's finger tighten on the trigger, and he cried out, "No, don't shoot!" Sweat appeared on his brow, and he said, "Boys, do as they say." He unbuckled his gun belt, allowing it to fall to the dust, and when Hines hesitated, Longly cursed him. "Drop it, you fool! You want to get blown to bits?"

When the four had shed their gun belts, Amos ordered, "Throw the rifles on the ground." When that was done, he said, "Get off this place."

"What about our guns?" Hines demanded.

"I'll leave them with the sheriff," Amos said. "But if I see any of you close to this house, I'll shoot you. Now—git!"

Deuce and Peace mounted and rode out quickly. When they were out of shotgun range, they stopped and cursed, Longly threatening loudly, "You'll see us again, old man!"

Amos paid no attention but moved to where Hope was holding Zane's head. "How is he, Daughter?"

"Oh, Pa, he's hurt bad!"

Amos saw that Zane was unconscious. "He may be hurt inside. We'll take him to see Doc Matthews."

They carefully lifted Zane and put him on the bed in the wagon. Og wanted to stay and defend the place, but Amos argued. "No, I don't want you here alone." Ozzie insisted he'd be all right, and finally Amos got in the wagon, sitting down beside Rosa. They waited until Cody was on his horse, then looked back to Hope, who was holding Zane's head in her lap. "All right, Daughter?"

"Drive easy, Pa," she said quietly. When they drove out, she looked at the house, thinking it might be the last time she'd ever see it. *Arrow may come back and burn it to the ground,* she thought sadly. Then she concentrated on carefully holding Zane's head.

CHAPTER FIFTEEN

ACTION AT THE PALACE

★ ★ ★ ★

Dan spent three fruitless hours trying to pick up Rosa's trail through the myriad tracks of cattle that dotted the range around the ranch. Finally he said to Sid, "You go back to the ranch and wait. Someone might have found her and brought her back."

"What will you do?"

Dan pointed toward the low-lying hills that lay westward from the ranch. "I'll start there and work my way around to the flats. Maybe I'll have luck and cross her trail. If I don't find anything, I'll head for town and try to get some help so we can comb the country."

He wheeled Duke around and rode off without giving Sid a chance to speak. For the next two hours he rode slowly along, his eyes fixed on the ground searching for signs, and finding none. He wanted to ride as fast as he could, shouting and hoping to find Rosa by blind luck, but he forced himself to be patient. Several times he ran across the tracks of horses, but none of them were made by Rosa's mare. He was thankful now that her horse had never been shod, for that made her prints easily recognizable.

The sun rose higher and higher until it was almost directly overhead, and he was beginning to feel the dull throb of despair. He knew well the possibility of disaster for man, woman, or horse on the open range. She could be lying at the foot of a hidden canyon, dead or so severely injured she couldn't crawl out—or her horse could have been spooked by a grizzly, throwing her and leaving her to the fury of the animal. Nor were wild animals the only dangerous species on the range. The men of the country could be far more vicious than any four-legged breed, and it was this that he feared the most.

He had set the edge of the hills, where they ran down to flat country and then shaded off into the driest part of the long valley, as the terminal point of his ride. Then he would have to admit that he'd missed the trail and turn back to town.

He crossed a small gully, and as he urged Duke up the sloping side, he caught a glimpse of a set of tracks that paralleled the depression. A thrill of hope ran through him as he looked closer. *Unshod horse!* he thought. *Got to be Rosa!*

The tracks were plain in the dusty ground, and he was glad that no rain had fallen to wash them out. He spurred Duke to a gallop, leaning over to follow the trail. It ran along the edge of the gully for a mile, then turned and entered a section marked by broken hills and dotted with occasional stunted oaks and brush. The tracks were still evident, but when the earth turned to packed ground, then to even harder terrain, he was forced to slow his pace. He lost the trail once, was forced to backtrack and dismount in order to pick up the prints of the horse again.

Finally he stopped in some thicker timber, mostly fir, where the ground was covered with dead needles that obscured the trail almost completely. He moved slowly, searching the ground for signs, until he was at least a mile into the timber. The trail led through some thick undergrowth, and he wondered why Rosa would try to ride through it.

He came at last to a section of ground where the needles had been disturbed by movement—not by a horse, but by human movement. He circled the area slowly, studying the telltale needles, and became more puzzled when he discovered two sets of tracks. Rosa's mare had gone straight on into the thickets, but another set led away to his left. He hesitated, then followed the strange prints and found that they led to a campsite. He examined the remains of a fire and noted some cattle that were grazing a few hundred yards away. The ground was easier to read here, and he saw the print of Rosa's boot—along with those of a man's tracks.

"She was here," he murmured. "But who made these other prints?" His mind worked furiously, and finally, after circling the area several times, he made a decision. "Only one set of tracks leaving here—so whoever it was must have taken her."

He mounted at once and followed the trail, noting as he left that the cows close by wore an anchor brand. "Must have belonged to the man who took her," he reasoned, and decided that if he lost the trail, he'd be able to find out whose brand was an anchor.

But the trail ran due east and was simple to read. It was late afternoon when he came to a small ranch, the trail leading right to the front door. He checked the loads in his gun, rode into the yard, and dismounted. As he did, a voice cut across his nerves: "Just hold it right there!"

Winslow turned quickly, finding a man of fifty with grizzled hair and faded blue eyes holding a shotgun. "You an Arrow hand?" he demanded of Winslow.

"No. My name's Dan Winslow. I'm looking for a girl named Rosa Mann."

Ozzie lowered the shotgun instantly, a look of relief in his eyes. "I'm Ozzie Og. The girl was brought here early this morning."

"Is she hurt?" Dan asked instantly.

"Just a bump on her head and a twisted ankle. She's in town now." Og hesitated, then asked, "You know Deuce Longly and a big yahoo named Ollie?"

His question brought Winslow's head up with a startled gesture. His eyelids crept down until his eyes were half-closed. "They been here?"

"Yeah, till we run 'em off with shotguns!" Ozzie sketched the conflict in a few words, then said, "The boy, Zane, he's hurt bad, so they took him into town to see Doc Matthews." He added gloomily, "He's been holdin' this place together since his stepfather got killed a while back. Don't know how the folks will do for help now."

"My horse is about used up," Dan said. "Maybe you could lend me a fresh one. I want to get to town in a hurry."

"Yeah, I can do that." He led Winslow to the corral and nodded toward three horses that watched them approach. "Take your pick."

Dan chose a tall, rangy chestnut gelding, slapped his saddle on him, and turned Duke into the pen. He mounted at once, saying, "Thanks, Og. I'll be back to get him."

"If you see any of that Arrow bunch, I'd be obliged if you'd put a bullet in 'em," the cook said savagely. "No tellin' what they'd have done to that girl if they'd took her off."

"I'll see what I can do," Dan said with tight lips. "Which way to town?"

"That way—'bout ten miles."

He spurred the gelding and sped out of the yard, taking the turn that led toward War Paint. Ozzie Og watched until he was out of sight, then looked at the horse he had left. "Well, he looks like he could be tough," he addressed the animal. "I hope he stomps a mudhole in that bunch!"

★　★　★　★

Zane twisted on the narrow bed, the movement sending a shock of ragged pain through him. Despite his efforts, a groan escaped his lips, and at once Hope put her hand on his forehead, whispering, "Try not to move, Zane."

They were in the room Doctor Matthews used to keep patients overnight. Zane occupied one of the three beds; the rest of the furnishings consisted of two mismatched chairs, a small battered table on which sat a kerosene lamp, two tall cabinets packed with odds and ends of the doctor's supplies, and a washstand with a pitcher and a basin. The single window had no covering, and the flies came and left at their leisure.

"What's wrong with me?" Zane whispered. He glanced down at the white bandages that encased his body, then looked up at Hope. "My chest hurts, Sis."

"You've got some broken ribs," Hope said quietly. Rising, she moved to the washstand, poured water into a glass, then returned and lifted his head carefully. He drank thirstily, then she lowered his head and went back to fill the basin with water. Placing it on the small table, she took a clean cloth and began bathing Zane's swollen face.

He was disoriented, for Matthews had given him a large dose of laudanum before working on him. The doctor finished taping his chest and treating the cuts on the boy's face, then had said, "He's going to have to be still for a while, Hope. I don't want those ribs taking any more punishment." When she had nodded, he'd asked, "How will you make out without Zane to work?" She'd put him off, and he'd insisted on her using the room for the night.

She'd sent to get something to eat, and now she sat beside Zane, who blinked his eyes and asked, "What about Rosa?"

"She's all right," Hope said. "She's at Mr. Edwards' house. They offered to keep her and Cody for the night."

"I should have shot 'em!" he said bitterly. The drug was still having its effect, and his speech was slurred. "I will when I get well!"

"Hush, now!" Hope whispered. "Don't talk about it."

A thought occurred to him, and he looked up at her and asked, "How we gonna take care of the place, Sis?"

Hope smoothed his hair back from his forehead and smiled. "God will help us," she said softly.

At that moment a tap came on the door, and she rose and crossed the room to open it. A big man she'd never seen before stood there, and she said, "Doctor Matthews isn't here right now."

"Mrs. Malloy?" He removed his hat and stood there watching her.

"Why—yes."

"I'm looking for Rosa Mann. My name is Dan Winslow."

At once Hope said, "Come in, Mr. Winslow." She stepped back as he entered. "Rosa isn't here, Mr. Winslow. She's with Mr. John Edwards. We were planning to bring her home, but— we've had some difficulty."

"I stopped by your place," Dan said. "Your man Og told me some of it." He lifted his eyes to take in the young man on the bed. "This the young fellow who got hurt?"

"Yes. This is my brother, Zane."

Dan moved across the room, coming to stand over Zane. "Guess I owe you some thanks, for finding Rosa and bringing her in," he said.

Zane blinked his eyes. "Aw, it weren't nothin'." A streak of bitterness tightened his lips. "I didn't do so good protectin' her from those Arrow hands."

"You did your best, Zane," Dan said gently. "That's all any man can do. How do you feel?"

As Winslow spoke with Zane, Hope had an opportunity to study him. There was, she saw at once, a vigilance about him, despite his easy speech. He moved with a loose-muscled slackness, but she saw that he was very strong. His chest was deep, and the muscles in his upper arms and on the broad flats of his shoulders filled the thin shirt he wore. He had a quiet manner, but there was a quickness in his eyes, a remote and angular shining, and behind such surfaces Hope caught a hint of the toughness the years had beaten into him. And as she watched him, the intense masculine vigor that she sensed in him caused a sudden fear. She had stayed away from men since Willis had died, and now without intending it, a resistance to Winslow built up in her.

Winslow was saying, "You did fine, Zane, real fine. I'm grateful and so is Rosa, I'm sure." Then he turned and put his eyes on Hope. "Like to talk to you, Mrs. Malloy."

"Yes, we can go in the other room." She led him into the doctor's main office and turned to face him.

"Like to hear about what happened," Dan said. He listened as she recounted the details of the fight. She was younger than he had expected, and he admired the steadfastness of her manner. She was, he noted, an attractive woman, with hair the color of honey and a smooth complexion. She was wearing a worn brown dress, but it didn't conceal her upright carriage nor the smoothly rounded lines of her figure. There was some quality in the woman he couldn't quite identify—a sort of distance that she kept. She seemed aloof, and there was a kind of warning in her clear blue eyes that puzzled him. He decided that it was the strain of her brother's beating, and when she was finished, he said, "Hard on you, Mrs. Malloy."

"I'm used to hard things," she answered. She hesitated, and Dan sensed a gentle spirit that lay beneath her distant manner. "But I'm afraid of Arrow. Those men will come back."

Dan Winslow said softly, "No, they won't."

His quiet words were so firm that Hope was taken aback. He was very sober and added, "I'll have a word with them. And until your brother gets better, I'll be around to help you keep the ranch going."

"But—you have your own ranch to take care of!"

A wry light that could have been amusement came to his eyes. "Well, it's shrunk up, you might say, so I've got some time on my hands."

"I couldn't let you do that, Mr. Winslow," Hope protested.

But he merely nodded, saying, "I'll be back. Where does this man Edwards live? I'd like to see Rosa."

She was telling him how to get to the Edwards' house, when the door opened and a man entered. "Smoky!" she cried out in a glad voice.

"Heard Zane had some trouble," the man nodded. "Come to check on him."

"This is Dan Winslow," Hope said. "And this is Smoky Jacks, an old friend of ours."

Winslow nodded, saying, "Glad to meet you," then left the office. He went at once to the Edwards' house. He was met at the door by a woman who stared at him coldly until he identified himself and asked for Rosa.

"Why, she's in the living room, Mr. Winslow. Come with me."

Rosa was sitting on a chair, and her face lit up when Winslow walked in. "Dan!" she exclaimed and struggled to her feet. He caught her as she grabbed at him. "You better take it easy," he grinned.

She pulled him down to the couch, her eyes wide as she began to talk. "My horse raked me off," she began, and went through the story of her rescue by Zane. "If he hadn't found me, I think I'd have died!" she exclaimed. She recounted the events of the fight with Arrow at Anchor—the new name Hope had given their ranch after Willis' death—and her hand squeezed his arm urgently. "Dan, we've got to help them! Zane got hurt trying to help me, and now they've got nobody to watch the cattle."

"I guess we can be of some help there, Rosa," Dan said. "Are you all right?"

They talked briefly, Dan filled with relief that the girl had come to no serious harm. But he was also angry, and soon he said, "You're staying here tonight, I guess?"

"Yes, they're very nice people," Rosa nodded. "But tomorrow—"

"Take it one day at a time, Rosa," Dan advised. He got to his feet, but paused to put one hand on her shoulder. "You gave me quite a scare, you know it? I had all kinds of thoughts while I was riding around looking for you."

She reached up and put her hand on his, a smile on her lips. "I'm all right, Dan."

He hesitated, then said gently, "Rosa, I want to tell you something."

She took a look at his face and knew instantly what it was. "It's about my father, isn't it? He's dead, is that it?"

"I think he is, Rosa. If he were alive, he'd have gotten word to us by this time." He put his hand on her shoulder, adding gently, "He was a fine man. I'll try to help you all I can, but I can't make up for a father."

He left the house, his face losing its easy look. It was in his mind to ride to Arrow at once and take up the matter with Silas Head, but he decided instead to pay a visit to Sheriff Rider. Making his way to the main street of War Paint, he was hailed by a rider and looked up to see Sid Kincaid pulling alongside.

"Dan, I came in to find out what's happening," he said at once.

"She's okay, Sid," Dan said quickly, and saw a tremendous relief come over Kincaid's face. Winslow explained quickly, and when he was finished, said, "I'm going to pay a visit to Arrow."

"Good! Let's go."

Dan studied the smaller man. "May be a rough visit, Sid. I'm not feeling charitable."

Kincaid's hazel eyes were hot with anger. "We're wasting time, Dan," he said. "And don't try to talk me out of it," he added stubbornly.

"I guess I won't," Winslow said. "Let's go see the sheriff first. It won't do any good, but if we're going on the rampage, I guess we ought to let him know."

But Sheriff Rider was out of town, they were informed by his deputy, Ray Shotwell. The stocky deputy stared with a truculent air at the two men, but asked, "Anything I can do for you?"

"I guess not, Deputy," Winslow said. "Just tell the sheriff that some Arrow hands beat up young Zane Jenson. We figure to take it out of their hides."

A startled look sprang into Shotwell's eyes. "Why, you can't do that!"

"Why can't we?" Kincaid demanded; then the two men left the office with Shotwell calling out for them to stop.

"No help there," Sid commented. "You ready to go?"

Winslow nodded, and they started back down the street. When they were almost as far as where their horses were tied, Winslow heard his named called. He turned quickly to see three men standing in front of a barber shop. He identified two of them at once as the men who'd brought his cattle back—Gus Miller and Dave Orr—and the third was the cowboy named Jacks that he'd seen in Doctor Matthews' office.

"Winslow, what's this about your girl and Zane Jenson?" asked Gus Miller, who spoke quickly as Winslow and Kincaid approached. "Smoky says the Arrow bunch beat him to a pulp." Miller had a set of hard black eyes, which now revealed a wicked temper.

Smoky Jacks broke in. "Hope said you told her you was gonna go after the bunch that done it, Winslow. Well, count me in! That Zane is a good kid!"

"Now wait a minute, Smoky," Dave Orr said quickly. "If you go after Arrow, they'll come down on us hard—all of us." He had a nervous look on his thin face, and of the three men, he alone carried no gun.

Smoky glanced at him impatiently. "Well, I quit, Mr. Orr. And I'll tell Mr. Ash Caudill I'm on my own hook when I take a bite of that bunch."

Orr frowned. "Now, don't be so hasty, Smoky. I agree we can't let this go by, but we can't fight Arrow. There's too many of them."

"You got any ideas, Dan?" Gus Miller demanded. "Them yahoos are over at the Palace Saloon right now."

Winslow glanced in the direction of the saloon across the street that Miller indicated, and rank anger burned in him. He knew that he should stay clear of the trouble, but he couldn't stop the swing of his temper. It was a weakness for which he had been punished more than once, as the scars on his face testified. Nevertheless, he said, "I'll take a hand," and turning, forged across the street.

"Hey, Dan—!" Sid was beside him, and the suddenness of Winslow's response startled him. He stretched his legs to keep up with the larger man. "Look, we gotta be smart, Dan. There's probably a big bunch in there. Let's catch 'em when the odds are better."

But Winslow appeared not to hear him, for he didn't answer but shouldered his way through the double doors of the saloon. Sid followed, but then faded off to one side, his eyes sweeping the crowd. The place was packed, for it was a Saturday, and the smell of tobacco smoke and whiskey was strong. Dan spotted Deuce Longly and Ollie Peace instantly, sitting at a round table filled with other hands—Arrow hands he judged. He noted the way that Longly spoke to the others and how their glances swung to meet him. And then he saw Ash Caudill far toward the back of the room, sitting at a table with one other man. Caudill lifted his head, but showed no friendliness. He had a cigar clenched between his teeth, and Dan caught his slanting, sly glance, which didn't hide the catlike alertness of his interest. *He heard about the trouble*, Dan thought. *He'll stay out of it—let the crew do me in.*

Winslow moved to the bar and laid his arms on it. He felt a growing pressure in the place; it was like a steady force on his shoulder blades. He made a circle on the bar with one forefinger, watching the pale imprint show on the scarred hardwood surface, and he saw Gus Miller drift in through the front door and take a place at the bar not far from where the Arrow hands sat.

The barkeep, a burly man with pale blue eyes, came to stand before him. "What'll it be?"

Winslow lifted his voice so that it carried over the hum of talk that filled the Palace. "I'm looking for the yellow curs who beat up Zane Jenson. Part of that yellow-bellied Arrow outfit."

The barkeep, tough as he was, blinked and looked flustered. He shot a nervous glance sideways toward the Arrow crowd, but said nothing.

"Well, are the dirty sons in here, or not?" Winslow demanded. Then when the barkeep shook his head and moved away, Dan turned and put his eyes on the Arrow crowd. "Well, well, look what we have here!" he said in the absolute stillness of the room. "These men work for you, Ash?" He shifted his gaze to Caudill.

Caudill got to his feet, the man across from him doing the same. "I'd be a little careful, Dan," he said tersely. "Let's you and me have a quiet talk about this thing."

"Be glad to, Ash," Winslow said, "just as soon as I settle up with these skunks." He moved away from the bar and kept his hand close to the gun at his side. "Peace, you don't learn very fast do you? But you're about to get an education right now."

Suddenly Deuce Longly stood up, fury on his face. As he did, the men with him all rose and moved away. Three of them moved to the left of Winslow in front of the door, while two more edged toward the bar. Those five, plus Ash and the man with him formed a threat that Dan couldn't handle. He kept his eyes on Longly and saw the gunman's eyes run around the room. Deuce liked what he saw and brought his gaze back to Winslow.

"You've got in my way too often, Winslow," he said. "I aim to see you don't do it again." His hands hovered over the butts of the twin .44s in his holsters, and one twitch would set him off, Dan saw.

Winslow knew the moment he touched his gun, the other Arrow hands would draw, but he kept his eyes focused on the savage face of the gunman. He thought suddenly of the many times he'd been at this point, often in the war, poised and waiting for the signal that could bring death to him. But he said only, "You're a dog, Longly."

His words brought a crazy light into Longly's eyes, but at that moment Smoky Jacks stepped through the front door. Smoky lifted his gun and said to the three Arrow hands who were facing Winslow, "You fellers scratch for it."

Suddenly, Gus Miller drew his revolver and held it on the two hands who'd moved toward the bar. "Jack, you and Mott are out of it." The two riders half turned, but were frozen by the sight of Miller's gun trained on them.

That left Ash Caudill and the man at the table with him. But Sid had seen that and now moved away from the bar. He took a position to the left of the table, his gun still in his holster, but Caudill could not mistake the look on his face. "Better stay out of this," Caudill snapped, but saw that the man was standing there like a cocked gun.

Winslow shifted his glance and shot another look toward Ash. The foreman, he knew, was no coward, but he was smart. The balance of power had shifted, and Winslow gambled that he would stay out of it. He turned to face Longly, and at that moment, the hands of the gunman shot down toward his guns.

Longly had seen Winslow's gaze move away from him, and was confident that he could draw and shoot before Winslow looked back. The slap of his hands on the butts of his guns was heard by every man in the saloon. Ash had anticipated the move and was expecting the crash of Longly's guns—but it didn't happen.

Longly had his guns half-drawn, but the Colt in Winslow's holster had appeared in his hand like magic and was pointed right at his chest. Longly flinched and stopped his draw instantly. He threw his hands up over his head, and a hoarse cry of fear came from his lips. He knew he was a dead man—as did every man in the saloon.

Winslow, however, held his fire. He moved forward until he stood before the terrified man. He pulled Longly's guns from the holsters, tossed them to the floor, then slapped the man's face with a force so sudden it drove him sideways. When Longly caught his balance, Winslow said, "Get out of my sight, you scum! The next time I see you, I'll kill you."

Longly seemed to be drunk, for fear had destroyed his nerve. He turned and scrambled out of the room, his hoarse breathing cutting the silence of the room. He hit the door blindly, and his heels made a staccato sound on the board walkway, and then his horse left at a wild gallop.

Winslow turned to Ollie Peace, who was staring at the door with shock. "Now, Peace," he said, slipping his gun back into the holster. "It's your turn."

Peace suddenly grew pale. He had seen the lightning draw of Winslow and knew he had no chance at all. "No, not me!" he cried out. "I'm not drawing on you!"

Caudill's voice came across the room. "If you shoot him, it'll be murder, Winslow!"

Winslow stood there, a tough figure with every man's eyes on him. Slowly he unbuckled his gun belt and laid it on the bar. "All right, Ollie," he said. "This will be a treat on me."

He moved toward the hulking form of Peace, who stood there in shock. He was a brutal saloon fighter and could not believe that Winslow was offering to fight with his fists. He was sly and unpredictable, a giant of a man with brutality throbbing through him. Now he was pleased with himself for he had no doubts as to his ability. He studied Winslow in a way a man might measure an ox for a slaughterhouse sledging. His confidence and malignant enjoyment was clear to every man in the room. Then he grinned and dropped his gun belt. "Watch this, boys," he leered. "I'll drive him around a little before I drop him!" Peace needed fights as other men needed food, and his breath grew shallow with anticipation. "Winslow, I'm gonna bust you up good—!"

He tried to surprise Winslow by throwing a powerful right hand that would have ended the fight had it landed. But it didn't land. Winslow parried the blow, and as Peace missed and was thrown off balance, Dan lifted his arm and brought it down with all his might on the back of Peace's thick neck.

The sound of it striking went through the saloon, and it drove Peace to the floor. His face struck the boards, and he rolled there, his wits addled. It would have broken the neck of a lesser man, but Peace was a burly brute with bones like those of a grizzly, with an oxlike vitality. All his victories came from the thick shield of bone and muscle, this insensitivity to injury. He crawled to his feet and came up facing the wrong way as Winslow said, "Over here, Ollie."

Peace was confused, and before he could move, Winslow stepped forward and threw a tremendous right hand. Dan knew that the skull of the man would break his fingers, so he drove another blow into his thick throat. It was only partly successful, for Peace ducked and the blow only caught him indirectly. But it did turn the big man's face crimson, and he began gagging. Winslow pushed forward, and a blow he never saw struck him on the chest, the force of it driving him backward.

Peace yelled, "I got you!" and fell forward to grasp Winslow. But Winslow drew back his foot and drove his sharp heel directly into the man's mouth. It stopped Peace cold, driving his head back as he rolled off to the floor. Winslow got to his feet and watched with amazement as Peace slowly staggered to his feet. The man should have been unconscious. His eyes were bulging from the blow in the throat, and there was a gap in his teeth, with bloody froth blowing out of his smashed lips.

But still he moved forward. Winslow felt a moment of despair, for he knew if Peace ever got a grip on him, he'd be torn to pieces. The vitality of the man was a frightening thing! Winslow moved backward, avoiding the big hands of Peace, who had given up on hitting with his fists. His hands were like great claws reaching out for Winslow. Winslow knew there was enough power in those hands to rip him apart. He also knew that he could shatter his own hands without putting the man down.

Then he felt the bar at his back. He couldn't run. But as Peace closed in, Winslow sent a tremendous kick at the man, the tip of the boot striking Peace on the right knee. He thought he heard the bone snap, and Peace went down as though struck by a scythe.

Yet still Ollie Peace was not whipped! Grabbing the bar, he ignored the agony of the broken knee and pulled himself upright. Winslow picked up a full bottle of whiskey and brought it down on the iron skull. The bottle broke, leaving a ragged remnant that scraped down the side of Peace's face, leaving a bloody red track.

Peace fell loosely to the floor, his body jerking, but with no sign of consciousness.

Winslow moved across the room, picked up his gun belt, and strapped it on. Then he moved to stand in front of Ash Caudill. The only sound in the room was the ragged breathing of Peace, and Caudill thought that Winslow intended to draw on him.

But the battle fury was gone, and Winslow took a deep breath. "Caudill, I'll be staying close to Anchor. If one of your men touches it, I'll kill you out of hand."

He turned and walked out of the saloon, followed by Jacks, Orr, and Sid Kincaid. When they were gone, Jack Hines walked over and looked down at Ollie Peace. "Hey, Ash, we better get Ollie up to Doc Matthews—"

But Caudill stared at him without a word. He knew that he'd

been bested. Up to this point, Arrow existed by force, and Winslow had shifted that balance. He walked across the saloon and paused to look down at Peace. He was silent, then nodded, "See to him, Jack. I've got an errand."

When he left, Jack stared at the door, then said bitterly to Luke Mott, "Like to hear how he explains this thing to Silas Head!"

Mott nodded slowly. "You know what he'll say to that, Jack. He'll tell Caudill to wipe out Winslow—and I ain't sure Ash can cut it!"

CHAPTER SIXTEEN

AT THE ANCHOR RANCH

★ ★ ★ ★

When Dan Winslow put the run on two of Arrow's toughest hands, the news spread out over the valley with astonishing speed. By nightfall of the next day, the news had spread to practically every rancher, settler, and sheepherder in the county. But then the reports of the eyewitnesses began to reflect different views, rumors spread quickly, and within a week, the simplicity of the thing had been lost.

By the time Silas Head returned from the cattlemen's meeting in Cheyenne, there were plenty of men to warn him that his absolute dominance of the valley had been badly shaken. He heard it first when he got on the train, from the conductor, A.B. Tettleman, whose son-in-law had been in the Palace Saloon when the confrontation had taken place. Silas Head knew the man to be an inveterate gossip, but when Tettleman sat down and told him the story, he felt uneasy—though he waved the gossipy conductor off with a shrug, saying, "Just another saloon fracas, A.B."

But he thought about the matter more than once, and when he got off the train, he immediately went to Lyle Coppenger, his lawyer, to find out the truth of the matter. Coppenger, a rotund man of forty-five who knew everyone in the central part of the territory, was a shrewd politician. He rolled his cigar around thoughtfully, removed it, then said, "Silas, it's funny how things run along, not changing much. Then one thing happens—and the whole thing is turned upside down."

"Just one man whips a couple of men in a saloon brawl," Head shrugged his heavy shoulders. "Don't mean much."

"I think it does," Coppenger said quickly. "Some men just seem to be natural leaders. Men just follow them, watch them to see what they're going to do. Now every two-bit rancher and fifty-acre sodbuster in this part of the world has seen Arrow get knocked for a loop by Dan Winslow. And they're watching him like a hawk to see what he's going to do next." Coppenger shook his head. "That fight changed everything, Silas. Before it happened, Arrow was the big outfit who'd never been put down. Now a man has taken your best shot, and he's made you look pretty weak. If I was you, Silas, I'd look at my hole card pretty close."

Silas Head had not made himself a king in his world by ignoring danger signs, and when he got back to his ranch, the first thing he did was greet his daughter—who kissed him and asked at once, "Did you hear about Longly and Peace?"

"I want to hear it from Ash," Head nodded. He sent for the foreman, and when Caudill entered, Head said, "Diane, why don't you go do some sewing?"

Diane shook her head instantly. "I want to hear about it, Dad," she answered. "Ash won't tell me a thing."

Head frowned, but as usual gave way to his strong-willed daughter. Turning his frosty blue eyes on Caudill, he demanded, "What happened?"

Ash Caudill had been burning with anger ever since the fight in the Palace, for he was not a man to take defeat easily. But now he knew that he was in for a bad time from Head. He spoke quickly, telling about the fight, then said, "Winslow and his bunch played it smart, Mr. Head. Next time—"

Head glared at Caudill, anger roughening his speech. "No, they didn't play it smart, Ash—you played it *dumb!*" He proceeded to give Caudill a tongue lashing that left the foreman pale, his lips tight, and his eyes filled with fury. Yet he had enough control to keep from lashing out at the owner, and finally Head finished by saying, "I pay for an army to keep these sodbusters and two-bit cow outfits in line—and you let one man buffalo the whole crew!"

Diane had listened carefully, and now she asked, "Dan Winslow beat Longly to the draw that bad, Ash?"

"He's as fast with a gun as any man I've seen," Caudill admitted.

"Faster than you?" Head demanded at once.

"Won't know until it happens."

Diane wasn't finished. She leaned forward and asked, "I can't believe Dan Winslow destroyed that brute Ollie Peace. That brute's half killed every man he's fought. Did Winslow get hurt much in the fight?"

Caudill glared at her but didn't dare to lie. "No, but he didn't use his fists. He used his boots and busted Ollie over the head with a full bottle of whiskey."

Diane smiled suddenly. "You mean he didn't fight *fair*, Ash? I didn't know that you were interested in a little set of rules. I guess from now on you'll count to see that we have the same number of men in a fight as they have! I don't remember that you ever thought of doing that before."

Her taunt brought two spots of color to Ash's cheeks. "It may be funny to you now, Diane, but it won't be when we start losing our graze to these little fellows!"

"Diane, I want to talk to Ash," Head snapped.

Diane walked to the door, but paused to give the two men a smile. "Maybe you ought to hire Winslow." A thoughtful look crossed her face, and she murmured, "He must be quite a fellow!"

As soon as she left the room, Head said, "This won't do, Ash. I've spent my life building Arrow into the biggest spread in this part of the territory. I don't propose to lose it because you can't handle your job."

Caudill stared into Head's eyes, then nodded. "I told you it would be easier to buy Winslow than to fight him. Now it's too late for that. But there's only one way to stop him, Mr. Head. Don't waste your time thinking on anything else."

Head was a hard man. His life had been spent among hard men, and he had outlasted them. Violence had been as much a part of his early days as the air he breathed. He had taken his land and held it against Indians, drought, and as tough a set of roughnecks as can be imagined. But for a long time he'd been so strong that it hadn't been necessary to carry on a full-scale war. Now he was thinking of the old days, and it was only after a long silence that he said, "All right, Ash. A man's got to fight for what's his. Always been that way, and I reckon it'll never change."

* * * *

After the fight at the Palace, Winslow, heading for Doc Matthews' office, had found himself flanked by Gus Miller, Smoky Jacks, and Sid Kincaid. Jacks, his eyes still bright with the excitement of the fight, said, "Been waiting a while to see them jaspers get the skids put under 'em!" Admiration shaded the glance he threw at Winslow as he warned, "Don't walk past any dark alleys, Dan. Ash Caudill won't let this thing go."

"Smoky's right about that," Gus Miller put in. His dark eyes glinted, for the fight had pleased him as well as Jacks. "You can count on trouble, but call on me anytime. I've been waiting for a man to stand up to Arrow for a long time. I thought Willis Malloy was the man, but he got himself killed."

"That would be Hope Malloy's husband?" Dan asked.

"Yeah, he was a tough one," Miller nodded. "Mean as a snake to his wife and kid, but ready to face up to Silas Head." A thought came to him, and he said, "This is gonna make it rough on Miz Malloy. With Zane laid up, she's got no way to run her place—and it'd be my guess that she'll have trouble with Arrow."

Sid had listened to all this and now said, "Dan, with just the two of us, how are we going to handle it? I mean, we've got Rosa to think of. You and me, we can risk it, but if Arrow starts throwing lead, she could get hit by some fool just as easy as we could."

The three of them watched as Winslow stood there listening. His nerves were well-insulated, not easily touched by little disturbances or rumors. He gave the impression of a man wholly confident of himself, but now he seemed troubled by deeper things. He had been a tough man as he had thrown himself recklessly against Peace's fists and Longly's guns, but now he turned away from those fighting instincts. The stout bones of his face and his tight-closed lips betrayed the inner turmoil; everything in him that had any fancy or lightness he seemed to have put aside.

Finally he said, "I'm thinking it was Rosa being at the Malloy place that got the boy beaten. She's my responsibility, so I'll have to do what I can to help, at least until he gets better. I've already said something to Hope, but I'd better go tell her what I've got on my mind."

"Looks like I'm out of a job," Smoky Jacks said at once. He didn't seem to be troubled by that fact and added, "Malloys are good friends of mine. Reckon I'll give them a hand until Zane gets better."

Winslow nodded, pleased with Jack's decision. "That'll make things easier. Let's go tell her."

They crossed the street, and five minutes later Hope met them at the door. She stepped back, her eyes wide with surprise at the delegation. When they were all inside, Winslow said, "Mrs. Malloy, I feel responsible for what happened to your brother, so I'd like to help with your place until he gets up and about."

Hope looked at him, but shook her head. "You can't leave your own place, Mr. Winslow. What about the young woman? You couldn't leave her alone there, could you?"

"No, but I've got an idea—maybe not a good one." He hesitated, then said, "Rosa's going to be laid up for a few days with that bad ankle. If she could stay with you for a while, Sid and I could handle my place and yours, too."

"Why, she'd be more than welcome," Hope said at once, but then she added, "I don't know how safe it would be for her. Those men who beat Zane up may come back."

"Not them fellers, Hope," Smoky Jacks grinned. "Dan here run that fancy gunman outta town, and Ollie Peace won't be doing any fightin' for quite a spell, and *never* with Dan." He nodded when she looked at him with some confusion, adding, "That's right, and the job was done complete. And by the way, I'll be hanging around your place for a while if you can put up with me."

"But—I can't pay you, Smoky."

"You can still bake them pies, can't you?" the muscular young rider grinned. "That'll do me for a while."

Hope knew that he was doing it out of friendship and said gently, "That's like you, Smoky, to do a thing like that. God bless you for it!" Then she said, "We'll be taking Zane home in the morning, Mr. Winslow. If you want us to take Rosa, we'll be glad to have her."

"Fine! And it's Dan, by the way." Winslow smiled, the first one Hope had seen on him. It made him look younger, and when he said good-night and left with the others, Hope went to the window and watched as they moved down the street.

When they disappeared from view, she sat down on one of Doc Matthews' chairs, thinking about the visit, and rose only when Amos and Cody came into the room. Quickly she said, "Dad, Dan Winslow just left here—" She reported the visit, including his determination to help with the ranch.

When she finished, Amos said at once, "Why, that's wonderful, Daughter! We can make it fine with a little help. And I've been praying right hard that God would send somebody to give us a hand."

A shade of doubt clouded Hope's eyes. "I'm not sure Dan Winslow is sent from God, Dad. He's very hard. As a matter of fact, he's already run the two who hurt Zane out of town, so they say. I didn't seem to feel that he was a godly man."

Amos studied his daughter, then said gently, "Well, maybe God sent him our way to help us—and so that we could help him."

"Did he shoot 'em, Ma?" Cody demanded, his eyes big with excitement. "Them two who hurt Zane?" When she shook her head, he said with disappointment, "Dern! Wished I could've seen it!"

"I hope you never see any shooting," Hope rebuked him. Then she said, "Rosa will be coming to stay with us for a time— and Smoky Jacks, too."

Amos smiled at that, saying, "We'd better get some more supplies, then. You know how that cowboy can eat. But it'll be good to have him around." He saw the faint doubt in Hope's eyes and asked, "Don't you like the man, Hope—Winslow, I mean?"

A trace of color came to Hope's cheeks, and she said hurriedly, "Why, he's nice to offer to help us, Pa." But Amos knew that something was behind her hesitation, and a thought came to him: *This Winslow is pretty tough—and Hope's afraid to trust strong men. Two of them were enough for her, I guess.* The thought saddened him and he said no more, but went in to see how Zane was doing.

★　★　★　★

For several days after moving Rosa to Anchor, a tension hovered over all of them. Winslow sent Sid to watch the Circle W, with a stern warning, "If trouble comes turn tail and run. I mean that, Sid. I don't want you getting killed over a few head of cattle." He and Smoky Jacks had taken turns keeping a night watch over Anchor, both of them half expecting some sort of retribution from Arrow.

Rosa's injury healed rapidly, and after a week, she had only a slight limp. With Winslow gone most of the time, she fitted herself into the family with surprising ease. She had never been in the midst of such a warm family circle, and after an initial stiffness, grew fond of them all. She liked Amos from the start, and when he offered to teach her how to play the dulcimer, they spent much time on that project. Cody was shy of her at first, but after a few days pestered her constantly with questions and requests to play checkers—at which he was quite good. As for Hope Malloy, there was a kindness in her that Rosa had hungered for all her life, and had never found in her difficult life back in Texas.

Much of her time she spent with Zane, who was able to sit up after three days, but still in severe discomfort. Hope was busy with her work, and it was natural that Rosa would take over waiting on the injured young man. At first he was tremendously embarrassed when she came to wash his face and arms, but she laughed at him, saying, "You're a dirty boy, Zane Jenson! Now, be still!"

She read to him, though the choice of books was small. She had bogged down on some of the volumes of sermons that Amos Jenson loved, but discovered a real pleasure in reading aloud a thick novel entitled *Ivanhoe*, which Hope had given her. Zane was not much of a reader himself, and at first the two of them struggled through the book. But then they were both drawn into the story, and night after night Rosa sat beside Zane, reading in a low voice that grew excited when the action occurred.

It was almost eleven o'clock on one of these nights that Rosa reached the part where the beautiful Rebecca is carried away by the villain. Zane was sitting up in his bed, braced against a pillow, and his light blue eyes flashed with outrage at the cruelty of the false knight. "By golly, I hope that Ivanhoe don't put up with that!" he said angrily.

"Shhhh—don't be so loud!" Rosa warned him. She smiled at him, saying, "It's just a storybook, Zane."

"Well, I don't care!" Zane protested. "It makes me mad for a nice girl like Rebecca to get carried off by that guy!" He twisted in the bed to look more directly at her, then said, "You reckon that Ivanhoe will come to get her?"

Rosa's face was suddenly sad, and the amber glow of the lamp made her soft complexion stand out even more. Her lips were rounded and soft as she shook her head, saying in answer to Zane's question, "I don't think so, Zane. He'll marry Rowena."

Her answer was so prompt that Zane was silenced for a moment, but then shook his head. "You don't know that, Rosa. You ain't read the end of that book yet."

"No, but I know it," she said. She closed the book, putting a marker in place, then lifted her eyes to him. "Ivanhoe will marry Rowena because she's his own kind."

"What does that mean—his own kind?"

"Why, Rebecca is a Jew, and Jews are different from other people. She's from another race, Zane, but Rowena is blonde and from the same race Ivanhoe's from. It's real sad. Rebecca's in love with him, but she won't get him."

Zane stared at her, then shook his head stubbornly. "That's crazy, Rosa. Why, that Rebecca is a beautiful woman, prettier than Rowena! And she's real nice, too. I'll bet you're wrong. I'll bet Ivanhoe picks Rebecca. Go on, read some more."

"No, it's too late." Rosa stood up, placed the book on the table, then asked, "Do you want anything? A glass of water?"

"I'm thirsty, all right." Zane watched her as she left the room, then returned with a glass of cool water. He drank it, then looked up at her. "Hate to have to be waited on like this. You must get sick of it."

"No, I don't," Rosa said. She seemed subdued, not at all lively as she usually was. "I'm glad to do it. Not just because you saved me out there in the hills, but because it was my fault you got hurt." She smiled at him, and put her hand out to take the glass. "I thought it was the finest thing I ever saw, Zane, the way you stood up for me."

"Didn't do much good," Zane mumbled. "Got myself all punched out and didn't stop them."

"But you tried," Rosa nodded. "I'll never forget it."

Zane asked suddenly, "What's wrong, Rosa? You don't seem happy tonight. You worried about something?"

"I guess it was the story," she said slowly. She sat down beside him again and shook her head sadly. "Isn't that silly? To be sad about a story that never happened when there's so much real trouble."

"I don't know why you should be sad. It's a great story."

"It's what we were talking about," Rosa said slowly. The lamp was turned down low, and her face was thrown into high relief by the golden light it cast over her. Her dark hair glowed and her eyes seemed much larger as she sat there looking at him. "All the time I was reading about Rebecca, I was thinking about myself."

"Why, what's she got to do with you?"

"Oh, Zane, she's a foreigner and so am I!" Rosa cried out impatiently.

Zane stared at her, shock in his thin face. "A foreigner? You're no foreigner!"

"I'm a Mexican!" Rosa said, her lips growing thin. "Don't tell me you never noticed!"

Zane shook his head, saying, "Why, I never thought about it!"

His words brought a warmth to Rosa's face, and her lips grew soft. "That's sweet of you, Zane," she said, then something came to her, and she shook her head. "But people do notice. No man will ever look at me and want me—not like I'd like to be wanted."

"*I* would!" Zane blurted out, his fair skin burning as a blush rose to his cheeks.

Rosa smiled then, and moved by an impulse, reached out and put her hand on his cheek. "Yes, you would, Zane—but you're still young. When you get older, you'll want a gringo woman."

She rose to her feet and left the room before he could answer. He struggled to get down in the bed, but sleep came slowly. He had never been around a young woman before, and her behavior troubled him. Punching the pillow, he lay back and went to sleep, muttering, "I'll ask Sister about it. She'll know—"

At dawn, awakened by the sound of voices, he got out of bed painfully, pulled on his pants, and moved carefully into the kitchen. He found Winslow and Smoky at the table, with Hope and Rosa moving back and forth from the stove. Winslow turned as Zane entered and smiled at him. "Come on in before Smoky and I eat it up, Zane." He eyed the young man's slow, painful movements, then nodded. "Horse fell on me once, right after the fight at Chancellorsville. Broke some ribs and hurt like the devil. You're taking it better than I did."

"Zane, I was going to fix your breakfast and bring it to you," Rosa scolded.

"Aw, I cain't lay in that ol' bed forever!"

"Better take her up on it, Kid," Smoky grinned. "You ain't gonna get many offers like that from a young lady!"

Hope smiled at Zane's obvious discomfort at Jacks' teasing. "Don't pay any attention to Smoky, Zane. He's just jealous."

"Lady, you're shore right about that," Smoky nodded. "I been on my lonesome so long, I get plumb starved for personal attention. What I been thinking about doing is finding a widow lady whose husband died right convenient like and left her a good-sized bunch of cash. I figure I could sort of *manage* it for her, and she could wait on me all she wanted to." Jacks looked at Hope and asked, "You seen any rich widows lookin' for a handsome young feller to take care of?"

"No, Smoky," Hope said, laughing at his plaintive tone. "I think you'd have to get in line, though, if there were such a woman."

Rosa fixed her plate and sat down beside Dan, asking, "Can I go with you today? My ankle's almost well."

Winslow shook his head but grinned at her affectionately. "Maybe next week. Doc Matthews said for me to take good care of you till then, and I aim to do it." He studied her and asked, "You fixed your hair different?"

"Yes, Hope did it for me."

"Looks real good," Dan smiled. He turned to Hope and winked so that Rosa could not see it. "I'd be pleased if you didn't give this girl any more help like that. If she gets any prettier, some long-legged galoot of a puncher will run off with her."

Winslow didn't notice the flush of pleasure that came to Rosa's cheeks, but all three of the others did. All through breakfast, Zane was quiet, saying almost nothing. Hope said, "Dan, I'm going with you this morning." When he gave her a surprised look, she added, "I want to get out of the house—and you and Smoky can't do all the riding."

She went to change into a riding outfit, and when she emerged, the two left. Zane watched them go, then noted that Rosa was throwing the dishes into the pan with what seemed to be unnecessary roughness. He said nothing, but sat there talking to Smoky, who was drinking coffee. Finally Rosa turned and walked out of the room without a word.

"What's wrong with Rosa?" Zane asked.

Smoky grinned and shook his head. "Jealous of the big fellow," he commented.

"Jealous!" Zane glared at Jacks as if he had insulted him. "That's crazy, Smoky! Why, he's at least thirty years old!"

Jacks studied the face of his young friend, knowing at once what the problem was. However, he said only, "Mexican girls marry lots younger than girls this side of the border." He sipped his coffee, noting the distress on Zane's face. *Youngster's stuck on the girl*, was his thought. *Well, be odd if he wasn't, pretty as she is.* He got to his feet, saying, "Guess I'll catch me some shut-eye, Zane," and left to go to the barn, where he and Winslow had fixed up a tack room to sleep in. As he left, he slapped Zane on the shoulder, saying, "Be glad when you get all healed up, Zane." Outside, he spotted Winslow and Hope just cresting one of the rolling hills, and gave them a thoughtful look. Finally he shook his head and moved on into the barn.

Hope rode beside Winslow, listening as he spoke of the condition of the cattle, but her mind was not on that. He saw that she was only half listening, and he fell into a silence. Finally she said, "Dan, what's going to happen? About Arrow, I mean?"

"Hard to say," he said thoughtfully. "I been expecting them

to do something to offset that business in the saloon. I know Ash Caudill, and he's a hard nut. He lost a little of his reputation in that fracas, but he's not a man to quit." He sat in the saddle easily, his tanned face constantly surveying the terrain.

They moved ahead, coming to a natural draw, and he nodded at the cattle grazing there. "You've got some good stock, Hope," he remarked. "You'll have a good herd this year."

"My husband knew cattle," she replied, and he looked at her quickly.

It was the first time she'd mentioned her husband, but he'd picked up on some of the problems. For one thing, Cody had followed him around a great deal, and had given away the fact that he had hated his stepfather. Then Amos had spoken guardedly of his son-in-law, revealing a little more. But it was Ozzie Og who had given the clearest picture of Willis Malloy. "Mean as a snake," the cook had spat out. "Treated that woman and those boys like dirt. It ain't Christian of me, but I'm glad the sucker's dead!"

Winslow was watching her, and she turned so suddenly that he had no chance to avert his eyes. His look of obvious admiration disturbed Hope, and she said quickly, "We're all grateful for your help, Dan—but I hope you won't have to stay here too long." Then she said, "I guess that sounds ungrateful, but I—don't want—"

She broke off, embarrassed by her own thoughts. "You have your own life to live, and the sooner you can get back to it, the better. You can't nurse us along forever." Her words had struck him, she saw, and quickly she changed the subject. "Rosa's a nice girl. She's worried about her father, isn't she?"

"I can't say for sure, but I believe she knows he's dead."

"Oh, Dan!"

He glanced at her, saw the pain in her eyes, and said, "She's probably right."

"What will happen to her?"

"I'll take care of her. The ranch isn't much, but it's hers for what it's worth. I owe that much to her dad—and to her."

"It's awkward, isn't it?"

"Well, it is for a fact. I don't know anything about children—not a thing."

"Rosa's not a child, Dan," Hope stated flatly.

He gave her a surprised glance, then nodded. "No, I guess not—and that makes it more tricky. I guess I'll have to hang around to see she gets a good husband." A thin smile pulled at the corners of his lips, and he added, "Now that's something I never thought I'd be doing—trying to keep a bunch of cowboys from a young lady. Makes me feel like Methuselah!"

Hope thought of the look on Rosa's face when she had left the house with Dan, and said thoughtfully, "You may have an even bigger problem than that, Dan." When he gave her a questioning look, she said, "Nevermind. Let's ride around by the flats. I always liked that country."

CHAPTER SEVENTEEN

A MAN CAN'T RUN AWAY FROM GOD!

★ ★ ★ ★

"Aw, Dan, I don't wanna go to church," Cody protested. "I'd rather you and me take ol' Buck and go see if we can get us a wild turkey over by the river."

Winslow pulled the straight razor down through the white, frothy lather on his throat before he answered. His beard was tough and his eyes watered as the blade raked across the flesh, making a rasping sound. He wiped the lather from the razor and looked across the porch where Cody leaned against the outer wall watching him. "We'll do that tomorrow," he said, then grinned at the boy. "Now, I like listening to your grandpa preach. Guess I missed out on things like that for too long."

Cody brightened up at the mention of a future hunt and stood there watching Dan finish shaving, talking with excitement about how he planned to get his gobbler. He was wearing his church-going clothes, and his hair was pasted down with water. Winslow listened to him, inserting a comment from time to time, speaking to the boy as if he were another man. He had been amused at the manner in which Cody had attached himself, but then had realized that there was something pathetic about it. He had been at Anchor for three weeks now, except for trips to his own ranch and to town, and Cody had become his shadow. "The boy's never really had a father and he looks up to you," Smoky had remarked, noting Cody's insistence on following Winslow as closely as possible.

"Guess I better put on a clean shirt," Winslow said. He dried his face, then threw the shaving water out. It splattered Buck in the face, drawing a startled bark. Winslow laughed with Cody, and as he went to the small room he shared with Smoky, Cody stuck close to his side. As he put on a white shirt and a pair of clean gray pants, he answered the questions that Cody fed him in a steady stream, amused at the boundless curiosity of the boy. He put on his good boots, tied a string tie around his neck, then brushed his heavy black hair.

"Guess I'm ready," he said. "Let's go to church and get skinned."

"Grandpa does lay it on pretty hard, don't he, Dan?"

"Sure does. But that's the way it should be, I reckon. Too many preachers seem to be afraid to tell their congregations they're going to hell if they don't repent." He smiled wryly, adding, "Your grandfather doesn't have that problem."

"Are you saved, Dan?"

The simplicity of the question might have offended Winslow if it had come from an adult, but as he looked down at the boy, he saw only an innocence and a concern. "I reckon not, Cody."

"Me neither. Guess we'll both go to hell, you reckon?"

A shock ran through Winslow such as he had seldom felt. He had slipped into his coat and had just settled his low-crowned black hat on his head as Cody spoke, and the question hit him hard. He turned quickly to Cody and studied the boy. Cody stood there matter-of-factly watching him, and finally Winslow said, "I hope not, Cody. You need to listen to your grandfather—and to your mother. Don't look at fellows like me."

Cody frowned, his brown eyes wide and careful. "Well—I guess so, Dan."

The scene bothered Winslow, but he could not think of any way to say what he was thinking to the boy. He left the room, and they found the rest of the family coming out of the house. Amos was sitting on the seat of the wagon, and Dan got there in time to put out a hand and help Hope climb in. She was wearing a white dress with small yellow flowers and a small white hat with yellow lace around the brim. Her hand was firm and cool in his, and she gave him a smile, saying, "Thank you."

Winslow saw with surprise that Zane was coming out of the house. He watched as the young man moved slowly and carefully down the porch, and said as he approached the wagon, "Feel like spreading your wings?"

Zane shrugged, and his answer was brief. "Sure." He grasped the wheel of the wagon, took a deep breath, and climbed onto the back seat, his lips tight.

But when Amos said, "You sure you can make it, son?" Zane grinned and nodded. Then Rosa came out, wearing a dress that Winslow had not seen—a light green frock with darker emerald embroidery around the bodice. Dan handed her into the back seat, then Cody scrambled in to sit beside her. When Winslow climbed in to sit beside Hope, Amos said, "Giddap," and the wagon moved off.

"Weather's changing, ain't it?" Amos remarked. "Think there may be some cold over behind those hills."

"I used to like fall back home," Hope said, "but now it reminds me that winter is coming. I'm sure not looking forward to another winter here." She was acutely aware of Dan Winslow. He had surprised them all by going to church on his first Sunday and had not missed a service. Now his arm pressed lightly against hers, and there was no way she could move away from it. The impulse to do so brought a sudden feeling of disgust, for she had been aware since Winslow had come that she was not comfortable in his presence. And yet, it was not a simple dislike, for she did like him—very much. She was pleased that Cody had taken to Winslow and was amused at the persistence with which her son followed the big man.

She was aware also that Zane disliked Winslow—and it bothered her. She would have called Zane's attitude toward Rosa puppy love, but somehow she could not. They were both so very young, and she was afraid for them. Once she had tried to talk to her father about it and had discovered that he was very much aware of the problem. But he had only said, "Nothing to be done, Daughter. Young people will be drawn to each other."

The air was cool as they drove along the slopes of the hills, and there was a stirring in the earth. Hope said, "I like spring best. In the fall everything dies. I like it when the grass comes up and the trees start budding. Fall and winter are just too gloomy for me."

"I always liked them," Dan remarked. "A change after the hot summers. Good to feel the bite of cold after sweating all summer. I remember how we all nearly died in the summer, trying to keep up with Stonewall Jackson. That man was a driver! Then at Fredericksburg we had snowball fights. I'll never forget that."

Hope said hesitantly, "I feel so strange, Dan." He turned to look at her, noting that the sun had given her fair skin a golden tan, and that a line of tiny freckles was sprinkled across her cheeks and nose. She was usually a solemn woman, but there was a streak of humor in her that often took a strange turn. She would laugh at Buck when their new kitten scratched his nose— a happy laughter like that of a very young girl. But now she was sober, and added, "I feel like something's going to happen. It's like this time of year, when the sun's shining, but you know sooner or later winter will come."

"Know the feeling," Dan nodded. He sat idly on the seat, his face relaxed as he spoke. "I guess it's natural enough. Life's mostly trouble, with a few good times in between. The war was like that for me. No matter how much fun a fellow had, we always knew sooner or later we'd be in the middle of the dying. Guess old Job was right when he said, 'Man is born to trouble as the sparks fly upward.' "

Amos looked across at Winslow, saying, "You know the Bible, Dan."

"Know it—but don't do it," he replied laconically. He was uncomfortably aware of the woman beside him. Aware of her profile, the curve of her shoulders, the rich yellow gleaming of her hair—even of the lovely turnings of her body. He had been aware of her since coming to Anchor, and his sense of her presence had grown in him. He had known women, but somehow this one particular woman with her strong, straight eyes and her concealed warmth and humor had gained some sort of admiration in him that puzzled him.

He shook his shoulders slightly and went back to her statement. "I guess I know what you mean, Hope, about feeling something's going to happen. I figured we'd have trouble long before now. Can't see Arrow just folding up and start handing out Christian charity."

"Maybe they will," Hope said, and for the rest of the trip she was quieter than usual.

The streak of fatalism that made up part of Winslow's character would not permit him to hope for any mercy from Arrow, but he put the thing out of his mind.

They arrived at the small frame building just off Main Street as the congregation was gathering. Dan leaped to the ground and helped the women out, then resisted the impulse to give Zane a little help. He let the family go in, standing outside to watch the people arrive and file in, then entered and took a back seat. It was a small building, no more than twenty feet wide and perhaps twice that long. Two rows of pine benches ran from the back to the low platform that held two chairs and a simple pulpit, and most of them were full. Yellow sunlight filtered through the high windows that broke the front wall, and the smell of sawdust and rosin hung in the air.

Several people spoke to Dan, and he was somewhat puzzled as to his presence in the place. He had not been to a service more than five times since the war, but somehow he had wanted to come to this place. Part of the reason, he understood, was his admiration of Amos Jenson, for the man was genuine to the bone. But other than that, he was aware that something in his life was out of joint; and over the years he had thought often of the simple faith of his parents, what a completeness it brought to them—and it seemed to him that he saw that same simplicity in Amos and Hope.

He especially enjoyed the music, which was different. Amos played the fiddle and Hope the dulcimer, and the two had played together so long they complemented each other perfectly. There was a charm in the sounds of the instruments, and Hope's clear contralto voice blended perfectly with the accompaniment.

The rest of the congregation joined in heartily, singing, "Nothing But the Blood of Jesus," "Shall We Gather at the River?" "Amazing Grace," "Rock of Ages," and other favorite hymns. To his surprise, Dan discovered that he knew the words of most of them, that after all his years of wandering, the songs he'd sung in church as a boy had not left him. He began singing quietly, unaware that Hope saw this, as well as Amos.

When the singing was over, Hope took her place with Zane, Cody, and Rosa. A silence fell over the congregation as Amos stood up, his worn black Bible in his hand. He was not a shouter, but spoke in a warm, casual manner—which had displeased some of the congregation at first, those who liked the fiery evangelists who came from time to time. But over the months most of them had come to realize that Amos Jenson was a man who heard from God—and who would deliver fearlessly any message that God gave him.

Amos looked calmly over the room. He was not an impressive man to look at. He wore a simple, worn black suit, a white shirt, and a string tie. His face was thin, and there was a fragility about him as he stood there quietly, but when he spoke his voice was clear.

"All over this country people are meeting to worship God. Some in humble buildings like this, others in big, expensive buildings. Preachers are standing before their congregations, just as I'm standing before you, and I suppose texts will be preached on from every book in the Bible. There'll be sermons on heaven, on hell, on infant baptism, on the beast in Daniel rising out of the sea that looks like a bear with three ribs in his mouth—and on just about every other subject the mind can imagine."

A big black bug chose this moment to fly in through the window. It flew to Amos, circled around his head with a loud buzzing hum, and Amos paused to brush it away with his hand. A smile appeared on his lips, and he said, "A preacher friend of mine was giving his message once, and one of those big black bugs flew right into his mouth. Well, sir, he had to decide to make a spectacle out of himself and try to cough it up and spit it out—or to just swallow it and go on." He scratched his head, ignoring the giggles of the young boys, and said, "He finally decided to just swallow it—which he did—and went right on with his preaching. But after the sermon one of his deacons came to him intending to have some fun out of the pastor, and he said, 'Now, Pastor, you've always got a scripture from the Bible to fit anything that happens to you. Now what scripture you gonna find about swallowing a bug?' "

Amos paused, then smiled, "My preacher friend didn't even have to think about it. He said, *'Deacon, he was a stranger, and I took him in!'* "

Laughter swept over the congregation, and Dan Winslow grinned broadly. He admired Amos as a preacher, and was aware that few men had the ability to put the gospel in terms that these unpretentious people could understand. The simple jest won them over, and they settled down to listen as Jenson began to speak seriously.

"This morning, I want to speak about the most important thing that ever happened on the face of the earth. It changed everything, and I mean, of course, the death of Jesus Christ on the cross. You've read the story of that death many times, but it makes me tremble every time. Turn to Luke's gospel, chapter twenty-three, beginning with verse thirty-three." He waited until those who had Bibles found the place, then read slowly:

"And when they were come to the place, which is called Calvary, there they crucified him, and the malefactors, one on the right hand, and the other on the left.

"Then said Jesus, Father, forgive them; for they know not what they do. And they parted his raiment, and cast lots.

"And the people stood beholding. And the rulers also with them derided him, saying, He saved others; let him save himself, if he be Christ, the chosen of God.

"And the soldiers also mocked him, coming to him, and offering him vinegar, and saying, If thou be the king of the Jews, save thyself.

"And a superscription also was written over him in letters of Greek, and Latin, and Hebrew, THIS IS THE KING OF THE JEWS."

Amos looked up and began to tell of the miracles Jesus did, of the holy life led by the Savior. He spoke of the hardships Jesus suffered, and of the poverty He endured.

Then he described the betrayal by Judas, the unjust and illegal trials that Jesus suffered through. And finally he described the crucifixion, dwelling on the agony of the nails that crushed the fragile bones of the hands and feet, the terrible jolting as the cross was dropped into the hole, and the awful torture that forced the crucified to pull himself upright on the nailed palms in order to catch a breath. He described the swarm of flies that must have been drawn to the scene, the mockings of the crowd.

"What was this man doing on that cross?" Amos asked, and there were tears on his cheeks. "Was He a criminal? A vile sinner? No, He was the only perfect man the world had ever seen since Adam fell."

The crowd was absolutely still, and Winslow was beginning to experience a strange sensation, not fear exactly, but not far from it.

"Jesus was there," Amos declared in a ringing voice, "to put back together what Adam had torn apart. Not since the sin in the Garden had man been able to go to God. He could sacrifice and pray, but the scripture tells us that the blood of bulls and goats can never take away sin. For thousands of years devout Jews had taken a lamb and slain it, the Passover lamb. But not one sin had the blood of those thousands of lambs ever taken away!

"But when John the Baptist saw Jesus," Amos lifted his voice, "what did he say?"

One of the older ladies in the church could not contain herself. "Behold the Lamb of God, which taketh away the sin of the world!" she cried out with tears running down her cheeks.

"That's it, Sister!" Amos nodded as amens echoed the woman's statement. "Jesus is *the* Lamb of God. It took innocent blood to take away the sin and guilt of man, and that's why we sing:

"What can take away my sin?
Nothing but the blood of Jesus.
What can make me whole again?
Nothing but the blood of Jesus.

"Oh, precious is the flow,
That makes me white as snow,
No other fount I know,
Nothing but the blood of Jesus."

Dan Winslow had heard those familiar words a thousand times. He could not remember a time when he hadn't known them, for it was his mother's favorite song. He had been rocked to sleep hearing those words, but as Amos spoke them, it was as though he'd never heard them before. *Nothing but the blood of Jesus.* He had a sudden thought that swept all else from his mind. "Why, that's *true*! There is no other way to get to God except by Jesus!"

He appeared calm as Amos continued to preach, but he felt as if every nerve in his body had been laid bare. He'd taken religion to be a thing a man *did*—such as joining a church, being baptized, paying his tithes. Now he saw that all those things were nothing in themselves, mere activities that a bad man could do just as well as a good man. It was as if he'd come to a sudden drop-off in the middle of a road, and he was about to plunge off into some unknown and awesome chasm.

He dropped his head, stared at his feet, and did not know that his fists were clenched so tightly that the fingernails cut into the flesh. Nor did he know that Amos Jenson saw this, though he did not let his gaze linger on Winslow.

Finally Amos said, "What does all this mean? The death of God's own Son on a terrible cross? Let me read you verses thirty-nine to forty-three of this same chapter. They tell us why Jesus died:

"And one of the malefactors which were hanged railed on him, saying, If thou be Christ, save thyself and us.
"But the other answering rebuked him, saying, Dost not thou fear God, seeing thou art in the same condemnation?
"And we indeed justly; for we receive the due reward of our deeds: but this man hath done nothing amiss.
"And he said unto Jesus, Lord, remember me when thou comest into thy kingdom.
"And Jesus said unto him, Verily I say unto thee, Today shalt thou be with me in paradise."

Amos closed his Bible and put it down gently on the pulpit. Then he said, "A man can't run away from God. He may go as far as a horse can take him, then get on a ship and go as far as the ship can take him. But when he's gone as far as he can go— he'll find out that Jesus Christ is right there." He paused and bowed his head, and a stillness came over the room. "Some of you have heard about Jesus for a long time. But you've run from

Him. He wants to do you nothing but good, but you've acted as though He was your enemy."

A young man sitting halfway down to the front suddenly bent forward and put his head on the bench in front of him; muffled sobs rose from his chest. An elderly man with silver hair sitting next to him put his hand on the boy's shoulders, leaned forward, and began to pray.

Amos said, "What will you do with Jesus? That's the only question that's of any eternal importance. Get the answer to that right, and all the other things in life come around right. Some of you have made every mistake in the book, done everything you shouldn't have done. Well, you're like that thief. What did he do? Nothing! He just knew he was a sinner, cut off from God, about to face judgment. But he did one wise thing in his life— maybe the only wise thing he ever did. He asked Jesus for mercy—and he got it!"

The young man got up and staggered to the front of the building, falling on his knees; the older man was right beside him. Another came, a girl of no more than fourteen with tears streaming down her face.

As Amos urged anyone who needed salvation to come, Dan Winslow sat on the bench, feeling as though he were being torn in two! Part of him wanted to go, to fall on his knees and cry out to God. But there was something else in him, a pride that held him in his place. Finally, able to stand it no longer, he rose and stumbled over the feet of those sitting beside him, then turned and left the building.

Amos watched him go, and a sadness came to his eyes. He wanted to run after Winslow, to beg him to give in to Jesus Christ—but he was too wise for that. He knew well that it was the one decision that no man can make for another, so he began to pray with those who did come forward.

After the service there was a dinner on the ground prepared by the ladies of the church, but Winslow was not present. He had walked out of town as quickly as he could, taking refuge in a grove of cottonwood trees that lined a small pond. But he found no rest in the place; a heaviness like lead had come over him. Thoughts of his past deeds swirled through his mind, most of them deeds that were better left undone. He saw his mother's tears—his father's as well—and shame ran along his nerves.

Finally, he walked slowly back to the church and saw that the dinner was over. Most of the people had left, and he would rather have taken a beating than to face them. But when Amos saw him, he merely smiled, saying, "Ready to go, Dan?"

The ride home was long, and Cody did most of the talking. Hope was aware of Winslow's silence. Her father had told her briefly of the spiritual struggle the man was having. She turned once and examined him. But she could not read his expression. The sun caused him to narrow his eyes, so they were half-hidden behind the drop of his lids. His features were solid, with nothing to show that he was going through some sort of turmoil. She knew he was a man who could conceal his feelings, and wondered if a man like Winslow could be touched by great emotion.

And Winslow was trying to force his thoughts away from Amos' sermon. But he could not, and over and over he kept hearing the words: *A man can't run away from God!*

CHAPTER EIGHTEEN

CABIN RAISING

★ ★ ★ ★

For days after Winslow's experience at the church service, he was quieter than usual, but as far as Hope could tell, there was no other change in him. When she spoke of it to Amos, he replied, "Don't rush him, Daughter. When you plant a seed in the ground, you don't go digging it up in two or three days to see how it's doing. Remember the parable in Mark chapter four, the one that says a man casts seed into the ground and goes on with his life, but that seed comes to life? Well, I know God spoke to Dan, but we've got to wait." His thin face grew more thoughtful, and he spoke reflectively, "The seed's got to die before it can bring forth new life and growth—and I'm thinking something in Dan Winslow will have to die before God can do what He wants to with him."

"Have you noticed how Cody follows Dan around?" Hope asked.

"Sure. The boy is starved for a man's attention. I'm not able to go places and do things with him, and Zane's been too busy. Boy needs a father."

His words caused a flush to rise to Hope's cheeks, and she said quickly, "That can't be, Pa." The two of them were sitting in the kitchen, and she rose to go to the sink. Agitation stirred the smooth surfaces of her cheeks, and she kept her face averted. "We're doing fine as we are."

Amos said, his voice tinged with sadness, "It's troublesome to me, Hope. I can't be around too much longer, and I'd give a lot to see you find a good man. A woman needs a man, just like a man needs a woman. You've missed the best thing God's given to us on this earth—but I'm praying that you'll find it sometime while I'm still around to see it."

Perhaps it was the memory of that scene—Hope could never decide afterward if that were the case—but two days later when Hope let Cody persuade her to go fishing with him and Dan, she discovered that her feelings concerning Dan were not simple.

The three of them had gone late in the afternoon to a deep pool that lay sheltered within a grove of tall firs half a mile from the house. Cody, never patient with his fishing, had stated, "I'm gonna go down to where I caught the big catfish last week," and had departed carrying his pole and a can of worms.

Hope sat on a fallen log beside Dan, and in the cloistered silence of the grove, broken only by the gurgling of the stream, she remembered what her father had said. The memory made her uncomfortable, and she stirred restlessly, drawing a look from Dan. She had little knowledge of men, but she knew when men looked at her with admiration, and she saw something of this in Winslow's eyes now.

As for Winslow, he had been going through a difficult time, the words of Amos Jenson echoing in his mind almost constantly. He had managed to put God out of his thoughts for years, but the sermon had brought a stirring in him that was somehow uncomfortable—yet at the same time not completely unwelcome. And as he looked at Hope, it was not her physical attractiveness that drew him—though that was part of it—but the calm serenity that lay beneath her physical graces. She was wearing a pair of Zane's faded jeans and denim shirt, which surprisingly flattered her figure, giving her paradoxically a more feminine air than if she had been wearing a dress.

"Zane's doing well," Winslow said. "He'll be able to ride soon."

Hope nodded, and they spoke of the ranch for a time, but it was only surface conversation. Suddenly she felt a jerk on her fishing pole and saw the cork bobber taking off across the stream. She cried out with excitement, yanking hard on her pole, and a small catfish flew out of the water and plopped on the ground behind her. Scrambling to where it lay flopping, she made a grab at it even as Dan called out a warning, "Watch out for the fins!"

But one of the sharp spines pierced her palm as the fish flung his head around, and she cried out with pain, dropping the fish. She held her wounded hand with the other as the agonizing pain from the poisonous spine hit her. Dan came to her at once, took her hand and looked at it. The puncture was already turning red, and he pulled her to the side of the creek, where he scooped up a handful of cool mud and smeared it on the wound. "This helps a little." He held her small hand, pressing the mud against it, adding, "Nothing hurts much worse than poison from a catfish."

Hope had her eyes closed, and her lips were drawn into a straight line. The throbbing pain seemed to run all the way up her arm to her brain, and she grew faint with the agony. Unconsciously she leaned against him, and he held her with his free arm. It was an involuntary gesture, and there was comfort in leaning her head against his chest.

Finally the pain grew bearable. She lifted her head and he released her at once. "Better?" he asked, his eyes filled with concern.

"Yes, it's not so bad." She gave him an embarrassed glance, adding, "Sorry to be such a baby." She had no way of knowing how appealing she was at that moment, or how the touch of her slender form had stirred Winslow.

He shook his head, and regret tinged the edges of his tone. "Wish I could take the pain from you, Hope."

It was the most personal thing he'd ever said to her, and she thought for a moment, then asked, "Why would you want to do that, Dan?"

The question seemed to embarrass him, and he looked down at the ground for a moment, as though seeking for an answer there. Then he lifted his gaze and said quietly, "Just don't like to see you hurting."

The simplicity of his answer moved her, for she had never known such concern from men, except from her father. Wonder came into her eyes, but at the same time, the caution that she'd let control her grew stronger. She shook her head quickly, saying, "I guess we all have to hurt for ourselves, don't we?" She stooped down, washed the mud from her hand, then drew a handkerchief from her pocket and wound it around the wounded hand.

There had been a moment of sweetness as she had leaned against him, bringing a longing up from the depths of her spirit, which she had thought long-buried. She was a woman capable of great love, and one who longed for love as well. But her experience with two abusive men had forced those feelings into a dark closet someplace in her mind and heart, and it would take more than the spine of a catfish to bring them out.

Turning from him abruptly, she said, "Take that fish off for me, will you, Dan?" And as he moved to do so, she knew she had closed the door on something tender and fine in the moment.

★ ★ ★ ★

Ash Caudill was a cautious man by nature—a trait that had kept him alive when others he had ridden with were dead. So when he came to a conclusion about Dan Winslow, he said nothing to Silas Head, to anyone else. For weeks he had been seething under the opinion of some that he had been bested by Winslow, and in his younger days he would have simply killed Winslow or had him killed.

The worst of it for Caudill had been the taunts of Diane Head, who had missed few opportunities to put a verbal barb into Arrow's foreman. The hands knew better than to ridicule him, and Silas Head had merely warned him gruffly, "Ash, it's you or Winslow. Valley's too small for both of you."

Now as Caudill eased his horse through the thick timber that surrounded the Littleton ranch, he was able to smile for the first time. He spoke aloud, his voice causing the gelding's ears to prick backward. "Reckon I've waited long enough to let Winslow settle down. Now we'll see what happens." Soon he rode up into the clearing where the ranch house sat, and called out, "Littleton! Hello the house!"

"Who's there? Stand fast!"

Ash spoke up at once to the challenge. "Charlie? It's me—Ash Caudill."

He waited quietly, and finally a reluctant voice muttered, "Ride in, Caudill." Ash touched his horse's flanks, rode up to the house, and stopped to look down at four men who had emerged from the cabin.

"Little late for a social call," Ash said. "But maybe you can offer me a cup of coffee."

Charlie Littleton studied Caudill carefully, his green eyes flickering over the trail. Seeing no one, he nodded. "Get down. Beans in the pot."

Ash walked inside the cabin, feeling somewhat tense. But he was a man of cool nerve, and sat down in the chair Charlie Littleton indicated. The table was set, and Charlie said, "Moon, give the man something to eat."

They all sat down, and a short, round-faced puncher pulled a steak out of the skillet, added a baked potato, and put it in front of Caudill. Ash cut a bit off with the knife provided, ate it thoughtfully, then said, "That's a good piece of beef." Then he grinned and added, "Not your beef, I'd guess, Charlie."

Charlie Littleton returned the grin. "Never was a man to disregard the custom of the country."

He began to eat, and the meal was quickly over. Ash spoke lightly of conditions on the range and in the market, adding that he'd been out looking for strays and thought he'd drop in. None of the men at the table believed that, nor did Caudill expect them to. When he was finished with the meal, he said, "Charlie, I been thinking about that gray mare you tried to sell me a few months back. She still for sale?"

"Sure. Price ain't gone down though."

"Mind if I take a look at her?"

Charlie rose and winked at the others. "You boys get ready for a bonus. When a man comes to me to buy a horse, I know I can do him."

The two men walked out of the cabin and strolled to a corral a hundred yards east of the house. When they got there, Littleton stopped and turned a hard glance on the other. "What's on your mind, Ash?"

"How many cattle you rustled from Arrow, Charlie?"

The blunt question caught Littleton off guard, but only for a moment. "You ain't never caught me rustlin', Caudill."

"I'd hang you if I did. You're a crook, but that's all right with me. I aim to see you do your rustlin' from some outfit besides Arrow—most of it, anyway. But I got a proposition for you, Charlie."

"Like to hear about it," Littleton said promptly. "Always looking for a way to go up in the world. What's on your mind?"

"Dan Winslow."

Littleton took that in, studied the face of Caudill, then nodded. "Yeah, I know. He's a burr under your saddle, ain't he, Ash?"

"He's getting in my way. I want him taken out."

"Why don't you do the job yourself? He's just one man."

Ash's lips tightened, but he was honest. "I could take him one-on-one . . . but it would be a close thing. Why risk it when there are other ways?"

Littleton squinted his eyes, then asked bluntly, "What's it worth to you, Ash?"

"The widow Malloy's got a nice herd—and there must be over one hundred head of prime stock at Winslow's place. You shouldn't have any trouble moving them when you've put Winslow out of the way. And to sweeten the pot, I'll add fifty head."

"Of old man Head's cattle?" Littleton grinned. "Make it a hundred and you got a bargain."

"Good enough," Caudill nodded. "Now, it's got to be done right. Don't try to face him, Charlie. Somehow you've got to lure him away by himself and take a potshot at him." Now that the deal was made, Caudill was anxious to leave. He walked back to his horse, mounted, and said only, "I'll be waiting to hear something."

After he left, Littleton entered the cabin. "What did he want, Charlie?" Dion grunted.

"Just a business deal, Dion. Tell you about it when I've thought on it some."

★　★　★　★

Any sort of gathering was an enticement to the small ranchers and settlers, and a cabin raising was as much a social gathering as it was a utilitarian affair. Young Dale Browning and Carolyn Stone, therefore, found the future spot of their cabin filled up with people early one crisp October morning. As the pastor of the church, it was necessary for Amos to be at the affair, and he arrived with his family at the clearing in time for Winslow, Sid, and Smoky to help with the work.

There were over a hundred people congregated, some of them coming from as far away as thirty miles, and there was a holiday air about the gathering. Saddle horses and wagons were led to a nearby meadow, and men were soon notching and setting up the log walls of the cabin, while others with wedges and froes were riving out the cedar shakes to be used on the roof. One crew worked on the windows, arguing vociferously concerning slanting the frames for better protection against Indian attack. Another crew worked on the fireplace, which was a tricky affair. The man in charge of this task, Lowell Cox, spoke with authority. "You got no draw," he stated firmly, "and you got no cabin." He looked down at the clay gathered to set the stone and shook his head. "Wished I had some animal blood to mix with this clay."

The young couple themselves had little authority in the matter. Young Browning requested that the cabin face the creek, but he was overruled by several older heads who informed him that every cabin should face northeast.

The women worked on the food, the sound of their laughter and talk rising above the sounds of hammer and saw. Hope helped set the food out as the cabin grew near to a finish, each lady bringing her own favorite dishes—pickled peaches, huckleberry pie, blackberry pie, cider, fresh butter molded in pretty patterns, homemade cheese, summer sausage, Indian relish, cucumbers in cream and vinegar, and jellies, jams, and fruit butters.

Finally a fire was lighted, and they all crowded in to see if the chimney drew. A hearty cheer went up when it did. The bed was made, a rug was laid down, and a lamp placed on the table beside a Bible opened to the Psalms.

"Now," Amos said with a wide smile, "let's have the wedding." He stood bareheaded in the open yard and married the pair. Then he put his Bible away, and people gathered around to kiss the bride and wring the groom's hand.

Hope helped serve the food, then clean up the dishes. Finally the sound of a fiddle rose, and Mrs. Miller, a pretty red-haired woman of thirty-two, said, "Now's the time for frolic, Hope."

The fiddler was joined by two guitarists and one banjo player, and soon men and women were moving over the grass in a lively fashion. Dave Orr came and stood before her, tall and better dressed than his neighbors, saying, "Let me have this dance, Mrs. Malloy."

"Oh, I don't dance!"

Orr smiled and insisted. "Come now, I know you must." He led her to the circle, and soon Hope found herself enjoying the music. Dave Orr was a fine dancer, and so was Smoky Jacks, who claimed her next. The dance went on for two hours, but Hope withdrew after only a short time. She went over to sit down, watching the others. Cody was playing with several boys his age, and Zane was leaning against a tree.

Rosa had been chosen at once, and now she was laughing as Sid Kincaid spun her around. Hope rose and went to stand beside her brother, asking, "Are you too sore to dance, Zane?"

He turned toward her, and she saw the unhappiness in his eyes. "I don't want to dance."

"Why, you do so!" Hope said and pulled him to the edge of the grass. "Now, let's show these people how Arkansas people can dance!"

Zane moved somewhat awkwardly, but when the dance was over, Rosa came to him at once, saying, "Why, Zane Jenson! I'm put out with you. Now, you dance with me or I'll poke you in the ribs." Hope returned to her seat, noting that Zane was smiling.

"Would you take a chance on me, Hope?"

When Hope looked up, she saw Winslow waiting, a smile on his tanned face. He added, "I can't guarantee anything. Might step on your feet."

Hope wanted to refuse, for she was still not willing to trust herself to this man. But there was no way she could do that, so she rose and they began to dance. She said after a moment, "You've had lots of practice at this."

"A long time ago," he admitted. They moved gracefully

around the grass, and he was aware of her slim beauty.

When the dance was over, she said, "Dan, I want to talk to you." She walked away, and he followed her to the edge of the circle, then out to the meadow where the horses and wagons were tied. There was a glow in the west where the sun was sinking below the line of hills, and her smooth cheeks picked up a rosy tint as she turned to face him.

"Dan, I think you should go back to your own ranch," she said, speaking quickly as if it were a speech she had practiced. "Zane is better now, and we have Smoky to help. I don't want to impose on you, though I don't know how we'd have gotten along without you."

Winslow said quietly, "What's your real reason for wanting me to leave, Hope?"

"Why—that *is* my real reason!"

"First dishonest thing I've ever heard you say," Winslow answered almost roughly. "What you mean is, you're afraid of me."

Hope gasped, and her lips grew firm. "I am not!" she exclaimed. "What makes you say a thing like that?"

He gave her a long look, then said, "You're afraid of men. That's why you want me to leave."

Hope's face burned, and she turned to leave. But he grabbed her and was about to say something when a movement caught his eye. A man he'd never seen before had appeared and was walking straight toward them. When he drew close, he reached into his pocket and pulled out a piece of paper. "For you, Winslow," he said, then turned and walked away. Dan watched him with curious eyes as he mounted a horse, then rode away.

He looked at the note, then his eyes went back to the horseman. "Know who he is?" Dan asked.

"No. I've never seen him before." She was still angry, but the interruption had given her a chance to regain her composure. "Dan, let's not quarrel. I've had—bad luck with marriage. That's all it is. Don't be angry with me."

"No," he said gently. "I just hate to see you missing out on things."

"I've got a son to raise," she said quickly, her tone defensive. "And Pa isn't well."

He shook his head, but knew that arguing would not break

down the wall she had built around herself. "You'll have to face up to it someday, Hope. And I wish the best for you."

He turned to go, and she asked, "Was the note bad news?"

"Can't say. I'll have to go now, though." Then he walked away toward his horse. She stood watching him. The scene had disturbed her, and she wrestled with her thoughts until he stepped into the saddle and rode away. She started to go back to the dance, but a slight movement on the ground pulled her eyes down. A piece of paper was blowing over the grass, and she picked it up. It was a message printed in large letters with a blunt pencil: IF YOU WANT TO KNOW ABOUT YOUR PARTNER BE AT THE OLD INDIAN CAMP AT EIGHT TONIGHT. DON'T TELL ANYBODY—AND COME ALONE.

Hope looked quickly toward where Winslow was now a small figure on the horizon. She put the note in her pocket and went back to the dance, troubled by the message. *He doesn't need to go alone*, she thought. It occurred to her to tell Sid or Smoky about the note, but decided that she couldn't. Later that night, after they got home, she lay awake for hours listening for the sound of his horse—but it never came.

★　★　★　★

Everyone knew the Old Indian Camp, for it was a storied place. There were several mounds where one could pick up arrowheads and bits of pottery, and it had been one of the spots that Dan had visited with Cody on one of their hunting trips.

The site lay in the folds of the hills beside a large creek that meandered through the hills, then made its way across the flatland. Several men had tried to homestead the place, but Arrow had made it too unpleasant, so it was now used by hunters and punchers for night camps.

Dan made a quick trip, and when he pulled up beside the creek, was disappointed to find no one there. It had occurred to him that he might be walking into a trap, so he kept his eyes open and listened carefully. An owl hooted to his right, and something about the sound didn't seem normal. He dismounted and walked along the edge of the timber, and at that moment, a man called out, "That you, Winslow?"

Even as the voice struck him, a sudden explosion came from

across the creek, and a bullet smashed into the tree beside him. At once he drew and fired on the rifle flash, but he saw the shapes of several men appear. Little yellow and purple rosettes of muzzle light began to flash from their guns.

Winslow stepped backward, whirled, and raced toward his horse, but the barrage of fire was so heavy, he knew he would never make it. Ducking into the trees, he raced away, drawing fire. When he came to a small gully, he turned, threw two shots, then dropped into the gully. It was rough and lined with loose stones, but he ran as fast as he could, hoping to find safety in the darkness.

He heard someone yell from behind him, "He's headed that way!" and knew that if a man were in front of him, all he'd have to do was wait for a shot. The gully was no good, so he scrambled up the side, fell clumsily, and heard a yell to his right, then saw the flare of the man's gun.

He ducked and whirled, plunging into the thickets. The branches scratched his face, and he suddenly splashed into the creek—but just as he did, a bullet struck his right leg, feeling like a huge scythe, cutting him off his feet with one stroke and dropping him to his knees. He felt no pain, but shock ran through him as he rolled over. He heard the sound of crashing through the brush, and rolled over the slope into the creek itself. The water was cold, and the pain from his right leg hit him.

"Watch out!" someone was yelling. "He's doubled back on us!"

As Winslow settled into the water with just his head above the surface, two men ran by less than a yard away. He pulled himself along to a deeper spot where a huge cedar had fallen across the stream. The length of the tree spanned the creek, making a large pond, and undergrowth had sprung up around the upper section. Winslow pulled himself out of the water, dragging himself along until he was hidden by the bulk of the tree on one side and surrounded by saplings and vines on the other. The sounds grew fainter and fainter, but the pain in his leg was a searing fire.

He lay there gritting his teeth against the waves of pain, then when it grew even worse, dropped into a black pit where there was no sound and no light and no pain.

PART FOUR

WAR IN THE VALLEY

★ ★ ★ ★

CHAPTER NINETEEN

A CRY IN THE NIGHT

★   ★   ★   ★

Overhead the stars glittered like cold frozen points of light, and a night breeze cooled by the hills reached into Winslow's hiding place. The cold air had brought him back to consciousness, and he stayed awake for hours, his leg stiffening and becoming increasingly more painful. At times the silence would close in, so that he could hear only muffled sounds of water flowing over stones and occasionally a lonely coyote's anthem to the night.

He was lying flat on his back on the broken stems of reeds, with stones punching his flesh, but the cold and the pain that shot through his leg when he moved—or even when he didn't—made all other discomforts seem slight. He thought once of trying to get his boots off, but when he bent over and pulled at his right foot, the pain hit him like a sharp knife, and he gave up.

Not going to get dry, anyway, he thought, and lay back to endure the rest of the night. Yet even that was not certain, for the voices of men and the movement of horses came to him more than once as the night passed. Once he heard a voice not more then twenty-five feet away say, "Hey, Dion—look around that big cedar. He could've crawled in there—!"

Dan recognized the voice of Charlie Littleton, but he had no time to think of that, for he heard a horse plunging into the creek.

He pressed backward into the cedar, rolling over until his body was wedged beneath the body of the tree and the damp earth. He could do no more, and when he saw by the light of the moon the reeds and willows part and the forelegs of a horse appear, he thought it was over.

But the horse moved on, passing so close that Dan could almost have touched it if he had stretched out. He thought of a time in Virginia, at Spotsylvania, when he had been pinned down by Union sharpshooters in thin cover. The sun had baked him dry, almost cooked him, and he could see the muzzles blaze as his foes took their shots. He could not expose even a hand. Night had come then, and he had crawled off. He remembered the tiny creek he'd found, no more than a foot or so across, and foul with the passage of men and horses, yet that water had been as sweet as any he'd ever known as he'd lapped it like a dog.

Then, heat and drought had been the enemy; now it was damp and cold, and he knew that even when morning came, his adversaries would be watching both sides of the stream. The night breeze was cut off by the cedar tree, and the absence of the wind gave the sensation of warmth. He knew this was an illusion, that the cold was sapping his strength as much as the loss of blood. At Fredericksburg the wounded had been left on a field for two days, neither side willing to call a truce so that they could be moved. Some of the members of Dan's own company had died not of their wounds, which need not have been fatal, but of the cold and lack of care.

He knew well that he might die under the cedar, for there was no hope that those who sought him would show mercy. The deadly ambush had almost succeeded, and those who prowled all about him would kill him on sight.

Time moved on, and he began to tremble with the cold. At first he could will himself not to shake, but soon that ability passed, and his body moved involuntarily, only mildly at first, but later with a series of violent spasms that almost made him groan aloud as his leg was stirred.

Finally he dropped off again into a fitful coma—not sleep, but more a state of unconsciousness such as comes to the very ill. And in that sleep, dreams came, fragments from his past that seemed to touch him with ghostly fingers as they brushed across his mind. He heard again the muted echoes of distant guns swelling into a furious storm, such as he had not heard since the war, and after that the rattle of musket fire, much like the snapping of thousands of dry sticks, just as he had heard it at Antietam and Gettysburg and dozens of other bloody fields.

Along with the sounds, he seemed to see those who had lain in shallow graves for a decade—men he had marched with, shared the comradeship of battle with. The face of Billy Simms—who had always been able to find food—came to him, as clear as a daguerreotype! A thin, cheerful face with a pair of bright blue eyes and a wide grin. Billy—who fought in every major battle in Virginia, from Manassas to the end—who had died of a musket ball in the stomach on the last retreat from Richmond to Appomattox.

Dan moaned faintly, trying to speak to the memory of a friend long dead, but could not. Other faces—long forgotten and blurred by time—floated by, and finally faded.

Then other dreams came, mostly of his boyhood and young manhood. His father, Sky Winslow, as he had appeared the day when Dan had killed his first buck. His mother, Rebekah, her face rapt as she sang in church, and in his dream he could almost feel her warmth as he had pressed against her when he was very young, sitting on the hard wooden pew as Reverend Sanderson preached. This dream was the most vivid of all, for he could smell the polish on the floor and hear the rustle of pages as his mother used the hymnbook. Amazingly enough, the voice of Reverend Sanderson came to Dan as he lay under the tree, and the sermon he had heard twenty-five years ago came back. Not all of it, but fragments that came to him as though filtered through some sort of fragile covering: "Whosoever liveth and believeth in me shall never die!" This he heard many times, not only in the high tenor voice of Reverend Sanderson, but in the warm voice of his mother, for it was a favorite of hers.

Whosoever liveth and believeth in me shall never die.

As the words came to him, Winslow dreamed that he was in some sort of big open field, and that he was not alone. Many, many people were with him, young and old—and of every race, it seemed. At one end of the field was a tremendous canyon, so deep that the bottom of it could not be seen but lay wreathed in dark wisps of clouds, and thunder rolled distantly from the depths.

Many of the people moved to the edge of the field, and when they came to the lip of the canyon, instead of stopping—they stepped right off. And as they did, they seemed for the first time to become aware of the great gulf and began to scream as they fell, their terrible screams fading as they plunged into the darkness that swallowed them up.

Winslow saw others in the crowd who seemed to become aware of the danger, and who struggled to turn back, or twist aside. For some this awareness lasted only for a brief time—and then they joined the others moving blindly toward the abyss and plunged off with them.

Others seemed totally aware of their danger, and some of them were attempting to persuade others to avoid the edge of the field and the dark chasm beneath, but these were for the most part ignored by the hordes milling around them.

And then over the voices of those in the field came one loud, clear voice like a trumpet that said, "He that liveth and believeth on me shall never die." Many in the field seemed to respond to the trumpet-voice, to become aware of the terrible danger at the end of the field.

The dream faded, but over and over Dan Winslow heard the voice, saying, "He that liveth and believeth on me shall never die."

Winslow came awake—not all at once, but in the manner of a man coming out of the depths of the sea into the light. Out of an ebony darkness to just a few feeble bursts of light; then his eyes opened to see that morning had come. He tried to roll over to get from beneath the log into the sun, but at once it felt as though someone had thrust a white-hot sword through his thigh. He fell back, closing his eyes, sick with the pain of it. Finally he moved very slowly, coming out into the sun, and the touch of it warmed him a little.

His throat and lips were dry, and it took him twenty minutes to drag himself to the edge of the stream, where he drank deeply of the cold water. There was no sound except a bird singing, and he lay still, letting the warm sun begin to dry his clothes and drive the chill away. Finally, he took a grip on a thick sapling and pulled himself upright. The effort brought the pain in his leg alive, and he looked down to see that he had caused the bleeding to start again. But he saw also that the bullet had passed through the fleshy part of his thigh on the outside. The knowledge that the bullet was not imbedded brought some relief.

Gritting his teeth, he ignored the pain, and when he looked around, saw no one. He thought of moving to drier ground, but if he did, anyone searching for him would see his trail—and besides, he knew he would eventually have to drag himself back to the creek for water.

Carefully he lay down again, rolling over to let the sun dry his clothing completely. By late morning, he was dry, all except his feet.

Got to be dry or I'll freeze tonight.

He pulled his left boot off with little trouble, removed his sock and wrung it out, placing it in the sun to dry. The right boot took half an hour, and when it was finally off, his face was pale with the agony of the effort. But by noon, the socks were dried, though the inside of the boots were still damp. *Better let the sun dry the inside*, he thought, and lay back to rest.

He had no intention of sleeping, but suddenly found himself waking up with a sharp jerking motion. He heard the sound of hoofbeats, and he dragged himself as quickly as he could back to the hiding place beneath the cedar tree. Shoving himself under, he could see little, but the sound of voices floated to him, though so far away that he could not make out the words.

A thought occurred to him that it might be a friend looking for him—but he had told nobody where he was going. Then he considered the possibility that it might be some hunters or fishermen rather than his killers returning.

Got to take a chance, he thought, and he noticed as he carefully stood up, holding the slick side of the cedar, that his thoughts and movement were slower. Carefully he came upright, putting all his weight on his left leg and holding on to a naked branch with a bend like an elbow. The weeds and undergrowth were chest high. He could see three men on horseback, about fifty yards downstream.

But one glance was all he needed, for one of those men was

Ash Caudill, and the other two were the Littleton brothers, Charlie and Dion. At once he lowered himself to the ground, despair closing in on him. They moved away downstream, but an hour later they came back, this time so close that he could hear part of their conversation.

" . . . got to be around here someplace! He's not a bird, Charlie!" The speaker was Ash Caudill, and there was anger in his voice.

Charlie Littleton answered him, and he, too, spoke sharply. "He got away into the timber, Ash. No place else for him to go."

"Without a horse? We'd have found him long ago. He's still here, I tell you!"

Dion's voice came then: "He ain't here, so he had to move up the creek or down. He just got farther away than we looked, that's all."

Caudill shouted, "Then send men both ways! You two botched this thing, and it's up to you to finish it!"

They moved away, and Winslow sat down and tried to think. He was basically a man of action, and inactivity made him restless. But now there was absolutely nothing he could do. All afternoon he waited, once hearing the sound of men calling, but when one of them said, "We ain't found him downstream—" he knew it was his enemies.

Finally the sun sank, cooling the air. The night, he thought, would be colder, though he couldn't be sure. He got a drink, then moved back under the cedar tree, and soon the darkness was complete.

He could not sleep and made up his mind that at dawn he would have to move, to try to find help. *Rather go down trying than to snuff out like a dying animal in a hole*, he thought grimly.

But after a fitful nap, he awoke feeling hot—which meant fever. He felt clammy and his face was flushed. He grew thirsty and went for a drink, but the cold water made him sick, giving him stomach cramps. He knew he needed warmth and food, for the cold and the wound were sucking his vitality. Crawling back to the log was much more difficult, so much so that he had to rest on the way, and when he got there, he fell asleep at once.

He had been right about the temperature, for a cold breeze swept down from the hills that night, chilling the air. The feverish heat of his body ebbed, and he found himself awake again and shivering with the cold. He drew his body into a ball but was helpless against the elements. The pain in his leg was not so savage, but he knew that he could not travel at dawn, not more than a few yards.

He lay there, swept by trembling spasms so fierce that they knotted his muscles. He tried to think but was so weak that his mind began to wander. The stars were hidden for it was a cloudy night, with a hint of rain in the air, and the blackness seemed to press down on him like a thick blanket.

He slept fitfully, but at some time before there was even a trace of dawn in the sky, he awoke, his head clear, though he was miserable from cold and hunger. For what seemed like an hour, he lay there, the cold clamping him like iron bands, convinced that he was going to die.

It was not the first time this had happened to him. Both during the war and later in the range wars, there had been occasions when death had seemed inevitable. He had always handled it by putting the significance of it out of his mind, but somehow this time his usual reaction was not possible. He had been a brave man, his courage proverbial among his fellows, but now as he lay helpless in the thick darkness, he felt the cold taste of fear.

Not of death, for he was not afraid of dying. But the dream he had had was clear in his mind, and he thought of it with dread. He had no doubt about what it meant. Not that he put much stock in dreams—but this one had been the clearest one he'd ever had.

It was not so much death, but what happens to a man *after* death—that was the thing that began to rise in him.

And he could not escape what he had heard about that destiny since his childhood. For years he had buried the knowledge that all men and women must go from this life to another. He had never had anything but contempt for atheists, for it seemed folly to him to deny that man was different from beasts.

He thought much of his parents, how they faced any and all difficulties with peace, and he knew that their serenity was—as they confessed—due to their faith in Jesus Christ. And as soon as he thought of Jesus, he was suddenly filled with an overwhelming sense of his own weakness. The very thought of Jesus brought a sudden fear—and a hope just as abrupt.

But he could not help but think of the years of running from God, nor of the sin that had controlled him during that time. Shame filled him, as it had never done before, and he knew that the shaking of his body was not just from the fever but from the sobs that rose in him.

For a long time he lay there, filled with despair as he thought of his wasted life. He longed to cry out to God, but could not. *What can I do, now that I'm about to die? A man can't ignore God all his life and then go whimpering for mercy when it's too late for him to do anything for God.*

Then he was startled, for he remembered his mother singing:

> Forbid it, Lord, that I should boast,
> Save in the death of Christ, my God;
> All the vain things that charm me most—
> I sacrifice them to his blood.

He thought about those words, and the meaning came to him with a burst of clarity. "Why, a man can't *do* anything! It's all got to be of God!"

And then he was flooded with scriptures he had heard—and thought he had forgotten—all speaking of God's grace. "For by grace are ye saved through faith . . ."; "Not by works of righteousness which we have done, but according to his mercy hath he saved us." These and others came to him, and then as in his dream, he seemed to hear the words:

"Whosoever liveth and believeth in me shall never die."

The night was still a stygian blackness, and the pain was ripping at him. There was no hope for survival as he lay there— but somehow he slowly came to a point when he did the one thing he'd fled from for years.

"Oh, God!" he whispered, and he felt that he was speaking to a deaf heaven, for his spirit was crushed, and hope of living had fled. "I've run from you all my life. Now I'm dying, and it seems like a cowardly thing to do—but I'm asking you to help me. I don't have any right to call on you, but I call anyway. Give me what my mother and father have! Forgive me for my sins— and in the name of Jesus Christ, save me—!"

In the blackness of the night he cried out with a fervor that shook him. He was not conscious of time but continued to pray and to seek God. Finally he grew quiet, and there seemed to be nothing.

And yet there was in Winslow a growing consciousness that something was very *different*. He could not explain it, not even to himself. He was still sick and dying—but the deadly *pressure* that had been pulling him down was gone.

He lay there, only half-awake, conscious that the sun was coming up. A light was growing in the east, and as he watched, he suddenly understood that what had changed was his spirit— a guilt had been lifted that he had vaguely known was there. Now he knew that he had been struggling with it for years, but suddenly it was gone!

Reaching up, he touched his face, brushing his hands across his eyes. *I feel all clean!* he thought with wonder. *It's all gone—all the weight!* He began to thank God, not that he was out of danger, but that no matter what happened, he had found a peace that he knew would never leave.

As the light grew, the fever came back. He started to tremble as the chills returned, and as he began to slip away, he was aware that someone was coming. He thought he heard someone calling his name—and just before he lost consciousness, he called out, his voice reedy and frail: "I'm here!" and then he knew no more.

CHAPTER TWENTY

A DESPERATE SEARCH

★　★　★　★

Hope rarely dreamed, and even when she did, she usually never remembered what she dreamed. However, shortly before dawn, she awoke with a start, her body lunging with an abrupt jerking motion, and she sat bolt upright. She even cried out, an involuntary reaction to the fear that came to her in the darkness.

She stared around in confusion, somehow convinced that someone had called out to her, and the first thought that came to her was: *The house is on fire!* However, there was no other sound, and as she peered through the darkness, she saw nothing. She twisted to look out the window, but the night was very dark, and all she could see was the vague outline of the barn.

And then the dream came flooding back—though it was not a visual thing as much as a sound. She seemed to see herself, asleep in the bed, as though she were overhead looking down. Then she remembered that she had heard a voice calling her name—*Hope! Hope!*—and she saw herself beginning to twist and writhe on the bed. Then the vision faded, and she knew that she was lying on her bed, and the voice was calling, more urgently than before. In the dream she began to try to sit up, to move, to open her eyes, but it was as though she were frozen, for she lay there helpless. The voice came again, calling her name, and for one moment, she had a fleeting impression of Dan Winslow's face. She seemed to see it vaguely, and the sight of it frightened her, for he was pale, his eyes glassy, and his lips twisted with either pain or fear. He seemed to focus his eyes on her and then cried out, *Hope—Hope, come and help me!*

It was fleeting, but the intensity of it drove sleep from her, and she rose and lit the lamp. The room was cold, and she shivered as she began to dress. When she was dressed, she went to the kitchen, where she rekindled the fire in the cookstove. She fixed coffee, then sat down at the table and tried to shake off the unpleasant sensation that the fragment of the dream had brought.

For thirty minutes she sat there, then Amos came in, his eyes bleary from sleep. He was in pain, Hope saw, but he would never mention it. "You're up early," he observed.

Hope said, "Sit down. I'll fix breakfast." Getting up from the table, she began making breakfast while he sat there, listening to him as he spoke occasionally. When the meal was ready, she sat down but was unable to eat, for the dream had disturbed her.

Finally, she said, "Pa, I had a strange kind of dream—" She related it, then asked, "Do you think dreams mean anything?"

Amos shrugged his thin shoulders. "Not usually—but sometimes I think God uses them. Like when He wanted to tell Mary and Joseph what the child that was coming meant."

"Oh, this wasn't anything like that!"

"No, I guess not." Amos thought for a while, then said, "In one way, I guess it's natural you'd think of Dan, since he's been so much a part of our lives. And as for dreaming that he's in trouble—why, that's generally true. He's had his share of it, losing his partner and his herd."

Hope hesitated, then reached into her shirt pocket. Drawing out the piece of paper that Winslow had dropped, she passed it to her father. "I guess this is why I'm worried. A man gave it to Dan at the cabin raising. He didn't show it to me, but it fell out of his pocket, and I found it after he left." She bit her lower lip nervously, then added, "He didn't come home—hasn't come home yet, Pa."

Amos slowly handed her the note back, his eyes troubled. "That's strange—but he could have gone to his own place. He does that sometimes."

"I guess he probably did." Hope gave a slight laugh, then said, "I'm getting to be a regular worrywart!" She rose and began clearing the table and said no more about Winslow.

At nine o'clock, Gus Miller rode into the yard, but did not dismount. When Hope and Amos went out to greet him, he nodded, "Howdy, Parson—Hope," he said. "You know that new family that moved in north of me?"

"The Amboys?" Amos asked. "Sure, Gus."

"Well, they had a fire last night. They all got out, but lost everything."

"What a shame!" Hope cried at once. "Where will they live?"

"There's a cabin about three miles down from their place— not much, but it'll keep the rain out until we can do something better. But like I said, they lost everything. I'm riding around to see if we can't get them some food and clothes—and maybe some bedding."

"I'll take some food and blankets," Hope said at once.

"Fine! I'll stop at the Coxes and the Shultzes."

As soon as Miller rode away, Hope began to gather some food. "I'd better go along," Amos said.

"No, Pa, you stay here," Hope said, knowing he was unfit for the trip. "You help Ozzie and take care of Zane. But it may be too late for me to drive back. I may stay over and come back tomorrow."

An hour later, she left in the wagon, with food and blankets packed in the bed. It was a long way, but when tragedy came to anyone, there was no question as to what to do. They were dependent on one another, and Hope knew that others would be coming to the aid of the distressed family. It was a good feeling to know that they had ties, and that none of them were alone.

She drove along the base of the plain, the hills rising to her left, and by two o'clock had made good enough time that she knew she could make the Amboy place well before dark. But when she passed through the timberline into a country broken from time to time by draws and canyons, she saw dust rising in front of her and recognized that a horseman was coming toward her.

She watched him carefully, pulling the rifle up beside her on the seat, and as he drew near, she saw that it was Ash Caudill. When he called out, she pulled the team to a halt, and he rode up within a few feet of her. His clothing was stained with dust, and fatigue had etched lines in his smooth face. "Seen anybody back that way, Mrs. Malloy?" he asked, and there was a tense quality to his voice that made her suspicious.

"No. Who are you looking for?"

"Oh, just thought you might have seen some of my hands. We've been combing these draws for strays." He studied her from under the cover of his hat brim, his eyes driving at her with a force that was unsettling. "You're a long way from your place," he commented. "Going to be dark soon."

"Yes. But I'll be at the Amboy place before then." She had a sudden uneasy feeling but had no intention of letting Caudill know it. Calmly, she explained, "Their house burned down yesterday. I'm taking them some food and blankets."

Her words seemed to satisfy him, for he touched his hat and said, "Don't get caught out in these draws after dark. Not safe." Then he pulled his horse's head around and rode off abruptly.

Hope slapped the reins and called out, "Hup, Babe— Butcher!" and the horses obediently began to move ahead. The encounter with Caudill disturbed Hope, and as she moved along the road, which was now following the edge of a shallow canyon, she considered what his agitated state might mean.

She had no trust in the man, and almost at once she thought: *He came from the direction of the Old Indian Camp.* And that thought brought back the memory of the dream that had awakened her. She knew the enmity that lay between Caudill and Winslow and slowly a plan began to take shape. It was born out of a vague uneasiness, for she was still unhappy that Dan had not returned. Now to see Ash Caudill riding out of that same location where Dan had been told to rendezvous with an unknown man—it seemed wrong, somehow, and her alarm grew steadily. Soon, she nodded, saying out loud, "I'll have to have a look at that place."

She turned the team to the right and slapped them with the reins, bringing them to a fast trot. Two hours later, the sun was far down in the sky, sending shadows creeping over the bluffs that bordered the river where she turned the wagon northward. As she drew near, she thought she heard someone and stopped the team to listen. At first she heard nothing, but then from up ahead, she heard the sound of a voice, faint and dim but growing stronger. Finally the sound of horses approaching came to her. She quickly pulled hard on the reins, bringing the team around and directing them off the road into the timber. She leaped off the seat, tied the team, then picked up the rifle and moved back to the road. She stopped behind a large tree, and soon two riders came into sight. They were, she saw, looking down at the road, and more than once one of them would leave the road and go to ride along the banks of the stream, while the other would search the timber. One of these came within thirty feet of the spot where Hope stood rigidly behind the tree, but then he moved back to the road.

"Nothin' here—" one of them said, his voice barely audible to Hope. "We'll ride on to where the road turns, then make a sweep on the other side of the creek—"

Hope waited until the two disappeared, then went back to the wagon. She stood there, uncertain and confused, for it would soon be dark, and she had no idea what was happening. Finally she spoke aloud, "They're hunting for him—and he's got to be somewhere around here."

She got into the wagon, turned the team around, and decided that the two she had seen were the only riders she might encounter. When she got to the site where the old ruins of an Indian lodge lay, she stopped the team and dismounted. Pulling the rifle from the seat, she walked toward the lodge. It was only a skeleton of wooden poles now, and she gave it scarcely a glance. Fifty feet beyond the ruins, the stream gurgled over smooth stones that made up its bed. She paused at the brink, looking both directions, then turned to her left. When she had gone fifty feet, she lifted her voice and called, "Dan—are you here?"

Hearing no answer, she walked almost a quarter of a mile, calling as she went. If there were other men, they would hear her and come, but she knew of nothing else to do.

Finally she turned and retraced her steps, then moved downstream. She called his name often, sometimes pausing to listen, but she only heard the sibilant murmur of the water. When she had gone for some distance, she stopped, and a feeling of helplessness came over her. *I could walk this stream for hours—and he may be ten miles from here.*

She stood there, wondering if she should return, for by now the dusky shadows in the trees were blotting out the last dim rays of the sun. She had no idea when the men might return, and in desperation she prayed, "Oh, God—help me find him!"

For a few seconds she stood there, once almost turning to go back to the team, but she decided to look down the stream once more, seeing in the dim light a bend ahead. *I'll go as far as that bend—and then I'll have to go back.*

She stumbled along the edge of the stream, for the underbrush had grown thicker, and called Dan's name as she moved toward the bend. When she reached the curve of the bank, she saw a huge old tree that had fallen across the stream. By the time she reached it, her face was scratched by briars that she had not seen in the waning light. She stepped off into a boggy hole, soaking her feet, and finally stopped, the dark bulk of the tree barring her way.

"Dan!" she called out, desperation in her voice. "Dan—can you hear me?"

Again she waited, hearing only the whisper of the water. The wind was beginning to rise, making a keening noise as it moved across the reeds that lined the banks.

"Dan!" she cried, as loudly as she could. "Please—answer me!"

Her voice made a slight echo over the water, and she stood absolutely still, listening so hard she gritted her teeth with the effort.

And then—she heard it!

Only a faint sound, or cry, but she knew it was a voice, and she cried out, "Dan—where are you?"

"Over here—"

The voice came from her left. Whirling, she stumbled through the shallow water, almost falling. When she had gone a few feet, she paused and looked around, straining her eyes in the darkness. "Where are you?"

"Over here—by the log—"

This time the voice was close enough for her to pinpoint, and she moved toward it, feeling her way along the log. She struggled through a thick clump of reeds clustered by the log—and then as she peered downward, she saw Dan lying almost hidden by the bulk of the fallen cedar.

"Dan!" she cried, falling down beside him. There was only enough light to see his face, and as she knelt next to him, pulling his head up and cradling it in her arms, Hope saw that his worn features looked exactly as they had looked in her dream!

CHAPTER TWENTY-ONE

HONOR IN THE DUST

★ ★ ★ ★

When Ash Caudill had encountered Hope south of the Old Indian Camp, he had just left the Littletons and their crew with a warning: "Don't leave until you're sure of Winslow. That's your end of the bargain."

"Where you headed, Ash?" Charlie Littleton had asked.

Ash had answered, "I'm going to get my crew and put the run on these sodbusters. Without Winslow to hold them together, they'll run like rabbits!"

Caudill had ridden directly to Arrow after leaving Hope, arriving at the ranch just as darkness was beginning to close in. His horse was exhausted, and he threw the reins to Shorty Ellis, saying, "Shorty, tell the boys to get to bed early. We'll be pulling out in the morning."

"What's up, Ash?"

Caudill shook his head, saying only, "We'll leave at sunup— and don't forget to bring your guns."

He left Shorty staring after him, going directly to his room— a separate section of the bunkhouse—where he washed and changed clothes. Leaving his room, Ash crossed the yard and stepped up on the porch of the main house, where Lionel, Silas Head's body servant, was standing. "Where's Mr. Head, Lionel?" he asked.

"Him and Miss Head, they eatin' supper, Mister Ash."

Caudill nodded, walked into the house and down the wide hall that led to the dining room. He entered and found Head and Diane seated at the heavy oak table.

"Come in, Ash," Head said. Nodding to the black maid, he added, "Miranda, bring an extra plate and some silverware." He motioned to a chair, "Sit down—sit down."

Diane examined him, noting the lines of fatigue on his face. "You've been gone two days, Ash."

"Had some chores to do," Caudill said. He took the plate that the maid brought, helped himself to the beef and potatoes, then said, "I'll be taking the crew out tomorrow."

Head stared at him, a question in his eyes. "What's going on? You stay gone for two days, ride in and tell me you're leaving with the crew. I'd like a little more information."

Ash had been cutting the roast beef, but now he looked up, and both Head and Diane saw a smile on his lips. The foreman had not smiled since before the fight in the Palace, but now he seemed to be different. His slate-gray eyes were bright, though he was obviously tired. He was a closed man, keeping his own counsel, and since what he did was always good for Arrow, Head let him have his own way in most things. Lately, however, he had been short with Caudill because of his anger over Winslow. No man could make a laughingstock of Silas Head and get away with it.

"It's time to move some people," Caudill said. "There's been four or five new families move onto our graze in the last few weeks. They can't stay, and some of the others who've been crowding us will have to leave."

Diane asked, "Why the rush?" There was a directness in the glance she put on Caudill, as if she were weighing the qualities that lay beneath the surface of the foreman's smooth exterior. She was, in some respects, like her father, having his intense drive and unwillingness to fail at anything. She asked with curiosity, "You've been doing nothing since that scene in the Palace. What's changed your mind?"

Caudill's cheeks reddened at the reference to the fight, but he said at once, "I don't mind losing a battle now and then, Diane—not as long as I win the war." His eyes narrowed, and he shrugged his muscular shoulders. "I know what you've both been thinking since that fracas. That I couldn't handle the job."

Silas nodded his massive head in agreement. "In that, you're right. It takes a strong man to handle Arrow's crew, and you lost something when Winslow put you down. And it's not just Diane and me who've been wondering," he added. "The whole valley's been waiting for you to take him on."

"They don't have to wait anymore."

Caudill's blunt statement caught both Silas and his daughter by surprise. "What does that mean?" Head demanded.

Caudill's eyes gleamed, and he said, "Don't worry about Winslow. He won't give us any more trouble."

"Did you face him down?" Head asked at once.

There was a slight hesitation in Caudill's answer, which both Head and Diane noted. "He's out of it—take my word on it."

"It would have been better if you'd let the valley see you face him, Ash," Diane said thoughtfully.

"I'm not interested in any of those fool shoot-outs you read about in the dime novels," Caudill shook his head. "Some men spend a lot of time practicing their draw. They get good at it, and I expect that Winslow has practiced until he's a fraction of a second quicker getting a gun out of his holster than most men. Why should I risk everything on a thing like that?"

"Maybe because in this country men get measured by things like that," Head said thoughtfully. He was not entirely pleased with his foreman but could not put his feelings into words, though he tried. "I spent my life building up this ranch, and I did some things I'm not proud of." He paused, his thoughts going back, and a heaviness came to his features. "But one thing I never did was to dodge a man I had trouble with. I met him straight on, no dodging around!"

Caudill felt Head's disapproval but refused to argue, saying only, "Times have changed, I think. This isn't just one man against another. It's a question of whether this will be open cattle range or broke up into little farms surrounded by wire fences."

Head could not escape the logic of Caudill's words, but he left the table soon afterward, saying, "Come and talk after you get the job done."

When he was gone, Caudill stared down at the food, but

found that he had lost his appetite. Shoving his chair back, he said suddenly, "Let's go out on the porch."

Diane rose and walked beside him. An eight-foot porch wrapped around three sides of the house, bordered by a low bannister. Caudill and Diane stopped, and he turned to face her. It was almost completely dark now, and he leaned forward to see her more clearly in the light that shone through the parlor window. The sound of men's voices carried from the bunkhouse, and one of the hands was playing a guitar.

"Do you agree with your father?"

"Do you mean about facing Winslow?"

"Yes. He thinks I'm afraid."

Diane's face was smooth, but there was doubt in her eyes. "Oh, Ash, I don't know!" she said, agitation in her voice. "You've faced men before. I've never questioned your courage."

"But now you do, I think." Caudill stood there, his lips drawn tightly together, his shoulders suddenly tense. "If I'd known you felt this way, I'd have done it," he admitted suddenly. Then he slapped his fist into his palm, adding in an angry voice, "Winslow's a tough one, but so am I, Diane. And I'm not afraid of him. It would be close, matching draws with Dan, but I was never afraid of getting killed."

"What stopped you, then?" Diane asked.

"You did." Ash put his hands on her shoulders, gripping them hard. His words shocked her, he saw, and he added, "I've wanted you for a long time, Diane. You don't know how much! I've stayed here because of you, and I've thought of nothing but marrying you for years! Now if I faced Winslow and lost—I'd lose you forever. That's what made me draw back, and I was wrong!"

"It's not just for my sake you've stayed on," Diane said. "You want Arrow."

Caudill stared at her, then said, "You're tied to Arrow, Diane, just like your father. I've always known you'd never leave here. But if you think that, just agree to marry me. I'll ride away from Arrow with you, and we'll start someplace else." He paused, then smiled as she blinked at his offer. "You see? You can't do it, can you?"

Diane Head was an honest young woman, so she said at

once, "No, I don't want to leave this place. I want to marry here, raise my family here, and be buried here."

"Sure, I know, Diane." Caudill put his arms around her, drew her close, and kissed her. There was a hunger in his kiss, and she stayed with him, enjoying the response that came to her.

Finally she drew back, and her eyes were soft. "I want you, Ash, but I'll be honest. I can put up with a lot from a husband, but he's got to be strong. I want the man I marry to be able to hold this place together."

It was a promise, Caudill understood, and he felt a thrill of triumph. He didn't try to kiss her again but said, "We'll talk about this in a few days, Diane. Then you'll be able to judge if I can be the man you want."

Diane reached out and ran her hand down his arm, then said with a slow smile, "All right, Ash—we'll have another talk."

★ ★ ★ ★

Gus Miller was inside his barn, working alone at his forge. The sound of his hammer on the anvil drowned out the sound of the approach of Arrow's crew. The first he knew of their coming was when he turned to plunge a horseshoe into the steel bucket of water. Even as it hissed, emitting a small cloud of steam, he looked up to find Ash Caudill and Jack Hines facing him.

The sight of them sent a shock along his nerves, but he concealed it well enough. Placing the tongs on a bench, he turned to face them, saying, "Hello, Caudill. Didn't hear you ride up."

Caudill grinned slightly. "Careless of you, Gus. Should make you realize how hard it is to keep yourself safe."

Miller studied the pair, thinking of his gun that was hanging from a nail on the wall. His glance touched it, and Ash, following his gaze, ceased grinning. "It ever occur to you, Gus, how a man can get killed real easy?"

"It occurs to me now," Miller said, not taking his eyes off the pair. "What's on your mind, Caudill?"

"I've warned you before to keep your stock off our graze," Caudill said. His eyes grew cold, and he said, "I've come to see you do it."

"Not your graze," Miller said. "It's public land, and I was

using it before you and Head decided you wanted it."

Caudill said in a wicked tone, "Miller, I'm not going to argue. Step outside."

"What for?" Miller asked warily.

"Just do it."

Having no choice, Gus Miller walked through the door. He saw at least fifteen riders, all armed, and he turned to face Caudill who said, "We'll be back in two days, Miller. If your cows aren't gone, we'll cut them down."

"We'll cut you down, too, Gus," Jack Hines put in. "I say we might as well do it now, Ash."

"No, Gus isn't stupid," Caudill said. He went to his horse, waited until Hines was mounted, then nodded to Miller. "Two days, Gus."

The crew rode out, and Miller, tough as he was, drew a hand that was not quite steady across his brow. "Now that was a close call, Gus, old boy!"

★　★　★　★

Lowell Cox was digging a posthole when the Arrow crew arrived at his place. At once he put the post-hole digger down and turned to face the riders. He made a slightly ridiculous figure, balding and fat, dressed in a faded pair of overalls. He watched as the horsemen pulled up and turned to Caudill, who said, "Luke, cut that fence."

Luke Mott, a thin rider with a hatchet face, pulled a pair of wire cutters from his saddlebags and dismounted. He walked to the fence that surrounded the spring and snipped the wires. A *pinging* noise signaled each cut, and the barbed wire recoiled violently.

"Now—the rest of them," Caudill commanded, and Mott went to cut the fences that held Cox's three milk cows.

He drove them out by waving his hat and shouting, "Git outta here!" then returned to his horse, a grin on his thin lips.

"Sodbuster," Ash said harshly. "Be off this place by the end of the week."

Cox's round face grew red, but he held his temper. He was the mildest of men, although in his youth he had gained scars by a streak of impulsiveness. Now after a lifetime of trouble, including a war, he was in better control of himself.

"This is my place," he remarked. "You can cut my fences, but I'll put them up again."

Ash drew his gun with a practiced ease and put a bullet through the head of one of the brown milking cows. The cow's head rocked with the impact, and she took one or two faltering steps, falling dead without a whimper.

The wickedness—and efficiency—of Caudill's attack made Cox's lips draw together into a thin line. When Ash saw that the fat man didn't intend to speak, he holstered the gun, saying, "If you're not gone in a week, Cox, I'll kill every animal and burn your house to the ground."

Cox watched silently as Caudill pulled his horse around and led the crew away. Then he turned to his wife, who came from the house, her face pale.

"What are we going to do, Lowell?" she asked quietly.

Cox stared at the dead cow, then said evenly, "I'll butcher the cow and fix the fences, Lorene. Then we'll go see how bad the others are hit."

"The others?"

Cox stared at the dust raised by Arrow's crew. "They'll all be having a visit from those fellows. We'll get together and decide what to do."

★ ★ ★ ★

"We've hit every two-bit spread in the valley, Ash," Jack Hines complained. He lifted himself in the saddle, stretched, and then spat on the ground. He was tired, as were the others, most of whom had dismounted and were looking to Caudill for the signal to head for the ranch. They had been riding hard, covering the valley from one end to the other, and now were hungry and tired.

"Just one more stop," Caudill said grimly. "I know what these people will do, and I want to get them all into one place so we can show them what to expect."

"How you gonna do that?" Luke Mott demanded. "They're too scared to do anything now." He laughed crudely, his catfish mouth drawn wide into a grin. "I thought that old lady Shultz was gonna faint when we shot up her settin' hens!"

"They're scared," Caudill admitted, "but they'll all get together to try to figure out how they can hang on."

"Get together where?" Hines asked.

"They've always run to that preacher's house—Amos Jenson. They figure that Winslow's there, so they'll all be there. Come on, we'll pay them a visit."

Two hours later, they pulled up on top of the hill that overlooked Anchor, and Caudill grunted with satisfaction. "I was right. Look at all the wagons and horses. They're all inside. Let's go."

"Want to shoot 'em up a little, Ash?" Jack Hines asked.

"Not unless some of them get brave." Ash spurred his horse, and the rest of them followed him down the hill.

Inside the house, it was Ozzie Og who heard them first. He rose and went to the window, looked out, then said sourly, "Well, here they come!"

"Arrow crew?" Dave Orr asked in alarm.

"It ain't Santa and his little helpers," Og replied.

He picked up a rifle and started for the door, but was stopped by Amos, who said, "Leave the rifle here, Ozzie."

They all stared at Amos, alarm on every face. They had done exactly what Caudill had expected, come to Anchor as if at a signal. They had arrived one by one, all of them expecting to find Winslow there, and when Amos had told them he was missing, they had talked for hours. They were angry—and afraid. Most of them were in favor of pulling out, and even Gus Miller could see little hope of winning in a pitched battle with Arrow's hard-bitten crew.

Now the men rose in alarm, and Amos said, "Men, we want no trouble. Leave your guns inside." He stepped outside, followed by a dozen or so men, as the Arrow party dismounted and came to stand in front of them. Some of the women came out to stand on the porch and watch with fearful eyes.

"What do you want?" Amos asked. He was pale, but he held himself in place by sheer force of will.

Caudill gave him a hard look, then said, "Old man, you know what we want. We want you out of here."

"You can't drive people as if they were cattle," Amos said. "Go back to Silas Head and leave us alone."

"You own the land this house is on, Jenson," Caudill responded. "You can stay on it. But your cattle will have to go. I'll make you a fair offer for them—market price."

"We won't leave," Amos insisted. "Now, go and leave us alone."

Caudill shook his head. "This is Arrow graze. We've made a visit to all of you—now I'm telling you, get out!"

Smoky Jacks demanded, "Who died and made you king, Caudill?" He stepped forward, the only man among the settlers except for Gus Miller and Zane Jenson who was wearing a gun. Coming to a stop in front of Caudill, his eyes were bright with anger. "You're rough on women and young'uns, Caudill. Why don't you try it on a man?"

Zane and Gus Miller stepped forward, and the Arrow hands at once zeroed in on them. Caudill settled back on his heels, saying, "All right, you can have it if you want it!"

But Amos moved forward and caught Jacks' arm. "No!" he protested. "It's what they want, Smoky!"

"Put your guns on 'em!" Caudill called out, and at once every Arrow hand drew a gun. "Now get their guns." Caudill's men jumped to obey his command. When the three men were disarmed, Caudill shouted, "Burn that barn down!"

Zane's face went white, and he cried out, "You're a dog, Caudill!"

Jack Hines was standing beside Zane. He lifted his fist and drove it into the back of the boy's neck. Zane collapsed, and lay there struggling to get up. Rosa ran off the porch and came to his side, putting herself between Hines and Zane. The sight of her brought a laugh from the bruising Hines, who reached down and dragged her away from Zane. "Now, you just hold still, little lady!" he said.

Zane staggered to his feet, shouting, "Let her go, Hines!"

But Hines shook his head. "Make me," he taunted Zane.

Zane threw a punch at the big man, which Hines pushed aside; then, thrusting Rosa to one side, he growled, "I'm gonna have to show you, I guess—"

But as he drew back, Amos Jenson moved forward. "Let the boy alone," he said.

"Stay out of it!" Ash Caudill said loudly, but made no move

to stop the thing. He had come to provoke these people and saw his chance. Amos Jenson was no fighter like Winslow, but he had the confidence of the settlers.

With contempt, Jack Hines grabbed the thin arm of the sick man, turned him around, and drove a blow into his back, which sent Amos' slight form rolling to the ground. A mutter went up, and Miller cursed Ash and moved to stand between Jenson and Hines.

Ozzie Og leaped to Amos' side, turned him over carefully, and saw at once that he was unconscious. Ozzie looked up, anger in his eyes as he glared at Arrow's foreman. "Go on, Caudill, why don't you shoot him? He's an old man with a bad heart. Shouldn't be hard for a hairpin like you!"

Rosa ran to kneel next to Amos, followed by Zane. "He's dying!" she cried out. "We've got to get him to a doctor!"

Caudill blinked, not wanting this to happen. He knew that killing a preacher would be going too far, that the town would demand action, probably in the form of a federal marshal.

"All right," he called out quickly. "It's his own fault. Get him to a doctor. But you've had your warning!" He swung to the saddle and led the crew out of the yard, toward Arrow. When they were out of hearing distance, Caudill whirled and cursed Jack Hines. "You dumb fool! Why'd you have to pick on Jenson! We can't get by with killing a preacher!"

At the Anchor ranch, the group gathered around the still form of Amos Jenson, and Gus Miller said, "I'll go get Doc Matthews."

As he rode away, the men picked up Jenson and took him into the house. Lorene Cox had been restraining Cody on the porch, but now she let him go. He came running to Zane. His eyes were frightened, and he asked, "Zane, where's Ma—and where's Dan?"

Zane shook his head. "I don't know, Cody."

The boy looked at the limp form of his grandfather, then asked, "Is Grandpa gonna die?"

Zane put his hand on Cody's shoulder. "I hope not."

Rosa put her arm around the boy, saying, "It'll be all right, Cody." She looked at Zane, and there was fear in her own eyes.

Later, when she was alone with Zane, Rosa admitted, "I'm like Cody, Zane. I'm afraid."

"I know," Zane replied. "You're afraid something's happened to Winslow, aren't you?"

"Yes—and to your sister! Where can they *be*?"

They had left the house, coming outside to stand on the porch. The men were inside, and the women were taking care of Amos. Zane was afraid, too, for his father. His face was pale, and he said, "You shouldn't have come off the porch to help me, Rosa."

"Well," she said, shaking her head, "you shouldn't have tried to fight with that bully, you with broken ribs!"

Zane looked at her with a queer expression. "I—didn't want him to put his filthy hands on you," he said simply.

Rosa looked startled, her eyes opening wide. "Why—Zane! You can't fight a man like that! Not over me!"

"Why can't I?" Zane was not himself, and now he said what he would never have said ordinarily. "I love you, Rosa. Don't you know that?"

Rosa stared at him, her lips parted with surprise. Then she said, "You're only a boy, Zane!"

"And you're only a girl!" he retorted, then turned and walked away. Rosa stood there, still and motionless, watching him walk away—then a small smile touched her lips, and she stepped off the porch to follow him.

CHAPTER TWENTY-TWO

A MAN AND A WOMAN

★ ★ ★ ★

He emerged from a warm sea of soft, cushiony blackness—not willingly, for the voice was drawing him back to the cold and pain. He longed to sink down into the comforting oblivion—but the voice kept calling his name, and hands were pulling at him, shaking his shoulders until he opened his eyes. The intense cold struck him, and he began to tremble, but he stared at the face in front of him until the kaleidoscope of images faded and the face of Hope Malloy swam into focus.

"Dan, can you understand me?"

"Hope—it's you?" He saw relief sweep across her face, but the darkness was so dense that he could see nothing else.

"We can't stay here, Dan," she said. "I'm going to get the wagon. Sit up and stay awake until I come back." She tugged at him until he was sitting up, then disappeared into the darkness. The fever was raging in him now, and the temptation to lie down and close his eyes was as demanding as any need he'd ever known; he realized, however, that he had to stay awake. Chills ran through him, but he concentrated on keeping himself upright.

He sat until he caught himself slumping, almost falling over, and knew that he could not stay awake unless he stood up. Rolling over, he put his hands against the side of the cedar and gathered his good leg under himself, and with a tremendous effort pushed until he stood upright. The pain from his right leg was so bad that it made him nauseous, but he was able to turn around and brace himself against the tree while he waited for Hope to return.

Time ran slowly, and the murmur of the creek had a soporific effect, lulling him to sleep, but he fought against it with all his strength. Finally he heard the sound of horses, then a voice saying, "Whoa up!" Then a silence broken by the sound of Hope moving through the undergrowth, her boots splashing in the shallows.

She appeared, almost phantomlike, at his side. "Oh, Dan, you can walk!" she cried. "I didn't know how I was going to get you to the wagon!"

"Well, I can stand—can't say about walking. Got a bum leg."

"Lean on me, then. We've got to get out of here."

He put his right arm over her shoulder, gritted his teeth, and took a step forward. When he had to put his weight on his right leg, however, it almost collapsed so that his full weight fell on her. Hope staggered, but he managed to throw himself forward on his good leg, and they both remained standing. "You can't do it, Hope," he whispered. "I'll have to crawl."

"No! It's all right, Dan," she protested. "Come on, we'll take it slow."

As sick as he was, Winslow was filled with admiration for the woman. But he said nothing, saving his strength for the formidable task ahead. "Let's go," he said grimly, and they lurched forward, this time not stopping until they had gotten out of the waters of the stream and were on dry land. Both of them were gasping for breath, but Hope said, "Just a few feet more to the wagon—"

Dan fell forward until he felt the back of the wagon strike him. Hope had let the tailgate down, and he leaned forward, almost spent by the effort of the short journey. "I'll have to hurt you, Dan," Hope said. "I'll be as careful as I can—"

He felt her lifting at his bad leg and helped all he could by rolling to one side. With a mighty effort he sprawled onto the bed, his breath coming in short, tortured gasps. Then she was beside him, and he felt the roughness of blankets cutting off the cold air. He also felt her hands on his face, felt her pushing the edges of the blankets under him, and heard her say, "Try to keep the blankets over you." The wagon shifted as she moved to the seat, then she spoke to the horses, and the wheels creaked as the wagon lurched forward.

Exhausted by his efforts, Winslow passed out at once, lulled by the rhythmic movement of the wagon and the warmth of the blankets. He had no sense of the passage of time as he lay in the bed of the wagon. It could have been a week or five minutes, but the sound of Hope's voice and the touch of her hands on his cheek brought him out of the comalike sleep.

"Dan, can you get out? I've got a fire going," Hope said.

He raised himself up to a sitting position, and saw a flickering light. His mind moved slowly, and all he could do was mutter, "Sure—" He scooted himself to the rear of the wagon, gritted his teeth, and rolled over on his stomach. She helped him lower himself to the ground, minimizing the jolt to his wounded leg. "Lean on me," she commanded, and he limped across, once again forced to throw most of his weight on her. He was able to notice that they were entering some sort of a cave, or at least a crevice cut deeply into the earth, with an overhang that blotted out the faint stars.

"Sit down here, Dan," Hope said, and he lowered himself onto the blankets she had arranged next to the bank that formed the back of the crevice. He gave a long, gusty breath as he settled down, putting his legs out straight with relief. Looking around, he took in the fire burning in the center of the crevice, then managed a grin. "All the comforts of home."

She looked at him carefully and came over to kneel beside him. Putting her hand on his cheek, she paused, then nodded. "Your fever's not so high. I've got to look at your leg." She took a pocketknife from her pocket, opened it, and cut his pants leg off a few inches above the wound. She started to close the knife, but he reached out and took it from her. He looked at it closely, then turned his eyes on her. "Where'd you get this knife, Hope?"

"Why, from Zane. He bought it from one of the Littleton brothers, the big one. Why do you ask?"

When she looked puzzled, he said, "This knife belonged to my partner, Logan Mann. He got it from his father, James." Dan touched the knife with his free hand. "Look at the silver initials— JM." He turned the knife over in his hands, his eyes gone hard. "This means that Logan is dead. He'd never sell this knife; it was the only personal thing he had from his dad."

"Oh, Dan, I'm so sorry!"

He gave her back the knife, a sadness in his face, but said no more. She took a look at the leg and glanced at him with relief in her eyes. "No infection, but I'm going to clean it and put a bandage on it."

She did so, washing both the entry and exit wounds with strong soap, then tearing into strips some sort of cotton garment, which she used to cover the wound. Then she put the blankets over him, saying, "Now—you need something to eat. Don't go to sleep."

"You've gotten pretty bossy—" Winslow said, but she was gone. He lay there soaking up the heat of the fire, which seemed to go to his bones, and was assaulted again by weariness. But he fought off the desire to sleep, and she returned soon with a large box, which she put down close to the fire and began unloading. He watched with interest as she drew out a skillet, a sauce pan, a coffee pot, and a canteen, placing them on the ground. She put the coffee pot on the hot coals, poured water into it from the canteen, then searched through the box until she found a small can. Opening it, she poured coffee into the pot. She rummaged through the box and came out with a large piece of bacon wrapped in a cloth. Using the pocketknife, she sliced the bacon into strips, threw them into the skillet, and made a place for it over the fire. Winslow watched her as she worked, filled with wonder at what she had done. The flickering light of the fire threw her features into relief, but he made out the roundness of her cheeks, the firm set of her full lips, and her deep-set eyes hidden by the shadows. She worked efficiently, as though she were in her own kitchen preparing a meal for her family, not hidden in a cave with a wounded man and in danger from desperate men.

"How'd you find me?" he asked as the aroma of the meat began to come to him, stirring his hunger.

"You dropped the note that man gave you at the cabin raising," she replied. "When you didn't come home, I got worried."

"Now, that's an odd one," Winslow mused after a long silence. "If I hadn't dropped that note, I'd still be in that creek."

The bacon was soon sizzling, popping in the frying pan with a cheerful noise. Hope used the knife, stabbing the pieces and putting them on a tin plate. She handed Dan the plate, warning, "Don't burn your mouth!"

He took the plate, picked up a piece of bacon, and juggled it until it cooled. As soon as he put it into his mouth, hunger rose in him, and he chewed and swallowed so eagerly that Hope said, "Don't strangle yourself, Dan! You've got plenty of time." She filled a large mug with coffee and handed it to him. He raised it to his lips, savoring the steamy warmth. It was the best thing he'd ever put into his mouth. The bitter brew almost scalded his lips, but at once it warmed his stomach in a most satisfying way. He ate several pieces of bacon, then she put her hand out to stop him as he reached for another piece. "Wait a while. I don't want it to make you sick. Just finish your coffee."

He leaned back and drank the coffee, savoring every drop, then handed the cup back. "Mighty fine," he murmured. "I want to tell you—"

"Lie down and sleep," she said. Putting the cup down, she moved to his side and helped him down onto the blankets. When he was comfortable, she tucked the blankets around him, saying, "You need to get some rest now—"

He wanted to speak to her, but his eyelids closed as though weighed down, and without preamble, he dropped off into a sound sleep.

★　★　★　★

When he awoke, there was a sharpness in his mind, and he realized that his fever was almost gone. He sat up, aware of the sharp bite of hunger, but ignored it. Rain was falling and the sky was a dull gray. He noted with satisfaction that the pain in his leg was now bearable. The fire had burned down to embers, but he saw several chunks of dead limbs stacked against the wall. Throwing back the blankets, he moved carefully, pulling some of the smaller sticks onto the coals. He nursed them until they began to blaze, then built the fire up with larger pieces. The box she had brought was pulled back away from the fire, and he managed to get to it, finding not only bacon but some cans of food. The canteen was filled, which told him that she had replenished it, and he drank deeply then began to fix a meal. He kept looking for her to return, but by the time the food was cooked, she still had not appeared.

He ate slowly, relishing the meal, then sat back and drank coffee from the mug. It was, as far as he could tell, somewhat past midday, but with the rain blotting out the sun, he could not be certain. "Where could she have gotten off to?" he spoke aloud, and when she still had not returned two hours later, his concern grew acute. "She took the wagon, but where to?" Uncertainty gnawed at him. What if she ran into some of Littleton's men and they took a shot at her? His thoughts tormented him, and he pulled himself to the brink of the overhang where rain dripped like a screen, but could see no sign of the wagon.

Winslow was not a man who could endure an enforced time of passivity easily, for there was a restlessness in him that craved action and activity. Now, again—as when he was trapped under the log—he could do nothing but wait, and by the time dusk began closing in, he was almost out of his mind.

Then he heard the muted sound of something approaching, and in his eagerness, pulled himself to his feet and watched. He hadn't considered that it might be Arrow closing in. Then he saw the wagon appear from the timber and a great weakness washed over him, a relief that left him almost faint.

Hope leaped from the wagon and entered the cave. He grabbed her arms, his voice ragged with worry. "Hope—where have you been?"

Hope was taken off guard, and her lips parted with surprise at his greeting. "Why—I had to get word to Pa that I was all right—" she began, but to her shock, he suddenly pulled her close and held her so tightly that she couldn't breathe. His embrace stirred a small spark of fear, but at the same time, she felt strangely safe in his arms.

He drew back, his face drawn tense, and shook his head. "Don't *do* that again, Hope! I nearly went out of my mind!"

"I—I'm sorry, Dan," Hope whispered. She was confused by his obvious fright—and aware that she had some of the same feelings, for she had been apprehensive that he might have gotten worse. Now, however, she saw that he was better. "I had to get word to Pa. Now, you sit down." He put his arm around her to brace himself for the short journey to the blankets. "You're better," she said, noting how much easier he could put his weight on his bad leg.

"Yeah, guess so." Dan lowered himself to his side, then asked, "How'd you get word to your father?"

She picked up the coffee pot, poured some into the mug, and took a long draught before she answered. "I went to the Shultz place. Nobody was home, so I left a note." Worry touched her eyes, and she shook her head. "I couldn't be sure Arrow men wouldn't find it, so I just asked them to tell Pa I'd be gone for a few days. Maybe I can go back tomorrow and leave word that I'm with you. Pa's worried about you."

Suddenly Dan realized that Hope was exhausted. She'd been up all night, struggling with him, and now had made a hard trip. There was, he saw, a vulnerable expression on her face, and he said, "Here now, you've got to rest."

"I'm all right—" she protested, but he ignored her, and she finally smiled wanly. "All right, Dan. I'll take a nap." She spread out some more blankets, pulled her boots off, and stretched out. She put her head back, sighed deeply, and almost at once was sound asleep. If she had been able to think clearly or to reason, Hope would have been shocked at what she had done. To be alone with a strange man far away from everyone—that in itself would have been enough to put her on her guard. But to lie down and sleep with a sense of perfect safety with a man not five feet away?

Dan Winslow watched as the lines on her face began to disappear then smooth out until they were gone entirely. Her hands had been clasped together tightly over her chest—but slowly they relaxed, falling open. Dan crawled over to her, put her arms at her side, and covered her with a blanket. Then he put out a rough hand and touched her hair so lightly that she never stirred. He lay back on his blanket and watched her as she slept.

★　★　★　★

"We'll pull out of here in the morning, Hope."

Dan had been sitting in front of the fire as Hope cleaned the skillet, scouring it with sand brought from a nearby creek. "We've been here three days, and I'm fine now." He grinned at her, his eyes bright with humor. "Shows what a good nurse I've got."

Hope smiled back, saying, "You're a terrible patient. I think you'd have tried to leave that first morning if I hadn't sat on you."

Winslow nodded. "You were right. We wouldn't have gotten far." He peered out into the darkness. "I think they've given up on me."

They had remained hidden while his wound healed, and more than once they had heard gunshots—obviously signals. His fever had not come back, and except for soreness, his wound had not given any serious problems. Now they sat at the fire, and he said, "The rain saved us, I reckon. Washed out the wagon tracks."

"God is good," she replied.

He glanced at her sharply, then said, "Yes, He is." He poked at the fire, his thoughts sober and long. "The food and blankets you were taking to the Amboys—if you hadn't had them, we'd have been in poor shape." He glanced up at her suddenly. "Makes you think God's in control more than we think, doesn't it?"

"I've always thought He cared—but sometimes it doesn't look like it to our eyes."

"That's just what my mother always said." He tossed the stick into the fire. "I want to tell you something, Hope—" He began to speak of how he had called on God when he was pinned down and thought he was going to die. He spoke slowly, halting at times to think more clearly, and as he told the story her eyes grew warm.

" . . . so I didn't ask God to get me out of the mess I was in," he said, his voice soft and tinged with a sort of wonder. "I'd given up on that—thought it was all over. And that part wasn't so bad, Hope. I gave up on myself so many times during the war when better fellows than me died and I lived—well, I was pretty sure I wasn't going to make it." Then he looked up at her, and his blue eyes were wide with an emotion she'd never seen in him. "But what I did ask God for was—to forgive my past."

He paused then, thinking of that moment, and Hope asked gently, "What happened, Dan?"

"I can't say what it was like," Winslow said slowly, but then he smiled and shook his head. "But whatever it was—it's still working! I got rid of some kind of heavy load, Hope. I can't ever go back to being the way I was." He shook his head regretfully, "Can't go back and undo the things I've done—but I know God's forgotten them."

"That's wonderful, Dan!" Hope said. She had drawn her knees up and placed her arms around them, with her chin resting on her forearms. "Your people will be so glad to hear you've been saved."

"Yes, they will." He smiled again. "Wish you could be there when I tell them. If it weren't for you, they'd be out one prodigal son."

His words made her uncomfortable, and she rose to her feet, saying, "Oh, that's not true."

He got up stiffly, went to the overhang, and looked out. Then he came back to stand beside her. "We'll be leaving here tomorrow. Might be I may not get as good a chance as this to tell you what it meant—your coming to get me."

"Oh, Dan, I don't—!"

He put one hand on her shoulder, and with his other hand closed her lips. "Hush now," he smiled. "Never interrupt a man when he's trying to say thank you." Then he dropped that hand to her other shoulder and stood looking down at her. She felt very small as she looked up at him, and the gentle pressure of his hands on her shoulders made her feel somehow very shy and uncertain. While he had been sick, she had had none of those feelings, for he had been almost like a child.

Now he seemed very big, and the lean masculine strength of his features held her fast as he went on speaking. She felt, somehow, very young, very vulnerable, much as she had felt at times when she was growing up through that stage that marks the borderline between childhood and womanhood. She remembered suddenly how it had been, that time when she still moved with the aura of innocence about her and in her. Everything had been touched with wonder—the world around her of trees and streams and clouds—and the world that lay before her. She thought of the nights when she had gone to sleep dreaming of marriage, of a man, of a home, and even of babies to hold and nourish. That had been the wonder time of her life, and now as she stood in front of Dan Winslow, some of that came back to her.

"Hope, I'm not sure I would ever have come out of it," Dan was saying. "It was like—like slipping away from the world. And then when I heard your voice and felt your hands, it was like coming back to life! I'll never forget that moment!" His smile was gentle, and he nodded slightly. "I still can't believe it, Hope," he went on, his eyes fixed on her. "That you came for me—and when you found me just about gone, you got me out of there and brought me here. No other woman in the world could have done it!"

The cave had been a haven of safety for them, shielding them from the dangers of the world outside. The hours that they had passed there had drawn them together—more than either of them knew. For Dan, coming after his experience with God, it had been a time of growth, for he had discovered the reality of prayer, and the miracle of the presence of God had been beyond anything he had experienced. For Hope, the days had brought a sense of release. She had been tense in the beginning, her old fear of men rising as a threat. But perhaps because of Dan's weakness—his helplessness—she had discovered a sense of ease that she had never known with any man.

Now as they stood there, the silence of the cave was broken only by the rhythmic patter of rain falling on the soaked ground. He had been smiling, but now the smile faded, and he became aware of Hope in a different way. She had been his protector, his nurse—but she was more than that, and he was aware of the simple beauty of her face and form.

Hope saw something come to Dan's eyes, and when he pulled her close, the old fear came. But there was a gentleness in his touch, almost a reverence—such as she had never known to be in any man. He drew her close with his left hand, lifted his right and cupped her face gently. Then as she looked up at him, he said huskily, "I didn't know a woman could be like you, Hope."

For some reason, tears came to Hope's eyes. They overflowed and ran down her cheeks, and with them she shed some of the pain that she had known. A strange and wonderful thing was happening inside her, so unexpected that she could not move. Her spirit was like a frozen river, hard and fixed, made so by the ill treatment she had known at the hands of the two men she had tried to love. But the gentle pressure of Dan's hand on her cheek and the kindness in his eyes seemed to bring a thaw to her spirit. Emotions she had long forgotten began to stir, and as he held her lightly, making no move to do more than that, she began to feel free. The coldness and the hardness that she had allowed to build up began to fade away, and she understood then that there were men who were not brutal and demanding.

What happened then was a miracle, and later she could not believe that she had done such a thing. Slowly she reached up and put her hands around his neck, hardly conscious that she was doing so. She pulled his head down and kissed him on the lips, softly at first, then with a firmer pressure.

Dan Winslow was shaken by her sudden caress, but even as the softness of her lips sent riotous emotions along his nerves, he knew how fragile this woman was. He tightened his hold on her, pressing her close, but as soon as she drew back he released her.

"Dan—!" Hope whispered, unable to say what was happening to her. She placed her hand on his chest, and he covered it. "I don't know why I did that," she said, wonder in her eyes.

Dan took her hand, held it between his own, marveling at the firmness of it. He let the moment run on, thinking of Hope's past. Then he said quietly, "I guess we'll always be close, won't we, Hope?"

"Yes!"

They stood there, but there was nothing tense about the way they looked at each other. Hope knew that if he had pressed his advantage—as most men would have done—she would have been rigid with fear. But now Dan did something he'd never done in his life. It was just not done by the men of his family. He took her hand, lifted it to his lips, and kissed it. Then he said, "You're like no other woman, Hope!"

The simple gesture was so unexpected, so foreign to all that Hope had known, she stood before him in shock. Then the gentleness of it brought fresh tears to her eyes—hot and scalding.

She turned quickly to stare out into the darkness. Dan said nothing, for he could see her shoulders shaking as she tried to control her tears.

Finally she turned back and lifted her eyes to him. "I—think it'll be good for us to leave here, Dan."

"Are you afraid of me?" he asked.

"No—" she said slowly, "not of you." She turned away again to face the darkness outside, and he didn't hear the rest of what she said, for she whispered softly, "I'm afraid of me!"

CHAPTER TWENTY-THREE

"WE'LL TURN WOLF!"

★ ★ ★ ★

When Hope and Dan got into the wagon at dawn, both of them turned to look back at the cave. "Guess I'll never forget this place, Hope," Dan said. Shaking his head, he added, "Kind of a Garden of Eden before the Fall. Now we've got to go back to face all the problems."

Hope was feeling much the same way, but she managed a smile for him. "It'll be something to remember—one of the good things."

He slapped the horses with the reins, and they made their way through the trees. The rain had stopped, but the air was still cold. As the wheels made a squashing noise in the soft ground, Dan said, "We'll go to Gus Miller's place. I'll get a horse from Gus, and you need to get back home."

"Aren't you going with me, Dan?"

"No. I've got to lie low for a while. I want to do some prowling around. Find out what's been going on."

Hope had been worried about what Dan would do concerning the ambush, and now she put it into words. "Dan, you know who tried to kill you, don't you? What will you do about it?"

Winslow sat loosely on the seat, his eyes searching the trees ahead in an alert fashion. For a few moments he remained silent, then spoke in a manner that contained an odd note of hesitation.

"Well—it's a funny thing about that, Hope," he finally replied. "From the time I got hit, I was planning on a manhunt. That's the way I've always lived—when you get hit, get the man who's behind it. The old eye-for-an-eye business, and I know that game pretty well. And what made it worse was the fact that it had to be the Littletons who killed my partner, Logan Mann. No way they could have had his knife unless they took it off his body. It belonged to his father, the only personal thing he had from his dad. I may never find his body, so the law won't ever do anything about his murder. But he was my friend, and where I come from, we have a habit of taking up for friends."

A white-tailed deer suddenly stepped out of the brush over to their left, and his snort of sudden surprise set Dan's impulses off. He drew his gun and aimed at the animal, acting with lightning reflex—then chuckled as the deer whirled and fled in that beautiful rolling gait common to the breed.

Dan laughed shortly and holstered his gun. "Guess I'm a little jumpy," he said. He gave her a smile, then shook his head with a puzzled motion. "But the thing is, ever since you pulled me out from under that tree, I've been thinking about this thing. And what I've come up with is—something in me is different. I just don't hate those fellows like I would have before."

"So you won't be taking revenge on them?" Hope asked.

"Guess not. Funny thing."

"That's the way it is with Christians, Dan," Hope said quietly. She was happy for him and put her hand on his arm in an open gesture. "I'm so glad for you!"

He was embarrassed by his confession, but the sight of the warmth in her eyes made him feel a release. "I'll probably stub my toe a few times," he said. "Feel like a baby in a lot of ways."

"Pa will be so happy to hear about it," Hope said. She realized she was still holding his arm and quickly let her hand drop. There was still a shyness in her toward him, but she had thought for a long time about the tenderness of his caress.

They spoke of the problems that lay ahead for a time, then fell silent. Three hours later they came in sight of Gus Miller's place, and as they drove out into the clearing, Dan said, "There's Gus—"

Gus Miller ran forward to meet them, his face tense. "Dan,

get into the house!" He grabbed the cheek straps of the team, throwing out his words rapidly. "I'll put the team in the barn— Hope, get inside with him."

Dan helped Hope to the ground, and the two of them ran up the steps and through the door that Betty Miller held open. Her two children, Stonewall, age ten, and Eileen, eight, stood back watching them carefully. "Hope—!" she said, agitation on her face. "Are you all right?"

"Why yes, Betty," Hope answered. She started to speak but turned to the door, for Gus came in, breathing hard, relief on his face.

"What's happening, Gus?" Dan demanded.

Miller stared at him, his black eyes going hard. "Arrow hands been nosin' around the place the last few days," he said. "I don't think any of them saw you. You see anybody on the road?"

"No," Dan said. "I figured they'd be looking for me. I need a horse, Gus, and I'll get out of the way."

Miller shook his head. "No place for you to run, Dan. Caudill's got the crew movin' like an army. You know what's happened here?"

"No. What's going on?"

Miller's lips grew thin, and he allowed the bitterness that had been building up in him to tinge his tone of voice. "Head's done what I always said he'd do—clean out the valley." He spoke rapidly, sketching out the visits Arrow had made to all the settlers and small ranchers. He ended by saying, "The chips are down now, Dan. If we don't move, Caudill will turn that crew loose on us."

"I need to get back to Anchor," Hope said instantly.

"Hope—" Betty Miller said, then paused and gave her husband a helpless look.

There was something in the exchange that made Hope's heart grow cold. "What is it, Betty? Is it Cody? Has he been hurt?"

Betty hesitated, compassion turning her lips soft. "It's your father, Hope. He's very sick."

Miller slapped his hands together, anger in his rigid back. "Jack Hines beat him up! I'll lay a gun on that dirty dog for it, though!"

Hope said, "I've got to go to him!"

"Sure," Miller nodded. "But you've got to keep out of sight, Dan." He paused and a thought came to him. Narrowing his eyes, he asked, "You gettin' out? Wouldn't blame you much with that Ash Caudill on your trail."

They all looked at Winslow, but he shook his head, his lips forming a stubborn line across his tanned face. "No, I won't be leaving, Gus. But I can't stay here. If you'll lend me a horse, I'll clear out." He turned to Hope, saying, "I'll be in to see Amos tonight. It'll be late, but I'll be there."

"Be careful, Dan!" Hope whispered, her eyes on him. Then she turned and they all went outside. Dan helped Hope into the wagon, then paused and gave her an odd look.

"Thanks for taking care of me," he murmured. Then he slapped the horse, and as the wagon pulled away, he turned to Gus. There was a hard, careful look in his eyes. "Let's have that horse, Gus."

"Yeah, sure." Miller roped a fine-looking bay, put a saddle on it, then noticed for the first time that Winslow was limping badly. "You took a bullet?" he demanded. He listened to Winslow's quick review of the ambush, then nodded. "The Littletons? Not too surprised about that, Dan. But you can't do much with a bad leg."

Winslow shook his head, saying, "I'll make it. You hear anything about my place?"

"Saw Kincaid yesterday. He came by to see if I'd laid eyes on you. Said Caudill and his bunch came by. Gave him a week to move your stock, just like they did me."

Winslow eased himself into the saddle. It was a painful process, but he endured it with only a grunt. "What will you do, Gus?" he asked.

Miller looked up at him, and there was a black despair in his eyes. "I'd fight if there was a chance, Dan. I can't make it without the graze Arrow's taking over—and Head knows that." He shoved his hat back, revealing a shock of coarse black hair. There was a wildness and a recklessness in Miller that he had to fight to contain, and now he exploded, "Blast it, Dan! What's a man to do? I've got Betty and the kids to think about—but it sure does grate me to hunker down before Silas Head!" He shook his muscular shoulders in a gesture of suppressed rage, then gave

Winslow a sudden look. "You gonna buck Arrow, Dan?"

Winslow lifted the reins, but said only, "Meet me tonight at Anchor, Gus. Can you get the word around to some of the other men?"

Miller brightened instantly. "Sure, Dan, most of 'em are pretty down. They sort of gave up after you disappeared, but most of 'em will come for sure."

"See you, Gus."

"Keep yourself out of sight, Dan—" Miller called out after Winslow. He turned and walked to the corral where he saddled a well-muscled black gelding, then swung into the saddle. Riding up to the porch, he called, "Betty—!" When his wife came out, he said, "I'm gonna get everyone together for a meeting at Anchor. It'll be late when I come back."

"Gus, will we be able to stay on this place?" Betty asked anxiously.

Miller gave a quick glance toward the disappearing figure of Dan Winslow, and then looked back to his wife, saying, "We got a chance, Bet. It all kind of hangs on what that big fellow does." He leaned down, and she came to take his kiss. She clung to him, whispering, "Be careful! Oh, be careful, Gus!"

*　*　*　*

The living room of the house was far too small for the group of men that showed up at Anchor. When it became apparent that they'd have to meet somewhere else, Hope said, "Zane, take some lanterns to the barn."

"Sure, Sis," Zane agreed. He hesitated, then asked, "You think Dan will do something?"

Hope turned to look into the youthful face of her brother and wished that she could help him through the bad time she felt was coming. "I don't know, Zane."

"Well, you must have talked about it," Zane persisted. "I mean, what did you *do* all that time you were hid out with him?" He saw a flush rise to Hope's face and quickly blurted out, "Oh, my gosh, Sis! I didn't mean—!"

Hope smiled at his confusion, went to him, and gave him a hug. "I know, Zane. But Dan is changed. He found God when he was shot and thought he might die." She frowned, then bit her lip in a puzzled fashion. "If that hadn't happened, I know what he'd have done—but now, he's different."

"You mean he won't fight?" Zane demanded.

"Go on to the barn, Zane," Hope said. "I'll be down as soon as I see to Pa."

Zane left and Hope heard him say, "Let's go to the barn. More room there."

She turned and went to the bedroom where her father lay, and found Cody sitting beside him. He had spent much time with his grandfather, and it seemed to Hope almost as if the boy feared that if he left Amos would die. Now she went over and sat down on the other side of the bed. "Pa?" she said quietly. "Are you awake?"

The flesh had withered away on Amos Jenson's emaciated body, and his face had a skeletal appearance. Doc Matthews had made three trips, and each time he had been less optimistic. "Nothing I can do, Hope," he had said on his last visit. "Not much we doctors can do anyway—except set a broken bone or take out a bullet."

"Will he live, Doctor?" Hope had asked.

Matthews had carefully scrutinized her, as if judging her in some way. Finally he shook his head, saying gently, "No, Hope, I don't think so. He's weaker every time I see him—and there's only one end to that." He had added, "I love your father, Hope—and it's my prayer that he'll go quickly. He'd hate to be a burden on anyone. He's ready to meet God."

Now Hope saw her father's eyelids tremble, then open. He had been alert and clear in his mind almost constantly. Now he saw her and smiled faintly. "What are the men here for?"

Hope hesitated, then explained. "Gus Miller rode all over the valley. Dan wanted all the men here tonight."

"I want to see Dan as soon as he comes," Amos said. He turned his head toward his grandson. "Cody, will you go watch for him?"

"Sure, Grandpa!"

Cody left at a run, and they heard Buck bark suddenly as the boy left the house. "How do you feel, Pa?" Hope asked.

"I don't complain," he said, reaching out and taking her hand.

"You never do," she murmured. "Why do you want to see Dan?"

"I want to ask him to do something for me," Amos said. He looked at her, then said, "You know, Daughter, I never had much tact—but now that I'm short of time, I don't have any at all." She tried to protest, but he cut her off. "I'm going to die, but every one of us has to do that." He shifted in the bed, then seemed to gather his strength. "Hope, do you love this man Winslow?"

His abrupt question took Hope by surprise, and she lifted one hand quickly to cover the flush that rose to her cheek. Thoughts fluttered through her mind like butterflies, but she put them aside resolutely, looked down at her father's wasted face— and knew she must give him the truth.

"He's—the most gentle man I've ever known, Pa." She told him a little about what happened when they were together in the cave, then swallowed hard and said, "I guess you know I've been scared of men for a long time. But I'm not afraid of Dan. I don't know if that's love, Pa." He was watching her intently, and she continued, "I feel—oh, *safe*, I guess is what I feel. Now that he's been saved, I want—well, I feel like I could trust him with anything."

"That's not a bad way to think of love, Daughter," Amos mused. Each word came slowly, for he was like a man with a limited number of coins, and he spent them sparingly. He let the silence run on, then said, "He's a strong man. Zane and Cody both know that. Cody, especially, is drawn to him, though he don't know why. The boy's always wanted a father, and I've tried to fill in as best I could. But I've watched the two, and if you could love the man, it'd be good for Cody to be raised by a man like that." He seemed to grow weary and closed his eyes. She had to lean forward to catch his words: "Dan Winslow's the kind of man you should've married in the first place—"

Hope sat beside him, holding his hand, and ten minutes later she heard the door open. Turning around, she saw Dan enter. She motioned to the chair on the other side of the bed, and then turned to whisper, "Pa—Dan's here."

Amos opened his eyes slowly, took in Winslow and said, "Glad you got here, Dan."

"Sorry I wasn't here to help, Amos." Dan was shocked at the sight of the elderly man, for he saw at once that Jenson was dying. He pulled the chair close to the bed and sat next to Amos. "Let me tell you what happened—" He related his conversion experience, concluding, "I think if I hadn't been around to listen to you preach, I wouldn't have made it, Amos. And I'll always thank you for that."

Amos smiled and nodded. "That's the best thing I've heard in a long time, Dan. I thank God you're in the family." He coughed, seemed to strangle, and Hope quickly got a glass of water and held him up to drink it. When Amos lay down again, he seemed stronger. His eyes fixed on Winslow, and he asked, "What are you aiming to do about this trouble, Son?"

Winslow looked up to meet Hope's eyes, then back to Amos. "If I was the same man I was before I met God, Amos, I'd fight Arrow to the last breath. But now—I don't know what to do." He looked sad as he sat there, the strong planes of his face harsh in the shadows of the lamp. "The Bible says 'Thou shall not kill.' And I don't see any way to fight without killing."

Amos said, "Son, every good man I ever heard of had to fight that out within himself. Weren't there a lot of Christian men in your outfit?"

"Sure, lots of them."

"Well, they fought, didn't they? Do you think they weren't saved men?"

"I know they were Christians, Amos." Dan sat there trying to make up his mind, then asked, "Are you telling me to fight?"

Amos nodded. "I hope you will, Dan. This is a terrible world, not what God intended it to be. Not what it will be when Jesus comes back. But until He comes, men have to defend their families. Soldiers have to fight for their country. Peace officers have to carry guns to protect the weak. Do you see that, Son?"

Winslow nodded slowly. "I guess I do, Amos. And it's what I've made up my mind to do. I hate the thought of it, and if it was just me, I'd ride on. But I can't leave you and Hope and the boys to face trouble." He looked up again, meeting Hope's eyes, then said, "I've got to tell you, Amos, I've got a strong feeling for your daughter. She probably won't have anything to do with a man like me, but if I get through this thing alive, I'll probably be coming around a lot."

Amos had listened to Dan carefully, and when he heard this, he seemed to relax. "Son, that's good news for me. I been lying here praying that you'd stay. Now I don't need to worry about anything." He lifted his hand, and Dan took it. "Now, go do what you got to do. You'll be in God's hands—but Hope and me, we'll be here praying for you all. Here, I'd like you to have this—" He picked up a small black Bible, thick and dog-eared with use, and handed it to Dan. "I've carried this many a day, and I hope it'll be as precious to you as it has been to me."

Dan took the Bible, held it for a moment, then put it in his shirt pocket. "I'll treasure it, Amos." Then he reached out and took the hand of the old man, saying quietly, "I wish my dad were here. Maybe you'd like to give me the blessing he can't, Amos." He knelt beside the bed and leaned forward; then a holy light came to the eyes of Amos Jenson, and he reached out, placing both his hands on Winslow's head. He began to pray, invoking the blessings of God on the big man.

Hope bowed her head, tears coming to her own eyes, and then she sensed a movement behind her. Turning, she saw Cody, who had entered and was staring at his grandfather and Dan Winslow. His eyes were big, and his lips were clenched together tightly. As Dan got up, Cody kept his eyes fixed on him. Winslow leaned over and whispered something to Amos; then when Winslow moved away from the bed, Cody asked, "Dan—can I go with you?"

Winslow glanced at Hope, then nodded. "Sure, Cody." The two left, and when Hope turned back to her father, she saw that he was smiling and that there were tears in his eyes.

"Thank God!" he was saying over and over, as she held tightly to his hand.

As Cody walked beside Winslow to the barn, he asked, "Is my grandpa gonna die, Dan?"

"I think he will, Son," Dan replied. He stopped and put his hand on the boy's shoulder, looking down at him. "But you mustn't be afraid. He's going to be with Jesus."

"I know—but I'll miss him!" Then Cody reached out and took Dan's hand. "Will—will you be here?" he asked in a small voice.

Dan squeezed the boy's hand and said, "I'll be around if the Lord spares me. But there's going to be a fight, Cody. Some of us are going to get hurt, maybe killed."

"Dan—try not to get killed!"

Dan Winslow gave the boy a hug. "I'm a pretty tough fellow, Cody. And I'm going to try harder to keep myself in one piece than I ever tried before. Now—let's go see what we have to do."

He stepped into the barn and saw at once that everyone gathered there was expecting something from him. "Cody, go stand with Zane," he said, and when the boy went to Zane, Dan looked around carefully. This was his army, and it was not a large one. There were no more than twenty men in front of him, and most of those had never fired a shot in anger. He ran his eyes over them, noting those who were good fighting men: Sid Kincaid, Smoky Jacks, and Gus Miller were all he could count on. Others, such as Dave Orr and Zane, were unknown qualities, and farmers like Dutch Shultz and Lowell Cox had been in the war, but Dan had no idea if they could stand fire or not. Some of the men he hardly knew at all, such as Leon Amboy, a tall, thin man with a pair of mild, blue eyes. Despite the odds, Dan knew he must not let any doubt appear.

"I guess you all know what we've got to do," he said. "And maybe some of you think it can't be done. You're thinking that Arrow's got a crew of fifteen tough men—and I'm telling you that the Littletons will throw their crew into the fight, so you can figure we'll be up against at least twenty men—and Head can get more. Most of you are farmers, not gunmen, so you're feeling pretty much like letting the thing go."

"Well, it's a long shot, isn't it, Dan?" Dave Orr spoke up at once, voicing the doubts of several of the men. "I've never shot at a man in my life. How can I go up against a man like Caudill or Jack Hines?"

Several of the men agreed, but Lowell Cox said, "This won't be a shoot-out between two men, Orr. I wouldn't stand a chance in a thing like that, no more than you. Most of us wouldn't. But there's a way to do these things, and I figure Dan Winslow's the one to turn the trick."

"Guess I agree with that," Dutch Shultz said instantly. He was a slow-moving man and a slow speaker as well. He was, moreover, a solid man—one who was not impulsive—and Dan had sense enough to know that it was men like Cox and Shultz who would have to draw the more fearful men into the fight. He stood back, letting Cox and Schultz answer Orr's arguments, saying nothing at all.

Finally the tide swung, and even Dave Orr was convinced. Orr was the only educated man in the group, and though education would be of no use in a fight, these uneducated men had respect for learning and were impressed when Orr agreed, "All right, we'll do it. Now, Dan, how do we go about this thing?"

Winslow stood still, every man watching him. His lips made a long, faintly smiling line; but it was the wistfulness of that smile which stirred the wonder in some of them. Winslow was tough, and he had a streak of raw courage that most men lacked. Yet now, behind the smile and steady blue eyes of the man was something like profound knowledge and profound regret. It made him different—it set him apart. Maybe it was loneliness that came out of knowing and seeing too much.

"Silas Head has put a bounty on us," Winslow said slowly, almost idly. "It's like to him we're a bunch of lobo wolves, so he's paying Ash Caudill and his crew to hunt us down for the bounty."

He paused and let the silence run on so long that Zane finally burst out, "Well, Dan—what will we do then?"

Winslow looked around the room slowly, then nodded as he said, "Why, Zane—we'll turn wolf!"

CHAPTER TWENTY-FOUR

A NEW BEGINNING

★ ★ ★ ★

"You boys set right still and none of you will get your heads shot off—maybe!"

Only four of Arrow's crew were on the ranch, including Ash Caudill, Jack Hines, Shorty Ellis, and Luke Mott. And all four of them were in the middle of breakfast when they looked up to see two men standing at the head of the long table, guns drawn and aimed at them.

"What in the—!"

Smoky Jacks cut in, a thin smile on his lips. "Just settle down, Caudill. Zane, take their guns. We wouldn't want these cut-throats to be tempted."

Caudill was the only man who had come to breakfast wearing a gun. Now he had a burning desire to draw the gun—but the steady muzzle of Jacks' .44 discouraged him. As Zane Jenson took Caudill's weapon, the foreman tried to bluff the two men. "You two are making a big mistake," he said. "We've got twenty men in call."

"No, you ain't, Caudill," Jacks grinned. "You got your crew scattered all over creation. Now, you fellers get outside." Zane kept Caudill's weapon in his left hand and gave Jack Hines a hard look. Hines turned slightly pale as he remembered the last time he'd seen the young man. But Zane only motioned with both guns, and the four of them walked out into the yard without further argument.

In the big house, Diane and her father got a similar shock. The servant came to the table where they were also at breakfast, saying, "Gentleman to see you, sah."

"Who is it?"

"It's that Mistah Winslow."

Silas Head shot a look at the man, then shifted his gaze to Diane. "I'll see about this," he said quickly. "You'd better stay here."

Diane paid him no heed but went with him, following as he stepped out on the porch. The first thing she saw was Dan Winslow standing on the ground looking up, then she looked across the yard and saw Ash and three of the crew being herded toward the house.

Head saw this as well, and said frostily, "I take it you're here to rob us, Winslow."

"No, Head, just to collect a debt—and to lay down a little rule for you."

"What debt—and what rule?" Head shot back. He was not wearing a gun—had not for years—and it grated on him to be helpless before his enemy.

Winslow's eyes were hard as flint as he said, "Your man Caudill took a crew over the valley lately. They made a stop at Lowell Cox's place. Caudill killed one of his cows." Dan turned and asked, "That's right, isn't it, Ash?"

When Caudill remained silent, staring at Winslow with hate-filled eyes, Smoky Jacks gave him a sharp dig in the ribs with his revolver. "Speak up, Ash, I'm hard of hearing."

When Caudill nodded slightly, Winslow said, "That's the debt, Head."

Silas Head said in a grating tone, "You won't take one of my animals, Winslow."

"We've already got one." He turned and waved his hand, and a big, heavy bull trotted out from behind a barn, driven by Sid Kincaid. "I'll get him started to his new home, Dan," Sid yelled, and turned the huge animal toward the road.

Head's ruddy face grew crimson. "You can't take that bull!" he shouted. "That's a champion breeder I had shipped all the way from the East. He cost more than Cox's whole ranch!"

"Beef for a beef, Head," Winslow said evenly. "Which takes care of the debt—now we come to the rule." He paused to look at Diane. "I regret to speak like this before you, Diane."

Diane stared at him, then shook her head. "You'll die for this, Dan Winslow. Don't you know that? We can't let you take that bull—and we can't let you get by with coming here. If we did, we'd be—"

Diane broke off abruptly, and Winslow finished the sentence. "You'd be just another ranch, not the king and his princess lording it over the poor serfs." He noted the flush in her cheeks, but she had opened herself up for his barb. He turned his eyes back to Head, saying, "This rule, here it is. Whatever you do to us— we do to you. You take one of our cows, we take one back from you. You shoot one of our people, we shoot one of yours. Burn one of our houses, we burn this one."

"You're crazy!"

Dan shook his head. "Head, don't make any mistake about this. There's nothing you can do to us that we can't do to you. I mean that." He turned and said, "Zane, take Caudill to his bunk. Have him bring his personal belongings out here."

Caudill's head jerked, but he had no time to argue. Zane forced him across the yard, and as they left, Head began cursing and blustering. He was ignored by both Winslow and Jacks, and as soon as the two men were back, Winslow said, "Keep an eye on them, Smoky," and stepped into the house.

He was back at once with a coal-oil lamp in his hand. He walked across to where Caudill had thrown his belongings on the ground, removed the chimney of the lamp and poured the clear oil carefully over the pile. He set the lamp down, found a kitchen match in his pocket and struck it against a rock. Giving Caudill one look, he tossed the match on the pile, and it caught the oil afire at once. As the blaze grew, Dan said, "Get out of the country, Ash." Then he turned around and walked back to where Head and Diane were watching, their eyes filled with shock.

"Go get the horses, Zane," he said, and while the young man was gone, he addressed the big cattleman again. "I hope you show a little sense about this thing, Head. Your day is over. There's room enough for all of us—but you've been a hog."

Head choked and began to shout, but Dan ignored him and turned to his horse. He mounted, as did Smoky Jacks, and Dan said, "Don't send any raiders after us. I'm going home, and if you send men to hit it—or any other place—you'll go to your grave sorry about it."

The three wheeled and rode out of the yard at a gallop. At once Ash began cursing, but Head bellowed, "Shut up!" His face was set now with an anger that went to the bone. "Why didn't you keep a watch on this ranch?" he demanded of Caudill. "You've let them make a laughingstock of me!"

Caudill was wild with rage, but he got hold of himself. "Nobody will be laughing—they'll be too busy burying people!" He spun around, shouting, "Jack, go get Littleton and his crew. Luke, go get the boys over at Black Canyon, and you, Shorty, ride like the devil to the river. I want every man of our crew here by noon!"

"What are you going to do, Ash?" Diane asked.

"*Do?* I'm going to get that bull back," Caudill snapped. "And while I'm at it, I'm going to burn Dan Winslow's place to the ground—and a few more to boot!"

Head said at once, "Be careful. Winslow's no fool."

"He won't carry through," Ash said. "Look at the chance he had here. He could've shot us down and burned the house. Instead, he just burns some of my clothes and takes one animal."

"He's smart," Diane countered instantly. "We can't have the law on him for burning your clothes—and you shot that farmer's cow in front of witnesses." Ash glared at her but had no ready comeback. "He's beaten you every time," Diane added cruelly. "Don't let him beat you this time—or it's all over."

Caudill strode over close to Diane and thrust a defiant finger in her face. "He'll be dead by sundown," he said through clenched teeth. "And anybody else that's fool enough to stand against me and the boys!"

★ ★ ★ ★

Dan Winslow watched as Sid carried the last of Rosa's things out of the house and dumped them in the wagon. Sid had, at Dan's order, loaded all their personal things, and now he asked, "What's this for, Dan? Where we moving to?"

"This place won't be safe, Sid. Caudill will be here as soon as he can get his crew together. We'll take the stuff over to Gus's later. For now, put the wagon over in the meadow under the shed, then come up on the bluff."

Winslow wheeled his horse and rode around the garden that Sid and Rosa had planted, then up the steep path that led to a bluff overlooking the clearing. When he got to where the men waited, he said, "Dutch, take your three men and get started. You may not have anything to do, but I'm thinking that when he busts them up here, the stragglers will either go down the road to get away, or they'll take the old trail beside the river. Lowell, you take Amboy, Keyes, Sanders, and seal off that road."

Gus Miller said, "Dan, I don't like splitting up like this. We need all the men right here. This is where they'll hit, and we need to hit back with all we got."

Dan shook his head. "Gus, we've been over that. I want this thing over and done with. If we let them get away, it'll be all to do over again. This way no matter which way they take, they'll run into us."

"All right, Dan, you're the captain," Miller shrugged. "I just hope you're right. Those boys are tough."

"We've got the high ground, though," Dave Orr commented. "They'll have to climb this ridge to get us. Pretty hard going for them."

"It's kind of like Lookout Mountain," Lowell Cox said. He grinned at Dan, saying, "That was one time us Yankees put the run on you Johnny Rebs. I was one of the fools that made that climb, right up into the guns of the rebs." He shook his head with a puzzled look. "We should've lost that fight. Never could figger out why you fellers let us git up that hill."

Dan said, "When men get fired up, Lowell, they can do most anything. And if we want it bad enough, we can finish Arrow here today. But it's going to be a close thing. Now, get going, you men, and remember—we don't want any heroes. Hear me?"

"Sure," Lowell Cox answered. "Keep your head down, Dan." He led his little band away, and Dutch did the same with his three men. When they were gone, Sid came back, and Dan looked over his force. There were seven of them, including Zane, Smoky, Sid, Orr, Pie Dutton, Birch Bingham, and himself.

"We're going to have company pretty soon," he said. "There'll be at least twenty or so, all Ash can get together. I'm going to put you all in the spots where you can do the most good. It's what's called 'enfilading the enemy.' Which means shooting at them not only from the front, but from both sides."

He walked around the small bluff placing each man, warning them all, "No matter what happens, don't shoot until you hear my first shot—no matter *what* happens! Then when I start firing don't waste your shots. They'll be caught in the open, but Caudill's tough and smart. He'll know there aren't many of us, so he'll try to rush this ridge. But if we keep up a steady fire, those Arrow boys won't be able to stand it."

Finally he returned to the end of his thin line and lay down on the ground. He went to sleep almost at once, after saying, "Sid, wake me up when you hear them coming."

He stirred later at the sound of Zane's voice.

" . . . don't see how he can sleep like that, Smoky! It ain't human!"

"Well, he's a nervy cuss, Zane," Smoky responded. "Never saw a nervier one."

Zane was silent, unnerved himself at seeing Dan continue to sleep through their conversation. Then he asked, "This don't look right to me, Smoky. Why don't we wait for Arrow away from the house?"

"Why, that's what they'd like for us to do," Smoky said. "That way they could—Wait a minute! I think they're coming." He turned and shook Winslow. "Dan—wake up."

Winslow was up at once and took a look at the horizon, where a group of tiny horsemen were making their way cautiously up to the house.

"Well, you figgered right, Dan," Smoky murmured, his eyes gleaming. "Must be about twenty-five of 'em."

They watched as the riders approached the house, and Dan ordered, "Smoky, go along the line. Pass the word to wait for my signal." When Smoky scrambled away, Dan said, "Zane, keep your head down."

"Sure, Dan." Zane paused awkwardly, then said, "I don't expect to get killed in this fight—but guess I better get something off my chest." Dan turned his gaze on the young man and saw that Zane was tremendously embarrassed. But he waited until Zane finally spluttered, "Well, shoot! I *gotta* tell you why I been acting like a bull-headed fool toward you!"

Dan felt a wave of sympathy rise in him and smiled at Zane. "You've been jealous about Rosa, haven't you?"

Zane's mouth dropped open, and he stared at Winslow with astonishment. "You knowed it all the time?"

"Zane, young girls are real impressionable. They fall in and out of love pretty fast—or think they do. I was able to help Rosa, and she's been grateful. She's young and been treated pretty badly—and she was looking forward to having a father. When she lost him, I was there. She was just looking for security." He turned and put his hand on Zane's shoulder, saying, "She's a fine girl, but you're both young. Maybe something will come of it. I wouldn't be too surprised—because you're quite a man, Zane. Rosa would be fortunate to get you."

Zane's face flamed, and he turned his head quickly. When he spoke, his voice was husky. "Thanks for that, Dan. I—I needed it!"

Dan cut the moment short by saying, "Look sharp, our friends are busy." Smoky came back, his eyes bright, but then when he took a look at the scene below, he gasped, "Why—them vultures are burnin' the house!"

Winslow smiled and asked softly, "What d'you expect them to do, Smoky? Give it a coat of paint for us?"

Zane stared at Winslow. "You knew they'd do that, didn't you, Dan?"

"What you forget is that we've got to have a reason for this fight. Head can hire fancy lawyers to get out of shooting us. He's a powerful man, and if we give him any excuse, he'll have us posted outlaws by morning. But I doubt that anybody's going to have the nerve to blame us publicly for anything we do to a gang of men we catch burning our house!"

Even as he spoke, the flames caught, and Winslow knew coal-oil had been used to cause such ignition. He felt a pang of grief, for the house had been a haven to him, short though the time had been.

Dan watched Ash Caudill, who never got off his horse but directed the operation. Finally when the house was ablaze, Caudill called out, and the men who'd set the house ablaze mounted. Dan lifted his rifle, saying, "Get set—" He drew the hammer back to full, the sound striking on his nerves, and heard the same sound from the rifles of Zane and Smoky.

He had gambled that the riders would pass close to the bluff, following the trail beside the river, and that was exactly what happened. He could hear them laughing and talking now, with all the clinking iron and leather noises that attended the movement of a large group of horsemen. The leaders were splashing across the creek, and then it exploded—a sharp, hard smash of sound from his left, and two more rifle shots right on the heels of that.

Dan shouted, "Let 'em have it!" and drove his first shot at Caudill. But the foreman's horse had reared at the first burst, catching the bullet in its chest. The animal fell kicking into the creek, and Caudill fell face down into the water. He staggered up and grabbed one of the other horses, then swung on behind its rider. He was looking up at the bluff, and Dan heard him yelling, "They're up there! Get 'em—!"

As much as Dan Winslow disliked Ash Caudill, he had to admire the man's nerve, for he was yelling orders and firing as he rode behind his man. The shooting grew intense, and Zane was firing too fast. Winslow noted this and wished that he had a good sergeant to chew the boy's ear off. But just then Smoky Jacks said roughly, "Ease off, Zane—!" and the nervous young man settled down.

Down below, two riderless horses galloped off, and though the Arrow crew was raking the bluff with a steady fire, they could not find their target, and firing from a running horse is not easy. Dan heard a cry of pain from one of his men, but could not turn to see who it was, for Caudill had spotted his little group and sent his force against it. The three of them kept firing, and soon the pressure grew too great. The man in front of Caudill dropped to the ground, the front of his shirt blossoming crimson, and Caudill tried to lead the others to the crest—but they were taking too much punishment. They turned, and Caudill was forced to follow.

When Caudill's crew reached level ground, Dan shouted, "Pour it on!" It was Caudill who led the survivors away.

When the firing ceased, Dan moved down his own line, finding Dave Orr with a bullet in his forearm, but he was the only casualty. As Winslow was binding up the wound, a faint echo of heavy gunfire came to his ears.

"They ran into Dutch and his bunch!" Orr exclaimed. His face was white with the pain of the wound, but he looked up at Dan with wonder. "You figgered it all out, Dan!"

"It's not over yet," Dan said, his lips tight. He could not help but think of the bloody forms that lay on the ground below, and of the carnage that he knew had taken place when Arrow's crew had run point blank into the smashing rifle fire of the ambush he'd set. *I left the door open*, he thought sadly. *No one forced you to walk in, Ash.* But this brought no comfort to him, and he said evenly, "One more call to make."

"Where's that, Dan?" Orr asked.

"We'll go to town and report this to Sheriff Rider. I want him to see all this so there'll be absolutely no defense for Arrow."

* * * *

Sheriff Rider's old eyes had seen many rough sights, but as he stared at Dan Winslow, who'd come into his office, there was an odd wonder in them. When Dan had given him the facts of the fight, he shook his head, saying, "Son, you done turned hell over and built a fire under it! Doc Matthews has been patchin' up Arrow riders, and the undertaker's got two of 'em. Now you tell me there's more out at your place." He asked suddenly, "What kind of punishment did *you* fellers take?"

"Dave Orr got shot in the arm, but he's all right."

Rider stood up and walked over to the window. He stared out at the hotel and then turned, saying, "Silas Head was in here an hour ago. He's a whipped man, Winslow! I guess he ain't had no heart attack—but he's got no stomach for any more fightin'. It didn't help him none when I told him I was gettin' a U.S. Marshal here from Cheyenne to check into what he's been doin'."

"You think he'll quit then?"

"Already quit, Son!" Rider said, spreading his hands wide in an eloquent gesture. He started to speak, but at that moment, the door to his office opened, and Hope burst in, Cody at her side. Something in her eyes alarmed Dan, and when she walked over to him and leaned against him, he put his arms around her. "Is he gone?" he asked quietly.

Hope nodded. She leaned back and looked up at Dan, tears in her eyes, but she said, "He went out praising God, didn't he, Cody?"

The boy had red-rimmed eyes, but he said strongly, "He sure did, Ma—and just about the last thing he said was, 'Cody, you mind Dan—and take care of your ma.' "

"I wish I could have been there—" Dan said quietly. He put his hand on Cody's shoulder and would have said more.

At that moment, Sid Kincaid broke into the office, shouting, "Dan—!" He looked at Hope and Cody, obviously keeping something back.

"What is it, Sid?" Dan asked at once.

"It's Ash Caudill," Kincaid said. "He's down the street, and he says if you don't come and meet him, he'll hunt you down."

"It's not Head's doin'," Rider spoke up. "I'll go down and talk to Caudill."

"He's a mad dog, Sheriff Rider," Sid warned. "He'd shoot you without a thought."

"I expected it," Dan said. "Ash was always a stubborn fellow."

"Don't go, Dan!" Cody begged.

"Why, a man has to stand for something, doesn't he, Son?" Winslow smiled down at the boy briefly, then said, "I'll be back, Hope."

Hope watched him as he left the room, then the others followed him. When she went outside, too, she saw Caudill standing in the middle of the street. As Dan stepped out to meet him, men began scurrying to take cover.

Winslow walked steadily toward Caudill, stopping about twenty feet away. "Wish you'd have left town, Ash," he said.

"Not likely!" Caudill said coldly. Anger was burning in his eyes, and he spat out his words. "You may have won up until now, Dan, but you won't live to enjoy it."

"It's all over, Ash," Dan shook his head. It was quiet in the street, so he spoke in a conversational tone. "Arrow's still a big ranch. Go run it and be satisfied."

But Ash had seen the scorn in Diane's eyes and had heard the old man tell him to leave the ranch. He was stripped of all his hopes and dignity, and now he stood there with one single idea—to kill the man who had robbed him of them.

Dan didn't move but kept his eyes fixed on Caudill. His nerves were tight, and he watched the eyes of the gunman steadily. But the shot came before Caudill moved. Winslow felt the impact strike his chest, driving him backward. Even as he fell, he spotted a figure with a rifle in an upstairs window—and knew it was Jack Hines. He tried to draw his gun, but the force of the bullet had sapped him of strength. In one split second he saw Caudill draw and bring his weapon to bear, and he knew that in the window above, Hines was ejecting a shell, ready to fire again. . . .

Even as Dan struggled to breathe, he knew there was no hope, and he thought with regret of Hope and Cody and what might have been.

The muzzle of Ash Caudill's gun looked like a tunnel, but at the moment he saw Ash's finger tighten, two shots rang out, so close together they seemed to be one. Caudill was struck in the heart and fell back, dead as he hit the ground. Dan shifted his glance in time to see Hines fall forward, blood spurting from his throat.

Rolling over in the dust, Dan saw Smoky Jacks and Gus Miller, their guns smoking. Jacks had shot Caudill, and Miller had potted Jack Hines.

And then there was a loud cry, and Dan was aware that Hope was next to him, crying his name and holding his head in her arms. Winslow was still having trouble breathing, and then Doc Matthews was there, tugging at his coat. The doctor stared at Dan's shirt, then pulled at something, exclaiming, "Talk about a man shot with luck—look at this!"

Dan slowly sat up, holding on to Hope's hand, and saw that Matthews was clutching a black book, the little Bible that Amos had given him. He reached out and touched the flattened bullet that had smashed against it. It was hot, and he slowly got to his feet, staring at the Bible.

"This happened to a fellow in my company at Shiloh," he whispered. "Never thought it would happen to me!"

Then he turned to Hope, and saw in her eyes the thing he'd been looking for all his life. And she saw that same love and desire in the eyes of Daniel Winslow. She put her arms around his neck, ignoring the stares of those about, and kissed him on the lips. "My dear!" she murmured. "I thought I'd lost you!"

Dan looked down to see Cody, and when he held out his free hand, the boy came to him at once, his eyes big and filled with love. "Lose me?" Dan said with joy in his voice. "You'll never lose me—and I'll never lose you two!"

Zane felt a touch on his arm and turned to find Rosa standing beside him. She looked lost and forsaken, but he knew exactly what to do. He put his arm around her and felt her response at once. "Now Sis won't ever have to be alone again," he said. Then he added, "And neither will you, Rosa!"

She gave him a startled look, then a smile spread over her face and the gloom fled. "You talk pretty large, Zane Jenson. But I'll expect a little more than fancy talk—!"

Hope saw the pair turn away, and said, "I hope they fall in love, Dan. Really in love!"

"So do I," he said. His grip on her tightened, and he smiled at her, then at Cody. "I've got me a family—a wife and a son. Let's go home and start living!"

"All right, Dan," Hope smiled, and they walked down the street, the three of them, each putting away the past and walking into the future with a special kind of joy.